SHELF LIFE

A Hearts &
Crafts Story

KELLY JENSEN

I0563817

RIPTIDE
PUBLISHING

Riptide Publishing
PO Box 1537
Burnsville, NC 28714
www.riptidepublishing.com

Shelf Life

Cover art: L.C. Chase, lcchase.com
Editors: Veronica Vega, Carole-ann Galloway
Layout: L.C. Chase, lcchase.com

ISBN: 978-1-62649-973-7

First edition
January, 2023

Also available in ebook:
ISBN: 978-1-62649-972-0

A Hearts &
Crafts Story

KELLY JENSEN

For my fellow bagel shop survivor, Jason.

Life is a song—sing it.
Life is a game—play it.
Life is a challenge—meet it.
Life is a dream—realize it.
Life is a sacrifice—offer it.
Life is love—enjoy it.
—Sai Baba

TABLE of CONTENTS

Chapter One

T he bell over the café door jingled. Grayson didn't want to check to see how many people had slipped inside, but he did. And groaned. Too many. The line winding away from the counter, between the tables, and along the front window of the café was already long.

As he pulled his phone from an apron pocket, Gray entertained a fantasy about turning the sign from Open to Closed. He hit Redial. The call cut out before the first unanswered ring. Did that mean he'd been blocked or that the phone he was trying to call had been switched off?

Patty would know.

Except Patty was busy grilling with one hand, somehow cutting a sandwich in half with the other, all while taking an order over the shop phone. Gray counted the number of people in line for lunch again and selected a new number on his phone.

His best friend, Oliver, answered after one ring. "What's up?"

"I don't suppose you have an hour free?"

"Is that Clery-speak for three hours?"

"It's lunch, it's a rush, and the damned college student I hired yesterday isn't answering her phone."

"Wonders will never cease. So, I'm down in Allentown right now. I'm heading back, though. I could be there in forty-five minutes."

Another groan worked its way up from Gray's gut. He trapped it below his throat, where it sat like a bubble of unexpressed air.

"You could try Cam," Oliver suggested. Cam was Nick's brother, Nick being Oliver's boyfriend. Cam had a job but worked flexible hours and always seemed oddly happy to help out elsewhere.

"I will. Thanks." As Gray ended the call, the bell over the café door jingled again. He didn't want to look but he did. Speaking of oddly happy people...

Sporty McSporterson had a name. One not made up by Gray's unhappy brain. Sporty was easier to remember, though, if only because the guy always wore coordinated sweats and always—*always*—seemed ready to run somewhere in an entirely too cheerful and energetic manner. Sporty was also cute in a way that had never appealed to Gray before.

Red hair? Freckles? Cheekbones? Broad shoulders, narrow hips, long legs?

Yes, Gray had looked. The often vibrantly colored sweats invited his gaze to linger.

But Gray didn't do cute, redheaded, sporty, or cheerful. Especially not cheerful. He also barely had time to breathe, let alone think. No time for casual chats or the more-than-casual attention he often caught from Sporty.

He had a café to run, a college student to murder, and—

"Gray!"

Gray glanced over at the service counter where Patty might as well have been holding back a flood of humanity with nothing but her too-short arms. Thankfully, she'd put the knife down.

"Do we have any Kaisers left?"

Gray pocketed his phone and ran for the oven, where the timer beeped merrily away. He shoved a thick mitt over his fingers and grabbed the oven door. Heat rolled out into the kitchen, carrying the scent of overly toasted sesame seeds. He ground his teeth together and flipped the switch at the side of the oven to halt the rotation of the shelves. Tension throbbed along his jaw as Gray reached inside for the first tray. If he hauled them out quickly enough, he might be able to save this batch. The ones at the back? Toast, quite literally. But these could be okay. Too dark but not completely awful. And honestly? On days like today? He didn't care.

He wanted to finish rolling out the dough for tomorrow's bread and then go home.

Of course, that was as likely to happen as little green men poking their heads out from the other side of Jupiter to offer the answer to life, the universe, and small business staffing issues.

Gray rescued what he could from the oven and turned the temperature down. He should cycle a few pastries through before shutting it off entirely, but first he needed to give Patty a hand behind the counter.

"Where do you want me?" he asked, though he was technically the boss.

Patty was his cousin and his savior. She turned up to work when no one else did. Also, she'd been working the counter solo for about the past half hour and had a rhythm going. He'd step in where she needed him most.

"Can you take over the grill?"

"Sure." Gray glanced at the line of dockets tacked to the wall beside the flattop and hauled in a deep not at all calming breath. A sharp jolt of pain shot through his torso. He'd been experiencing heartburn on and off for weeks, now. *Note to self: eat less bacon.*

He rubbed at his sternum before picking up the spatula and a pair of eggs. Four bacon, egg, and cheese sandwiches, one with the egg cooked hard, two cheesesteaks, a chicken parm, three BLTs—

A blur of motion added another docket to the wall: a grilled chicken, and two more bacon, egg, and cheese sandwiches. His phone buzzed with an incoming text: Cam was on the other side of Milford but could get there in about an hour.

Don't worry about it, Gray texted back. *But thanks.*

Gray slipped the phone into his apron pocket. "When a call gets cut off before the first ring, does that mean I've been blocked or the phone is off?" he asked as Patty retreated to the counter.

"It means we're never hiring another college student, ever. Did you get in touch with Oliver?"

"He's in Allentown. Is Jared actually sick today, like really sick?"

"He sounded pretty awful."

"Call him if you get a chance. Maybe his girlfriend could come in for an hour?"

"Last time she worked here she somehow got the cord to the can opener looped around the blade of the deli slicer."

"Desperate times, Patty."

"I'll give her a try." Patty glanced toward the crowd milling behind the counter. Gray followed her gaze. The crowd gazed back, each and every person waiting to order vying to meet the eyes of the people supposedly working at the café, as though making contact would hurry everything up.

At the end of the line, Sporty offered a cheerful smile and wave.

A groan broke free and seemed to tear something loose with it. Gray's heart skipped a beat, tapped double time for a bit, and then squeezed tight. Sweat broke out across his forehead. The heat from the flattop buffeted his face, and the kitchen floor shifted beneath his feet. It was only the first of April, but already, spring had proved warm.

Gray slapped together the first few sandwich orders and delivered them to the counter. Patty wrapped, rang up the tickets, and continued taking orders. Together, they moved through the dance they'd practiced hour after hour, day after day, over the past nine months. Orders were filled, more orders were placed. Time ebbed and flowed in unsteady waves, minutes disappearing only to reappear later—mostly when Gray needed additional room on top of the grill. Eventually the line behind the counter dwindled and discarded plates, coffee cups, and napkins collected at the center of each table. Gray muttered curses. There were trash cans by the coffee dispensers and near the door.

"Is there any coffee?" someone called.

Gray smothered another groan. His molars ached and the tightness in his chest had yet to loosen. He pressed his palm to the muscles lurking beneath the winter layer he'd packed on somewhere between the turn of the century and now, and massaged the ache spreading toward his shoulder. He must have pulled a muscle lifting a sack of flour. Normally, his back complained. But shoulder pain wasn't new. Nor was stomach pain, or the feeling the shop van was parked across his chest. Sometimes, it felt as though he carried the weight of the entire row of buildings. Mostly, this one—his parents' café and the apartments upstairs. The thick stack of bills on the desk in the office, the responsibility for it all. A dream that wasn't his but could be. His mother's legacy and the burden of his father's current apathy.

"You okay?"

It was Sporty. Hadn't he picked up his sandwich and left yet?

His dark orange eyebrows were pointing toward the center of his forehead. His eyes—a quieter shade of light brown than the bright blue or warm hazel one might expect from a redhead—reflected concern.

"Was there something wrong with your order?" Gray didn't mean to bark, but he didn't have time to chat.

He turned to survey the row of coffee urns and noted with dismay that four of the six were empty. *Jesus, lord, help me.* He hefted the first and winced as the pain in his shoulder flared.

"My sandwich was great. It's always great."

Turkey, beets, alfalfa, and avocado on a gutted wheat roll. Gray would roll his eyes at the alfalfa if Sporty was the only one who ordered it.

"Have you put any more thought into a line of gluten-free bread?" Sporty continued. His gaze flicked to the urn. "Here, let me help you with that."

"I'm fine." Gray tugged the urn out of Sporty's grasp and coughed as the movement wrenched his shoulder further. A muscle in his upper chest spasmed. His stomach rolled. "I hear you on the gluten-free bread. But as you can see, I'm a tad busy right now."

"Of course." There went the eyebrows.

Why was he so obsessed with Sporty's eyebrows? Because looking down meant noticing the color of Sporty's eyes again. And the freckles. All the freckles. The cheekbones. His wide mouth. His lips. The hint of ginger stubble along his jaw.

Gray had dated white guys before, but never one this white. And never one who seemed to have an inexhaustible wardrobe of coordinated sweat suits and sneakers. Definitely not a guy who sparkled with such good health.

Gray was more into nerds like himself and Oliver. Guys who wore their middle age comfortably (sometimes a bit too much so) and owned maybe one pair of sneakers, purchased at least ten years ago and only ever worn . . .

Gray couldn't remember the last time he'd worn sneakers.

"Is there anything else I can help you with?" Gray yanked open the cupboard beneath the coffee stand to retrieve a pouch of coffee grounds. He sorted through the different flavors for French roast.

Or was he supposed to be making decaf? And who put the coffee away last? There was a system: French roast to the left, decaf to the right, flavored coffee in the drawers underneath.

He found a double-sized pouch of French roast and straightened. The shop did not follow him up. In fact, the shop seemed to be moving in a slow circle away from him. Gray gripped the edge of the counter, waiting for the circle to stop. It didn't—not quite.

"You don't look so good," Sporty said.

"Been a busy day." Why was Sporty still standing there?

"Gray!"

Oh, dear lord. That was Patty's something's-broken-and-we're-all-going-to-die voice.

"What now?" he called.

"The flattop's acting up. Gas has cut out on one side."

A murmur traveled along the small line of customers still waiting for their lunch.

"Be right . . . there." Gray rubbed at his chest, right over his heart. Decided the pain wasn't there but up toward his shoulder. Or kind of down his arm? The floor shifted beneath his feet again, and his stomach performed a queasy roll. His teeth sent a sudden ache along his jaw, and the coffee filter he'd picked up drifted from his hand. He pincered numb fingers together, frowned, and bent to retrieve the filter. Stars flashed in front of his eyes as his head collided with a hard object.

"Oh my God! I'm so sorry. I was trying to help."

It was Sporty. Had been Sporty. Sporty's head. He now had a red mark in the middle of his forehead, one he stroked with long fingers, each topped with a very square nail. In fact, Sporty's fingernails were disturbingly neat. All of them the same size and shape, as though he spent his evenings filing them next to a ruler. And they were pink, which made no sense, or maybe it did. Also, he had freckles on his hands. Not many, but enough to notice.

The coffee stand hit Gray in the back. The floor was still moving. He was sitting on the floor and the weight parked across his torso had rolled onto his chest.

"Can't breathe," he said, gripping one of Sporty's hands. "Can't—"

The café grew dim. What was up with the lights? Had he forgotten to pay the electricity? Maybe the grill—no, the grill was gas. Had he forgotten to pay the gas?

He'd meant to catch up on everything this morning. Now all of Stroudsburg had landed on his torso and he could not get off the floor.

Chapter Two

Aaron hadn't imagined his first physical contact with Grayson Clery would be so painful. The center of Aaron's forehead throbbed, and the corresponding mark on Grayson's forehead was starting to form a visible lump. That Grayson seemed to be having difficulty breathing worried him, though. They hadn't hit their heads together that hard, had they?

When Gray slumped to the floor, eyelids fluttering, and started tugging at the collar of his polo shirt, Aaron switched from dazed bystander to concerned citizen. Gray rasped about a bill before clamping a hand to his chest, right over his heart.

Aaron switched into panic mode and yelled, "Someone call 911!"

The remaining customers in the café stared at him with exactly two expressions: *What did you say?* and *Does this mean I can't order lunch?* Then the woman at the head of the line pulled out her cell. Behind the counter, Patty grabbed the shop phone.

Aaron knelt next to Gray, who continued to clutch his chest. His breath rasped and labored, and his usually warm brown skin had taken on a decidedly ashy cast. Despite the terror welling inside, Aaron ran down the emergency checklist drilled into him once a year when he refreshed his CPR certification. As a gym instructor and personal trainer, he took the health of his clients seriously, including adverse reactions to exercise.

Gray was suffering more than an adverse reaction. He looked like he was having a heart attack.

Keep him calm, loosen his collar. Ask about medication.

"I'm going to unbutton your shirt collar," Aaron said. "It might help you breathe. Are you taking any medication for your heart? A daily aspirin?"

Gray's lips moved. A gasping sound came out.

Aaron leaned closer. "What was that?"

"Sporty."

Shaking his head, Aaron rocked back on his heels to call to Patty. "Anything?"

"I—" Her attention diverted to the phone and she started speaking quickly.

Gray tugged on Aaron's hand. "Sporty."

"What?"

"'M fine. Just need some coffee."

The absurd urge to laugh welled inside Aaron's chest. "Yeah, no. I think coffee is the last thing you need right now. How's your breathing?" He eyed the lump in the middle of Gray's forehead. Should he hold up fingers for Gray to count? "Are you allergic to aspirin?" he asked instead.

Gray was shaking his head when Patty called out, "They said to ask if he's currently taking any medication for his heart."

"For God's sake," Gray wheezed. His eyelids fluttered.

"Gray?" Aaron put a hand to his shoulder. "You still with me?"

"They want me to stay on the line," Patty said. "Can you make him comfortable?"

Aaron answered with a jerky nod. "Gray." He squeezed the broad shoulder beneath his palm. "You still there? Can you tell us about medication or aspirin?"

"I can take an aspirin," Gray whispered, eyes still closed. "Might help with this headache."

This time, Aaron did laugh. Guy was making a joke right when he might be . . .

Please don't die. I haven't gotten to know you yet.

"They're saying the EMT is five minutes out," Patty relayed. "Is he breathing okay?"

"He says he can take aspirin."

Patty glanced from the phone, to Gray, to somewhere toward the back of the shop.

The customer who'd pulled out her cell phone stepped up. "Want me to get it?"

"In the office at the back," Patty said. "Right inside the door, white tin. Should be a jar inside."

The customer hurried past the kitchen into the back of the shop. She reappeared almost instantly with a bottle of water and a jar of aspirin. She broke the seal on both, knelt next to Aaron and Gray, and dispensed a pill.

Gray allowed the aspirin to be pushed into his mouth and drank from the bottle when Aaron held it to his lips. After swallowing, he said, "Coffee would have been better."

Aaron shared a chuckle with the woman kneeling next to him.

"Three minutes," Patty called out. "How's he doing?"

"How're you doing?" Aaron asked.

Gray locked eyes with him and a chill jolted down Aaron's spine. He grabbed Gray's left hand and squeezed his fingers. "Gray?"

"It's all blurry," Gray said.

What?

Gray's eyes drifted closed.

Aaron cupped Gray's suddenly slack hand and slid a couple of fingers to the inside of his wrist. He barely registered the sound of sirens outside the café or the bustle of the EMTs as they pushed through the door. His entire focus had narrowed to the near nonexistent rasp of Gray's breath and the fact he couldn't find a pulse.

Then Aaron was being gently set aside while the EMTs formed a loose huddle. The other customer helped Aaron to a nearby chair, and Aaron sat heavily. Tears stung his eyes, and his sinuses burned. His breath felt about as shaky as his hands, and if the band around his chest didn't loosen soon, he'd be on the floor beside Gray.

Someone patted his hand. Aaron glanced over to find the woman who'd gotten the aspirin and water smiling faintly at him. "You did great," she said.

"I . . ." Aaron shook his head.

"I'm choosing to believe he'll be fine."

Aaron let his head bob up and down instead of shaking side to side. Then decided all motion should cease before he regurgitated his lunch.

One of the EMTs materialized in front of him. "Sir?"

"Yes?"

"Are you okay? You've got a pretty big bump on your forehead. Can you tell us what happened?"

The next few minutes passed in another blur of motion. Gray being lifted onto a stretcher. Patty yelling at one of the technicians. Questions, answers, the determination that Aaron did not have a concussion, but had suffered a shock and might want to consider asking someone to pick him up.

"What about Grayson?" Aaron asked.

The EMT squeezed his shoulder. "He's in good hands."

Aaron watched them steer Gray out through the door and into the back of the van. They'd just closed the van doors when a familiar man blocked Aaron's view.

Patty ran toward the café door. "Oliver! Gray collapsed. A heart attack, maybe."

"What?" Oliver swept the café with a glare, as though one of those remaining inside was responsible. His gaze landed on Aaron. They knew each other from the gym. Aaron taught classes; Oliver provided some of the food for the small onsite café. "Where are they taking him?" he asked.

The EMT van pulled away.

"Which network is he with?" Aaron asked. Did Gray have insurance?

"Lehigh Valley." Patty turned to Oliver. "They'll probably take him to Pocono Medical." The closest local hospital had been renamed Lehigh Valley something or other a couple of years ago but no one from the area called it that. "I need to contact his dad and maybe get over there, unless you want to? And we need to close the café."

"I can help," Aaron put in. "Here, at the café. I'll help whichever one of you close up." He'd prefer to follow Gray to the hospital, but despite his currently addled state, Aaron understood that wouldn't be appropriate. Gray didn't even know his name. At least, Aaron didn't think he did.

Would he ever?

Now was so not the time to ponder romantic fantasies.

A buzz against his thigh distracted him. Aaron fished his cell phone out of the pocket of his sweats and stared dazedly at the picture of his sister on the screen. Devorah did not have red hair and freckles. She had the perpetual tan of their parents' Mediterranean heritage as well as their dark hair and eyes. Aaron's adoptive family often teased him about his almost transparency, but always in a way that made him feel welcome and loved. They'd chosen him because of his red hair, his mom always insisted. Not in spite of it.

He was still staring at his phone. Aaron gathered his wits and answered the call.

"Aaron, dude, it's after one o'clock. Did you forget you had a class? Where are you?"

He blinked at the café windows. "What?"

"Where. Are. You?"

"Oh, shit. I'm so sorry. I was at Clery's getting lunch and asking about the gluten-free bread and Gray—Grayson Clery. The baker? He had . . . I think he had a heart attack. Right here. He was standing next to me, and then we bumped heads and he collapsed on the floor."

Feeling a prickle of attention, Aaron glanced up. Oliver was giving him the side eye. Thankfully, Patty pulled on Oliver's sleeve and the pair of them disappeared toward the kitchen.

Over the phone, Devorah was saying, "Are you okay?"

"I'm fine. Stunned, I guess? I mean, we run through that course every year on what to do, but it's very different when it's happening. I'm glad we've never had a serious incident at the gym, because I don't think I did everything I was supposed to."

"I'm sure you did fine. He's okay, right?"

"I don't know. They took him to the hospital, but they didn't have the siren going when they left. Is that good or bad?"

"I'm not sure. Wait, Grayson Clery? The guy you've been crushing on?"

Aaron didn't answer.

"Oh—kay," Dev said. "So, your two o'clock class."

"I'll be there."

"Are you sure? Leilani is here. I can ask her to cover it." Leilani was Devorah's partner in every sense—life partner, business partner, and coconspirator in making Aaron's life simultaneously wonderful and awkward. It was like having two sisters for the price of one.

"No, I think I need to be there. To do something usual. The exercise will be good for me." His head chose that moment to throb. Aaron inspected the lump with his fingers. Maybe he should let Leilani cover the two o'clock. There was also the matter of having volunteered to help close up the café. "You know what? Ask Leili if she'd mind. And the three thirty. Add it to the babysitting bill." Not that watching his nephew was ever a chore. "I want to hang here and help them clean up the café. They were understaffed today and it was nuts."

"Should I ask about our bagel order?"

"We can check back tomorrow. If not, we'll have time to order from Metzgar's. Heck, we could buy a few bags of bagels from the supermarket if it came down to it. We don't sell a ton."

"We can chat about it later. You going to be all right?"

"Yep!"

"All right. Love you, bro."

"Love you too."

They rang off and Aaron slipped his phone back into his pocket.

Oliver was looming over him again. "Can you help Patty close? I'm going to head over to the hospital and check on Gray."

"Sure. Anything to help."

Oliver's countenance softened slightly. "Thanks for sitting with Gray. Patty told me how you helped out." His gaze wandered upward. "You might want to put some ice on that."

Aaron touched his forehead. "I'll be fine."

"Hey, about your bagel order. It's all good. Don't worry about it."

"I wasn't—"

"I'll be making sure Gray's café remains open. He needs to not worry about this place while he recovers."

Oliver's faith that Gray would recover was heartening, as was his desire to keep the café going in his absence. But Aaron couldn't help thinking that closing the door for a month or whatever might be kinder. The café was always busy and nearly always understaffed. Today, though. Today had to have been every small business owner's nightmare.

Thank God Aaron didn't have a stake in anything like it. Devorah and Leilani seemed happy enough building their small fitness empire, but for Aaron, working a daily schedule of classes and personal training sessions was enough. He did his thing, then he went home and did some other thing. Aaron had had enough complication at the start of his life to not want any in what were supposed to be his best years.

That being said, he wouldn't mind some company now and again.

He glanced around the empty café, at the tables piled with leftover plates and napkins. The coffee pot sitting on the floor. An image of Gray, ashen and panicked, flashed to the forefront of Aaron's mind. Taking a deep breath, Aaron sought the moment before—and got instead the moment after, when Gray had been lying on the floor cracking, literally, coffee jokes.

He'd take it.

Chapter Three

When Gray was a kid, a vacation had meant he wasn't allowed to leave the hotel alone and that he could eat French toast for breakfast every day. When Gray was in his twenties, a vacation had meant he could leave the hotel any damn time he wanted to.

His first adult vacation, he hadn't left the hotel for three days. When he had left the hotel, he'd slept on the beach. He'd bought postcards at the airport and told everyone he'd had a great time. Couldn't wait to go back.

Waking up in the hospital the morning after someone parked the shop van on his chest felt a bit like that vacation. He was tired. Very tired. The previous day was a smear across his memory, a blur of endless tests and the dawning knowledge that fear only lasted so long before morphing into a complacency that was somehow worse.

Gray was blinking at the ceiling, his mind working to slot the events of the past day into a sensible timeline, choosing what to keep and what to discard, when a face popped into view. A nurse with warm brown eyes and a wide smile.

"Look who's awake."

Gray croaked in response, and when he blinked, the nurse's face slotted into the kaleidoscope of his memory.

"I know." She patted his shoulder. "You're tired. And no wonder. Last night wasn't fun, was it? Now, in case you don't recall, my name is Evie, and I'm about to head off shift. My friend Eric will be taking care of you until you go home. Which will be soon." She delivered another pat. "Dr. Kassel is going to have a lot of information for you when she comes in, but I've been working this unit for five years. I can always tell."

Tell what? And whatever it was, shouldn't he assume she could tell simply because it was her job? His eyebrows must have declared his doubts.

Evie clucked. "Mm-hmm. You go on and believe I don't know what I'm talking about." She activated the cuff encircling his upper arm. "That's fine. All types end up in here. Those who think I don't know my job and those who take comfort from what I have to say."

The blood pressure cuff squeezed tight. Gray tried not to hold his breath. Tried to will his blood pressure toward a reasonable state. Evie frowned at the display.

"High or low?" Gray rasped.

"About right," she reassured him, checking the bandage wrapped around his left wrist.

Gray issued a warning grunt.

Evie smiled gently. "Imagine how you'd be feeling if we'd used the femoral artery instead."

They could have opened a hole in his chest and he might not have felt worse.

Evie frowned at the display again. Then she was back by his shoulder, her grip firm. "Deep, slow breaths. Easier said than done, I know."

"When can I go home?" Gray asked.

"Oh, honey. As soon as your blood pressure stabilizes. We're nearly there. Dr. Kassel will be by soon. Can I get you some water?"

Gray shook his head, his thoughts sloshing from one side to the other. He was so done with peeing in bottles. Fatigue landed on his chest and spread out like an octopus. With a sigh, Gray let his heavy lids fall closed.

The next time he woke, Dr. Kassel stood over him holding a tablet computer.

"There you are." Her smile wasn't quite as warm as Nurse Evie's.

Gray instantly decided he was not a fan.

"Worst April Fools' ever, am I right?" she said.

Really not a fan.

"I know, my humor sucks. Luckily for you, it's not an essential component when it comes to your treatment."

Why were all the staff at this hospital so talkative? "When can I go home?" Gray asked, his voice as strained and broken as before.

"Let's talk about that."

I thought we were?

Gray didn't consider himself a terse individual. He could be sunshine itself. He'd patented the wide and warm smile. But the past couple of years had been a trial, and now the universe had played a practical joke that he failed to see as funny: he'd just suffered from the same ailment that had killed his mother—after moving home to take over the business that might have proved her end.

"Okay. Talk." He meant to say more, to maybe try for a modicum of politeness, but Dr. Kassel's was not the only humor that currently sucked.

"It's all right to feel whatever you're feeling at the moment," she said. "You're probably tired, sore, overwhelmed, anxious. All of the above." Thankfully, she didn't squeeze his shoulder. "So, let's start with the good news."

Dr. Kassel began with a recap of what he'd experienced the day before. He'd suffered a myocardial infarction, commonly referred to as a heart attack, and they'd used the highway from his wrist to his heart, the radial artery, to clear the blockage and place a stent. The procedure had gone well, and he might have been sent home last night if not for the fact his blood pressure refused to stabilize.

"What's the bad news, then?" Gray asked.

"Statistics. But we're going to buck the trend."

"What do you mean?"

"African Americans have a significantly higher risk of heart disease and high blood pressure. We're going to look at hereditary and lifestyle factors and do what we can to minimize the impact of both."

"Meaning..."

"I'd like you to monitor your blood pressure at home until we're sure the medication is doing what it's supposed to do. I'd also like you to examine your diet. Losing weight and making healthier choices, both food-wise and regarding exercise, will go a long way toward addressing your hypertension and high cholesterol. The medication will do its part, but will work better if you do yours."

"What about my job?"

"You'll want to take it easy for the next couple of weeks. Your wrist may be sore, but the incision is small and should heal nicely. Keep it clean. Otherwise, avoid stress and get lots of rest. Fresh air if you feel like it. A quiet walk if you feel up to it. No driving right away and no heavy lifting."

A bag of flour weighed fifty pounds.

"I have a business to run. A bakery."

"Someone else is going to have to do that for a while."

"What?" Had the cuff around his arm started squeezing him again?

"Unless you'd like me to book time right now for your bypass?"

"Bypass?" More squeezing.

Dr. Kassel's eyes twinkled. "I'm kidding. Mostly."

"I liked the April Fools' joke better."

"See? My humor's not all bad." She smiled briefly before consulting her notes. "If you're good and follow all the rules"—*don't leave the hotel alone*—"you'll be back up to speed in no time. Many heart patients are healthier than they've ever been after recovery."

"That makes no sense."

"A better diet, adding exercise and medication, and a new appreciation for the little things. For some, it's a wake-up call. For others, it's a much-needed change of perspective. For you, it's your body saying you need to slow down and take care of yourself, especially considering your family history. Think of the next couple of weeks as a vacation."

Heh. "Can I eat French toast?"

Here came the wide, warm smile. "In moderation."

Gray had no idea how much time had passed when he next opened his eyes. The cuff around his upper arm had been removed, which allowed a much deeper sleep, even if someone had woken him up to check his pressure anyway.

A scuff caught his attention. He rolled his head and saw Oliver seated in the chair next to the bed.

"Hey," Oliver said.

Gray issued the grunt he planned to trademark once they let him out of the hospital.

"How are you feeling?" Oliver lifted the small box resting in his lap. "I brought cookies."

"Are they free of everything that makes the good things in life good?"

"If you're referring to animal products, yes. But they're still chocolate chip cookies. You could even call them legal chocolate chip cookies."

"You're going to tell me that they're heart-healthy. Aren't you?" The very thought of eating a vegan cookie caused him distress.

Oliver set the box down on the table next to the bed and wheeled it over Gray's midsection. "Try one."

"Maybe I don't feel like a cookie."

"You don't look like one, either."

"What is it with hospitals and bad jokes?"

Oliver's eyes glistened.

"Don't you dare."

After drawing in a deep breath, Oliver managed to compose himself. "Hospitals are the scariest places on Earth," he said, voice quiet. "Bad humor is par for the course, my friend."

"True that." Gray pushed his palms into the mattress and winced at the pressure on his bandaged wrist as he scooted back against his pillows in an attempt to sit up.

"Don't you have some sort of control to lift up half your bed?" Oliver asked.

"Dunno. Maybe. Give me a cookie."

Before Oliver could open the box, Eric arrived. Eric was a large man. And hot. He had the patented wide smile, but also warm brown skin, merry brown eyes, and a fade that would require weekly maintenance.

Gray could remember when he and Oliver had had cool, up-to-date haircuts. Now he let his hair grow out until it touched his ears, at which time his dad was usually ready for a mutual barbering session.

Nurse Eric also had broad shoulders and large hands. And he and Gray had already been intimate. He'd helped Gray to the bathroom earlier that morning.

"Are those cookies?" Eric asked.

"Heart-healthy cookies," Oliver answered in a slightly dreamy tone. He must have noticed Eric's shoulders and hands. His smile. Eric was the whole package. Much more Gray's type (and Oliver's, apparently) than Sporty McSporterson.

A flash of light brown eyes beneath dark orange eyebrows teased his memory. The bump corresponding directly to the fading mark on Gray's forehead. The cadence of Sporty's voice, the fact he'd been down there on the café floor with Gray, gripping his hands.

Back in the present, Oliver was ticking off the benefits of his un-fun cookies. Eric was frowning and chewing on a full lip. "I dunno, man. How about if I take the cookies back to the nurses' station and give them to Mr. Clery when he's cleared to go home?"

"I guess that'd be okay." Oliver tore his gaze away from Eric's assets to check in with Gray. "Sound good to you?"

"Sure. So, the café. How—"

Eric's tut sounded suspiciously similar to Evie's.

Oliver patted the air with his hands. "All under control. You had enough bread dough to cover the weekend, and I've worked with you often enough to prepare for next week. I'm going to show Patty's husband how to mix dough this afternoon, and Nick took care of the bills on your desk. Aaron's been scrubbing everything from the front door to the back."

"Who's Aaron? Where's Patty?"

"Patty's keeping the lights on. Making sandwiches for your ever-loyal public. Aaron's the guy who was with you yesterday. Red hair?"

"Sporty."

"Sporty?"

"Always wears coordinated sweats."

"He's an instructor at Leilani's gym."

"I know. Drops off the bagel order in person, twice a week, even though there's a thing called email. Always orders the same sandwich: turkey, beets, alfalfa and avocado on a gutted wheat roll. Asks when I'm going to start doing gluten-free bread." Dispenser of smiles that revealed a dimple in each cheek. How did Gray know this? Because Sporty was always cheerful and chatty.

"Sounds like someone has a crush," Oliver murmured.

"Don't I know it," Gray all but sighed in reply.

Eric was pretending not to listen, but he was totally listening.

"I'll tell him you said hi." Oliver was grinning now.

Gray scowled. "What about my dad?"

"He was here last night. We weren't allowed to see you until you were asleep. Want me to give him a call?"

Gray's thoughts fluctuated: Was his dad watching over him while he slept annoying or sweet? And how long had he stayed? Maybe he'd simply checked the heart monitor, tendered one of his gruff nods, and left. Or had he sat in the chair awhile?

Gray shook off the questions, his shoulders rustling against the pillow. "No. I should be getting out of here today."

"Call me when you're ready for a ride home."

Already tired but not willing to show it, Gray offered a sharp nod. "Will do."

Chapter Four

"G reat class, everyone! Thanks for being here." Aaron raised his hands in a double clap and the class clapped back. The energy he had pushed into the ninety-minute workout bounced right back at him, and he soaked up the high.

The Saturday freestyle class could be his favorite. Rather than follow a set routine, he got to change it up from week-to-week, varying between CrossFit type workouts to old-school kickboxing and step aerobics. The changes kept the class interesting while also challenging the participants. And him.

Aaron mopped his face with a towel and picked up his phone. Before he could wake the screen, a sneakered pair of feet stopped in front of him. He glanced up.

Focus Fitness attracted multiple types of people, but Aaron could almost always sort them into two broad categories: those who liked to work out and those who wanted to like working out. Contrary to the spirit of working out, Aaron preferred the second group. He loved witnessing that moment of change, when an exercise clicked or a goal was met. When one of his clients figured out that fitness wasn't a chore but a choice.

Kevin, the guy standing in front of him now, fell into the first group. He loved to exercise, attending nearly as many classes as Aaron taught, and regularly booked two private sessions a week. Kevin didn't really need the help, and if he was just after a workout buddy, there was always someone in the weight room willing to spot. Aaron assumed he simply liked showing off his admittedly impressive stamina and the body that came with it.

Still, Aaron greeted him with a smile. "Hey. Great work today."

"Thanks! It was a fun class. I felt like we were back in the eighties."

Aaron laughed. "Jane Fonda is a legend, even if some of her moves are a bit outdated."

"As always, you knew where to make the changes."

"I appreciate that."

"So, listen, can I change our Monday session to Tuesday?"

Aaron woke the screen on his phone to check his training calendar. "What time were you thinking? I have an opening at ten." He also had two open training spots after lunch that day, but would like to keep his afternoons free to help out at Clery's. Gray's friend, Oliver, was going to take care of the baking, and Patty seemed to know all there was to know about café management. But Aaron could work a broom and a mop.

Kevin consulted his phone. "Ten is great. See you then!"

"See you."

While watching Kevin work out might not be the highlight of Aaron's week, regular clients were essential to the gym's business. And Aaron had to admit Kevin put on a good show. Focus Fitness had gained a handful of new personal-training clients after someone had seen him and Kevin working together.

Aaron checked his calendar for the rest of the day. Only two people had signed up for the three o'clock session. Gym policy was to cancel any class with too few participants. Aaron rarely did, though. He enjoyed smaller groups because he got the opportunity to work closely with those who showed up. But Gray was still in the hospital, and Aaron wanted to visit.

After arguing with himself for thirty seconds, Aaron clicked Cancel. The app would text anyone who'd signed up, informing them of the change.

He was about to put his phone away, when it rang. His mother's smiling face filled the screen, and Aaron grinned. He answered the call. "Hey, Mom."

"Hey, yourself. How's my charming boy?"

"I think I know what I want for my birthday." It was two months away, but whatever.

"You do?" She sounded delighted.

"For you to stop referring to me as your 'charming boy.'"

"Aw. How's 'charming young man'?"

"How's *Aaron*?"

"My Aaron?"

Aaron laughed. They had the same conversation at least once a year. "How are you, Mom?"

"I'm about to step onto an airplane."

"Yeah? Where are you going this time?"

His parents had retired to Arizona about a year after Hurricane Sandy swept through the Northeast. They'd decided they were done with snow. Since moving, they'd continued to travel, apparently *not quite* being done with seasons. They'd cruised Alaska; toured the Sonoma Valley; trekked the Appalachian, PCT, and the John Muir; ridden donkeys through the Grand Canyon; and sailed the Florida Keys.

"Pennsylvania!" she chirped.

"Really? What's here that you haven't seen?"

"You, my charming young man."

Warmth built a nest in Aaron's chest. "I've missed you too. How long are you staying? Can I pick you up at the airport?"

"That's why I'm calling. Could you?"

"Of course. What time does your flight get in?"

She rattled off a flight number and arrival time, and Aaron plugged it all into his calendar before ringing off and pocketing his phone. Only then did he realize she hadn't mentioned how long she'd be staying. Huh. She'd fill him in on the way home from the airport, no doubt.

Next on his agenda was a shower. If he was quick, he could stop by the hospital before he picked up his mom.

Devorah caught him outside the locker room. "Do you have time for a chat?"

"Sure. Can I take a shower first?"

"Leili's on her way. Can you make it a fast shower?"

It'd have to be if he still wanted to visit Gray. "Ten-four."

Aaron assumed any chat involving his sister and her wife would have to do with the gym, and he wasn't wrong. He'd no sooner sat down across the small table in the corner of Devorah's office when Devorah pushed a glossy brochure toward him. She glanced at Leilani as Aaron picked it up. He blinked down at the trifold real estate advertisement for a commercial property development in a neighboring suburb.

"What's this?"

"That—" Devorah reached over, unfolded the brochure, and pointed to a large, blank square at the end of the development "—could be your gym."

"My gym?"

"Memberships at our Marshall's Creek expansion have nearly doubled over the past three months, far outpacing our first-year projections, so we're ready for the next step. We always planned to try for a property to the west. A gym for each of us!"

Devorah beamed. Beside her, Leilani beamed. They smiled at each other, and then turned their high-wattage happiness back in Aaron's direction. He felt his lips peel upward. His face forming the appropriate response.

Inside? He was not beaming.

Post-workout slump, probably. He needed a protein shake and fifteen minutes of positive visualization—otherwise known as a power nap. Still, he did his best to mimic his sisters' excitement. They were getting a new gym and they wanted it to be his!

"Wait, you mean you want me to run it?"

"Of course!" Leilani said. "What did you think we meant?"

Aaron massaged his forehead. "Sorry. Blanked for a bit there. Will I still be able to teach my classes? My clients, what about my personal clients?"

Devorah waved a hand. "We'll figure it out. Some of your clients probably live over that direction and will be happy to relocate with you. As for classes, it'll be up to you because—" she folded her elbows across the table and leaned in "—it'll be your gym."

Leilani extended a hand to squeeze his wrist. "I'm so excited for you!"

"I am too," Aaron's lips said. His brain had hit a hill of sand and was having serious doubts about its ability to get up and over. Time for a subject change. "Oh, hey, Dev, did you know Mom and Dad were visiting?"

Devorah blinked at him.

"She just called. Was about to get on a plane. I'm picking them up at Newark in a couple of hours."

"This is the first I've heard of it."

"So, they're not staying with you?"

Devorah glanced at Leilani, whose eyes widened. They turned their surprise on him. "Ah, no?" Leilani said. "Crap, I don't think they can. We literally have no wall on the back of the house. Why didn't she call sooner?"

"Maybe they got a last-minute deal," Devorah said.

"What do you mean 'no wall'?" Aaron asked.

"We decided to go ahead with expanding the kitchen and put a family room in too. Also, we, ah, need an extra bedroom."

Devorah grabbed Leilani's hand, and they kissed.

Aaron gaped. "Wait, an extra bedroom for . . .? You're pregnant?" he asked his sister.

She shook her head. "Leili wanted to do it this time. It's still early, so keep it to yourself, okay?"

"Can I tell Mom and Dad?"

"Let us do it when they're here. Did they say where they planned to stay?"

"No, but I guess I can keep them. Though I've been throwing shit into my spare room and closing the door without waiting to see where it lands for—" he checked his watch "—five years? I really need to get going." So much for stopping by the hospital. "About the gym, can I think about it for a few days? I've got a lot going on in my head right now, and I want to take a moment to sit and process this."

Devorah and Leilani exchanged a glance.

"Sure," Devorah said, her tone clearly saying, *Really? What's there to think about?*

Leilani squeezed his wrist again, and the meeting broke up.

Aaron pocketed his phone, collected his bag, and left the gym. The early April sunshine, weak and watery as it was, felt good against his skin but also prophetic. No, that wasn't the right word. *Relevant?* *Knowing?* Whatever the word, it was as though the sun matched his mood and his feelings about heading up the third gym in the Focus Fitness Empire.

He should be excited. He loved working out. He loved helping others reach their fitness goals. So why wasn't he dancing and singing? Why did he feel as though he'd skipped his post-workout shake and nap?

Because you did.

That wasn't all of it, though.

Chapter Five

Gray pushed his left arm through a sleeve and hissed as the bandage briefly caught. He paused with the bulk of the T-shirt wrapped around his face until the claustrophobic press of material over his nose and mouth spurred him on to finish poking his head out of the neck hole. After another breath that did little to refresh him, Gray sat on the side of the hospital bed and let his chin drop toward his chest. First order of business when he got home would be a nap.

He wanted to be annoyed but couldn't muster the energy. If Gray had learned one thing over the past two days, it was that anger was exhausting. He hadn't given up on his basic human right to be pissed off— He was saving it for when his blood pressure stabilized fully.

Today's next battle: his socks. He gazed down the length of his legs. Why were his feet so goddamned far away? He filled his lungs, which still felt like a miracle, and made the executive decision to pull his feet up onto the bed.

Why the socks Oliver had packed for him didn't match was a question for the ages. Gray tugged them on, fitted the sneakers Ollie must have dug out of a lost property box over them, laced everything up, and rested with his eyes closed for another handful of minutes.

At this rate, it'd be a year before he got back up to strength.

A hand touched his arm, and Gray opened his eyes.

Evie stood by the bed. "I wanted to come say goodbye because I know I'm not going to see you in here again."

Gray found a smile for her. "Yeah, how's that?"

"Because you're going to follow each and every instruction Dr. Kassel gave to you and take care of yourself. Aren't you?"

"If I say, 'Yes, ma'am,' will you release the cookies?" Ollie had delivered another batch last night—when Gray had thought he'd been going home. His blood pressure had had other ideas.

"Once a cookie enters the nurses' station, it's lost forever."

"Figures. Do you come to find every heart patient before they're released?" he asked.

"Only my favorite ones."

Gray smiled again. His second for the day. How about that? Then another wave of fatigue rolled over his shoulders and down the front of his chest.

"You'll feel better tomorrow," Evie said.

"I seem to remember you saying that yesterday."

"Not feeling like you're going to die generally means you're doing better, though it can work the other way around."

Gray laughed. "Is this the new bedside manner? Like reverse psychology?"

She chuckled in return. "Most patients report feeling more rested after a night home in their own bed. It'll be quieter and you'll be in your own place."

"Makes sense."

Evie patted his hand. "You take care now."

"I will. And thanks."

A shuffle in the doorway caught Gray's attention. Sporty stood there holding an oversized potted potato in one hand and a plush turtle in the other.

Evie glanced from the doorway to Gray and back again. Her eyebrows arched upward, and with a quick, soft pang, Gray realized he'd miss her. Having a heart attack was not on his list of recommended pastimes. Not an activity he'd care to repeat. But she'd made his hospital stay bearable.

She patted his arm again and moved to leave. Sporty stepped aside to let her pass.

Gray wanted to lie down and close his eyes again. But he had the potato to deal with, the turtle (*seriously, what the ever living . . .*), and the man holding both.

"I'm guessing you didn't know I'm about to go home," Gray said.

"I did, actually." Sporty seemed to chew on this for a minute, his lips pursing without sound. "Oliver sent me. He had to go into the City with his daughter or he'd have been here."

Oliver's daughter was studying theater in New York City. This weekend was her set-design debut or whatever.

"I told him I'd be fine," Gray said.

"I'm here and I have a car. Where do you live?"

"Over the café."

"Perfect. I was going to help close today, anyway."

"I don't—"

"I'm pretty sure Oliver would have stern words for everyone involved if I let you take a cab home from the hospital."

"I do have other friends." He hadn't been great about keeping in touch with the crew from down south, though. Calling them from the hospital to ask for a ride home might not be the best way to say hey.

He also had a father who hadn't seen fit to visit him while he was conscious. Then again, his dad didn't drive unless he had to. Calling him for a ride would probably be more stressful than either of them could handle.

Gray gazed wistfully at the equipment he was no longer connected to. How was he going to tell he was in trouble without seeing his heart beat? Of course, he was supposed to be getting his own blood pressure monitor. Yay.

Aaron's eyebrows were pinched together.

He opened his mouth to speak, and Gray cut him off with a noisy exhale. "Fine, fine. But I'm not taking whatever that is with me." Gray gestured toward the mysterious plant. "I have enough clutter. Also, that has to be the ugliest plant I've ever seen. It looks like a big potato. With legs." Gray tilted his head. "Or a dead dog. With legs. And green things sprouting from its paws."

Sporty must have the best sense of humor in Stroudsburg, because he merely smiled. "Yeah, it kinda does, doesn't it?" He offered the pot to Gray. "Apparently someone ordered it by mistake and no one wanted to buy it. I felt sorry for it." He held out the turtle as well. "This is for luck and longevity." A cloud passed over his face. "Which I could have thought about a bit more, I guess. But turtles. Turtles are cool."

Huh. "I would have figured you'd be into cheetahs or horses." What else was fast?

"The turtle is for you."

"Because I'm a slow old man?"

"What? No. It's a gift. Turtles also symbolize endurance and persistence." A blush seared Sporty's cheeks, rendering his freckles almost invisible. "Sorry. I can keep it. I just thought—"

Gray snatched the turtle, leaving Aaron holding the potato plant. "Thank you."

"Still want a ride home?"

"I never asked for a ride home, but seeing as you're here . . ." Gray shrugged. Sporty's smile was hard to read so Gray gave up trying. "Let's get out of here."

Someone was waiting outside the door with the obligatory wheelchair. Having watched enough television to know better, Gray acceded to being wheeled to the front entrance without argument. Sporty disappeared to go get his car and turned up at the curb a few minutes later driving the sportiest vehicle imaginable: a bright yellow Jeep Wrangler.

The color was enough to incite Gray's heart to infarction all over again. The thought of riding in it? *This can't be good for my blood pressure.* But he'd already accepted the turtle, meaning he'd entered some weird bargain with this guy he barely knew. A guy who made his chest feel weird and not necessarily in a good way.

In defiance of Gray's out-of-sorts mood, Sporty wore a grin as he got out of the car and raced around to open the passenger-side door. An adorable grin. With dimples. *Should be a controlled substance.* Gray climbed into the Jeep and pulled at the seat belt. Buckling the damn thing took too long and left him exhausted. So much for feeling better the moment he left the hospital.

"So, what do you want to do first when you get home?" Sporty asked as he pulled away from the curb.

"Check to see if my dad is still alive, then sleep."

"Ah . . ."

Gray shook his head. "Sorry, spoke before I remembered adults use filters."

"Adults under the age of seventy, maybe. I have my mom staying with me, and I'm still trying to forget some of the stuff she shared with me at dinner last night. Like, seriously, I don't need to know what cheese does to her insides now and how the gas feels exactly like menstrual cramps."

"Um."

"Sorry. So, your dad. Is he sick?"

Gray was still trying to separate gas pains from period pains. "It's just your mom?"

"My dad is on a walking tour of New England with his book club."

"What?"

"Yeah, my mom didn't want to go. Not that she doesn't like walking. Everyone in my family loves walking. They've sectioned most of the Appalachian and over half the PCT."

"I have no idea what that means."

Sporty stopped for a light and glanced sideways. "It's when you hike a trail in sections rather than walk from beginning to end in one season. It can take years to section a long trail."

"What you're saying is that your whole family is sporty."

Sporty shrugged. "Sure. So, what's up with your dad? Does he live close by?"

"In the same apartment. It's his café. I'm just running it for him."

"Oh?"

"Two years ago, my mom died. Of a heart attack, as it happens. Her second in two years. Afterward, my dad decided to check out. All he does is sleep, eat, play bingo, and complain about the additives in supermarket bread."

The car had slowed. Sporty's jaw was dangling. After a second, he shut his mouth and sped up in time to brake for another light.

Gray massaged his forehead. "Sorry. I forgot my filter again. I'm tired. Thinking about being depressed, but mostly tired. I've taken more tests over the past couple of days than I ever did in college, and all I want to do is curl up on my futon with a tub of Rocky Road and wake up sometime next week. Hopefully not with ice cream in my hair."

Sporty flipped on his turn signal.

"Where are you going?" Gray asked. "The café is on Main Street."

"We're stopping to get you ice cream first."

"Pretty sure it's not on the post-heart-attack menu."

Gray had an after-care summary in his bag and a dozen new bookmarks on his phone. Everything he'd read so far assured him he'd feel better than ever in a couple of months—as long as he developed some (new) healthy habits. And he got it, he did. His mom had not developed any (new) healthy habits and look what had happened to her. But running a small business hadn't left him a lot of time or space to plan changes. For that, he'd need to make sure the café was operating smoothly—which, in his world, meant getting through a day fully staffed and without equipment failure.

"Want anything else from the store?" Sporty asked, unclipping his seat belt.

They were in the parking lot of a barnlike supermarket Gray had never visited before. Thinking about the multiple aisles drew another blanket of fatigue over his shoulders. "I'm good."

Was the world ever going to feel real again?

He'd just started to slip into a dream about turtle plants when the door behind him opened. Sporty tossed a few bags into the back seat before climbing back into the driver's seat. He shot Gray a lopsided grin. "Next stop: home."

Gray closed his eyes.

He could have managed the stairs to his apartment without Sporty's help. Might have taken him an hour or so; he'd wanted a nap about halfway up. But he'd have managed.

The sight of his dad's face when he opened the door nearly undid him, though.

His dad pulled him into a rough embrace, and in that moment, the years drifted apart like tendrils of smoke to reveal a memory of the first time Gray had visited his mom and dad at this apartment. They'd just bought the building and opened their café; a lifelong dream finally realized. His dad had looked proud but also anxious, and it had been that glimpse of uncertainty that had finally made Gray feel like an adult. That he'd seen it and recognized it—and realized his father was a man. Real and fallible. Capable of as much emotion as any human being.

The only other time he'd seen his father as vulnerable had been the day of his mom's funeral. Robert Clery had loved his wife with every fiber of his being. Gray had known that, but he also hadn't known it, or appreciated it until then, when he'd again seen his father as a man.

The moment over, his dad let him go. "Who's this?" He was frowning past Gray's shoulder at Sporty, who stood there holding a shopping bag and that damned potato plant.

Sporty shuffled them into one hand so he could hold out the other. "Aaron Asher. How do you do?"

"Robert Clery."

After shaking *Aaron's* hand, his dad clasped Gray's shoulder and squeezed. "Glad you're home."

"Thanks." Facing Aaron, Gray jerked his head toward the middle of the apartment. "Kitchen's this way."

The apartment ran the width of the building from Main Street out front to the lane at the back, and afternoon sunshine spilled in a familiar puddle through the rear windows, across dusty hardwood floors, his dad's recliner, and a sectional couch that took up way too much space. The familiar scents of chicken and rice wafted from the central kitchen.

That his dad hadn't forgotten to cook in his absence came as a relief.

Aaron set his bag on the kitchen table. "Want any help with—"

"Thanks for the ride. I'm going to take my ice cream to bed and catch a nap."

"Sure." The lopsided grin was back, along with one dimple. "If you need to go somewhere— Oliver said you weren't supposed to drive for a bit? Anyway, if you need anything, will you call?"

"Why?"

"What?"

Too tired for this. "Why are you here?"

Aaron blinked. "Um. Well . . ." He licked his lips. "I was *there*. I feel like I owe you a life or something. Like . . ." The blush returned, full force. "Sorry, that's stupid. I was trying to be friendly. But I can stop. I mean . . . sorry."

Most awkward situation ever, and one entirely of Gray's making. Apparently having a heart attack also meant he no longer had control over his mood and temper, which made him feel as much an alien as he'd always imagined his father to be.

"No, I'm sorry," he said. "I'm . . . tired."

"It's okay."

"It's not, but thanks. And thanks for being there, at the café. If anything, I owe you."

"You don't. Not really."

Gray stuck out his hand. Aaron's palm was warm against his, the grip strong. The moment of connection between them weird and odd and every other iteration of strange. But also real. While their hands touched, the world stopped spinning, and Gray's fatigue didn't bother him as much. The sharp edges of his worry became fuzzy because he couldn't quite remember what he was worried about.

Then Aaron was letting go and making his farewells.

Gray closed the door behind him and ambled into the kitchen to find his ice cream. He pulled the tub out of the bag, read the label, and swore. Aaron had bought him low fat, nondairy, sweetened-without-sugar ice confection. It was Rocky Road, though.

Gray dug a spoon out of a drawer and took his *ice confection* to bed.

Chapter Six

Aaron startled awake to the sound of a jet engine. Once his heart stopped pushing through his ribs, he realized a plane had not landed on top of his house. His mom was vacuuming. He snagged his phone off the nightstand. His mom was vacuuming at seven thirty in the morning. What the . . .?

Groaning, Aaron tossed his phone aside and pulled his pillow up over his ears. The sound of the vacuum died away. He closed his eyes and tried to retrieve the dream he'd been enjoying a few minutes before. He and Grayson had been talking. No, walking. Sitting? They'd been at a park. Somewhere with a lot of greenery and a plant like a potato with sprouting legs.

The roar of the vacuum seeped back in. With a growl, Aaron let the pillow go and rolled out of bed. He met his mom in the hallway outside his bedroom. She jumped and might have made a sound, but the vacuum drowned it out. After she powered down the jet engine, she looked up with a smile.

"Good morning. Did I wake you?"

"I thought a 747 had landed on top of the house."

"I'm sorry! I spilled coffee grounds in the kitchen."

"So, you thought you'd vacuum the hall?"

"I started in the kitchen and moved into the living room and then figured I'd do the hall while I was at it."

"Makes sense."

"Your carpet is very unsatisfying, by the way."

Aaron glanced down at the muted pattern of light and dark beige between his feet and shrugged. "It's fine."

"No, it's not. I can't tell if the swirls are a design or a stain. And you can see the floor through some of the high-traffic areas."

"Where?"

And so began a tour of his house, from the short hallway to the open-plan living and dining area, with stops along the way to sightsee interesting stains, suspected patterns, and a worryingly threadbare patch near the front door.

"That's why there's a rug there," Aaron insisted, pulling the rug down from the stair railing and putting it back over the worn-through carpet inside the door. He'd known when he bought the house that it needed work, and he'd been meaning to get around to replacing the worn carpets for a while, but his first priority had been the damp smell that drifted up the basement stairs when the weather warmed. He stored a lot of precious artifacts in his basement. Most of them now that his mother was using the spare bedroom.

"You didn't go down to the basement, did you?" Aaron asked.

"Why? What's down there?"

"A lot of boxes. Just leave them. I know the house needs some love, but I've been busy."

"Maybe we can do a few projects together while I'm here."

"How long did you say Dad's walking tour was?" *And, again, why aren't you with him?*

Instead of answering, his mother slapped his upper arm, as though they'd shared a joke, and turned toward the kitchen. "What can I get my charming young man for breakfast?"

"I can—"

She turned back around. "I'm not here forever, Aaron. Let me spoil you while I am, okay?"

His mom got this look in her eyes sometimes. On her whole face. Aaron wouldn't describe it as needy or pleading. It was more determined than that. As though Hava Asher believed herself part of an order that should not be messed with.

"Do you remember how I made my smoothie yesterday?"

"How about if we make it together?"

"Sure."

Aaron followed his mom to the kitchen and stared at the blank space of counter where his blender usually lived. "Where's my blender?"

"Oh, I put it in the pantry. You don't have a lot of counter space, and it was taking up so much room."

"Uh-huh." He waved toward the refrigerator. "Grab a bag of spinach and the chopped-up pineapple, and in the freezer there will be some bags of frozen banana."

Aaron grabbed the blender and the rest of his ingredients—a ripe mango, chia seeds, and protein powder—and met his mom at the counter where he showed her how to blend the spinach with some water first to make sure it liquefied properly. Then they added the rest of the supplements, Aaron doubling the usual recipe, and his mom bent to watch everything whir into a bright green beverage.

"It's like algae."

Aaron laughed. "Hand me a couple of glasses?"

He poured out two servings and handed her one. "Here, have a taste."

After a cautious sip, her eyebrows shot up. "It's good!"

"Of course it is."

"It tastes like tropical sunshine."

Aaron clinked his glass to hers. "That it does." By the time he drained his glass, he felt better. His morning had normalized. "So, what are your plans for the day?"

"I thought I might walk to the library. They have a book-club meeting this afternoon. There's a café on the way I might try for lunch, and before and after I can wander along Main Street and refresh my memory."

"Have you read the book?"

She waved a hand. "No, but I want to."

Wasn't his dad on some literary walking tour?

"What time do you think you'll be back?" she asked him.

Aaron rubbed his chin. He needed a shave. "Probably not until eight. Thursday is my long day. Tuesdays and Thursdays. I have personal training clients at six thirty on both days. Classes before and after lunch. And I want to stop at the café to help close if I can. That's usually around three."

"You have a second job?"

"No, I'm helping out a friend." A fast image of Gray's handsome features entered his thoughts. The wide smile and happy eyes. The rich tone of his skin.

Her lips quirked into a curve just shy of a smile. "A friend or a *friend*?"

"A friend. I'm not seeing anyone at the moment."

"Oh, why not?"

Because my friend *is currently recovering from a heart attack. One I might have helped induce.* Not that Aaron believed that was true, but he had been standing right there and Gray had pretty much dropped as soon as their heads connected over the spilled coffee.

Spilled coffee was going to be the undoing of his life, wasn't it?

He checked the time on the microwave. "My first training session is soon, so I need to shower, shave, and skedaddle."

"I had no idea you were so busy."

Aaron touched his mom's cheek and bent to kiss her forehead. "I can shift some appointments around, make some time for you in the afternoons while you're here. And if you need a project, Devorah and Leilani have no back wall on their house."

"I know! I was there yesterday. Dev gave me a tour. They're considering laminate flooring for the new addition: a lovely light woodgrain. You can hardly tell it's not real hardwood!" She glanced at the carpet abutting the kitchen tile.

"Sounds great." Aaron kissed her again and then made his escape.

Kevin showed up for his rescheduled appointment wearing new clothes. Aaron played the usual game of *should I comment or not?* Kevin wasn't training to lose weight, so the new clothes weren't to celebrate a milestone. Then again, he had bulked up appreciably over the past few months, trimming fat and sculpting musculature. His shape could have changed. Would he appreciate Aaron's notice?

If Kevin was gay or bi/pan, Aaron wouldn't hesitate. They were working out together for this result. Aaron had never been comfortable complimenting his straight male clients, though. He worried they'd take it as a pass. But after letting a few seconds whizz by in slightly uncomfortable silence, Aaron decided to go for it. "Looking good, man. Is that a cotton blend or all synthetic?"

Kevin's eyebrows danced and he smiled. Then he glanced down at his tank. "Cotton blend. I know the synthetics are supposed to wick better, but it's hard to get the stink out in the wash. You ever find that?"

"Yep."

They spent the next few minutes comparing the merits of different materials while they stretched, and Aaron relaxed into the familiar routine of working out with a client who needed little instruction. The more time he spent with Kevin, though, the more he realized that while he only had to provide occasional guidance, his presence was necessary. Kevin was the type to push harder with someone watching. Someone invested (or paid). And some people performed better with frequent encouragement—and there was nothing wrong with that. The world could be a negative place.

Kevin's phone chimed in the middle of their second set of lateral squats. After finishing the set, Kevin put his weights aside, plucked the phone off the floor, glanced at the screen, and scowled.

"Bad news?"

"Good news, actually." Kevin thumbed the button on the side of the phone to silence it before setting it back beside his water bottle. "My date for tonight is canceled."

"That's good news?"

"In this case, yeah. Ever been out with someone who is smart, successful, capable in all the ways, but is like a completely different person after six?"

"'The night is dark and full of terrors.'"

Kevin's eyebrows flew upward over a grin. "'There is ice and there is fire!'"

"No, it's 'The day is bright and beautiful . . . hope—" Aaron waved a hand to indicate there was more. "'One is black . . . white,' then the ice and fire bit." He pressed his lips together, afraid he'd overstepped. Not so much in correcting the quote, but in revealing his extensive knowledge of the popular TV show. Everyone watched *Game of Thrones*, though, didn't they?

Still grinning, Kevin raised a fist to bump. "Rock on, man."

Aaron bumped.

"Did you read the books?" Kevin asked.

Should he admit he had?

Apparently not requiring a response, Kevin continued, "I wonder whether he'll ever write the rest of them. I mean, on the one hand, he's got the scripts to use as a guide. On the other, it might feel too much like he's novelizing his own show."

"I've wondered that too."

"Yeah. With as long as it seems to take him to write anything these days, we might both be wondering until we're old and gray." Kevin jerked his head toward the phone. "This is the sort of conversation I thought I'd be having Saturday night. Maybe it was my fault. I tend to talk a lot when I get nervous. She kept asking about me, though, and was all dismissive when I wanted to talk about her. Like she was the most uninteresting person in the world."

What would Gray be like on a date? Delivering him home from the hospital hadn't exactly gone well, and they had little in common other than a shared bump on the head. What would they talk about? Would Gray find Aaron as interesting as Aaron found him? Would Aaron be able to do more than blush and stumble over his tongue?

Returning to the conversation at hand, Aaron said, "Maybe she's shy."

"Maybe."

As Aaron led Kevin through the rest of the workout, their conversation remained on television and the programs they liked until they were both lamenting the failure of a show that had lasted only one season.

"The problem," Aaron said, "for me, anyway, was that they didn't know what to do with the planet once they got there. It was supposed to be a new world. But instead of exploiting that and considering what it would take to re-create a society from the ground up, they brought the political mess of Earth with them and then threw aliens or maybe other humans who'd been abandoned there some decades before—and don't ask me how—into the mix."

"How would you have done it?" Kevin asked, wiping his face with a towel.

"I want to see someone land somewhere with nothing but the ship they came in on. Kind of like the way *Lost* started. And they have to learn how to survive with what they have access to. Devise their own tools, build their own world. Create their own legends. Imagine a game that started like that. Where you begin with nothing and have to build it all based on what's at hand. Not a set of starting tools but what's on the ground."

"A game?"

Aaron blinked. Had he said that? "I mean, well, ah . . ."

"You mean like a computer game or a board game?"

He'd meant like a tile-placing, card-collecting RPG. One that existed within the rules of the most popular systems but wasn't bound by them. One where free thought was more valuable than any scroll memorized the night before. And now he was thinking about scrolls and stats when he should be thinking about Kevin and Kevin's needs. "Let's talk about what you want to do next. We've been alternating legs, arms, and core, and I think you're getting good results. How do you feel about the workouts?"

Kevin stared at him blankly for a second or two before seeming to focus. Then he smiled. "You can get nerdy with me." His face heated. "Totally not a come-on, by the way. But if I wasn't straight, it might be?" He frowned. "See, this is why I never get to the second date. Anyway, we secret nerds have to stick together. Hear me? Life isn't all about the packaging. What's inside counts too."

Aaron hardened his jaw so his chin wouldn't drop toward the ground. Who was this man and what had he done with Kevin?

Kevin laughed. "Did I break you?" He held his fist up for another bump. "Rock on."

Aaron bumped.

Then Kevin surprised him again. "How about yoga or Pilates? I want to work on my flexibility."

"That's a great idea." And one Aaron would have had if he hadn't been so caught off guard. "Let's check for a yoga class that fits your schedule, and I'll research some Pilates moves to incorporate into your routine."

"Sounds good." Kevin tossed his towel over his shoulder and picked up his water bottle. "Oh, and when you finish designing your game, let me know. I have a friend who is always looking for indie developers to invest in."

"I'm not designing a game," Aaron said.

Kevin winked. "Yeah, you are."

Then he left and Aaron stood there massaging his jaw. Huh. How did Kevin know about the game?

Just . . .

Huh.

Chapter Seven

A week after leaving the hospital, Gray opened his eyes and lay there in the early-morning silence wondering what was wrong. For the past seven days, he'd been dealing with a sense of overwhelm that started the minute he woke up and lasted most of the morning. A mini version visited after his post-lunch nap, and an itch skirted the edge of his consciousness at night, in the moments before he succumbed to sleep.

At 5 a.m., Sunday, April 11th, ten days after All the Fuss™, Gray did not wake with a sense of dread. He wasn't tired and he wasn't panicked, despite the fact he should have been downstairs heating the oven to bake bread almost two hours ago.

For a long, quiet moment, though, he didn't miss being at work. He made a different plan. One that would take him to a beach where he wouldn't spend a week sleeping in the shade of a palm tree. He'd visit all the sites on the postcards as if he was on a proper vacation. And after he flew back to Pennsylvania, he'd tell his dad he was done with the café. They were selling the place. Or paying someone to take a wrecking ball to it.

Except that would leave them both without somewhere else to live. So, not a wrecking ball.

Could he sell the business without the building? The fact his dad owned the building was the only reason the café was still in business, despite the daily chaos. The café did sustain itself. It made enough money to pay all the bills and salaries. Gray wasn't making what he had before he'd moved home, but it was enough to live on while he paid no rent. The rent he collected from his house down in Allentown paid that mortgage, and he'd been living quietly long enough to have substantial savings.

Maybe he could sell the business but keep the building. Rent the shop back to whoever was stupid enough to buy the café, and the apartment to whoever was stupid enough to live upstairs. Then he and his dad could roll themselves into tarps and ask Oliver to store them on the upper floor, the apartment that hadn't been renovated because, despite having a plan, no one had had the time to make the phone calls necessary to get anything started.

Gray slowly sat up and swung his legs to the side of the futon. The dizziness he'd almost become used to took over. He rubbed his face and peered around the small home office he'd been using as a bedroom for the past two years. When he'd first moved home, the top-floor apartment was going to be his. That had been the plan, anyway. Help his dad out with the café, part-time: bake bread in the mornings, strip and sand hardwood in the afternoons.

"Hah."

After he'd made the apartment habitable—including an updated kitchen—Gray had supposed he'd continue baking for the café in the mornings and bake for himself in the afternoons. Given the opportunity, the space, and the time, he'd finally create as he'd always intended to. Bake loaves that weren't meant for slicing and wrapping around cold cuts. Not that there was anything wrong with sandwiches, as long as the bread complemented the fillings, that was.

But Gray wanted to bake beautiful bread. Focaccia decorated like garden plaques and pretty babkas. Sweet and savory brioche. He'd like to play with challah again. See how many seeds he could put in a loaf of rye before the crumb collapsed. Make cheese twists, pull-aparts, sourdough, soda bread, fruit bread, milk bread, unleavened bread.

"'Do something you love,' they said. 'You'll never work a day in your life,' they said."

Gray rubbed his face again. Sighed. Then he pushed to his feet and ambled into the kitchen. It was time to check his blood pressure and swallow half a dozen pills. He sighed once more when he noted a pair of plates jutting up out of the dish rack beside the sink and the smudged glass wedged in behind them.

His dad was engaged in a decades-long campaign against the dishwasher. Wouldn't be so bad if he was any good at washing dishes by hand. Gray ran a finger over the back side of one plate and caught three crumbs of old food and a greasy patch.

Curiously, the irrational anger he'd normally summon over the fact his sixty-seven-year-old father did not know how to wash dishes failed to rise. The weird peace Gray had woken with continued to flow through his veins. Was this what they meant about feeling healthier than ever after a heart attack? Was he now impervious to being pissed off?

Gray checked the kitchen for triggers. The ring of grounds by the coffee grinder. Detritus on the floor, collected in the hidden space under the cabinets. The spray of food particles inside the microwave door, visible through the glass because it hadn't been wiped out before the next use. The fingerprints on the refrigerator door.

Then he scanned the photos tacked between the smeared prints: His mom and dad at a family barbeque, standing closer together than any two people, their smiles for no one but each other. Gray with the cousins. Gray's adolescent self and his dad at the beach. Gray and his mom picking apples. The three of them at his college graduation.

Mixed emotions battled for dominance as he turned away from the photos. Love for his family, pain over his mom's passing. The fact they never talked about her. Confusion regarding his current relationship with his dad.

He caught sight of the giant potato with legs sitting in the middle of the kitchen table, and his heart finally made a small leap. Because he was smiling.

"Goddamn it."

He worked at narrowing his lips, but the smile refused to budge.

Gray had finished stacking the dishwasher, when his dad shuffled in.

"What are you doing?" his dad said. "I did the dishes last night."

"I spilled coffee on them," Gray lied. "Figured I'd put the dishwasher on now that we have enough to fill it."

His dad eyed the full racks with suspicion. "We only used two plates last night. And no bowls. Never that many glasses."

"Just giving everything a good, deep clean. The glassware needs it sometimes."

Gray met his dad's gaze, and they stared each other down for a few heartbeats.

His dad broke off first. "You're not supposed to be drinking coffee."

"I made it for you." Mostly. "Here, I'll pour you a cup so I can lean over the steam and breathe in the caffeine before I make myself a cup of dishwater." Gray did that, breathing so deep he nearly singed his nose hairs, before handing the full mug to his dad.

"They make decaffeinated coffee, you know," his dad said.

Gray scoffed. "They also make diet soda and fat-free yogurt."

His dad pulled out a chair and sat at the table. Nodded toward the potato with legs. "What is this thing, anyway?"

"No idea. What's on your agenda for the day?"

One shoulder shrugged. "Bingo over at Eagle Valley, then league night at the alley. I'll be eating there."

Gray was not aware his eyebrows had moved until his dad pointed a steady finger across the table. "Just because I'll be out all day doesn't mean you can sneak downstairs and check on things."

"I'm feeling pretty good today. I thought I'd head down for a bit. A few minutes. Look over the books. Make sure Patty ordered enough flour and so on."

"I'll call Oliver."

"You wouldn't."

His dad pulled a cell phone out of a pocket of his robe.

"You know, you could be the one to check the books and make sure Patty has ordered enough flour," Gray said.

His dad shot him a familiar look. "I haven't set foot in that café since the day your mother died."

Trust me, I know. "Why is that?" Gray had asked the question several times before, in several different ways.

His dad had supplied a variety of answers. Today's was a long, slow blink of sad, maybe haunted eyes. Then he got to his feet and hefted his coffee mug. "Going in to watch the news."

With yet another sigh, Gray finished cleaning the kitchen and went to take a shower. The same triggers lurked in every corner of the bathroom: dust on top of the toilet cistern and the glass shelves on the wall above. Three towels folded over the rails because putting a used towel in the washer, or even a hamper, would be too damned logical. An overflowing waste basket. The bathmat left on the floor, one corner dark and sodden with the water from only Poseidon knew when.

Something bit his foot. Hissing, Gray lifted his bare foot from the floor and picked at the small half circle of ouch embedded in his heel. One of his dad's toenail clippings. Great. Terrific. Just awesome. Given his new propensity for bruising, thanks to the blood thinners, his entire sole was likely to turn black. Thankfully, the nail hadn't broken his skin. He'd cut himself shaving last Wednesday and nearly called an ambulance.

The pressure in his chest refused to rise, though. He was dizzy—which seemed to happen every time he changed position—but not particularly stressed. Sitting on the closed toilet lid, he pulled his own phone out of the pocket of his sweats and dialed Oliver's number.

"Hey. I was on my way to see you," Oliver answered.

"Did my dad call you?"

"He texted."

Gray pressed the heel of one palm to his chest. "Something's wrong."

Oliver's reply came out in a rush. "Are you okay?"

"I'm fine. That's the problem. I'm too fine. My heart isn't racing, and I'm not upset about anything."

"That's . . ." The connection fuzzed. "Okay, so before you had a heart attack, that wouldn't have been weird, Gray. You're like the most level person I've ever met. Nothing phases you, ever. I've watched you deal with apocalyptic disasters day after day at the café and then sit down with the dregs of the worst coffee flavor you offer and tell Patty jokes. You are the King of Cool."

"I was pretending."

"What do you mean?"

"It was all a lie. On the outside, I was laughing, smiling, joking. On the inside, one long existential cry. You know that painting, *The Scream*?"

"Edvard Munch?"

"That's a portrait of me."

Oliver was quiet a moment. Then, "I don't know what to say."

"Yeah, neither do I. But the thing is? This morning? Today, I feel like the King of Cool. I just stacked every plate and bowl and glass in the kitchen into the dishwasher because my father can't wash a dish to save his life, and I'm cool. I have one of his toenails stuck in my foot, and instead of booking a rabies shot, I'm sitting here, in a bathroom that smells like it was last cleaned the day before Moses parted the Red Sea, and I'm *fine*."

"You don't sound fine."

"What do you mean? My heart rate is barely elevated. I've checked my pressure and it's good. And I can't wait to drink tea this morning. Eat oatmeal! With fruit! And I have six different plastic tubs of lettuce in the fridge all waiting for me to peel back those lids and mix them together for lunch! With a piece of chicken with no skin! And it's going to taste great, because it will taste like health. And did you know carrot sticks crunch like Cheetos?"

"Do you really have a toenail stuck in your foot?"

"No, I pulled it out."

After a brief pause, Oliver said, "I'm coming over."

"You don't have to do that."

"I kinda think I do. Be there in ten."

"Fine, whatever. I'm taking a shower, where I will most likely slip and hit my head because my father does not know the difference between shampoo and conditioner and the bottom of this tub has acquired a film. One I might spend today dealing with because I have nothing else to do."

Gray prodded the End Call button and tossed his phone onto the counter. Then he took his shower. Then he snuck into his bedroom, dressed, and tiptoed back to the front door. Oliver had arrived, and Gray could hear him and his father talking quietly over the news. Would they hear the door opening and closing?

Only one way to find out. Gray eased the handle down, pulled the door open, tried to slip through, remembered he had shoulders—one of which was already bruised—and opened the door a bit wider.

He was halfway down the stairs when the door opened again. Without turning to see who it was (it was Ollie, had to be Ollie), Gray raised one hand in a wave. "Just checking Patty remembered to order the flour."

At the bottom of the stairs, he faced the back entrance to the shop and keyed in the code. Pulled the door open and stopped.

The scent of baking bread and seeds filled his senses. Crust and crumb. Toasted poppy and sesame. The curling onion flakes from the everything mix.

He noticed the light, next. He'd forgotten how yellow it was at the back of the shop kitchen and how the bulb over the sink still needed changing. That the sink itself was too low for an adult to do dishes without dragging a chair out of the office, which some tall, lanky individual was doing now. Gray watched as the man (who was he?) positioned the chair in front of the sink, climbed over it, and plunged gloved hands into the soapy water.

An alarm chimed. Gray glanced at the oven in time to see Patty duck out from behind the counter and pull on an oversized mitt. She glanced up, saw him, and waved. Then she yanked open the oven and pulled out a perfect tray of kaisers.

A sharp pain shot through the center of Gray's being. Maybe near his heart, or maybe near some previously undiscovered organ. He backed up a step and bounced off Oliver, who was standing behind him. Oliver steadied his shoulder. Gray pressed his palm to his sternum.

"I am not fine," he said.

Without letting go of his shoulder—without saying a word— Oliver turned him around and guided him back up the stairs.

Chapter Eight

"**E**ven though it'd been moved six blocks away from the original location, we were still standing in the room where he'd been born."

Where who'd been born?

Pulling his thoughts from Gray, who presumably lurked somewhere upstairs, Aaron refocused on the cell phone in his hand. On the other end of the call, his dad had gone quiet.

"So, what's up next?" Aaron asked, willing himself to pay attention this time.

"More Hawthorne." *Aha.* His dad had been telling him about the House of the Seven Gables in Salem. *Right. We're back.* "And then we're moving on to Concord to look at a lot of graves. And another few houses."

"Sounds . . ." Not awesome. For his dad, maybe, but not for Aaron.

His father laughed. "Like my cup of tea."

"And Mom's," Aaron put in with a half smile, half-testing, half-questing.

After another beat of quiet, his father answered with, "Your mom wanted to catch up with you guys. Spend some one-on-one time."

"So—"

"Aaron, we're fine. How's she settling in?"

Breathing out, Aaron relaxed a little. "Well, she's about finished with the inside of my house. I might get her to check out the roof next. I think I lost a few shingles in the last storm."

His dad laughed. "I'm glad you're having fun with her." Did that really sound like fun? "What about you, Aaron? What are you up to?"

Aaron thought about what to tell his father—the *other* reasons he'd called. His anxiety regarding the gym and the question of the man upstairs who kept pulling his attention away from the task at hand: cleaning up after the day's baking and sandwich-making. Then, as had become habit, he swallowed his fears and put on his bravest face. He was the kid who didn't make trouble. Ever. "You know me. No fuss, no drama."

"Mm-hmm." Once again, quiet spread between them. "I'm always here if you do need to talk. You know that, right?"

"I do."

"Well, we're all gathering by the ferry for the trip to Boston for dinner, so I'd better get going."

"Okay. Take care of yourself and have fun."

"You too. It was good to catch up. We'll talk again soon."

Though tempted to spill some of the beans, ask his dad for advice, Aaron squashed the urge. He had time to sort stuff through on his own, the way he always did. He'd be fine. "Yep," he said. Then, "I love you."

"I love you too, son."

After tucking the phone back into his pocket, Aaron breathed into the quiet of the closed café for a few moments, then finished the sweeping, put the broom away, and picked up the two garbage bags waiting by the rear café door. He nudged the push bar with his hip. The door opened halfway and stopped as a hand grasped the edge. Aaron knew those fingers. Every time Gray had passed him a sandwich, Aaron had endeavored to brush those fingers with his own. Stupid, but so was lusting after someone who barely knew he existed.

"Sorry." Aaron stepped back.

"Sorry." Gray moved out of the way.

"I didn't hit you with the door, did I?" Aaron checked Gray's face for a mark. *Another* mark. Was he destined to keep injuring the man he was trying to get to know?

His scalp itched: the precursor to a blush. Aaron directed his gaze toward the floor and waited for the prickle to pass.

"My fault," Gray said. "I was . . ."

Aaron glanced up. "You were?"

"Lurking."

"Lurking."

"Thinking about coming into the café. Thinking about staying in the hallway."

"Why wouldn't you come into the shop?"

The bags were starting to weigh against Aaron's shoulders. He shifted them, and Gray waved toward the dumpster. "I'll get the lid for you."

"Thanks."

After dumping the bags, Aaron said, "That was the last of it. The cleanup. If that's what you were waiting for. I mean, if I was thinking about coming into the café, that'd be what I'd wait for. Cleanup to be done."

Gray's smile wasn't wide, but it did reach his eyes.

To Aaron, Gray was the whole package. Tall, broad-shouldered, and blessed with the grace larger men often developed—most likely from trying not to step on or squash their smaller brethren. Gray was also kind and generous and always seemed to have a friendly smile for his customers and employees.

His face was Aaron's favorite feature, though. The color of his skin and the roundness of his cheeks. The firm line of his jaw and the straight, no-nonsense nose. But while Gray's lips and mouth starred in his fantasies, Aaron liked his eyes the best. Gray always gave whatever or whoever he was looking at his full attention, even if only briefly. He was a man who saw and recorded. At least, that was how it seemed to Aaron, who, admittedly, lived for those brief moments.

Standing in the doorway at the rear of the shop, the odor of rotting garbage wafting over from the recently opened dumpster, shouldn't be another moment to add to the list, but it would be. Or maybe this would be the image that would finally break his fantasy.

I mean, rotting garbage? We are not having a moment.

"How was the bread today?" Gray asked. "Much left over?"

"Maybe two dozen assorted rolls and bagels." Which Aaron had dutifully transferred to the plastic tub labeled *Tuesday*. "A priest came by to pick it up before we closed."

Gray nodded. "What about the deli meat. Did anyone check the dates on those?"

"I don't know. Patty might have. It's not on the checklist she left for me."

"Patty's gone?"

"She locked the front door half an hour ago. Asked me to make sure this door was latched properly when I left."

"You're here alone?" Gray didn't exactly look worried. Okay, he looked worried.

"I'm about to leave," Aaron assured him.

Seconds stretched out between them before Gray said, "Thank you."

"You're welcome?"

"For helping out. I have no idea why you're here, but I'm sure Patty appreciates the assist." Gray rubbed a palm over the top and back of his head, scrubbing his short, dark hair. Hair dotted here and there with distinguished curls of silver. "I do too."

Aaron tried for a nonchalant shrug. "Sure."

"You want a cup of coffee or something?"

Tectonic activity did not suddenly rock Stroudsburg, but the Earth seemed to move between Aaron's feet anyway. His throat dried. The blush previously held at bay crept out of his hair and across his cheeks. Aaron fumbled his phone out of a pocket and checked the time. "I have a class in about an hour. A quick cup?"

Nodding, Gray led the way upstairs to the apartment over the shop. Aaron followed.

Once inside, Aaron said, "I don't actually drink coffee. Not in the afternoons, anyway. Water would be fine."

"What about tea? Day after I got home from the hospital, Nick brought me the sort of care package I could quite happily live without. He then made me sit at the table while he pulled every box of tea out of the bag, one by freaking one, and explained the health benefits. I can't remember which is which, but they all taste like fermented grass clippings."

"I happen to like the taste of fermented grass clippings."

Gray let out a classic *harrumph* and pulled a kettle off the stove. While he filled it, Aaron poked through the selection of tea stacked at the end of the counter. "I'm going to guess the green tea is for morning, the peppermint for lunch." He glanced up. "Do you suffer from indigestion? Peppermint could aggravate it." Aaron grinned at the next box. "I see Nick already thought of that. You've got ginger lemon here as an alternative."

"That's not the nighttime tea?"

"No." Aaron held up a box of chamomile. "This is. You've also got a honey chamomile blend, and one called Sleepy Time."

Gray *harrumph*ed again.

Aaron chuckled.

"We're both having green because it's the only one that tastes halfway like real tea, which isn't saying much."

Aaron handed over the box, and their fingers connected briefly. Remembering the fantasies he'd had and squashed over a silly lunch bag, Aaron swallowed against rising attraction. They'd barely touched. Gray probably hadn't even noticed.

The water boiled, and Gray sloshed it into two mugs and set them on the kitchen table. Aaron sat. Gray sat across from him. The plant sat between them. Not that it actually *sat*. It was already there.

Aaron smiled at it.

Gray scowled.

Aaron cleared his throat. "How are you?" He winced. "Are you sick of people asking you that yet?"

"You're the first person to ask in a while. I think everyone else is too afraid."

"I'll take Awkward Conversation Openers for two hundred, Alex."

Gray finally smiled again and it was glorious. His eyes sparkled.

Aaron tried to hide his return smile behind his tea and succeeded only in burning his lip. "Damn it."

"Want some water?"

"No. It's cool. I'm about to blush so hard I won't be able to feel anything for half an hour."

"Is that a redheaded thing?"

"An Aaron thing. You'd think I'd have grown out of it by now." Explaining that he blushed six hundred percent more around Gray would only exacerbate the situation. "I'm . . ." Aaron shook his head. "Anyway, you never answered my question."

"It's complicated."

"I can imagine."

Gray licked his lips, and Aaron fought more skin-heating thoughts. Maybe this wasn't a good idea. He'd resolved to get over this crush on Grayson Clery, hadn't he? Or had he only resolved to resolve?

Aaron fiddled with his mug handle. "I've heard, or read, that heart patients often feel better than they have in years after recovery."

"Yeah, they tried to tell me that at the hospital, before, during, and after telling me about all the exercise I should be doing and what I shouldn't eat."

"How are you doing with that?"

Gray's eyes narrowed. "Did Ollie send you up here?"

"No, you invited me for fermented grass."

Another smile.

Aaron grinned and something very, very interesting happened. Gray's eyes widened and narrowed. Then he turned his gaze toward the floor, deliberately away from Aaron. It was only when Gray scrubbed his palm over the top and back of his head again that the tell clicked. He was not the only one who still blushed as an adult.

What, why, how—

"I've been walking," Gray told the floor.

"Walking is good."

"I'm supposed to be doing more, like, when I feel up to it. But honestly? I've never worked out a day in my life. I mean, there was gym class in high school and the occasional pick-up game." He frowned. "Wait, there was this year back in the nineties when Ollie and I went in search of our abs. He bought some torture device, this frame, and we both tried it about once before deciding we'd rather eat cookies."

Aaron laughed and then made an offer that had his heart racing, "I could create a program for you." He tried to keep his tone balanced between upbeat and casual.

"A program."

"For exercise. You don't want to start too ambitiously. You'll either hurt yourself or end up so sore you'll never workout again." Also, the guy had just had a heart attack. Aaron made a mental note to research any restrictions Gray might have so he could design a program around them. For when Gray came into the gym.

If Gray came into the gym. Currently, he did not seem all that interested.

Aaron pushed on. "The difference between working out and working to a program is knowing when to start challenging yourself, to build up your strength and stamina. And doing it efficiently. Not wasting ten minutes or half an hour on an exercise that's not helping you reach your goals."

"Huh."

"And every body is different. We all have different strengths. Different goals too. Like, you might be more interested in finding your abs than bulking up. Or want to strengthen your lower back. Work on endurance. Coordination. Flexibility."

Gray now wore a curious expression. "You actually sound like you know what you're talking about."

Aaron laughed. "I should. I've been training for, like, fifteen years? And let me tell you, exercise and what we know about it has changed a ton over that time. We're constantly learning about how the body works and what health and fitness mean. There's always new information."

Gray's eyes had started to glaze.

"But I'd start you out with a simple program, a lot of moves you're probably already familiar with, until we can figure out where your strengths lie and what your goals are."

And that, apparently, put the last nail in the coffin.

"I'm not sure I need personal training," Gray said.

"First session is free and if the program is a good fit, you shouldn't need me there." Though Aaron would want to be. Was already mentally rearranging his schedule so he could be, regardless of the fact Gray hadn't said yes yet.

Gray was quiet for a while, and Aaron let him think. He sipped his green tea, wincing only slightly as the still-hot liquid touched the burn on his lip. Let his gaze wander around Gray's kitchen. Rested his eyes on the weird potato plant. Had Gray figured out what it was yet? Aaron had meant to look it up, but kept forgetting.

Rather than try for more conversation now, Aaron tucked that one away for when they were working out. Because Gray was going to say yes; he just didn't know it yet.

Gray started nodding his head. "I guess I could use the help. I'd ask Ollie, but he'd be as likely to assign the task to Nick, who'd probably research exercise back to the Dark Ages and come up with a plan marked out to the second and full of moves no one but he had ever heard of."

"Nick sounds like an interesting guy."

Gray grinned. "You don't know the half of it. Ever seen his workshop? It's next door. He and Ollie share the space. Ollie has a kitchen in the back half, and Nick uses most of the front to build his dollhouses."

"Dollhouses."

"They're pretty cool. Very precise."

Aaron added the workshop to his list of things to see and moved on. "So, when would you like to get started?"

Gray exhaled heavily and lifted his cup for a sip of tea. Grimaced and put the cup back down. "I don't like tea."

"Have you considered decaffein—"

"I never drank a lot of coffee. At least, I didn't think I did. Maybe in the afternoons when I needed a pick-me-up to get through the rest of the day. Of course, now I'm sitting here doing a whole lot of nothing while everyone else runs my café for me, without a hitch, and I'm wondering why I nearly died doing the same job."

Aaron opened his mouth to offer a platitude, but Gray rolled over the top of him. "And all of this food I shouldn't be eating? None of it is that terrible. A piece of bacon isn't going to kill me, or a real cookie. Not one of Ollie's fake-everything numbers. But every time I see that package of Oreos my dad thinks he's hiding behind the rolled oats, I get this weird pain in my chest and I think I'm going to have another heart attack."

Rather than touching Gray's hand (they really didn't know each other that well yet), Aaron chewed on his lip for a few seconds. "It sounds to me like you have been and probably still are under a lot of stress. Listen. We don't guarantee results at the gym. That's a gimmick that only serves to hurt everyone involved. But what I will tell you is that exercise can help with stress. Not just by improving your physicality and health. A big part of it is turning your thoughts elsewhere for a while. Thinking about your body, and how a particular exercise is working the muscles and tendons. How it all links together. Even counting the reps. It can be meditative."

Rather than scoff, Gray offered a nod. "I could use some of that. I've been sitting here brooding for over a week now. And when I go walking, I take my brood with me."

Aaron grinned. "Then come to the gym and let me change your life."

Gray rolled his eyes.

"Come to the gym, then. Have you got time tomorrow?"

"Sporty, I got all the time in the world right now."

"Sporty?"

Gray absolutely, positively blushed. The warmth suited his brown skin. Gave him a glow. "I meant Aaron."

"Uh-huh. Maybe you can tell me exactly what you meant at . . ." Aaron opened the schedule app on his phone. ". . . ten o'clock tomorrow morning."

Gray had his own phone out. He tapped the screen. "Maybe I can."

Chapter Nine

G ray slipped his arm inside the cuff, folded the flap over to seal the Velcro, and activated the twenty-first-century home torture device. At some point, presumably, testing his blood pressure at home would become routine. At some point, he'd stop panicking as the cuff tightened around his upper arm. Cease worrying whether his anxiety over the reading affected the numbers. Or quit imagining the throb in his arm was a clot the size of a marble just waiting for him to release the cuff so it could travel to his brain and kill him.

That couldn't actually happen, could it? Monitoring his blood pressure twice daily was supposed to prevent that, wasn't it?

As a result of all his worrying, his numbers weren't good. And because he'd been absolutely oblivious to what his blood pressure should have been before it mattered, Gray had no idea whether he was getting better or not. He only had a set of fantasy numbers that he had to reach and maintain in order to regain control of his life—and to maybe stop taking so many damn pills and put bacon back on the menu.

Grumbling and discontented, he swallowed all his pills and turned his attention to the dish rack, which was once again stacked with badly washed plates. His cell rang, diverting him from the task of testing them for grease.

A face he hadn't seen for a while popped up on the screen: James, one of his friends from Allentown. Gray answered the call. "James! It's been a minute."

"Hey. Yeah, sure has."

"What's up?"

"I heard you'd had a heart attack or something and wanted to check in."

How had the news made it all the way down to Allentown? "Where'd you hear that?"

A warm chuckle floated over the line. "My wife is in some cooking club, or maybe it's a restaurant club. I don't know. With Manny's wife. They go out and eat for like six hours every Saturday. Why didn't you call?"

The cousin network. They'd all called over the past couple of weeks, no doubt alerted by Patty. Or maybe his dad had bestirred himself to reach out. Nah, had to have been Patty. "I haven't been doing much of anything, really." Gray side-eyed the dish rack. "Sorry I've been out of touch lately. With the move and all. Running the café."

"I guessed you'd been busy. I'm also guessing you're doing okay?"

"I'm fine. Tired. But fine. Wasn't no big thing." Gray mentally changed the name of All the Fuss to A Very Minor Fuss.

"Good to hear. So, we should catch up."

"We should. My schedule is probably less crowded than yours right now. A lot of sleeping, thinking about all the things I can't eat, and more sleeping."

James laughed. "Sounds like the life."

"Heh."

"Okay, I'll check in with the cooking club and see when my turn to head out is. I'll text you."

Gray snorted. "So, next year, then?"

"Maybe by summer."

"Whenever, it'll be good to see you, man."

"Same here. You take care now."

"Thanks, I will."

Gray stared at the warm phone in his hand for a while before returning it to his pocket and wondered whether he and James would actually get around to catching up. It'd been so long since he'd had room in his schedule for more than an occasional Friday night game with Oliver, it felt weird to contemplate making other plans. As though he'd have to shift mountains in order to find a river.

Yet, all he seemed to do was stack the dishwasher.

The front door opened and closed. Gray glanced up in time to see his father's back as he made for the living room with a paper tucked under his arm.

"Morning," Gray called.

No response.

Before All the Fuss (A Very Minor Fuss?), Gray might not have been offended, dependent upon his mood. His dad had never been an overly talkative guy, but before his mom's Fuss, he'd been mostly pleasant. He'd always been useless with household chores, though, and when Gray considered the individual messes around the kitchen, the sum of them together, he had to concede that he'd always understood his mom better. Had taken after her. She'd been a doer. His dad had been the thinker.

Gray had been doing a lot of thinking lately, though.

Huh.

On the way out of the kitchen, Gray tripped over the six pairs of shoes stacked around the front door. "If you do one thing today, can it be to pick up your shoes?" he yelled. "I don't need a concussion or a broken neck on top of a heart condition."

No response.

Gray stalked into the living room. His dad had settled into the recliner that bore a permanent imprint of his ass. He had the footrest up, the paper open across his lap, and his glasses perched low on his nose.

"What's with you today?" Gray asked.

"Trying to read my paper."

"Can you pick up your shoes? I want to vacuum later."

"You shouldn't be doing too much."

"If I don't do it, who will?"

His dad continued to read the paper.

"Dad?"

When his dad glanced up, Gray caught the haunted look in his eyes. He hated that look. His dad had worn it for weeks after Gray's mom had passed.

Gray pushed out a sigh. Everyone had down days. Today was one of his dad's. They were going to have to talk it out at some point, but now wasn't the right time. Gray backed off. "Hey, so, I'm sick of chicken and salad. I'm going to get a pizza on the way home. What do you want on yours?"

Apparently reading the paper again, his dad muttered, "I'll cook."

Gray could feel the ghost of a blood pressure cuff tightening around his arm. His pulse throbbed. Robert Clery cooking meant Grayson Clery cleaning. Again.

In a pocket, his phone chimed. Gray fished it out and saw the half-hour reminder about his appointment with Aaron. He went to find his wallet and keys.

The smell of the café caught him halfway down the stairs: rising dough, baking bread, yeast, flour. His heart felt weird, as though someone had wrapped a hand around the muscle and squeezed an extra beat out of it. He missed working. He missed worrying about the work and the business. He'd yet to make it through the door, though. To get inside the café.

He wasn't sure why.

Sporty was waiting at the front of the gym for him. As always, he wore coordinating sweats that showed off his physique, and his trademark cheerful smile. Gray instantly felt lighter and mildly turned on. Aaron also had a small name plate pinned over his left pec featuring a gay pride flag and what were presumably his pronouns.

"Nice badge," Gray said.

Aaron glanced down. "They were Leilani's idea. My sister's wife. Devorah suggested the flags if staff wanted to include them. All of the badges have pronouns, though. We want our gym to be inclusive and to feel like a safe space."

"You get any pushback?"

"There're always the few who side-eye anything queer. Then we get the folks who want to start an argument about my cis-gendered pronouns. Like, why, you know? We've all had training on talking about inclusivity, though, and I think it helps that every staff member gives the same answer." He shrugged. "If someone doesn't like it, they can leave." A dimple briefly creased his left cheek. "Are you ready to work out?"

"I'm here."

Aaron clapped him on the shoulder. "Good attitude!"

"Really?"

"You'd be surprised how many people skip their first session."

"Heh. Probably not. The ratio couldn't be any worse than the number of people who don't show up for their first day of work at the café."

"No." Aaron looked horrified. "Seriously?"

"I don't know if the phenomenon is limited to Clery's, but it's definitely a thing."

"Who does that?"

"College students, mostly. Older folks too. About a third of the people who interview for a job at my café."

"I had no idea your staffing issues were so bad." Aaron said as he waved toward the interior of the gym.

Gray followed him inside. "If I'd known having a heart attack would fix everything, I'd have tried it sooner."

Aaron stopped and faced him. "I . . ."

"Too soon?"

"You're the one who"—he rolled a hand through the air—"you know."

"Nearly died in front of the coffee station? Yeah, I do know." Gray checked out Aaron's forehead. "Your head was okay? I forgot to ask. I also can't remember if I thanked you for sitting with me while my heart flailed."

Gray breathed out slowly. He didn't spend a portion of his days reliving All the Fuss. He did wake from nightmares now and again, though. Dreams where he wasn't sure whether he'd made it to the hospital.

"Are you up for this?" Aaron asked. "We can reschedule."

"No. I think I need this. What you were saying about stress? I need to learn to manage mine. I also need to lose weight and work on my cholesterol numbers. If I can kill three beasts with one sword, all the better."

Aaron was nodding. Dimpling. "Going for the AOE attack. Nice move."

What did Aaron know about area-of-effect attacks? He did not have the physique of a gamer. Not that all gamers were couch potatoes—his friend James could probably bench-press Aaron. But when did Aaron have time to play? When was he not working out?

"I haven't thanked you for helping out at the café, either," Gray said.

"I'm just sweeping and mopping at the end of the day. Taking out the trash. It's not much."

"It's a lot. Trust me. And I appreciate it."

Aaron's freckles disappeared. One moment they were there, the next moment, swallowed by a blush. Gray likely wouldn't ever get tired of witnessing that particular phenomenon. Especially on the face of a mature man.

Aaron seemed to become aware of the scrutiny, because he cleared his throat and glanced away. Started pointing around the gym.

Gray nodded along to the introduction to various stations without fully absorbing the information. He figured he could ask again if and when they visited certain equipment. But once he stopped thinking about Aaron's blush, he noticed how clean the gym was. How bright. How not intimidating. Mirrors flanked a couple of stations, but Gray could turn around and not see himself reflected in 360 degrees. If he concentrated, he could catch a whiff of sweat, but it came from people, not the equipment. The carpet wasn't sticky or dingy. The benches lacked strips of duct tape. The lighting didn't glare, but there were no dark corners. The music . . . There was no music.

"This is not what I expected," Gray said.

"What were you expecting?"

"A bad movie."

Aaron grinned. Basking in the warmth of another of Aaron's wider smiles, Gray decided he wasn't as annoying as he used to be. Couldn't, in fact, remember exactly what his objections to this guy had been. Nor could he remember when he'd started to find Aaron so damned attractive.

The first fifteen minutes of the session were given over to questions about Gray's health, what he thought he was capable of, and what he wanted to achieve. Aaron had obviously done some research, and when Gray tried to play down the fact he'd just had a heart attack, Aaron gently suggested they scale a certain goal to his current level of fitness. Which was going to be less than zero.

Aaron outlined a comprehensive warmup: jogging in place, jumping jacks, side bends, toe touches. Gray remembered the moves from high school and the occasional movie about people who did such wild things as work out regularly and win medals.

Aaron also demonstrated a modification to every move. For the jog, it was a high-step.

Twenty seconds into the jog, Gray's heart started banging hard enough to rock him off his feet. As dizziness gathered in the corners of the vast room, threatening to close toward the middle, he reached for the wall behind him. Aaron didn't leap to his rescue, which saved a little of Gray's dignity, but he did put on a concerned expression.

"I'm fine," Gray gasped.

"Switch to the high-step."

"I can do the jog."

"Strength comes from acknowledging what you can do before reaching toward what you want to do."

Aaron demonstrated the high-step again.

Halfway through the jumping jacks, Gray chose to switch to the side-step without the drama of clutching the nearby wall. A glance in Aaron's direction showed no pity, just a nod of encouragement and the next count. Gray began to understand why he was good at his job.

After the warm-up, Aaron introduced him to the workout bench. Gray had to lie on the damn thing every which way and bend his body in directions it didn't want to go. They were, apparently, testing his flexibility. Gray could have told Aaron before they started that his score would be negative whatever.

"You know, I'd have given up all of my bank account details, pin numbers, and social twenty minutes ago," Gray said when Aaron demonstrated the move he thought Gray would be trying next. "Also, I'm pretty sure my back doesn't bend that far."

"Show me how far it does bend."

Gray sat on the bench and gave it his all, which wasn't much. He was still feeling the warm-up. He had to draw his legs toward his abdomen and lift his torso at the same time so that his body formed a V. Aaron had started out flat as a board. He allowed Gray to start pretty close to the V-shape he was supposed achieve. Still, Gray's abs were not happy.

Aaron called for a break.

"Let's walk the perimeter of the gym. Bring your water, if you like."

"Why can't we lie on the floor and think about ice cream? Wait, you'd only think about that ice confection you bought me the day you drove us home from the hospital."

Aaron laughed. Gray was getting to like the sound of Aaron's laugh.

"I'd be more likely to think about the banana chocolate-chip nice cream I've got in the freezer at home," he said.

"Did you say 'nice cream'?"

"I got it from one of my favorite websites. Frozen bananas blended with stuff. Strawberries, pineapple, mango. Chocolate chips."

"You're kidding." Gray cut a sideways look at Aaron. "You're not kidding."

Aaron shrugged. "We advocate for all shapes and sizes and we have instructors of all body types. But I work hard to maintain what feels good to me and ice cream doesn't fit into that work. Not often."

Gray put a hand to his gut. At well over six feet, he could carry poundage that Aaron, who probably scraped 5'11" in shoes, couldn't. Gray had extra places to put it. But he was aware that he had a couple of inches here and there over his natural physique. It only bothered him once or twice a decade, usually around the same time Oliver decided to deep dive for some muscle group or another and enlisted his best friend Grayson in the adventure. Their attempts usually ended in an all-night board game marathon supplemented by potato chips and soda.

"Do you mind me asking how old you are?" Gray said.

"I'll be forty in June," Aaron answered.

Only five years separated them. Gray felt much older.

"Have you always been in great shape?"

They were on their second circuit of the gym. Aaron took a sip of his water before answering. "I was pretty gawky as a kid." While his smile still showed off his dimples, it felt reflective. "Red hair, freckles, all elbows and knees. Gay. Not overly effeminate, but I knew enough to know I was different. I didn't like sports. Team sports were my personal nightmare. My family were all super sporty, though, so I wanted to be too. It was my dad who started me with weights. He didn't force me into it or anything. He just invited me to workout with him, and I liked that it was an activity we could do together, *and* that my only competitor was myself. I also liked the results, which helped me learn to accept the way I was put together and work with it."

To Gray's eye, Aaron had a lot going for him, and it was hard to imagine anyone not agreeing. But he was fully aware that everyone saw themselves differently to how the world saw them.

"How about you?" Aaron asked.

"Always been tall, probably always bigger than I should be. I blame it on my mom. She's the one who taught me how to bake, and there isn't a carb I don't love and adore and want to make mine forever. I never felt like I had time to work out properly, though. It wasn't ever a priority. Especially over the past couple of years."

"It's not uncommon to ignore your own goals when you're helping someone else with theirs."

Gray didn't know what to say to that. He simply nodded.

"You're not in bad shape, Gray. You're strong. You've got muscle and you've been working a pretty active job. When we finish today, we'll talk about your fitness goals and put together a plan. I don't think it's going to be as arduous as you imagine it might be."

The look Aaron was giving him left a flush in its wake—and the maybe not-so-surprising knowledge that Aaron had checked him out at some point.

"Wait." Gray ripped his thoughts back to the gym. "We're not finished working out?"

"Nope. We're only halfway done."

"Kill me now."

Aaron laughed. "Now why would I do that?"

Chapter Ten

Watching Gray workout had been a rare treat and one Aaron had to stop going over in his mind if he ever wanted to finish updating his client notes and get back to work.

At the sound of a knock at the open office door, Aaron glanced up and smiled. "Hey."

"Hey, yourself," his sister Devorah said before flopping into one of the chairs in front of the desk. Her desk. "What are you up to?"

Aaron made to rise. "You need the computer? I can finish up later."

Dev waved one hand in dismissal. "I saw you signed up yet another new client this week. Membership and training. Go you."

Aaron glanced at the laptop. "He doesn't exactly know he has a membership. I'll cover it until he figures out what he wants."

Devorah's expression didn't change, which meant she was waiting for him to explain himself.

"Gray runs the café that fills our bagel order."

"Oh, right!" She nodded. "I thought the name was familiar. You know, as a vendor, he qualifies for a discount."

"It's not that he can't afford it. He's still thinking about it. He suffered a heart attack a couple of weeks back, and it's probably more that he's wrestling with how to approach his recovery."

"*That* Gray."

"You know many other Graysons in Stroudsburg?"

Dev chuckled. "No. Sorry. I've been spending a lot of time in my own head lately. Lining up dates. The house renovation, the new baby, the new gym. The fact Leili thinks we can do it all at once."

"She's a force of nature."

"She is."

"You said she's due in September, right? Are you going to find out the gender this time?"

"Why would we do that when the surprise is so much fun?"

Aaron leaned back in his chair. "Whoever it is, they'll be awesome. And you know I'm here to help out. Watching Cosmo if you need a break. Babysitting New Baby after the puking stage."

"That's, like, never. Cosmo puked banana all over the floor at Target yesterday. A complete stranger slipped in it. I didn't know whether to laugh, cry, or run."

"Oh my God." Aaron chose laughter.

"Laugh it up." She cocked her head. "When are you going to get yourself a family? You love kids."

"I *like* kids. Best part is being able to give them back when I'm done liking them."

"What about dating? You haven't been with anyone for a long, long while, baby brother."

"First of all, I am your only brother. The 'baby' designator isn't necessary."

"You're eight months younger than me. You'll always be my baby brother."

"You didn't know me as a baby." No one had. Aaron had been abandoned when he was six days old and passed around from home to home for ten years before the Ashers had decided to diversify their family.

"Eh, whatever," Dev said. "Answer my question."

"I've been busy."

"Is that why you're taking time to think about the new gym?"

Aaron glanced up from the desk where he'd been drawing circles with his finger, each one the frame to a vague impression of a face—the dates he'd had over the past few years. Not one of them had called him again. He bit his lip. "In part. Can I be honest with you?"

"Always."

"I haven't actually thought about it yet. When I try to push my thoughts there, my head goes blank. When I figure out why that is, I'll work it through. I promise."

Devorah smiled. "Of course." She reached across the desk, and Aaron met her hand with his, wrapping his fingers around her palm. She squeezed. "Whenever you're ready."

Aaron let go. "Okay, time to head home and find out which part of my house our mother has"—he made air quotes—"'tidied' today."

"Why is she cleaning your house? You're a neat freak."

"Because Dad is on a walking tour and she's here having a late-life crisis? I don't know."

"She sounded fine at lunch yesterday. Like she was enjoying having some time to herself."

"Awesome. Well, she only has the basement and the garage to go. Can I please send her to your place when she's done? She could help out your contractors."

Devorah's laughter followed her out the door. She raised one hand in a farewell wave and kept walking. And laughing.

Aaron grabbed his keys and hoodie and left the office. Nodded to the evening staff at the desk and stepped outside. A spring shower had left the parking lot sparkling, late sunlight glinting off puddles. The scent of wet blacktop and pollen hung rich in the air. Aaron breathed it all in, glad to be outdoors.

When he got home, he was relieved to note his mother had not yet made it to the garage. Everything appeared to be as he'd left it. The basement was a different story. Aaron opened the connecting door and stopped, breath catching in his throat, which seemed to be pulsing in time to a suddenly elevated heartbeat. She'd found his games. Not only that, she'd pulled them out of the closets and stacked them around the carpet. Why?

"Aaron, is that you?"

He called up the stairs. "Yeah."

"Dinner's about ready. You've a few minutes to wash up and change if you want."

Aaron took the steps two at a time, using the railing in the center of the split staircase to propel himself past the front door and up to the main level of the house. "Why were you in the basement? There's nothing down there but my gym equipment and stuff I'm storing."

She was standing outside of the kitchen, wiping her hands with a towel. "I had a spare hour this afternoon. I had no idea you were still interested in board games. I thought you'd grown out of them." *Ouch.* His mom soothed the burn with a smile. "Some of the boxes are quite attractive. I thought you could move them upstairs." She nodded toward the built-in bookcases lining the rear wall of the living area. "They'd be great there. You only have a handful of books, and all those turtles. Or are they tortoises?"

"Tortoises are turtles." He shifted from foot to foot. "I'm going to go take a quick shower."

Whatever she'd made for dinner smelled great. He'd miss coming home to delicious smells when his mom finally left. *Finally* being the operative word, because he still hadn't determined how long she'd be staying. Or what she was doing here. And now that she'd found his games—

Aaron didn't know what to think or feel. Not violated. That was too strong a reaction. They were only games. Boxes of pieces and . . . dreams.

That was it. He felt as though his mom had opened a closet and rifled through his dreams.

Had she found *his* game? The box of illustrated and hand-lettered cards he worked on when he wanted to disconnect completely from reality? The notebook with all his world-building ideas? He hadn't seen it. Then again, he'd rushed through the basement so fast, he hadn't seen much beyond colorful—and alphabetized—stacks of boxes.

He should be more worried about whether or not she'd found his manga collection. Some of it was pretty out there. Thankfully, he was beyond his tentacle phase.

Mostly.

Showered and changed, Aaron met his mom in the kitchen. The warm aroma of roasted vegetables and garlic assailed him as she pulled a casserole out of the oven and set it in the middle of the table.

"What do you want to drink?" Aaron asked as he opened the fridge.

"A glass of wine, please."

He emptied the bottle of white she kept in the refrigerator into a glass and grabbed some milk for himself. They sat and his mother bowed her head. Aaron did the same and they passed a quiet moment, each of them giving their own version of thanks. His dad was Jewish, his mom more philosophical than religious, and Aaron and his sister had been raised to believe that everyone and everything had a purpose.

Even after twenty years of living on his own, Aaron still felt that moment of pause before every meal, but particularly on a Friday night. It was nice to have his mom here for it.

"So." His mom picked up the serving spoon and gestured for his plate. "Why are all of your games hidden in closets in your basement?"

Because I should have grown out of gaming by now?

Her offhand comment still stung. Aaron knew she hadn't meant to hurt him, but the habit of keeping much of himself to himself had been developed years before he'd been adopted. Playing board games wasn't an objectionable hobby until everyone got tired of being asked to play or when they could try something new.

As for letting her know how he felt about his games? Foster families and group homes weren't places where one discussed their emotions. Even all these years later, Aaron had a hard time sharing.

So, he shrugged and said nothing.

His mom pressed the point. "It reminded me of that beach house we used to visit over the summer. Down at Cape May. They had a closet full of games, those dusty old boxes, most of them falling apart. You and your father only chose one game each visit, though, and played it over and over."

Aaron finally found a smile. "We had to keep playing until I won."

"He's a good man." His mom's smile was wistful.

Aaron accepted his filled plate, set it down, and fiddled with his silverware. Then he took a quick, shallow breath. "Is everything okay?"

"What do you mean?"

"With you and Dad."

His mom put her plate down and folded her hands. "Your father and I will be celebrating our fifty-fifth wedding anniversary this year."

Appreciative of the lack of glib in the reply, Aaron waited for her to continue.

"Love is hard, Aaron. But I do love your father. I married my best friend." His mom and dad had grown up together and married shortly after high school. "We've had good times and bad." After a moment, which felt like hesitation, she reached for Aaron's hand and he gave it to her. Squeezing his fingers, she continued, "You are one of our highlights."

Aaron rolled his eyes. "Mm-hmm."

Another brief pause ensued, as though she was considering sharing a secret. Her forehead creased. "Do you know how many miscarriages I had after Devorah?"

An uncomfortable flush worked its way up over Aaron's face.

"I know mothers and sons don't usually talk much about this sort of thing." Like the comparison between gas and menstrual cramps? "But you already know how much we wanted another child and how much we adored and still adore you. How lucky we feel to have found you. Our trials, though, us all becoming a family, were what cemented your father and me together forever."

Fair enough, but there had to be something else. Why was she here, now, alone? Again, Aaron exercised patience and again, his mother continued.

"After you kids left home, we drifted a bit. Not badly. Not out of love. But we had to redefine what we were as a couple. So, we started traveling. Then we retired and traveled some more." She squeezed his fingers again. "I'm tired of traveling, hon. I'll love your father until my last breath. But I don't want to walk Walden Pond with him. I wanted to visit my kids and do nothing for a while."

"Nothing except reorganize my perfectly well-organized house."

"Pssh." She poked at her meal. "I'm leaving almost everything where I find it. Mostly, I'm getting to know my son. We don't talk as often as we used to."

"I call you all the time."

"After I leave six messages asking you to."

"Not always."

"Then tell me what I can't learn by going through your things."

Had she been in his nightstand? *Dear God.*

His mom shot him an evil grin. "You're a healthy young man. Of course you like to keep yourself entertained."

Aaron choked. "Mom!"

Her expression softened. "Why aren't you seeing anyone? And don't tell me you've been busy."

Aaron filled his mouth and chewed. He wasn't sure what was happening with Gray. The workout had been great, but Aaron worried that his shyness in connecting with his crush meant he'd miss his chance. That he and Gray might end up just as friends.

He also didn't want to talk about it because he worried his feelings were somewhat immature. With forty approaching, shouldn't he be more decisive?

Then, again, there was the simple matter of sharing his feelings. Never easy.

The proprietor of Asher patience, his mother waited him out.

He swallowed some milk as another delaying tactic. Then decided to address the issue head-on. "My best friend is my sister and she's already married, so that's not an option."

His mom laughed. "Oh, Aaron. You know what I mean." She cocked her head to one side. "I didn't get the impression you were completely brokenhearted after you and Paul split."

"I wasn't. When we were good, we were good. Then we wanted different things. I've dated since." It'd been a few years since Paul, after all. "But the effort involved in getting to know someone feels like too much most of the time."

"You mean letting someone in."

He shrugged again. Filled his mouth with food in case she pressed for a better answer.

"Devorah told me about the new gym. The one they'd like you to manage."

Aaron swallowed awkwardly.

"You don't want to do it, do you?"

Panic formed a bubble in his throat, preventing anything from passing.

His mom reached across the table again. He did not take her hand. She offered a small smile instead. "It's okay to say no."

"I know," he rasped.

Thankfully, she leaned back and resumed eating. But after a short beat of blessed quiet, she poked the ant hill once more. "Will you tell me about the game you're making?"

Aaron was going to need a bottle of antacid after this meal. "What do you mean?"

She shot him The Look.

"It's . . . not much. A project I fiddle with." *When I'm not dating, which is all the time. So—*

"From what I could tell, you've put a lot of work into it. I'd love to hear the story." She caught his gaze. "Really. I would."

"It's not ready to play yet. I don't know if it will ever be. It's what I do in my spare time."

"If it makes you uncomfortable, we don't have to play it."

A great sigh welled up in Aaron's chest. He held it in for a few seconds before letting it go. Felt measurably better afterward. "I'll show it to you. But don't mention it to Dev or Leili, okay?"

"Why not?"

"Because they wouldn't understand."

His mom held his gaze for a long moment. When she turned back to her plate, Aaron expected her to say, *Give you sister more credit*, or *You don't know that*. Instead, she smiled a secret sort of smile and forked up another mouthful of casserole.

Aaron's gut was tied in knots. Forget the bottle of antacid, just back up a tanker.

His mom finished her mouthful and took a sip of wine. Then she said, "It's your life, Aaron. For you to do anything you want with. Don't ever forget that."

Chapter Eleven

The plastic covering the album pages creaked and crackled as Gray flipped through memories. He'd packed the album a couple of months after moving back to Stroudsburg, when he'd realized an overnight bag of essentials wouldn't be enough. Instead of sitting down with his dad to figure out exactly what they were going to do with the café, Gray had packed up his house and listed it for rent. He'd stored most of his stuff. Brought a little of it here.

The nearly two years that had followed felt about as displaced as the memories in front of him.

The album covered the latter half of Gray's childhood, the frequency of the photos diminishing as he got older. There were ten or so of him in eighth grade. Gray snorted at the picture of him and Ollie in costume for a talent show. They'd performed "Singing in the Rain." Together. Neither of them could sing nor dance, let alone tap, yet they'd been convinced their act would amaze.

It was a good thing they'd had each other or neither of them would have had a single friend in school.

The next page held two photos from ninth grade, the facing page a certificate of award from a short story contest. Gray chuckled again. He'd forgotten about that. His mother had been so proud. Yep, there she was in one of the photos, snugged against his side—already he'd been too tall for her to put an arm around his shoulders. She was holding both his story, printed on some long-ass paper and rolled into a scroll, and the certificate. His younger self looked somewhere between proud and mortified.

Gray touched his mom's face, blotting most of it out until he moved his thumb in a soft caress. His heart hurt with a different kind of pain. Two years. Some days it felt like longer. Other days, like no time at all.

The photo beneath showed him and his dad at the beach, and it took Gray a while to place the memory. It was a different sandy beach to the photo on the fridge. Perhaps a year or two later than that one. Huh. Gray hadn't remembered his dad liking the shore so much. Then the time and place clicked: Wildwood. Summer of eight-five. They'd played so many games on the boardwalk, Gray had zipped through his monthly allowance in less than an hour. His dad had been the one to sneak a few more dollars into his pocket.

With a sudden intensity, Gray missed summer. Not the upcoming season, but the summer of his youth. When his parents had taken time away from work to spend with *him*.

Maybe that's what had been wrong with his own beach vacation. His dad hadn't been there to wander the boardwalks with him. His mom hadn't been there to explore the local food.

His phone rang. Distracted, Gray inadvertently batted it off the futon and onto the floor. He glared at it a moment before deciding the futon was low enough that he'd be able to get down there without using his legs. They weren't stupidly sore, but he was aware that Aaron had exercised him more in one day than Gray had managed in the past decade. That all they'd done was warm up and stretch, check his flexibility, only added salt to the wound.

The album formed an uncomfortable wedge in his midsection. He put it aside and tried rolling forward onto his knees. His thighs complained. His calves burned. Gray gritted his teeth and swallowed a whimper. By the time he managed to collect his phone, the caller had left a voice mail. Rather than listen to the message, Gray hit Redial.

"There you are," Oliver answered.

"Here I am. What's up?"

"It's raining buckets out there, so we skipped the markets this morning." Oliver sold his joyless pastries and pies at various venues on Saturday mornings. "Want to come to yoga with us instead?"

"You do realize you're talking to Grayson Clery?"

Oliver chuckled. "The one and only. You said you were starting a program. This is me supporting your efforts."

"While I appreciate the gesture"—and he did with a warm, fuzzy, what-the-fuck sort of feeling—"I'm not sure I can. First of all, my legs are in full revolt. Yesterday wasn't so bad, but today? I can barely move."

"And second?"

"I can't believe you called to invite me to exercise. Who are you? Who am I? What world is this?"

The volume of Oliver's laughter rose and fell as though he was waving his phone around. A scuffling sound indicated he'd pressed it back to the side of his face. "Okay," he said. "Two points in return for you."

"Go."

"First of all, if you're that sore, this class will be just the thing."

"I did manage to get down to the floor to pick up my phone, but I'm not sure I can get up again."

More snickering. "Second of all, if you're that sore, this class will be just the thing."

"You already said that." Gray sat on his heels and scooted back toward the futon. That was better. Crawling around on the floor seemed to have loosened the tension in his thighs.

"For me, the day after the day after is always worse," Oliver said.

"I need my legs to work properly again by tomorrow. Maybe I should spend the day in bed?"

"You're starting back at the café tomorrow?"

"You all can't run the place forever."

"We don't plan to. Just long enough for you to get well."

"I'm not sick, Ollie."

"What does your doctor say?"

He'd had his first follow-up appointment the day before. Gray sighed. "I'm supposed to be listening to my body." Among less flattering suggestions. Like he shouldn't be listening to the thirty pounds he was supposed to lose. But the sore legs he'd used to limp into the office? He was allowed to listen to those. Apparently, the issue for a lot of patients Dr. Kassel saw was a lack of listening. Ignoring physical stress was not a sign of strength. She obviously had the same motivational poster as Aaron hidden somewhere in her office.

"And what is your body telling you?" Oliver asked.

"Are we really having this conversation?"

"Would you rather talk about aliens?"

"No."

"I have one word for you."

"Not two?"

"Yoga."

"Is it fat-free?"

"What?"

"I dunno, Ollie. I mean, isn't yoga mostly sitting around and farting?"

"Hah! No. It's stretching, basically, and breathing. And before you ask, we won't look out of place. I mean, there are some people in the class who could probably snap bones with their little fingers. But mostly, it's people like us. We won't be the only slightly used vehicles in the lot."

"Sounds enticing."

"C'mon, you know you wanna."

Heaving out a sigh, Gray considered his other options: continue flipping through pictures of his mother, flop back onto his futon—it was raining, after all—or try for an actual conversation with his father. "Sure. Let's do it."

Before leaving for the gym, Gray checked in with his dad. He found him in the living room, settled into his armchair with the paper across his lap. He looked comfortable.

Gray was jealous. "You good?"

His dad glanced up. "Yep."

"I'm heading out for a while."

"Okay."

Gray stood there a moment longer, watching his father read. Before All the Fuss he'd have said they had a fair relationship. Not the same as Oliver and his parents, but they got along. When Gray had first moved home to take over the café, his dad had seemed truly grateful. But while Gray couldn't say this current disconnect was new, his father had definitely become quieter over the past couple of weeks.

"Are you home tonight?" Gray asked.

"Yep."

"We should pull out some cards. Get a game going. Your choice."

His dad glanced up again. "All right."

Gray smiled. His dad did not. Gray hefted his gym bag. "I'll see you later."

"See you."

At the gym, Oliver, Nick, and Nick's brother, Cameron, awaited him. Oliver gave Gray a quick hug, Nick a quiet nod. Cam offered his hand.

"Thanks for the help with the café," Gray said.

Out of the two brothers, Cam always seemed the more cheerful. It wasn't that Nick didn't smile. To listen to Oliver, Nick's smiles were well-earned marvels. And Gray liked Nick, he did. But Cam was super easy to get along with. And though both brothers were generous with their time and attention, Cam truly seemed to enjoy helping out his friends. Gray had absolutely no doubt Cam had been rallied this morning in an effort to make this particular outing jolly.

The previous class let out, and Gray and the others stood aside while the studio emptied. Judging by the red and glistening faces, the session had been way more energetic than yoga.

"If you'd invited me to that class, our friendship would have suffered," Gray confided to Oliver.

Oliver answered with a hurt pout before grinning. "It would have been as painful for me as you."

Not for Nick or Cam, though. Both brothers were startlingly fit and way too energetic for a gloomy Saturday morning.

Aaron arrived dressed in a shiny, almost skin-tight long-sleeve T-shirt. The fit emphasized his perfect build. Underneath, he had on a loose pair of shorts over . . . not tights, but dark gray leggings? Should have looked stupid, but Gray could only find appreciative thoughts for what he could see of Aaron's leanly muscled thighs and calves.

Also, Gray's face felt weird. When he realized he was smiling, he almost reached up to squash his cheeks down. Since when was he pleased to see his cheerful torturer?

"Aaron." Cam was the first to offer a hand. "Good to see you." They shook.

While Aaron greeted the rest of the group, Gray worked through his irrational jealousy. Of course, Cam knew Aaron. They were both fit and . . . fit. And cheerful. And single, presumably. And why did he care? They weren't here to—

"Sorry, what?" Gray blinked at Aaron, who'd stopped in front of him and said something. At least, Gray had the impression he had.

"How's your body?" Aaron said. "Was I your least favorite person in the world yesterday?"

"Just about. Right behind whoever snuck into my apartment and cut the tendons in the back of my legs."

"Ouch. Did you stretch?"

"Yeah. As much as I could."

"Ice can help. Sorry if I pushed you too hard." Color swept over Aaron's cheekbones. "I'm glad you're here, though. Means I didn't put you off exercise forever." Dimples creased his pink cheeks.

Gray didn't know what to say. He certainly wasn't going to admit his lungs had suddenly constricted or that his chest felt tight. Why this guy? Just . . . why?

After waiting another beat, Aaron ducked his head and moved into the studio.

"Dude," came a soft drawl beside Gray.

He turned to see Cam grinning at him. "What?"

"Nick and Oliver told me about The Crush."

Gray hadn't imagined the capitals, had he? Also, "*Nick* said something?"

"Nick dutifully supported Ollie's hypothesis. After much unsubtle prompting."

Gray snorted.

Cam lifted his chin. "You into that? Red hair and freckles?"

"He's, ah, fit."

A wolfish grin. "Yeah. He is." Cam clapped Gray on the shoulder. "Let's do this."

Any concerns Gray had about trying to concentrate on a class taught by Aaron were allayed by the appearance of a new instructor, a woman who introduced herself as Stacy. His relief was quickly squashed by the appearance of another fit and reasonably attractive man (if you liked the athletic sort). The newcomer and Aaron exchanged a fist bump and rolled their mats out together.

Oh, joy. As if watching Aaron work out alone wouldn't have been fun enough.

"Today's class is meant to be relaxing," Stacy was saying. "Follow what you can, but always remember it's your body and your workout." She directed a smile toward the group. "Okay, everyone get a mat, a block, and a strap. Take a break when you need one, ask for a modification at any time, and remember to drink plenty of water now and after the class." She clapped her hands twice. "Who's ready to get started?"

A posse of excitable youths (they were somewhere south of thirty) near the front of the class clapped their hands in the air. "We're ready!"

So much for relaxing.

Stacy fiddled with a panel to the side of the instructor's area, and quiet music floated into the room. A pan flute and soft cymbals.

Gray had no doubt the musicians enjoyed tofu and granola.

He checked in with his friends. Cam was next to him, holding out a foam rubber block.

"What's this?" Gray asked.

"For support. Trust me, it's not as weird as it looks." Cam handed over a strap like a canvas belt, and Oliver tossed him a furled rubber mat. Everyone took a moment to set themselves up, mats unrolled to face the front of the room, blocks and straps to one side. Gray copied his friends, and they all made signs of encouragement. Nick offered one of his crooked smiles. Oliver said, "You've got this." Cam gave him a thumbs-up.

When Gray happened to glance over at Aaron, he caught a cheerful smile and had the uncomfortable notion Aaron had been watching him for some time. Aaron's companion was busy flexing and stretching his impressive physique.

Not sure what message a smile would send, Gray offered a nod, and then turned his concentration toward appearing as if he belonged. *Uh-huh.* He tried for less out of place, instead.

Thankfully, the class started with them on their backs. Hard to be out of place when everyone was lying down. The warm-up was actually relaxing. All Stacy wanted them to do was breathe. But before Gray could start to drift—what the heck was with this music?—Stacy had them bend their knees. Still not so bad. Even folding one of his legs to put his heel against his upraised knee wasn't all that arduous. Pressing on his hip wasn't great, but the stretch outside his upper thigh and around his calf felt much better than crawling around his bedroom floor after his phone.

Of course, no sooner had Gray decided he could do yoga than it all went sideways. Quite literally. They were still on their backs, both knees bent again, and Stacy wanted everyone to roll their knees to one side. As in, have them touch the floor.

Gray tipped his knees to the right and growled as muscles or tendons he hadn't known he possessed pulled tight.

"Use the block," Cam whispered.

Gray glanced at his neighbor and wished he hadn't. Cam's body faced one way, his head the other, as though someone had broken his head off his neck and set it on backward.

"How are you even talking right now?" he asked.

Cam grinned before jerking his chin toward the block. "Tuck it under your knees."

Gray did that and found he could lie on his back with his knees tipped a little to one side.

"When you go to pull your knees up again, use your hands if you need to. Don't want to put undue pressure on your lower back."

Using his hands to move his legs helped. Gray gave Cam a grateful nod and rolled the other way. Aaron's way. Thankfully, Aaron was also facing the other way and not performing Cam's dislocated-head trick. Gray spent the few breaths they were allowed on that side not admiring the straight line of Aaron's back and the curve of his ass behind the shorts he wore over the leggings.

Stacy moved the class through several other postures that involved lying on their backs and moving their legs around, and Gray decided somewhere between trying to remember his breath and trying not to arch up off the floor that yoga wasn't so bad. Also, no one had farted yet.

Next came a move performed on hands and knees: cat and cow.

Watching Oliver arch his back like a cat and then thrust his ass in the air (like a cow?) was almost worth the price of admission. Watching Aaron do the same thing stirred uncomfortable heat in Gray's groin. Aaron's body flowed sinuously between the two postures, making them elegant rather than contrived. Cam and Nick managed to flow nearly as well, but watching them didn't interest Gray as much as watching Aaron did.

And he wasn't going to examine why that was.

Downward dog, Gray had seen before. Doing it was anticlimactic until Stacy invited Aaron to move through the class with her to touch a hip here and there in aid of perfect posture. Aaron paused behind Gray, and all Gray could think while blood rushed to his head was that he should have worn something other than twenty-year-old sweatpants.

There'd been a time when he'd taken pride in how he looked.

There'd been a time when he would have laughed at a phone call inviting him to yoga. His friends down south would never have dared. Then again, they were all hitting middle age and had partners and kids. Who knew what they got up to in their spare time.

Aaron touched his hip. "Bend your knees a little, Gray. Keeping your back straight is more important to begin with. Use your shoulders and arms."

Heart pounding, Gray followed Aaron's instruction and found his posture did change for the better. It was subtle, but he felt his neck and spine loosening ever so slightly. His lower back didn't hurt at all.

What sorcery was this?

He glanced over at Ollie and met Cam's gaze instead. Cam offered a wicked grin.

Of course, when Gray looked back at Aaron, Aaron was touching his workout buddy's hip and murmuring encouragement. Gray was pretty sure he wasn't supposed to be feeling so much stress over their interaction.

A mixture of failure and success followed, with neither achievement meaning more than the other, and Gray came to understand that yoga—or this class, anyway—wasn't so much about perfecting a posture as striving for it. By the time they were on their backs again, almost an hour had passed and he felt warm, loose, and somewhat contented.

Stacy ended the class with a short meditation. "Close your eyes and check in with your body." She instructed them to find any tension and then to let it go. Easier said than done, but Gray did find fewer sore spots than he'd had to begin with.

Then she wanted them to "Imagine yourself outside. Somewhere quiet and peaceful." Gray drew a blank at first. After a moment, grass crept in from the edges to form a vague field. The field evoked no memory, and Gray could only imagine its absolute emptiness was what made him happy.

"Now imagine yourself as a tree. Every branch, every limb, every leaf turned outward and upward toward the sun."

Gray wanted to scoff. Him as a tree? But before he could find an excuse to mentally ridicule the exercise, his tree was there. Not as elegant as he'd like, but sturdy and solid. Dense bark the color of French roast wove tightly around the trunk, and his lower branches were slightly gnarled. The leaves took a while to form, but the magic of watching them unfold almost took his breath away. The warmth of the sun against their broad expanse of green? Like lying on the sand in Maui.

The lure of sleep scratched at the edges of his consciousness. Or that place between sleep and wakefulness—a drift of thought where what might have been important ceased to matter. There was only this moment, this breath, this warmth. Even the music seemed appropriate and restful.

Then Stacy began calling them back and Gray prepared to let go. To push back to reality. But a sense of the peace he'd gained stayed with him. It was weird . . . and not weird.

The class ended and Gray turned to his friends.

Cam looked serene. Oliver's sloppy smile had a sleepy cast. Nick's fidgets had lessened. Gray watched as Oliver touched Nick's shoulder, then looped an arm around his shoulders to draw him close. They touched their foreheads together and shared a secret smile.

A part of Gray envied their closeness. He was happy for Oliver (and Nick). But their happiness did sometimes remind him of his loneliness—of the fact that for too long, his world had consisted of little outside of work.

Maybe this was his opportunity to make some serious changes.

Well, duh.

But when Gray thought about what he'd like to change, he could only imagine more of the same. Dealing with the café while it was open. Dealing with the café when it was closed. His father's distance. His envy regarding Oliver's happiness.

"How are you doing?" a soft voice asked.

Gray turned to find Aaron standing close. His workout buddy was nowhere to be seen.

Gray opened his mouth, closed it, and shrugged. He didn't know what to say, except "It wasn't as weird as I was expecting. I mean, the music . . ."

A wide grin spread over Aaron's mouth, putting his dimples on full display. "Eh, it's kind of cliché, but it's expected, you know? If we played different music, it wouldn't fade into the background. It'd intrude on the mental space."

Gray nodded. "I get it."

"Of course you do. How are you feeling?"

"I feel good."

"That's great! I'm glad you could make it today." Aaron obviously meant every word.

Gray didn't feel like scoffing at him, though, or any of the curious resentment he'd had previously whenever Aaron showed up. His annoyance over Aaron seemed to have faded. Instead, all he could see was a man flushed with health and the satisfaction of a good class.

"You really like all this. Don't you?" Gray said.

"I do. Best part?"

Gray waited.

"It can get super busy at your café, but you always know what comes next. The way you move from oven to grill to counter and back again, always giving everyone what they need, it's like a dance. Being in a class, working out or teaching, can be like that. Everyone moving together. Everyone getting it."

Gray chuckled. "Maybe that's what I've been doing wrong. Running the café instead of watching myself work."

Laughter lit Aaron's eyes. "There you go."

The elation of surviving the class began to fade. At first, Gray worried he'd overdone it. That his heart had decided enough was enough and now would be a good time for him to lie down, even though he'd spent a good portion of the past hour on his back. He didn't feel dizzy, though. There was no pain. No queasiness or an impending sense of wrongness, as though the ceiling was about to give way, or the floor, or both. He just felt slightly untethered.

"Everything okay?" Aaron asked.

Gray directed his thoughts toward his plan to start back at work on Monday, which meant that tomorrow he should mix up and roll out some dough. The excitement he'd expected to feel—about the chance to slip back into the coordination of movement Aaron had mentioned—failed to register, though.

He glanced over at Aaron. Away again. "Yeah, 'm fine. Just . . ." He shot him a quick smile. "The, ah, one-on-one sessions. Can we set up that contract you suggested?"

Aaron's answering smile lit up the studio. "Of course. Do you want to book the same time as last week?"

"Do you have anything on Tuesday?" Tuesdays were quiet at the café, and he knew his friends wouldn't abandon him the first week back.

Mostly, though, Gray liked the idea of having an activity to look forward to. Something other than work. That the something was exercise, with a man he didn't know how to feel about? An issue to pick over some other time. But he did know that being here made him feel good.

That was enough for now.

Chapter Twelve

Aaron usually split his attention between a client's body and their expression; checking coordination and angles to make sure they didn't injure themselves, and whether they were smiling or crying. He'd never had a personal training client cry, but today Gray could be close. And his tears would not be ones of quiet suffering. Anger burned in his deep brown eyes. Frustration crackled along his limbs.

"Try not to snap your arms and legs out," Aaron cautioned. "You don't want to overextend your knees or elbows."

"It's a jumping jack. I'm meant to snap."

"If you put all of your energy into the warm-up, you won't have any left for our workout."

Gray's thunderous expression answered for him: He didn't care. About the workout, about injuring himself, about being there.

Aaron recalled Café Gray. The man who lit the store with a smile, even on the busiest and most chaotic days. That had been the Gray Aaron wanted to get to know. The man whose bright expressions lifted his entire face, suffusing his warm brown skin with a glow Aaron could never hope to achieve. And while he was on the subject of Gray, Aaron envied his stature too. He saw a lot of tall people who tended to stoop, as though they needed to bend down to interact with the rest of humanity. Gray lived his large frame. Even after his heart attack, he stood straight and kept his shoulders wide. And what shoulders they were. Rounded with muscle.

Gym Gray vacillated between quietly focused and quietly furious. Aaron didn't want to think it was his fault. That he was the Worst Trainer Ever. The warm-up routine obviously wasn't working for his client, however. So Aaron closed the tablet listing the next move and beckoned Gray away from the warm-up area. "Follow me."

With a grunt, Gray followed.

Aaron led him to one of the studios they used for group classes. A long, heavy kick bag hung from a ceiling beam in the far corner. Behind it, various pads and baffles stuck out of a rack on the wall. If Aaron knew Gray better—if he was working out with Café Gray—he might grab some handheld pads or a paddle. But Gym Gray looked as though he'd murder anyone who offered themselves as sacrifice. Aaron directed his attention toward the kick bag.

"What is it you want to punch?" he asked.

Gray stared at the bag, anger narrowing his eyes. Then he took a step back, shaking his head. "I'm good."

"No, you're not." Aaron swallowed a sigh. "I'm not going to tell you whatever you're feeling is okay. I'm not a licensed therapist. I'm not your doctor. But you are my client." And they might be friends. Sort of.

Gray made no answer.

"Right now, we're a party of two and between us, we have a certain set of skills." Aaron gestured toward the kick bag, the pads, himself, and Gray. "These tools. We're charged with . . ." He didn't want to completely game the situation, but they weren't in a Rocky movie here. "We're on a quest to defeat the big bad. Today's battle is your attitude. It's not good, it's not evil. It's chaotic. We need to nudge its alignment one way or another and then make a plan to deal with it."

Okay, he'd gone entirely too far because now Gray was blinking at him.

"Or we could punch and kick the bag until you feel better," Aaron said.

One corner of Gray's mouth kicked upward. "You're a tabletop geek." His gaze roamed over Aaron's form, head to shoulders to toes, leaving a warm flush in its wake. "Sporty McSporterson, secret nerd."

Ignoring the heat stealing across his skin, Aaron aimed a punch at the bag. A snappy jab. "You'll want to stand close enough to the bag not to—"

"I tried to make bread dough on Sunday. I thought I was ready. I wanted to go back to work this week."

Aaron straightened into a listening posture.

Gray continued, "But I'm still so tired. Sometimes I think this is how it's going to be, forever. That I'll always feel like I'm walking with twenty-pound weights attached to my arms and legs. That my joints will always be sore, that every inch of my skin will soon be one big bruise. That my motivation to do anything other than lie on the couch and listen to my father crack open pistachio nuts, yell at the TV, and fart, will remain nil."

Aaron's lips twitched.

Gray chuckled.

"It's only been, what, two weeks?"

"Two and a half."

"If I ask what your doctor has said, will you punch me?"

Gray glanced at the bag. Back at Aaron. "I'd think about it. She said I've been overdoing it for so long, my body is enjoying a much-needed break. Also, I'm on so many different kinds of meds—blood thinners, cholesterol, blood pressure stuff—it's taking me a while to adjust. But I feel like if I don't get moving, I'll never get moving."

"Let's walk and talk." Aaron gestured toward the perimeter of the studio and started walking. "I know you probably don't want to hear this, but walking is great exercise. If that's all you want to do at the moment, we can work with that. We can stretch before and after. Carry some light weights. Work up to a more aggressive routine if you want to build muscle."

Gray stepped up beside him. "I need to lose thirty pounds. I lost a couple in the hospital, but put 'em right back on when I got home. Eating dry chicken and greens. I'm so sick of chicken."

Aaron pulled in a slow but deep breath. "What do you like to eat?"

"Bacon."

Aaron laughed. "Okay, so how about turkey bacon?"

"It's not so much the fat as the sodium. Seriously, without salt, life is a lot less fun."

They were quiet for a circuit. Aaron let Gray set the pace and watched Gray's shoulders settle as they started on their second round.

He indicated the window. "Want to head outside? We have a track bordering the property."

Gray stopped in front of the hanging bag. Balled a fist. Threw a punch. Winced. "Sure."

The track outside the gym circled the parking lot before running behind the building to hug the edge of the woods along McMichael Creek. Two circuits equaled a mile, or close enough. They'd completed one before Gray huffed out, "I don't think it's so much the fatigue. It's that I didn't want to make bread."

"Why's that?"

Gray stopped walking. "I took over the running of my parents' café when my mom passed. I told you that, right?"

Aaron nodded.

Gray tipped his head back. Sunlight caught the planes of his face, highlighting the fullness of his lips and the furrow along his brow. Then he gestured toward the path. Aaron fell into step beside him.

"I was working at a bakery in Allentown. I quit my job and moved home to pick up the pieces, and that's what I've been doing ever since. But it's like every time I pick one piece up, two drop. Sometimes three or four. I can't keep a regular staff. My dad was supposed to be the one who kept the books. You know what I found? A cabinet full of receipts. The taxes hadn't been filed for two years. Some accountant kept getting extensions while my dad kept tossing paper into the drawer. On top of that, most of their agreements with vendors were handshake. As soon as I started trying to negotiate better deals, the prices went up and came with contracts and payment terms and shit I'm sure you need to go to school for an advanced degree to figure out."

Having sat with his sister and sister-in-law through enough meetings to know that running a business was not a walk around the parking lot, Aaron understood. "I get it. That's probably why I'm not sure whether I want to run my own gym. I'm not a businessman and I'd suck at being a boss. I want to teach classes and walk the track with my clients."

Gray nodded.

"What do you like about being a baker?" Aaron asked.

Gray glanced over. "I . . ." He swallowed. Stopped walking again. "My mom taught me how to make bread. Every Sunday we used to bake for the week. The café was her dream. She and my dad put everything into it. So I thought working there would make me happy and it does, but only sometimes." He met Aaron's gaze, his brown eyes searching. "I love serving customers. I didn't do that where I used to work and, if I'm honest with myself, my old job was boring me. When I signed on there, I thought I'd be developing new and interesting breads for a commercial market. There was a little of that, but mostly it was baking and testing. Doing the same thing, day in, day out. Moving home was going to be a chance to save my mom's dream and to maybe explore my own."

"Which is?"

"I want to make gluten-free bread for y'all. I want to make my grandmother's fruit breads. Apricot, raisins, and pecans."

God, that sounded good.

"Seasonal breads. I want to break out the artisanal flours and play." Gray's hands were opening and closing as though kneading imaginary dough.

"So why aren't you?"

"Because I have a business to run."

"Who's running it now?"

"Patty's on the books. Her husband is learning to bake, with Ollie's help. And you and Nick and Cam are doing everything else." Gray peered into the trees bordering the lot. "While I take a walk through the woods and complain about my life." He looked back at Aaron. "With a personal trainer who didn't ask to hear any of this."

"I did ask."

Gray blinked.

Aaron drew in a breath. "After knocking you on the head and thinking I caused your damn heart attack, I—"

"I was so annoyed at you that day." Gray's smile was wry.

Aaron snorted.

"You always bring in the bread order instead of emailing it," Gray said. "Why?"

"I like your sandwiches."

Gray held his gaze before clearing his throat and looking down. He started back along the trail. "What's the last tabletop game you played? Like an RPG or are you into board games?"

Resisting the urge to test the temperature of his cheeks—he could feel the flush without touching them—Aaron once again fell into step beside him. "I haven't played D&D or any sort of RPG for years. I used to have an online group." The heat of his blush intensified. "But we kind of fell apart after finishing our last campaign. Now I get together with a group for board games every other month or so. Used to be more regular, but two of them moved over the past year and one of the others has young kids now." *So, I've been collecting games I never get to play. Slowly designing one I'll likely never finish.*

"Same. I mean, I've lost touch with most of my friends from Allentown, but our gaming group had been suffering from the same fate."

"What did you play?"

Gray huffed out a laugh. "If it's printed on a card or a board, I played it. Ever heard of *Orcs & Swords*?"

"How do you know . . .?" Aaron's own laugh caught him by surprise. He gave into it. Glanced over at Gray to find all the rage had burned away from his eyes. Now he was twinkling. Smiling like the Gray who lit up the inside of a café with good humor, despite the chaos swirling around him.

Aaron got it, then, the reason why he was so fascinated with Grayson Clery. This was a man he'd follow into battle—imaginary, of course. Gray was the bard. The irreverent warrior who drew on an inexhaustible well of creativity to laugh in the face of danger. He was the backbone of any worthwhile campaign. Versatile and indefatigable. And open to the whispers of the world.

Lips twisting, Aaron gave up one of his nerdiest secrets. "Kickstarter. The original game and two of the expansions. I've unwrapped it and set it all up. But never played it."

Gray stopped walking. "Look at you. Sporty McGamerson."

"Who and what now?"

"Coordinated sweats? Shoulders, quads. Always smiling like you have no idea what it's like to catch your breath at the top of the stairs. Apparently, you game too. Also, I didn't know your name. Before."

Aaron stuck out his hand. "Aaron. Aaron Asher."

After leaving him hanging for a few uncomfortable seconds, Gray enclosed his hand in a warm grip. "Grayson Clery."

It didn't matter that Aaron already knew that, or that Gray already knew his name either. They were starting again. Not as the cheerful baker who smiled in the face of chaos and the fitness instructor who smiled the smile of the fit and healthy. But as game geeks who shared a secret passion.

"When are we getting together to play?" Gray said.

Are you doing anything this afternoon?

Aaron had to work to speak normally. He was a grown man. He shouldn't be this excited. He should also let go of Gray's hand. He did that, then cleared his throat and concentrated on answering in a cool, calm, and collected manner. "I'm free most evenings." All evenings, but Gray didn't need to know that. "I do work pretty late on Tuesdays and Thursday, though."

"How about Friday?"

"Works for me."

Gray took a turn at being uncomfortable. "I'd invite you over, but..."

"We can do it at my place. I've got plenty of room." He'd arrange for his mom to be at Devorah's.

Gray was nodding. "I'll bring over a couple of good two-player games. Maybe we can wrangle Oliver and Nick into playing sometime." His expression clouded. "They're both pretty busy these days, but it'd be good to get a regular group going again."

"I'd like that."

More nodding.

Aaron risked a touch. Clasping Gray's arm. "Gray?"

"Hmm?"

"I think you should bake what makes you happy. It's not going to solve the issue of a business that's overwhelming you—you'll get back to that when you're ready. But right now? While you're recovering and you've got friends to help out, pull out some of those special flours or whatever and play. Bake something fun. Rediscover the passion you've put aside."

Gray's smile was slow, but so worth it. Like watching the sun rise. "I think I might."

Chapter Thirteen

Gray took a moment to admire Aaron's house from the outside. He lived on the south side of Stroudsburg in one of the neighborhoods between the creek and the highway. Gray had grown up on this side of town and recognized many of the older houses, noting they were all neatly kept.

Aaron's place was a small split level. A sloping driveway led down to a garage wide enough for maybe a car and a half, or a car and some junk. Bedrooms would be over the garage, two or three steps up, maybe. There'd be open-plan living over a half basement and access to the garage and whatever he had out back.

Gray reached back into his car for the rosemary ricotta pull-apart he'd baked that afternoon and smiled as the yeasty scent of warm bread floated upward. All the good feeling of rolling out the dough, layering it, and cutting and shaping the loaf settled back over him.

The baking had centered him. The hour he'd spent grooming himself afterward? Forgotten bliss. He couldn't remember the last time he'd exfoliated. He kept his nails trim for the kitchen but hadn't taken time to smooth out the rough edges. And wearing something other than a café polo or sweatpants felt *good*.

It had been a happy and relaxing afternoon.

The front door opened before Gray was halfway along the path. Aaron stepped out and the setting sun lit his hair on fire. Gray almost winced. Much as he liked the color—wait, he liked the color?—he could imagine the crap Aaron had dealt with as a kid. Children were pack animals. When they sensed a difference in one of their number, they turned.

With his height and build, Gray had been able to hide in plain sight. No one had wanted to mess with the big Black kid. Aaron? His red hair and freckles wouldn't have been so easy to hide. He seemed to have turned out okay—though, if he'd blushed like that in junior high, he'd likely spent the lunch hour locked in a ball closet or another confined and smelly space.

"Hey," Aaron said now, his tone brighter and easier than the stain on his cheeks suggested. He glanced down at the baking dish. "Man, that smells good."

"Doesn't it, though?" Gray held it up. "It's the rosemary. Some garlic in the cheese."

"Oh my God. Cheese?"

"Ricotta. So, it's healthy."

Aaron grinned and Gray's heart gave a warning beat. Would it be weird to call a nearly forty-year-old cute? A couple of weeks ago, he'd thought Aaron was annoying. A couple of weeks ago, he hadn't really known him. And, if Gray stood on Aaron's doorstep to ponder awhile, he would probably end up admitting that part of his annoyance had been due to an inconvenient attraction. He didn't have time for cute redheads.

"Anyway," Aaron was saying. "Come on in."

"Want me to take my shoes off?" Gray eyed the tidy row by the door.

"If you don't mind."

Gray handed off the dish and sat on a step to pull his shoes off. It was then he noticed that Aaron was not wearing sweatpants. He was, in fact, wearing jeans. Dark denim hugged his leanly muscled legs, showing them to better advantage than sweats ever could. And from down there on the step, Aaron's ass was fine.

Clearing his throat, Gray hastily scrambled to his feet, grabbing the railing for support.

Desperate to focus elsewhere, he took in the interior of the house and nearly gasped. "How the heck is this place so clean?"

The carpet could use some love—as in, it needed to be ripped up and replaced. But it bore the marks of a recent vacuum, and if Gray were to run a finger along any horizontal surface, a window ledge or one of the bookshelves lining the sitting area, it was doubtful he'd find a speck of dust. Everything gleamed with quiet cleanliness.

Aaron's decorating tastes weren't terribly exciting, but he'd definitely made his mark. The walls were a soft honey shade, and the white trim around the windows and built-ins looked recently painted. Aaron's blush was adorable.

"My mom," he said. "Thankfully, she agreed to a night of babysitting for my sister, or she'd be here hoovering crumbs out of our mouths before they could drop to the floor." He rolled his eyes. "Don't get me wrong. I love my mom. But I keep a pretty clean house on my own." He glanced around, pride evident in his smile. "This is the first house I ever bought. I like to keep it, um, nice."

"I know exactly how you feel. I've got a house down in Allentown, about the same age. Could be a twin to your place, except yours is better cared for." Gray held up his hands. "These are bakers' hands."

"Meaning?"

"I like to specialize. I can cook and clean. I call a friend if I want to hang a shelf. Now, of course, I have a tenant who is quite happy to knock holes in walls."

"You're renting the place out while you live up here? Makes sense."

"Yeah."

A weird quiet bubbled up between them. Gray wondered if Aaron was thinking along the same lines as him. That Gray having a house in Allentown meant he lived in a kind of limbo, caught between two places.

Rather than address that subject, because this was supposed to be game night with a friend, Gray made a show of sniffing the air. "Something else smells good."

Aaron's eyes widened.

"Um, dinner?"

"Oh, right—"

"I'd say you also smell good, but, eh, fuck it. You already know you do. All woodsy and sh— This is not going how I planned it."

Aaron was grinning again. "Good, because it's not going how I planned it either."

"I think the fact we both had a plan works in our favor."

"Yeah?"

What was it about this guy? Gray rarely connected with someone so quickly. He drew in a fast breath, his shoulders rising with it, and then let it out. "Are we going to spend the evening standing around on your stairs? Might make playing a game a bit difficult."

Laughing, Aaron backed off, allowing Gray to reach the main floor. Then Gray followed him into the kitchen. The next hour passed easily—almost too easily—with them finding a practiced and purposeful rhythm. Gray sliding the pull-apart into the oven to warm. Aaron moving around him, between the counter and stove as he finished putting together a grilled salad layered with slender, perfectly seared strips of flank steak.

Gray's mouth watered. "You didn't have to cook for me."

Aaron's gaze bounced off the oven door. "Neither did you."

"I mean, we could have ordered a pizza." One of these days, he was going to enjoy a big, cheesy, salty pie, damn it.

"I like to cook. More so when my mom isn't here to snatch a dish out of my hand the minute I finish using it."

"She's been here a while, hasn't she?"

"She plans to stay for six weeks."

"She do that often?"

Aaron glanced toward the fridge. "Both of my parents visit about once a year. This is the first time she's come alone and stayed so long."

Gray checked out the photos pinned to the front by a colorful array of magnets. Aaron's red hair wasn't the only way he stood out from the family crowd. Aaron was about five shades whiter than the Ashers, who mostly had tanned skin and dark brown eyes. "One of these things is not like the others," he murmured before touching his lips closed with two fingers. *Not cool, Gray.*

Chuckling, Aaron leaned in close to his shoulder. "They adopted me when I was ten."

Gray shifted his attention to another of the photos, this one of a pair of women holding a bundled infant. He recognized Leilani from the gym. The other woman must have been Aaron's sister. "They look good together," he pronounced.

"Yeah, they do."

Gray flicked a glance at Aaron. "Your mom, the one staying with you, she's your adoptive mom?"

"Yeah. I never met my birth mother. She dropped me off at a church in Philly when I was six days old. No note, no nothing. My mom, my adoptive mother, thinks the sisters would have some idea who she was. She was probably from the neighborhood and chose that church for a reason, but I never had any interest in tracking her down."

"Because you had a family and they were good?"

"Better than most kids I grew up with, so, yeah."

Gray wanted to ask about the first ten years, but didn't. Whatever Aaron had been through before finding his "forever home" would have shaped him into the man he was today. Could have been awful, could have been barely worth mentioning. Gray suspected Aaron wasn't the kind to dwell on either actuality.

"What about you?" Aaron asked. "Any brothers or sisters?"

"No, only me. My parents had me when they were pretty young, like early twenties, and then decided they were happy with one kid, despite pressure from the rest of the family. My dad has six brothers—two of them live up here now—and my mom had two brothers and two sisters. Patty is on my dad's side. I think that's why she moved out here too, you know? To do her own thing with her husband and kids. We're the quiet Clerys."

"Sounds nice. The quiet part."

"Yeah. It was. I liked being the center of attention on summer vacations. Means I sometimes forget to think about others, though."

"I very much doubt that." Aaron finished serving out the food and held up the two plates. "Let's eat in the dining room. Then we can clear the table to play something."

Gray popped open the oven and pulled out the bread. He broke off a few pieces to put on the plate Aaron had set out for the bread and carried that into the dining room that opened off the kitchen, forming the corner of the living area.

When he sat at the table, he immediately felt at home within the warm-colored walls and the solid, unadorned furnishing. The only oddity in the whole place was the lack of gaming paraphernalia. Gamers usually filled their bookshelves with figurines, card decks, game boxes, and the like. Aaron only had the obligatory books, though not nearly enough to Gray's mind, and turtles. Lots and lots of turtles.

When he turned back to the table, Aaron was watching him. Gray offered a tentative smile. A flush darkened Aaron's hairline.

"Tell me about the turtles," Gray invited.

Aaron touched his forearm, covered by the sleeve of a long-sleeved T-shirt. "I've always been drawn to them for some reason. I think a part of it is that they carry their house on their backs, so wherever they are, they're home."

Given Aaron's background, that made sense.

"But I also love the mythology surrounding them. Usually, they represent age and wisdom. But there's also their vulnerability. The hardness of their shell compared to what's inside. I like the dichotomy of that."

Here, Gray had the notion Aaron wasn't talking about himself, but he could see that aspect of the man he was still getting to know. Aaron obviously lived his sportiness every day, but that wasn't all he was.

The conversation wandered from turtles to the places they'd vacationed as a kid, and they exchanged stories of memorable sunburns and near drownings in unpredictable surf. When their talk turned to the vacations they'd taken as adults, they discovered a theme: lots of sleeping and not enough vacationing.

"Someone forgot to teach us how to play hard," Aaron said.

"I think when you work a job that fits, you forget."

"Sounds about right."

Gray could almost hear the *until it doesn't* Aaron left hanging at the end. There was something in his expression. Something Gray felt reflected in his.

"We should play a game, then."

"We absolutely should."

They played a simple deck-building game first, then dug a mutual favorite out of Gray's game bag after he retrieved it from his car. Their third game was another of Gray's beloveds and he was thrilled to find it in the modest collection Aaron kept in a cupboard under the bookshelves. Sadly, many of the others seemed not to have been opened.

"We're definitely going to have to do this again." Gray gestured toward the other boxes as he put the last game away. "Who were you planning to play these games with?"

"No one. I mean, not . . ." Aaron sighed. "Not many people. Lately."

"Your family doesn't play?"

"My dad will, when he's here. But my family are not sedentary people. We're outdoor people. We camp and hike and fish. When we used to spend the day at the lake, we didn't laze about in the sun eating chips. We had races to the far side and back. When we picked berries at the farm where we stayed, the one with the fullest basket got out of doing the dishes. We learned how to sail, how to gut a fish, how to rappel down a cliff, how to navigate by the stars and bark and moss."

"Sounds like you had a great time as a kid."

Aaron's laugh was a tired scoff. "I did. But sometimes I wanted to curl up in front of a fireplace and play cards, you know?"

"I do."

Gray was about to close the cupboard when he saw a box without a label. "What's this one?" He reached for the box.

Aaron immediately stayed his hand. "Nothing. It's extra pieces and such. Blank cards. You know, all the odd bits collected from other games? Lost dice and so on."

It was obvious he was lying. The lack of flush gave Aaron away, the absence of color. Gray closed the cupboard door.

Aaron had moved toward the stairs and stood there fidgeting. Gray wanted to yank the cupboard door open again. Suspected he could and Aaron wouldn't stop him. But it'd be wrong. Or premature. Instead, he collected his things.

"I guess I'll see you Tuesday for our workout," Gray said when they arrived back by the front door.

"Not coming to yoga class tomorrow?"

Gray groaned. "If I can talk Ollie into going so I could watch him do falling warrior, maybe?"

Aaron flashed a dimpled grin.

Gray couldn't think of anything else to say, so he stood there, facing Aaron, saying nothing. Aaron licked his lips. Gray wrenched his attention away from Aaron's mouth and met his gaze. Was halfway to getting lost in the distinction between loam and smoke—halfway convinced Aaron's eyes might actually be gray—when Aaron looked away.

The moment was long and awkward until Aaron murmured softly.

"Did you just say the night is dark and full of terrors?" Gray asked.

Aaron blushed. "Not a reflection on you, I promise. I'm . . ." He turned his face ceilingward. Swallowed. The corded tendons in his neck called to Gray's lips and tongue. He almost salivated.

He needed to leave.

Aaron looked back down. "You could say I'm a little weird."

"I don't mind weird. I'm all about weird."

Another long, attenuated moment stretched between them and it was so painfully awkward, Gray felt like apologizing. He sucked a lip between his teeth, watched Aaron watching him, and finally blew out a breath. "I'm gonna go."

"Yep."

"Thanks for dinner."

"Thanks for coming over."

"We should do it again."

Aaron practically melted. "Yes, please."

Gray offered his hand.

Aaron's palm was warm and slightly sweaty. Their shake brief.

Outside, the night was cool . . . and dark. But not at all terrifying. Just kinda sad. As though an opportunity had been missed. When Gray glanced over his shoulder, he got the impression Aaron was standing behind his closed door thinking the same thing.

Next time, he promised himself. Next time, he'd make a move. He'd kiss Aaron. See if he tasted as good as he looked.

Chapter Fourteen

"Aaron!"

Aaron paused on the threshold of his sister's office.

Kevin caught up to him. "Here." He handed Aaron a slip of paper. "My friend's website. I was going to text it to you but kept forgetting. Luckily, I found this in my gym bag."

"Thanks." Aaron took the paper.

"Sure. Great class today!"

Freestyle had ended fifteen minutes before—long enough for Kevin to shower and change. He looked fresh-faced, energized, and ready to tackle his Saturday.

"What's on for the rest of the day?" Aaron asked.

"I have a date!"

"Oh, yeah?"

"The woman we talked about a couple weeks ago? I called her back and asked if we could get together for lunch. I apologized for being anxious and chatty, and she apologized for being anxious and not chatty and then we did some more chatting, figured out what we had in common, which was not *Game of Thrones*, but she's interested in watching it."

Aaron laughed.

Kevin continued. "We talked about a lot of stuff and agreed daytime was less intimidating." A thoughtful expression crossed his features. "I think we're both tired of the usual merry-go-round, you know?"

"I get ya."

Kevin nodded. "Okay. Have a great one."

"You too."

Aaron watched Kevin disappear into the parking lot before resuming course. Devorah wasn't in her office, so he sat at her desk, woke the laptop, and peered at the slip of paper in his hand. But instead of the URL, he thought about Gray. About how well their not-date had gone last night. How *not* well the last five minutes had gone. If prizes were awarded for awkwardness, that slice of time would take top honors. What Aaron couldn't decide was whether he should cringe at the memory or smile. Gray had been just as off-kilter. They'd looked at each other's mouths, for Christ's sake. And then shuffled their feet like teenagers who hadn't quite come to grips with the fact they were attracted to their own gender. Or anyone, for that matter.

What the ever loving—

"Always in my seat!" Devorah said from the doorway. "Anyone would think you'd want a gym of your own."

Speaking of awkward. Also, he had a half chub going. Yep, that was the current extent of his love life. He sat in other people's chairs and got a hard-on for a man he'd barely touched.

Dev flopped down in the chair opposite the desk. "You look out of it. Good date last night?"

"What?"

"You and the dude from the café. Did you tie one on, brother? Or tie someone up?"

"What!"

Devorah laughed, her head tipping back as amusement bubbled up her throat. "Oh, Aaron. You're too easy. But, seriously, how did it go?"

"It wasn't a date."

"That's not what Mom said."

"Mom doesn't know what she's talking about."

"Uh-huh." Dev leaned forward and patted her thighs. "What do you have on for the rest of the day? There's a trade show in Scranton. I thought you might like to ride up with me. I could use the company, and it'll be good experience for when you're running your own shop."

Gulp. "What's the show?" Aaron asked.

Dev waved a hand. "Sport science. New equipment, advances in tech, scantily-clad and buff models demonstrating it all to us."

"You're married."

"Just because I'm on a diet, doesn't mean I can't appreciate the menu."

Aaron chuckled. "That's one way of putting it." He checked his schedule. "I have two classes after lunch. Scranton, you said?"

"Stacy wouldn't mind picking up some hours. Want me to see if she'd like to take your classes this afternoon?"

"Sure." He wasn't entirely or even partway sold on the idea of running his own gym. Maybe a trade show would help move the mental matter along.

Half an hour later, heading west on Highway 80, Devorah said, "If it wasn't a date, why did you send Mom to our place?"

Aaron rolled his eyes. "Really?"

"I can tell you like him."

"And we're not in third grade."

"Aaaa-ron, talk to me." She glanced away from the road. "What's up with you? You've been all absorbed lately."

"I have?"

"Mom's noticed it too."

"Great. Did she happen to mention when she might be going back to Arizona?"

Dev tossed him a quick look clearly meant to convey she was bookmarking their place in the previous conversation before changing the subject. "I know. It's weird. I mean, like, why is she here?"

Aaron studied his sister's profile. "She didn't tell you she was tired of walking with Dad?"

"Something like that, but it seemed flimsy. I mean, they've been together forever. They know when to take a step back for air. That's all this is. Air is just as fresh in Arizona, though. That's all I'm saying."

"Maybe she wanted some unstructured time with her kids," Aaron suggested.

The sign for 380 flashed past, and Devorah merged into the right lane. "Let's talk about you and Gray. I don't know him all that well, but he seems like a solid citizen." Her brow creased. "How's he doing after his heart attack?"

"Good. I mean, he seems a little lost? Like, not used to not working. And he's stressed about his business. He's been running the café for his dad since his mom passed, but I don't think he loves it."

"That's too bad. His bread is to die for. Since we started stocking his bagels and Oliver's pastries, revenue from our café has doubled."

Aaron turned his gaze toward the side of the highway, the low trees rushing by, and let the words *to die for* run through his head. It was such a casual expression. The meaning diluted by overuse. The fact that Gray *had* nearly died for his bread didn't escape notice, however.

"He needs to reprioritize," Aaron told the side window.

"Mm?" his sister said.

"Gray. Figure out what's important to him. The bread or the café."

Devorah smiled. "I'm glad he has you to talk to, then. And to . . ."

"What?"

"Oh, come on. Not even a hint?"

"It wasn't a date."

"But did you want it to be?"

With a forceful exhale, Aaron returned to his study of the scrubby trees lining 380.

That evening, talked out and walked out from doing the rounds of the trade show and the drive there and back, Aaron slipped into his house and nearly melted into a puddle at the sight and smells awaiting him. He and his sister could complain about their mother's mysterious visit all they liked, but being able to come home to a cooked dinner and clean, cozy house was kind of nice. And Aaron knew that if he told his mom he was too tired for company, she'd keep to herself and let him be. His family had always been good about that. Giving him space when he wanted or needed it.

They were good about a lot of things.

His mom ducked out of the kitchen, a towel wrapped around one hand. "You're back! Just in time. Unless you want a shower? I can keep everything warm another ten minutes, no worries."

"I caught a shower at the gym before Dev and I left for Scranton. Let me drop my things downstairs."

After dumping his gear in the laundry, Aaron sauntered back up to the kitchen and watched his mother dish out another delicious meal. One thing he never had to worry about was her cooking. She was the one who'd taught him how to eat healthy, weaning her ten-year-old charge off of boxed macaroni and cheese, frozen nuggets, tater tots, and fruit roll-ups, all of which had been his golden standard when he'd arrived on her doorstep. He hadn't known the names of half the vegetables his new family ate until a year had passed. Back then it had seemed like they introduced him to a new one every few months until Aaron had become convinced that he'd eaten everything grown on this planet at least once.

They sat, observed their moment of thanks, and picked up their forks.

"So how was your date last night?" she asked. "I tried one of the rolls in the fridge. Was that ricotta inside? Very good."

Aaron's fork clattered to the table. He might have groaned.

"What?"

"It wasn't . . ." He exhaled so hard, his diaphragm almost cramped. "You know what? It went well until the end. Even though it wasn't a date. But I think we have chemistry and I would like to explore that, but we both got all jittery-teenager by the door and nothing happened."

"That's a shame."

"Yeah, it is." Aaron smoothed his frown as he looked across the table. "How about you? How was your night?"

"Oh, fine, dear. Leili and Dev are restful together, aren't they? And Cosmo is such a treasure."

"He is." The frown returned. "Mom?"

"Mm?"

"Is there another reason you're here? We love you, both Dev and I. I'm sure Leili adores you too. And having you here has been great. But it's weird. Or . . . not weird. Is there something going on?"

She put her fork down and took a sip of water.

Aaron waited for her to swallow. To talk.

His mom studied her plate a moment before starting. "Before I begin, I need to you to know that everything is fine. I'm perfectly healthy and I'm going to stay that way."

"Oh my God."

"We found a lump. In my breast." She patted her right side. "But we got on it quickly—a biopsy, tests. It was benign, but I had it removed anyway."

"Why didn't you say anything!"

"Because the tests were negative. Everything was negative. I'm a healthy human being." She took a breath. "But it got me to thinking about a lot of things." She met his eyes. "And one of those things was whether we should search for your birth mother. I know you weren't interested back when we gave you the files."

In a quiet ceremony after he'd turned eighteen, his mom and dad had turned over all of his birth records and foster and adoption paperwork in case he'd wanted to pursue his birth parents. Aaron had filed everything away and promptly forgotten about it. Couldn't say with any certainty whether he still had it.

"It's not so much now about something happening to me or your father," she said. "You've been able to take care of yourself practically since you arrived on this Earth. It's more about your health. Genetic risks and so on. I know you're not thinking about having kids anytime soon, but if you were to consider it, being aware of where you came from—"

"Mom." Aaron reached across the table and touched her hand.

"Yes?"

"I'm glad you're okay."

"Thank you."

He squeezed her hand. "And I'm good. I can get screened for whatever if I need to. Otherwise, I'm good. I have a family. One I love very much."

Her eyes shone with unshed tears. "Oh, Aaron. That's not—"

"For me it is."

And it was, except for one small thing. When he was younger, Aaron had had to deal with a lot. Every time a foster family had given him back, he'd hurt. Not being wanted had hurt. Not knowing why had always been the hardest part. But he'd had it better than most. Neglect and indifference had been a heck of a lot easier to bear than abuse. He had so much to be thankful for that not always wanting the same as his mom, dad, and sister, in terms of career and hobbies and a happy ever after, seemed selfish.

The exception to that rule, of course, was that he did want a happy ever after. Despite his family's love and support, he'd always felt a little apart. Aware he didn't match the rest of the set. Mostly, though, he wanted someone of his own to love. Someone who chose him as an adult. As a man. Not as a child who needed a family, but someone who could be the start of one.

His mom was still looking at him, concern in her eyes. Aaron squeezed her hand again. "Want to try a game after dinner?"

She smiled softly. "I'd like that."

Chapter Fifteen

A good focaccia bread started with good flour. Gray liked Farro but he'd splurged on some Enkir—supposedly the oldest of ancient grains. He'd chosen it for the nutty flavor, higher protein content, and lower gluten, the last factor bringing to mind a scattering of freckles and a dimpled smile.

He measured the flour into a large glass bowl and reached for the jar of sourdough starter he'd mixed up last Sunday. His father hadn't fed Thanatos while Gray was in the hospital, and Gray had forgotten about him until last week. He'd named this one Phanes after the Greek god of primordial life. Phanes was young but healthy.

While his hands did the work of preparing his yeast, adding it to his flour, and mixing the dough, Gray let his thoughts drift back over the weekend—specifically Friday night. Thinking about Saturday morning might raise his heart rate more than was good for him, and he didn't want to pop a boner in the kitchen while his dad was in the next room. But the slop of oiled and sticky dough against the side of the bowl sounded alarming similar to the slide of slick fingers around a hard cock. Ergo, Saturday morning.

He'd woken up with wood, thought about Aaron's mouth, and almost hadn't been able to get a hand around his dick fast enough.

Swallowing, Gray pulled a wrap over the bowl and set the dough into the warmest part of the kitchen to rise. He then palmed his crotch, specifically the hard poke at the center, and commanded his body to calm. It took a while. If his father wasn't in the next room . . .

I really need to get my own place.

He *had* his own place: A nice house. Or it had been before his current tenant had apparently failed to notice a leaky corner of roof.

A wave of sadness seemed to roll out from everywhere to push heavily at his shoulders and places less tangible like his soul. His erection deflated. So did his mood.

Gray grabbed the bowl he'd set aside the day before and pulled it close. The scent of risen dough wafted upward, evocative enough to redirect his thoughts. Again. The smell of yeast and flour, salt and honey took him back to a happier place. He'd flavor this loaf with pepitas and maybe sunflower seeds. A sprinkle of chia for extra protein and nuttiness. He turned out the sticky, almost bubbly dough, gave it a soft knead, and folded it back into the bowl for another rise. Then he washed his hands and cleaned up the kitchen.

The sound of voices drew his attention toward the front door. His dad and Oliver stood in the hallway. Gray hadn't heard a knock—a fact reiterated by the scowl on his father's face as he turned away and clomped back to the living room.

Oliver watched him get settled and then turned to Gray, his eyebrows forming two symmetrical arches.

"Was I expecting you?" Gray asked.

"Nope. I was supposed to be doing a market today, but Nick suggested I might like a day off. He and Cam are doing it. I thought I'd stop by to see how you were."

"If you're going to suggest another yoga class, I need to watch my dough rise."

Oliver snickered.

Gray checked his bowls and then jerked his head back toward the door. "Let's get some air." He shoved his socked feet into a random pair of shoes. "Heading out for a bit. Don't touch my dough," he called out.

The lack of response needled him. Gray shouldered his way through the door and led Oliver back downstairs and into the square of parking lot behind the building. There, he turned his face toward the sun, not quite visible over the rooftops but, gosh, the sky was blue and wide and beautiful. Gray closed his eyes and breathed. In and out. Tried to imagine the curls of frustration in his limbs straightening and sliding out with the used-up air.

When he opened his eyes, Oliver was standing by watching him.

"Trying to manage my stress," Gray explained.

"How's that working for you?"

"Good and bad, mostly dependent upon my father's mood."

Oliver lifted his chin toward the second-story apartment. "So, it's not my imagination that he's getting . . ." He paused.

"Worse?" Gray provided.

"I was thinking 'more withdrawn.'"

"Yeah." Gray sighed. "I don't know what to do."

"Have you tried talking to him?"

"Last night. He grabbed the TV remote and turned up the volume."

"Ouch. Do you think . . ." Another pause.

"I think a lot of things, Ollie, most of them not productive." Gray shoved his hands in the pockets of his pants and jerked his head toward the lane. "Let's walk. I haven't gotten my exercise in today."

"Are those your baking pants?" Oliver asked.

Gray patted the light gray chef pants that used to serve as his weekday uniform. It'd been weeks since he put a pair on, and they were a definite upgrade from sweats. Also, they had lots of pockets. "Yep."

"Are you still planning to start back this week?" Oliver's tone was careful.

"Yep."

"What does your doctor think?"

"That I haven't lost any weight, my blood pressure is still too high, and I'm apparently not doing very well at managing my stress."

Oliver's shoes scuffed against gravel as he stopped and turned to face him. "Gray."

Gray pulled his hands from his pockets. "I came home and baked and that helped."

"What did you bake?"

"A rosemary ricotta pull-apart to take . . ." A warning prickle moved across his scalp. Gray didn't know if he'd been wired to blush the way Aaron did. His form of embarrassment had always been a curious tightening in his chest and a tingle under his hair. Sometimes the tops of his ears buzzed as well.

"Are you blushing?"

Okay, apparently, he could do that too.

"Where did you take this rosemary ricotta bread?" Oliver asked, one eyebrow raised.

"Over to a friend's place. Game night."

"One of your friends from Allentown?"

"No, someone who isn't busy all the damn time," Gray grumbled.

Oliver rocked back a step. Then, because he was the kind of guy who rarely took offense, his posture softened. "I'm sorry."

"No, I'm sorry. You're busy because you're working at my shop while I mope around wondering why the medication I'm taking doesn't have me sitting in a purple golf cart in front of a sign pointing the way to happiness and enlightenment."

"Should I ask about constipation and bleeding from the eyeballs?"

Gray's lips twitched. "Ass."

"Seriously, though, are you experiencing a lot of side effects?"

"I honestly don't know. Some? Like the bruising and the aches. I get dizzy when I stand up, but who doesn't? And every time my heart beats a bit faster, I think I'm going to die. Most of my malaise probably comes from having my life turned upside down, and the fact my dad seems to have died while I was away, because the man walking around our apartment resembles an animated corpse more than my father. Then there's the inconvenient urge I have to kiss Sporty fucking McSporterson. To shove his shiny sweatpants down and see whether he has freckles on his legs. I'm pretty sure he does. They're on his ears."

And on the back of his neck. Gray hadn't spotted any in the gap between his T-shirt and jeans when he'd leaned over into the fridge, though. Only a vulnerable strip of skin.

Too late, Gray realized the direction of his thoughts. He shoved his hands back into his pockets.

Oliver cleared his throat.

Gray met his gaze.

"Want to talk about it?" Oliver asked.

Gray sucked on his lower lip and indicated with a shoulder that they should keep walking. He would kind of like to talk about it. Ollie had always been his closest gay friend: the guy he could talk about other guys with. Things with Aaron felt too new to share, though. Too tentative. Gray still had no idea whether his interest was purely physical or perhaps something more.

About a minute later, Oliver said, "Now I want to know if he has freckles on his legs."

"Kittens and kettles, Ollie. I just got it under control again."

Oliver laughed and Gray joined him.

"Sex is very good for stress."

"Fuck you."

"I'm not the one you want to get naked with."

Gray scowled, then released his cone of silence. "That's the thing. I don't know if I just want to sleep with him. I'm getting too old to cat around, even though it's been a minute, but I don't know if I'm ready for the part that comes after. Not presently."

Oliver considered him a moment before nodding carefully. "I get that. From my end, though? He seems interested in more than sex, and I think you know that. Why else have you avoided connecting with him for this long?"

"I guess now is also when I have time to explore a few options, right?"

"There is that." Oliver smiled. "So, do you want to talk about a schedule where we can make sure you coming back to work is as low stress as possible?"

"You're not going to try to talk me out of it? I mean, last week, I just stood there in the doorway." He hadn't managed to step across the threshold. Every time he'd tried to, sweat had broken out across his forehead and his stomach had cramped. His heartbeat had remained steady, but the rest of his body had gone into revolt. He hadn't felt right until Tuesday and his workout with Aaron—which had been more of a walk than a training session, but hey, they'd circled the gym four times. Gray couldn't remember the last time he'd walked two miles.

Then again, he probably racked up close to 10k steps a day at the café.

He let out a long, slow sigh.

"Where'd you go?" Oliver asked.

"Around and around in my head. I've been doing that a lot lately, which is why I need to get back to work."

"Or maybe you need to let the thinking happen. Your brain could be asking you to listen."

"Or saying 'Watch Me!' as it turns circles in the middle of the playground, arms all spread out."

"That's pretty specific."

"I'm tired, Ollie. I've done little else but sleep for three weeks now and I'm still tired."

Oliver curled an arm around Gray's shoulder and drew him against his side. "Lean on me awhile."

"It's not—"

"Listen. When I lost my job, you gave me another one and let me use your kitchen til I set up my own. Answered all the dumb questions I had about baking to a larger scale. You tasted every recipe I tried, including the failures."

They'd reached the end of the lane. As they turned the corner, Gray tossed a grin at his oldest friend. "There were a lot of those."

"There were. Point is, you were there for me, like you've been there for your dad the past couple of years. For Patty while she and her husband sorted out their move."

Patty had had to sell a house in one state while she lived in another. And Gray had made sure she could be there for her kids while still giving her enough hours to qualify for healthcare.

"I wouldn't have survived this long without her," Gray said. "When she came on, she didn't know the difference between chicken salad and tuna salad. Now she's practically running the place."

"She does more than show up for shift, that's for sure."

Gray acknowledged that with a sober nod.

"Her husband is a natural when it comes to dough. I've hardly had to coach him at all."

Gray looked up. "Yeah? I thought he had a job lined up for when he moved over here."

"Fell through, I think. He's been spending most of his time at Clery's."

"Huh." Gray stopped walking again. "Thank you for taking care of the place. I almost feel like I could walk away altogether, you're all doing such a fine job." And, damn, if that thought wasn't more tempting than the question of Aaron's freckle placement.

Oliver was quiet for a long moment, and the rumble of traffic up on Main Street filtered down into the pause. The growl of a truck along the interstate across the creek. A bird yelling displeasure at a cat. Street sounds. Town sounds. Familiar, sometimes too loud, but restful. The noise Gray was used to. Calm crept across his shoulders with the warmth of the spring sun.

Then Oliver said, "Maybe you could," and the calm kept creeping and warming, and the knot in Gray's chest untied by a single, glorious degree.

Chapter Sixteen

After updating his client notes and checking his schedule, Aaron stopped by the juice bar-slash-café at the gym. Over the past few months, they'd expanded the offerings from power shakes and green smoothies to include healthy snacks. Fruit, bagels, and a selection of pastries from Gray's friend, Oliver. Meat-free, dairy-free, and sometimes gluten-free, they were tasty. Aaron particularly liked the vegan spanakopita. They were usually sold out by the time he got to the café each day, though.

A pang of longing for a sandwich from Clery's swirled through Aaron's empty stomach. A smoothie would hold him long enough to walk up to Main Street, then he could get a sandwich and stay to help with cleanup.

The double beep of the gym doors opening and closing caught Aaron's attention. He glanced up and all but gaped at the familiar silhouette holding a carryout bag.

Gray stopped in front of him and shifted from foot to foot, which should have been awkward for such a tall man. His discomfort was endearing, though—if not only because Aaron felt the same.

"Hi! I didn't—" Aaron started, just as Gray said, "Hey, I brought—"

Gray gestured with the bag. "You first."

"I was going to say I didn't expect to see you today. It's Monday."

Gray smiled. "All day."

Aaron chuckled. "We're still on for tomorrow?"

"For our workout that isn't really a workout?"

"What do you mean? You've been working hard."

A shadow flitted across Gray's face. "I wanted to talk about that." He held the bag out. "And bring you this."

Any anxiety he might have had regarding Gray's future as a training client flitted away as he took the bag, opened it, and peered inside. "What is it?" Bread, obviously, and a promise of deliciousness. Slightly warm, yeasty, and . . . nutty?

"It's a focaccia loaf. A small one. Topped with seeds. Pepitas, sunflower, chia. Extra protein in every bite. The flour is low in gluten too. I thought—" Gray scrubbed a palm over his short hair. "I figured you might want to taste it."

The endearing discomfort coalesced into a targeted pulse. Gray had made him a loaf of bread. No, Gray had *designed* a loaf. For him.

"This is . . ." Aaron cleared his throat and leaned over the bag again. Inhaled. Closed his eyes. "Oh my God. It smells so good."

"Doesn't it?"

"I was thinking about a sandwich from Clery's when you showed up."

"Ah."

"What do you mean, 'Ah'?"

"You looked kinda like you were seeing a ghost." Gray's smile angled sideways in self-depreciation. "I almost wondered if I had died and all of this, the past three weeks, had been a dream. Then I thought I might be in a coma. *Then* I tried to talk at the same time as you because I'm smooth like that. Death thoughts, awkward thoughts." He tapped his chest. "Verbal diarrhea. I'd blame the medication but— Heh, let's blame the medication."

"Can you stay awhile?"

"Sure."

"Want to sit outside?"

Gray answered with a smile and a nod.

Aaron collected two bottles of water from the juice bar cooler and gestured toward the front door. They stepped out into the spring sunshine, circled the building, and crossed the lawn toward the bench on the far side of the walking track.

Once seated, Aaron spread the bag across his lap like a napkin and set the loaf on top. "It's almost too pretty to eat."

"It'll taste better."

The bread tore easily, the crust offering a little resistance before giving way to a lightly pocketed interior. The scent of fresh-baked *everything* rose up to greet him, and Aaron's mouth watered. He took a bite and moaned. Chewed and groaned. The texture, the almost-sweet-but-not tang of the crust. The salt and crunch. The nuttiness of the seeds and the bread itself. The *everything*.

"I think I just came in my pants," he said.

Gray laughed. "I knew I liked you for a reason."

"Yeah?" Aaron felt his mouth lift on one side.

Apparently, Gray noticed. "What?"

"Before Friday night, I'd have thought you found me more annoying than anything else."

Gray seemed to take that on board for a moment before muttering, "Whole wheat roll, gutted, turkey, avocado, alfalfa, and beets."

Aaron's ear tips warmed. "You remember my order."

Gray shrugged. "Of course. You're a regular."

"Whose name you didn't know."

"Eh, I give all of my regulars nicknames. Macy from the Appletree?" A clothing store across the street from the café. "She's Apple Cheeks. Not too original. Peter from the bank on the corner is Mr. Stripes. Not a suit in his closet without that banker pinstripe. Cherry from the ice cream place down past Fifth Street? Tray-Tray. That one's Patty's. The ice cream place sells sandwiches, but Cherry likes ours better."

"Then she should recommend your bread to her boss."

"She has. Her boss doesn't want to pay enough. I'm not a commercial bakery, and they don't want that kind of volume anyway, so the price has to go up."

"Sounds about right."

"Eh."

Aaron ripped off another piece of bread and offered it to Gray. He then tugged a second chunk away and folded it into his mouth. It was almost too much to chew all at once but Aaron didn't care. If he died eating this loaf, he'd die a happy man.

"I think it annoyed me that I'm attracted to you," Gray said.

Coughing, Aaron vacillated between continuing to chew and trying to tug the oversized chunk of bread from his mouth. He elected to chew and swallow. It took a while.

Finally he managed, "You, what?"

"Would you like to go out sometime?"

"Out?" Aaron met Gray's steady brown gaze.

"Like a date."

"You're asking me out on a date."

Gray shifted as though preparing to stand.

Aaron reached for his arm. "Sorry. I'm just surprised. We were still at me being annoying."

"You were still there. I was elsewhere." Gray's cheeks warmed. "Like Friday night. I had fun."

"I did too. Um. Yes. I would like to go out. What did you have in mind?"

Gray was staring at Aaron's hand. At the bitten-off chunk of bread. Not sure why the moment suddenly felt weird, Aaron checked out Gray's hands. They were pleasingly large, the darker skin around his knuckles scuffed, his fingertips rough. The skin on his forearms was smoother, and a warm brown beneath a vague curl of darker hair. Aaron dropped the bread back onto the bag and curled his fingers over Gray's arm, feeling for the strength he'd often admired from afar.

When he glanced up, Gray met the gaze, and his eyes seemed to smolder with thoughts other than dinner and a movie. Aaron nearly groaned again. Did they have to have a date, or could they fast-forward to sex?

It was only when Gray withdrew that Aaron realized how close they'd drifted. A spring breeze pushed between them, cooling Aaron's nascent flush. Still feeling awkward, Aaron snatched back his hand. He was about to dip back into the bread bag, when Gray touched his fingers. Aaron looked up to find him leaning close.

"Damn it, I really want to kiss you," Gray murmured.

"I really want you to kiss me." Stomach swirling, Aaron closed the distance.

Gray met his lips in a kiss so soft, Aaron almost thought he'd imagined it. That he wanted to feel Gray's lips against his so badly, he'd mentally divided the bare inch between them, divided it again, and—

Oh.

Gray flicked his tongue over his lips, moistening them, and then he and Aaron were connected again, mouth to mouth, and definitely not in a life-and-death situation. Aaron's heart wasn't so sure about that. A kiss wasn't meant to reach inside his chest and squeeze. A kiss shouldn't have his pulse rocketing into orbit. And the buzz in his throat wasn't just breath—he'd groaned.

Aaron pulled back, embarrassed, needy, embarrassed over his need, and mentally rearranging his schedule for the rest of the day because after a kiss like that he wasn't sure whether he could be seen in public.

Gray had a hand fisted in Aaron's zip-front hoodie. He hauled Aaron forward again, and the rocket left orbit. Aaron opened his mouth in invitation, and Gray deepened their connection. Aaron touched and petted, exploring firmly rounded shoulders, warm beneath Gray's soft T-shirt. The buzzed crop of his hair, and the familiar velvet prickle at his nape. Then there was the scent of Gray's soap and skin, talc and pepper, which should have been the oddest combination ever. The effect it had on Aaron certainly was. He was both soothed and turned on.

So completely turned on.

While glad for his sweats, Aaron wouldn't be walking anywhere soon. Not without a fist pushed deep into each pocket. But, hey, he didn't have to go anywhere because Gray was here and devouring his mouth and Aaron was totally committed to this feast.

The next time they parted, Gray leaned away completely and flopped back against the bench. Aaron did the same and they sat side by side, panting and adjusting. Aaron flicked a glance toward Gray's crotch. Felt the vague pressure of Gray's gaze against his own.

"We might need to sit here awhile longer," Aaron ventured.

Gray answered with a strangled chuckle. "Yeah."

The breeze ebbed and flowed between them, cooling the heat in Aaron's cheeks. He felt another prickle and angled his head sideways. Gray was studying him intently.

"What?" Aaron asked.

"Do you have freckles on your legs?"

Aaron conjured a lopsided grin. "I have freckles everywhere."

Gray's eyes darkened. "Dear lord."

Aaron chuckled breathlessly, then sucked in some air. "So. Our date. When were you thinking?"

"What are you doing tonight?"

Chapter Seventeen

G ray had just stepped out of the shower, when he heard a knock at the door. He wrapped a towel around his waist and ducked out into the hallway. All was quiet. Either his dad was ignoring the door or he'd already left for bingo. When he checked, the beat-up recliner sat alone in the corner of the living room. His dad hadn't left cleanly, though. The daily paper lay open across the extended footrest and three coffee cups lined up beneath. He'd also smuggled another plate in there and left it on top of the paper.

A second knock froze Gray in place, caught between several options, none of them immediately good. Throw on some pants, clean up his dad's mess, or answer the door. He chose answering the door, figuring he could do it quickly before excusing himself to get dressed. Also, if he didn't answer soon, Aaron might leave.

Gray opened the door. "You're early. I was in the shower. Almost didn't hear you."

Aaron's gaze immediately latched on to Gray's bare chest. "Sorry?"

His expression said, *Not sorry*.

Slightly uncomfortable beneath the scrutiny of a man who worked out for a living, Gray waved toward the living room. "I'll be out in a minute. Want to put some pants on."

"Don't hurry on my account." Aaron's attention still seemed focused on Gray's chest. He looked up and smiled. "Really."

Heat blossomed behind Gray's breastbone. He was tempted to drop the towel. Who said they couldn't start their date with sex? He'd be lying if he said he wasn't hoping it would end with sex. Or that some nakedness would occur at the very least.

Aaron invited himself inside, which was just as well. Gray's brain had stuttered to a halt. But when Aaron raised a hand to the side of Gray's face, fingers alighting gently against his cheekbone, Gray's thoughts restarted—for long enough to register the sound of Aaron's voice.

"What?" Gray asked.

"I want to kiss you."

"I want you to kiss me," Gray said in return, delighted in the echo of their first kiss.

The words had barely left his mouth when Aaron's lips were on his, feather soft, the touch so light it almost hurt. Gray had subconsciously braced for something more definite. For the hungry, needy drive building in his own lungs. Then Aaron was on him, backing Gray across the narrow hall to the wall outside the kitchen. He had one hand on Gray's chest, directly between Gray's pecs. With his other, Aaron cupped Gray's cheek again. His grip firmer this time, as though he would not allow Gray to turn away. Not that Gray had any intention of doing so. Or of moving.

Another glancing kiss, breath huffing between them, then a deep dive, lips parting, tongues flicking together in an experimental touch before sliding and tasting. The tightness in Gray's chest resolved into a deep groan. It was all he could do to keep a grip on the towel around his hips. It had slipped at the back. The wall was cool against his bare ass.

And Aaron still had all his clothes on. Hardly seemed fair.

Gray pulled out of the kiss to murmur against Aaron's lips. "One of us is wearing too many clothes."

Aaron's answering chuckle tickled his chin. "To think I spent almost an hour figuring out what to put on."

"I'm sure you look great." The idea of Aaron primping opened a kernel of warmth. Gray nudged him back another step and jerked his head toward the other end of the hall. "This way."

The apartment had two bedrooms, both facing the front. The one Gray occupied had been a home office until he'd moved in. Dissonance tickled across his shoulders as he prodded Aaron into the small space. It wasn't the bedroom of an adult. He'd been using the futon-style couch as a bed and the desk as a dresser. The room had a large closet, but it wasn't up to the challenge of the clothes, books, and games Gray had kept out of storage. Boxes lined the wall between the closet and the bed. The top row were all open.

But there was a bed and the sheets were clean.

Gray had hitched his towel back up and tightened the tuck. When Aaron started unbuttoning his shirt, Gray left the towel to the whims of friction and gravity and brushed Aaron's hands out of the way. "Let me." He wanted to count each freckle as it was revealed.

Aaron had chosen a purple shirt. Gray smiled at the mental image of this particular garment being surveyed, discarded, perhaps compared with a number of others, and finally winning the battle. "Why this shirt?" he asked as he released the third button.

"It's soft and the color doesn't clash too badly with my hair."

Gray considered the shade—a deep, richly hued violet—and had to agree. He got the fourth button undone and spread the material for a first look at Aaron's chest. "Where are all these secret freckles?"

Aaron laughed. "I never promised *secret* freckles."

Gray nipped at his lips. "It was implied." He undid the last couple of buttons and pulled Aaron's shirt down his arms. Grinned. "There they are."

They were clustered over the tops of Aaron's shoulders, the highest concentration being over the deltoids before scattering over his triceps.

"They follow the sun," Aaron murmured.

But Gray's attention had been caught by the lines of ink spiraling up from Aaron's forearms. Gently, he turned Aaron's right arm. "Is that an octopus or a squid?" he asked. "Never sure which is which."

"Squid. I have an octopus on my back."

"You don't say." Gray was mesmerized. Freckles, he'd expected. This? He took a step back to better appreciate the tattoos. Tentacles wrapped Aaron's right arm, turtles crawled around his left—sea turtles, their bodies and fins cleverly inked in bubble formations with ripples of water in between. The ink of the smallest turtle had faded to a dusty blue.

More tentacles wrapped his left side like a vine. Gray twirled a finger, and Aaron turned to show off the octopus on his back. It was centered over his shoulder blade with tentacles branching toward his hips.

The ink was so surprising, Gray didn't know what to say. Finally, he managed, "I had no idea."

Aaron had turned around again. "I went through a phase."

"Yeah?"

"I might still be in it. I was thinking about getting a ray somewhere, or a jellyfish."

"So, there's a theme."

Aaron's bashful grin was sweet. He shrugged. "Sorta. All started with this guy." He brushed his fingers over his left forearm, touching the smallest turtle.

Gray glanced at the turtle on the desk, the one Aaron had bought him in the gift shop. He was glad he hadn't thrown it away, until Aaron caught him looking at it, his lips quirked in a knowing grin.

Gray turned his attention to Aaron's impressive physique. "Man, you're in great shape."

Aaron flushed. Diversion successful.

Gray rumbled quietly. "And you're going to be fun."

"I am, huh?" A reedy thread broke up what might have been a cockier response.

Pressing a quick kiss to Aaron's reddened lips, Gray then murmured, "Heck, yeah."

He started on Aaron's belt. Aaron helped by kicking his shoes off, and a minute later, stood clad in nothing but patterned boxers—and miles of spangled skin. His tattoos were confined to his upper half. Everywhere else he had freckles. Like Gray, he wasn't particularly hairy, with only a scatter of crisp red curls over his pecs and abs. A heavier gathering toward the center formed a line straight down to—

Gray sputtered. Looked back up to meet Aaron's smiling eyes. "You didn't."

"I totally did."

"But why?" Gray couldn't help the whine.

"I figured if we got this far"—a flash of color warmed his face—"a break for some humor wouldn't go amiss."

"That makes no sense. And clowns are creepy."

"That was the point!" Aaron shuffled his feet and laced his fingers over the tented front of his obnoxiously patterned boxers. "I was nervous, okay?"

"That's cute." Gray untangled Aaron's fingers and glanced up for permission. When Aaron nodded, he cupped the erection behind the grinning mouths and painted eyes then lifted his fingers away. "You're killing me with these boxers. I don't know whether to laugh or cringe."

Aaron grabbed Gray's hand and placed it back over his clown-covered dick. "Shut up and touch me."

Gray touched him, feeling the heat through the cotton, the hardness. Groaning, he leaned in for another kiss, the rumble in his chest deepening as Aaron reciprocated by grasping him through the towel. Then time skipped forward, one or both of them directing the action toward the bed. Aaron's boxers dropped to the floor, joined quickly by Gray's towel. Gray collapsed backward, taking Aaron with him, and they lay side by side, using mouths and fingers to explore.

Gray brushed his fingertips over Aaron's freckled shoulder, marveling at the texture—not quite smooth but not rough. The skin of a man who lived in his body. He gasped as Aaron found one of his nipples and immediately redirected his own focus to the small, hard points below Aaron's pecs. Spent time tracing the cut of muscle and then a line of ink. Tasted Aaron's skin. Then he returned his attention to the erection poking him in the thigh and groaned in a series when Aaron did the same.

Aaron grabbed Gray's hand and brought it to his lips before licking a broad stripe across the palm. He did the same to his own hand and then they gathered their cocks together, Gray's fingers wrapped low, Aaron teasing up high. It shouldn't have worked as well as it did, but Aaron wanted it as badly as Gray did and it showed. They moved into a coordination of thrusts, hands tightening and releasing, a thumb pressed into his slit and then fingers at his balls. Then the glorious constriction of impending release arrived, along with the forgotten rush of sensation at the tops of his thighs, the small of his back. A body-wide flush, heat spreading and contracting, as though all his skin had a pulse.

Gray squeezed and tugged. Arched. Came with a yell that Aaron attempted to swallow with a kiss. Then it was Aaron's turn, his roar of release surprisingly deep, as though dragged from the tips of his toes and all the way up to his throat.

Gray's heart raced clumsily, and for the space of several breaths, he wondered whether this was it. He'd undone his careful recovery by falling into bed with a freckled, tattooed fitness instructor. What the fuck was his dad going to say? The ceiling wavered and the futon seemed to be rolling underneath him. Gray blinked through endless moments of fraught silence until he realized he wasn't going to die. Then the tightness in his chest eased.

He looked over at Aaron, sprawled beside him with one leg folded against the wall.

Aaron met Gray's eyes before cocking an eyebrow at the hand Gray held over his heart. "Everything okay over there?"

"Still breathing." He shifted and spilled half off the futon. "My bed is not big enough for the two of us."

"We managed," Aaron said softly. He grinned. "Damn well, if you ask me."

"Damn well," Gray agreed. Then, bending one elbow beneath him, he levered upward to gaze down the length of Aaron's body toward his spent cock. "Except I forgot to check you *all* over for freckles."

"You'll get tired of them soon enough."

Gray dropped a kiss to his shoulder. "Never."

Aaron brushed his fingertips over Gray's chest, his nails rasping against the short curls of hair around one nipple. "You are not without merit."

Glancing down, Gray took in his less than impressive physique. "Heh."

Aaron flattened his hand over Gray's heart. "Your body is beautiful. You're hard in all the right places, and I'm not just talking about your dick. Soft where you should be. The color of your skin is so rich and warm. You make me look like an afterimage."

Gray chuckled but inwardly, he was pleased by the compliments.

Aaron looked up. "Want to know what I first noticed about you?"

"Sure."

"Your mouth. When you talk, I have a hard time trying not to imagine your lips against mine." Aaron skated his palm up Gray's chest to his shoulder next. "Then your shoulders. They're so broad. I . . ." A sudden blush stung his already flushed face.

"What?"

"When I'm not thinking about your mouth, I imagine you're the kind of guy who gives excellent hugs."

Once again, Gray's heartbeat quickened. He did like a good hug. "I used to be. Can't remember the last time I hugged someone, though. It was probably Oliver." He gazed at Aaron, lying almost beneath him, and gave in to the sudden urge to fold himself around that lean body. To ignore the differences between them, their physiques, personalities, dreams . . . and simply hold him.

Aaron melted into him and it was *nice*. No, it was beautiful. To lie in the arms of a man scented with semen and sweat, to feel Aaron's skin warm and cool and sticky against his own. To be held in return.

The tightness Gray had been carrying for untold months uncoiled by another degree. It hurt—that loosening. As though something brittle had given way. Sadness ebbed around his heart. Not for the moment, or for what he had or didn't have but because he couldn't remember when he'd last felt this close to another human being. This cared for. This treasured.

He shouldn't. Now was so not the time for him to fall for someone.

But as Aaron let out a contented sigh, Gray exhaled alongside him. Timing wasn't everything, was it?

Chapter Eighteen

The workout after their first date in bed? Awkward as hell. Aaron couldn't meet Gray's eyes without having his cheeks heat. He also didn't want to touch him while needing, quite desperately, to touch him.

"No, hold your wrist . . . up. Don't twist, no . . . like . . ." Aaron sucked in a breath meant to hold in the urge to back Gray against the dark glass wall and ravage his deliciously full lips. Then he corrected the angle of Gray's wrist. No amount of air in the world could fortify him for the correction required to Gray's legs, spread apart and bent at the knees into a sumo squat. "Dear, God."

"Don't suppose you have a private office?" Gray asked, dark eyes burning with the same need carving a hole in Aaron's center.

Aaron made a sound he hadn't known he'd been capable of, high-pitched and keening. He then gathered more air. "Let's cool down with a couple of laps around the track."

"After we stretch." Gray's grin was lopsided and cheeky.

"After we stretch."

He managed to assist Gray without coming in his pants. Was a close thing.

But after completing the outside track twice, Aaron looking and not looking at the woods between the trail and the creek, Gray looking and not looking at the woods between the trail and the creek, Gray had only to say, "What are you doing for lunch?" before Aaron found himself in the passenger seat of Gray's Mustang.

If asked to recall the short drive back to the café, the journey up the stairs, and whether or not the bruise on his shoulder was from knocking Gray's bedroom door aside with more force than absolutely necessary, he'd have to admit he didn't know.

He was still trying to put together the journey from A to B when he registered the *click* of the apartment door closing. The echo of his orgasmic yell clashed with the absorbing quiet from the hall as he listened for additional sounds of life and heard none.

"Your dad was here?" Aaron whispered, afraid to disturb the silence.

"I guess he was."

Aaron considered Gray's replete form. His dark skin seemed to glow with satisfaction. A light sheen of sweat gleamed over Gray's brow. The soft, tight curls of his hair—even longer, now—glistened. A lazy smile flirted with his lips.

"Should I be, ah, having feelings regarding the fact your father was here?" Aaron asked.

Gray chuckled low in his throat. "Not unless you're planning to sleep with him too."

"Oh my God. Why would you say that?" Aaron scrubbed at his eyes. "I don't need that image in my head. Not that your father . . . Ugh. You bastard."

Hands clutched to his sides, Gray laughed until he could barely breathe.

Aaron eventually gave in and laughed along with him. Then he gave in to the urge to explore all of Gray's exposed skin. Again.

Their second training session, two days later, also nearly ended with an ill-advised walk in the woods. Gray veered off the path halfway through their first cooldown lap. Aaron followed only to find himself pressed up against a tree, his mouth ravished by the lips he couldn't stop thinking about. Gray kissed him thoroughly and deeply and the sound of the creek and the highway on the other side couldn't drown out the longing in Aaron's moans. Probably because he could also hear the moans in his head. Had heard them the night before as he somehow managed to jerk off after having enjoyed two orgasms, one right after the other, both courtesy of his hand.

And now his hand wanted a new conquest. He cupped the bulge at the front of Gray's sweatpants and squeezed.

"Fuck," Gray murmured against his lips.

"We shouldn't be out here," Aaron whispered back.

"Want . . ." Gray kissed the corner of Aaron's mouth, lipped at his jaw, and breathed over his ear. "To finish tracing those tentacles over your hips with my tongue."

"Fuck," Aaron all but whined.

"Need to see if those are suckers or freckles."

Aaron chuckled. "You and my freckles."

"You and your freckles." Gray kissed away his laughter.

When Gray pulled away for another breath of air, he bent to press his forehead to Aaron's in a manner that spoke of more than a need for closeness. He seemed to be leaning in, as though for support.

"Everything okay?" Aaron asked.

"Dizzy for a second. It'll pass."

Now more alarmed than turned on, Aaron put a hand to Gray's cheek and urged him to look up. "Do you get dizzy a lot when we're working out?" A helpless grin tugged at his mouth. "Ah, here or, um, in bed?"

"The way you get awkward sometimes will never not be cute."

Aaron rolled his eyes. "Uh-huh."

Gray offered a crooked grin in response. Then, "Dizziness comes and goes. Doesn't seem to be related to a particular activity."

"Have you asked your doctor about it?"

"Yes, Mom. I've mentioned it. Could be the new diet, the exercise, me not resting as much as I should be. Could be the pills I'm taking."

"Just—"

Gray cut him off with another kiss that weakened the tendons behind Aaron's knees—and rearranged a couple of his ideas about gender stereotypes, fainting spells, and all the myriad causes of dizziness. "Maybe it's a lack of oxygen," he suggested, somewhat breathlessly, into their next pause.

"Could be." Gray grinned again, before leaning back. "Can't remember the last time I necked like this."

"Me neither."

"Something to be said for it."

"It's definitely more innocent than what I'd like to do to you in these woods."

"I hear that."

With an expression of mild concentration, Gray traced a line low on Aaron's jaw with a callused finger pad. Aaron pictured the odd row of freckles he had there—on the left side of his face.

"It's the sun, when I drive with the window down."

Gray gave a soft nod.

Aaron studied the almost uniform brown of Gray's complexion. "You ever get a freckle?"

"Nope."

"I had this friend, in junior high, skin not quite as dark as yours, who freckled in the summer. I remember being jealous of how well his freckles complemented his color, as though he'd been designed properly."

Gray scoffed quietly and Aaron grinned. Then they were attached at the lips again, and like the trees surrounding them, their kiss seemed to put down roots.

Their workout ended *without* an impromptu visit to Gray's apartment, but it felt like a close thing.

They did not manage to leave Gray's apartment for dinner that Saturday, however. Thankfully, Gray's dad was out.

When Gray showed up for his session the following Tuesday, Aaron vowed not to touch him unless absolutely necessary. Even then, he'd keep an image of something gross in his mind, like the smell of the dumpster behind the café. Try to forget how Gray had been waiting down there for him yesterday afternoon.

Aaron had never slept with a personal training client before. He'd been tempted a couple of times: working out with a partner could be an intimate experience. A lot of closeness and testing of boundaries. A lot of skin and the measuring of impressive physiques.

Hard bodies didn't always do it for him, though. Despite his choice of career and the fact he worked regularly with clients who were solely focused on weight, body fat, and the cut of their abs, Aaron often felt detached from the physical attributes of the people he connected with most regularly. He *did* notice. With a single glance, he could start putting together a program designed to optimize a client's physical fitness. Decide on activity suited to their body type. But he didn't necessarily focus on certain attributes. Well, he did, but—

"Twelve?" Gray said.

Aaron's attention snapped to the present. "Sorry?"

"Counting." Gray dropped a pair of dumbbells back onto the rack. "And wondering why twelve? Instead of eight or ten or some other number."

"Oh. Um, I don't know. I . . . don't know. What?"

"You're cute when you're flustered."

"Again with the cute."

"And when you blush, your freckles disappear."

"I am aware."

Gray's grin spread wide. "Not making you uncomfortable, am I?"

"Mostly, I'm wondering whether or not I should assign you to another trainer. It's not like we have a rule, but I'm feeling less than professional at the moment."

"If it makes you feel any better, I don't actually need your help here. The routine's pretty simple."

"Oh, right." Aaron did not feel better. A sudden weird emptiness was moving in instead. "I can—"

Gray grabbed the front of his sweatshirt, then relaxed his grip to give a quick tug instead. "I didn't mean go away. I meant we don't have to be trainer and client. You could be a . . . friend helping me work out."

Aaron ignored the pause before *friend*. Regardless of what they were, friends didn't charge friends for their company. He pulled his phone from his pocket.

"What are you doing?" Gray asked.

"Canceling your contract."

"What? Why?"

"Because I don't feel right charging you for personal training if we're just going to, ah, hang out."

With a sigh, Gray sat on the workout bench. "I made it awkward, didn't I?"

"No, I think I did."

Gray murmured inaudibly.

"What?" Aaron asked.

"I was thinking about yesterday afternoon." A half smile flirted with the corners of his mouth.

Aaron allowed a grin. "Me too. On and off. Mostly on, which proved all kinds of interesting with my eight thirty session this morning."

"Oh?"

"Mrs. Barnes. She's eighty."

"Oh." Gray snickered.

Aaron sat on the weight bench next to him and gazed out across the gym floor. Between nine and noon, the gym always experienced a lull. The busiest hours were always from five to eight, at both ends of the day. Mornings and evenings, followed by a brief surge around lunchtime. He glanced over at Gray. "Seeing as we're taking a break, you want to talk about your program?"

"I thought my contract was canceled."

Aaron shook his head. "Only in practice. In theory, I'm still happy to help you achieve your goals."

Gray's smile faded. "If only."

"What do you mean?"

Gray looked around, as though checking for listening ears before sighing. "It's weird. Before . . . I don't like calling it a heart attack. But before then, I'd been experiencing this feeling of running in place, and I'm not entirely sure it started with me moving home after my mom passed. I liked my old job, but it hadn't turned out quite the way I'd wanted it to."

Aaron nodded. "I get that."

"Then I came back up here and it was chaos. I liked that for a while. Having to clean up the mess my dad had made of the café while my mom was in the hospital gave me a focus." He touched his chest. "Other than the grief, you know?"

Again, Aaron nodded.

"Then it took over my life. There was always something else to fix, something else to do, and it was easy to let go and fall into working all day, every day. Now? It's been . . . I dunno. Like, four weeks? And the fact the time has gone so quickly scares me. What scares me more, though, is the fact I can't seem to make myself go back to work."

Aaron sucked on his lower lip for a few seconds while he considered a response that might or might not be appropriate. But, what the heck. If what he and Gray were calling friendship was going to go anywhere, difficult subjects would arise. "Do you think it might have to do with the fact both you and your mom . . ." He gestured toward Gray's chest.

Rather than take offense, Gray nodded. "Only a fool wouldn't make the connection."

"Maybe . . ." *How to put this sensitively.*

"Hmm?"

"*Maybe* a part of it is that you haven't taken the time to properly grieve. I mean, like, I know you said being so busy at first helped, but maybe being so busy wasn't the greatest thing. And now, being so spectacularly not busy, a lot of stuff you've been putting off for the past couple of years is rising up and asking to be dealt with."

Gray's throat moved. He glanced away, his gaze resting low. Then he sighed, rubbed his cheek, and sighed again. "Yeah." One side of his mouth quirked upward. "And here I thought you were only supposed to help me feel better about the way I look."

"It's never all about the way you look. It's how you feel. Mind and body are connected. You could work out every day of your life and not like what you see in the mirror if you're not happy with what's inside."

Gray was nodding absently. "You're absolutely right."

He seemed so lost after that, that Aaron gave in to his next impulse. Or the one after that. Kissing in the woods behind the trail notwithstanding, he'd rather not be seen fondling a client at his place of work. "Super Villain Clue. Go."

Gray rocked back. "What?"

"Penguin, in the bathroom with an umbrella."

Gray appeared to repeat what Aaron had said, silently, then he laughed. He scratched the side of his head before offering, "Magneto, in the library, with a stapler."

"Ouch! Okay, how about Darth Sidious, in the bedroom, with . . . Yeah, no, I can't finish that."

Gray's shoulders were shaking. "So. Wrong."

"I know."

"Cool game, though." Gray's smile had relaxed. "You make that one up?"

"It's how I keep myself entertained on long car rides."

Gray gave him an appraising eyebrow raise. "You're not at all how you seem. I mean, you are, but . . . Heck, I'm not explaining myself properly."

"It's okay. I know what you're trying to say. First impression is jock, but I don't act like one."

"No, you don't."

"It's because I was the nerdy kid in school. Red hair, glasses. Gay. Into comic books. That was before my goth phase."

"You didn't."

"Black eyeliner and enough earrings to set off metal detectors a hundred miles away." He'd long since given up wearing any body jewelry at all, letting the holes in his ears mostly close up. "Even had a septum piercing."

"A nose ring."

"Mm-hmm."

Gray was squinting at his nose.

"Thankfully, my mom wouldn't let me dye my hair black. I was mostly an obedient kid and not entirely convinced black hair and freckles wouldn't be worse than red hair and freckles. The only curses I didn't suffer were acne and braces."

"Hah." Gray shared a rueful smile. "I probably had enough zits for the two of us."

"But were you a nerd?"

"Out and proud." Gray held up a palm. They shared a grin as Aaron slapped his hand. "What other games have you made up?" Gray asked.

Aaron's thoughts went immediately to his special project, the game he'd been working on for years, on and off. Talking about it would be different to admitting he'd worn nothing but black clothing, most of it artfully shredded, for nearly two years. He tried for a nonchalant shrug. "I've done a few riffs off of simple card games. Basically, Go Fish with different elements. Groups of minerals, farm animals, solar systems."

"That sounds fun."

"The farm one? Totally a drinking game because it's stupid."

"What else?"

"D&D with divergent rule systems."

"I miss those days. I need to reconnect with my old group. I lost touch with too many people when I moved up here, which is crazy. It's only an hour away. But most of them have kids, which limits their time."

"Same with my group."

With a grin, Gray stretched his legs out. "Best workout ever. I'm really feeling the burn."

Laughing, Aaron hopped up. "We were close to finished anyway. Let's stretch some before you cool down too much." He offered Gray a hand up.

After standing, Gray kept hold of Aaron's hand and squeezed. "When can I see you again?"

How about in half an hour, at my place? Was it wrong to be this obsessed? He was nearly forty, for Christ's sake. "How about tomorrow?"

"Perfect. We could do dinner first."

Aaron swallowed as heat zinged downward, spreading a flush over his skin. "We don't have to eat." *Not good for his health, Aaron.* "Er, unless you want to. I mean—"

Gray snorted. "What I want is to get you naked again. But I like talking to you too."

"Come to my place. We'll"—Aaron offered a sideways grin—"workout, and then we can head out or order in or, you know, whatever."

"*Whatever* sounds good. And I'd like to see some of your games. The one's you've made up."

"There aren't—"

Gray was shaking his head. "Don't even. I know you're holding out on me. Super Villain Clue? It's fun, but there's got to be more. I want to see what else you've got. All of it."

As though he'd taken a gut punch, albeit a gentle one, Aaron sucked in a breath. It wasn't fear, though, that someone might actually see him. The real him. It was surprise that Gray already had.

Chapter Nineteen

Having worn a towel for their first date and a combination of workout gear and not much at all on subsequent liaisons, Gray wanted to make a better impression on their second official date—not the least because he had to drive, and getting pulled over wearing next to nothing wasn't his idea of fun. He also wanted to wear something other than the jeans and long-sleeved T-shirt he'd worn to Aaron's house for their not-date. Now that he had time to groom, he was enjoying the process of getting ready to go out.

Also, on the last occasion they'd gotten together for an activity besides sex, they, well, hadn't been having sex yet. They'd been gaming buddies. Gray had always dressed for his gaming buddies, but tonight was about something more. *This* would be a date.

A part of him hoped he and Aaron would spend some time out of bed. It wasn't every day he met someone who had the same hobbies he did. He also hoped they'd spend some time naked. It'd been a while since he'd met someone he was this attracted to.

Gray surveyed the interior of his closet, hoping for a shirt that fell somewhere between casual and dressy. Where was his collection of denim shirts? They always looked sharp.

He found them in a box, tucked in beside the remnants of his Western phase. Gray shook out a shirt with an actual fringe and winced. Underneath, he found two bolo-style ties and a bandana. He grabbed his phone to shoot a quick text off to Ollie, the only friend he'd have worn them with. A theme night, maybe?

Gray: *Please tell me we did a Western-style cosplay at some point in our lives, or that I did not wear one of these bolos in public.*

Beneath his probable humiliation, he found the shirt he wanted. Soft indigo denim with contrasting stitching along the seams. A sniff test revealed two years of box must. Gray tossed the shirt toward his laundry basket and continued digging. His phone chimed.

Oliver: *I wish I could.*

Snorting, Gray tossed the phone aside and reached back into the box for the tissue-wrapped boots at the bottom—almost afraid to pull the paper away lest he reveal worked leather and spurs. He twitched the paper aside and grunted in surprise.

"I remember these."

They were almost a Chelsea, if memory served, though perhaps too high at the ankle. A deep burgundy leather with a darker detail at the sole and sides. The boots were scuffed and the soles a little gritty, but cleaned up, they'd look spiffy with his black jeans.

Or should he wear a tailored trouser?

Gray frowned at the boots. He could wear them with anything. Why the heck were they in the bottom of a box?

He glanced around his room. "Because I've done nothing but work for the past two years."

A heavy sigh deflated him, and the now familiar dizziness swirled up out of nowhere. Letting gravity take him down, he fell back onto the futon, boots clutched to his chest. He closed his eyes, tried to recall the last time he'd gotten dressed up for anything other than a casual game with friends, and couldn't—with the exception of his mother's funeral. The band around his heart constricted, the one he'd started noticing sometime last year and had successfully ignored until it had pulled tight four weeks ago, dropping him to the floor of the café in front of the coffee selection.

"I don't want to go back." He'd been thinking it but hadn't said it out loud before, and hearing the words didn't make them more real. Nor did the pronouncement feel like any sort of resolution.

But he'd have to figure his shit out soon; he couldn't rely on his friends to run the café forever, even though Patty and her husband seemed to be doing a better job than he ever had.

What would he do next, though? Go back to Allentown? He missed the circle of friends he'd made down there, mostly because he'd been a part of a vibrant Black community. But with as much family as he had around northeastern Pennsylvania, he'd easily connect with the community up here if he made time.

Time. He'd almost forgotten what it was to have time—just to think. To miss things. People.

If he didn't go back to work at the café, what would he do? Bake, definitely. Bread was in his blood. He'd had those plans, small ones, when he'd first moved back: to bake for the café in the morning and himself in the afternoons. To sell his bread—all of it, not only rolls and bagels—outside the café. To do what he loved and thrive on it rather than drown.

"Where would I sell my bread?" he asked out loud. To himself, he answered, "Anywhere. Who doesn't love bread?"

Something to think about when he wasn't marveling over how much time he had to think.

With another sigh, Gray pushed up and rolled off the futon. He collected his laundry basket, tucked it against his hip, and made his way to the laundry closet, half-aware he didn't have enough clothes to make up a load. After dumping the basket into the washer, he tucked it back under his arm and checked the bathroom. The hamper was empty; his dad's laundry must be in his room. He went to stand in front of his father's bedroom door.

His dad was out. He liked to walk along McMichael Creek before lunch. Keep an eye on the beavers who were building a dam under the Seventh Street bridge. What would it be like to pass his own days browsing the headlines of a newspaper so local, the rest of the world might not exist, to check in on beavers, and head out to bingo three times a week?

"It'd be like death," Gray muttered as he turned the doorknob and stepped inside his father's room.

The air hung heavy and close inside the dark room, and it felt as if it'd been a while since his father had opened the blinds. He flicked on the light to reveal an impression of half-hearted neatness: a bed sloppily made, a damp towel wrapped around a post at the end. Bureau drawers not quite lined up, nightstands cluttered with coffee cups, books, and notebooks. The closet doors stood open. Inside, clothes hung in seeming dejection, as though they'd hoped to go out today but had been left to fend for themselves yet again.

Acknowledging the sad clothes with a sense of accord, Gray circled the bed and spied the collection of undershirts, shorts, and balled-up socks propping the closet door ajar. He stooped to gather them into his basket and noticed another shirt poking out from under the bedcovers. He tugged it free and fell onto his ass, his back colliding with the other closet door.

A weird coldness opened up inside his chest. The blouse was his mother's. One of the floral numbers she'd liked so much, with satin-covered buttons and little cap sleeves. Gray was on the verge of balling it up beneath his nose to see if it smelled of her when a mental image of his father doing exactly that stampeded through his brain. Tears pricked his eyes as he got to his knees and gingerly pulled back the covers on that side of the bed. There was another blouse there, and he recognized it as her favorite. Similar to the one he already held, but not patterned. A peach silk with an ivory lace collar. Satin-covered buttons.

In an attempt to ignore the chasm of grief now digging its way into his torso, Gray recalled the weekend, about a year ago, when they'd boxed up his mother's stuff. Her sister, his aunt Sara, had come to oversee the task. As always, Gray had been busy with the café, but he'd managed to pop upstairs for long enough to accept a few tokens of memory, items Sara had put aside for him. Had she left these blouses or had his father pulled them back out of a box? Gray tried to imagine his father choosing them, the peach and the floral, and his heart broke.

No wonder the rest of the room felt as though it were waiting for someone to return and breathe life into it. The only important articles here were tucked beneath a pillow. Soft material set aside as an escape from reality.

Gray clutched one of the blouses to his chest and blinked into the still quiet as his eyes misted. Then his phone chimed, breaking the thick silence. Gray fished it out of his pocket and read a text from Patty: *Walk-in is making weird noises. Who is it we call?*

The familiar tightness was back. Sniffing back long-held grief, Gray stood and pushed the blouses beneath the covers on his mother's side of the bed. The tightness moved to his jaw as he grabbed the laundry basket, ferried the rest of the load down the hall, and got the washer started. He breathed in and out, using a practiced rhythm, as he jogged down the stairs to the café. Then he hung out behind the door until his phone chimed again.

Patty: *Is it Newman and Assoc?*

Gray drew in a deeper breath and tugged open the door. The familiar aroma of yeast and baked bread rolled over him. Crushed and toasted seeds. Bacon on the grill. The buttery scent of croissants. The clamor of noise from the kitchen cut over the burble of voices from the seating area. A phone was ringing, the chime interspersed with the jangle of the bell over the front door. Gray checked his watch. It was just after eleven. On a Wednesday. Nearly as peak as peak got for Clery's Café.

And the walk-in was probably about to die. Had anyone been called to repair it the day he'd collapsed? No, wait, that had been the grill. And someone must have taken care of that, or the café wouldn't still be in business.

Gray approached the walk-in to listen to the weird noise—he'd started a mental catalog of its odd sounds over the years. The door thumped open before he got there, and a tall, reed-thin man walked out. He was vaguely familiar: the deep, rich hue of his skin, the slope of his shoulders.

"Grayson!" The man stuck his hand out.

Frowning, Gray shook it.

"Wendell." Wendell cocked his head. "Patty's husband?"

"Wendell!" Gray shook his hand again, a bit more enthusiastically. "Good to see you, man."

"You too. You too." Wendell rocked his head back toward the walk-in. "I think it's the condenser."

"Yeah? A wheezy sorta rattle?"

"You know it. If we can get the parts locally, I can take a crack at it."

"Wendell Williams, you will do no such thing. Gray!"

Patty flew at him, spatula in one hand, knife in the other. Her breasts collided with his chest in what Gray assumed was an armless hug. Being that her husband stood beside them and that Gray was definitely gay, he tried not to look down. Though, Patty did have a rather substantial chest.

"Patty," he said, hoping the twist of his lips somewhat resembled a smile.

"I don't have time to ask how you are. Lunch rush is starting."

"I know how it is." He felt an urge to pull on a pair of gloves and jump in. Almost.

"Tell this fool here not to try to fix the walk-in." She aimed a glare over Gray's shoulder—a feat, as Patty was only about half his height. "And you, tell Gray what you did to our fridge at home."

"Whole different situation, sugar."

Their North Carolina accents, stronger when they spoke together, made Gray smile. As did the obvious warmth and love between their words. "Let me take a listen," Gray said.

Patty and Wendell turned to other tasks as Gray yanked open the refrigerator door and stepped inside. Cool air puffed up around him, carrying other familiar odors: Onions, celery, tomatoes, and cheese. The flatter scent of refrigerated dough, a tang of bacon from the boxes stacked inside the door, and the slightly sweet scent of refuse that tended to collect after a week or so, which was about when they'd haul everything out of the corners and mop the floor, wipe down the shelves, and restock the baking soda tray.

In a weird flash, Gray was back upstairs in his father's bedroom, clutching his mother's blouse. Then he was in the walk-in shop fridge again, reeling, as though he'd become unstuck from time. His heart hurt, but not with the tightness that had felled him in front of the coffee station. A weight hung there instead, one that wanted to break free. He was afraid of what might happen when it did, though.

Would he suddenly develop a need to keep up with the beavers of Stroudsburg?

A rattling wheeze broke through his thoughts, and Gray surfaced back into the present, his attention turning to the condenser unit mounted high over the back shelves. He pulled out a pair of milk crates and climbed closer. Poked at the cover until it came loose in his hands and peered inside, not sure what he was searching for. When a warm puff of air hit him in the face, he decided it was a sign and climbed down.

Back in the café, he made for the office and pulled open the filing drawer, intending to flip through folders of receipts until he found the one with the familiar red and black logo. But the folders were gone. A laptop rested at the bottom of the drawer instead. Gray had just picked it up when Wendell poked his head through the door. "Mia digitized everything."

"Who's Mia and what does that mean?"

"All the receipts. Scanned and filed. There's these folders on the desktop."

Gray glanced toward the desk. The empty desk.

"No, on the laptop desktop."

"Oh." Gray opened the laptop. "And Mia?"

"Our babysitter. Patty brought the receipts home and she did it over a few days, before getting the kids from school."

A sense of unreality was now unfolding inside Gray, and the competing emotions and sensations from the morning were starting to take their toll. This was why he'd spent the past four weeks cooped up in the apartment. All of this feeling couldn't be good for a body. Not that everything he felt was bad but . . .

He opened the laptop. A series of folders formed two lines across the middle of the screen. One was labeled *Repairs*. Gray clicked it open and scanned the receipts until he found the right one. He handed the laptop to Wendell. "Hewson and Associates. Cooling and heating people. They can fix the walk-in. We're probably going to need a new condenser. Current one has been repaired three times too many. I don't think there are parts for it anymore. In fact, we need a whole new walk-in. The insulation is deteriorating and the fans are sluggish. They either need replacing or cleaning. What are you doing?"

Wendell had put the laptop aside and pulled out his phone. "Making notes." He glanced up. "What else?"

"I . . . I don't know. What else has been acting up?"

"The sink was leaking. I took care of that. I also priced out raising it to a level where a man like me doesn't have to sit to do the dishes."

Memory clicked and Gray placed the man leaning in the doorway. It was Wendell he'd seen doing the dishes a few weeks back.

"You've been here all this time," Gray said.

Wendell shrugged. "Patty needed the help." He smiled. "You too. I know we've barely met, but family is family."

"I'm glad you're here."

"As am I."

Wendell held up his phone, and Gray had the sudden urge to say, *It's yours. All of it. Take it. Be happy with it.*

It would wear on them after a while—it'd have to. But right now, Patty and Wendell looked like they were enjoying themselves working together. Gray's mom and dad had loved it—which had to be why his dad seemed so adrift.

Did his father even care about the café anymore? Did he need to hang onto it the way he clung to his wife's blouses?

Gray would never know if he never asked.

Wendell cleared his throat.

Hauling himself back to reality took effort, and the weariness Gray had been battling since All the Fuss crawled over up his back. It was time for a nap. But first: "The deli fridge has to be defrosted once a month or the shelves start to ice over. The grease trap, under the sink: once a month on that too. Patty knows how to change the oil in the fryer . . ." The list went on, and as Wendell made a note of every task, the weight pulling down on Gray's shoulders started to lift. Degree by delirious degree.

He wasn't handing over the business. Wasn't sure whether he could do that. Didn't know what he wanted other than to not feel as though he'd been rolled out flat against the pavement day after day. But for the first time in a while, the scent of possibility hung close. The very real feel of options poked and tickled. He began to feel less . . . trapped.

More alive. And sadly aware his dad might not have been the only corpse haunting the streets of Stroudsburg.

Chapter Twenty

Aaron hadn't fantasized about sex with Gray. His crush had been oriented toward surface detail. Gray's looks—his smile—and personality. He'd also admired his dependability. His seeming good cheer in the face of chaos. He had imagined kissing Gray, though, or what it would feel like to be kissed by him. He'd thought about that a lot.

In retrospect, it might seem odd he hadn't taken his fantasies further than making out or the now-proven wonder of a Grayson Clery hug. But with Gray currently spread beneath him, knees raised, and Aaron locked between, buried balls-deep in a man he'd wanted for uncounted months, the realization that fantasy would never have matched reality caught him. He could not have imagined this feeling.

Their connection was more than sex, but this . . .

They'd been enjoying each other's bodies for a couple of weeks, now, but *this*. He was inside Gray. Even if he had indulged in a fantasy, he'd never have dared hope Gray might bottom for him.

"You okay up there?" Gray laid a palm against Aaron's cheek.

"Very much okay," Aaron whispered. He drew his hips back and rocked forward. Reveled in the way Gray's lips parted, chin tilted upward, eyes nearly closed.

"Do that again," Gray said.

Aaron did so. Pulling back and driving forward, the motion a little less gentle this time.

"Again."

And then again, Aaron moving faster, thrusting harder, testing Gray's resilience and willingness to be fucked.

Gray proved quite resilient.

It didn't take long for Aaron's climax to push close.

Bracing himself against the mattress, Aaron bent to lick and kiss the sweat forming across Gray's pecs. He teased a nipple with his tongue. Tested the texture of the sparse but crisp curls above and below.

"You slowed down," Gray whined.

"I was too close. Don't want to finish yet."

Gray wedged a hand between them to fist his hard cock. "We can do it again, Sporty."

They could.

The brush of Gray's fingers against Aaron's abdomen pulled his climax back toward the brink. With a deep groan, Aaron picked up the pace, thrusting, withdrawing, plunging, teasing, and just plain rutting, knowing how it must feel for Gray in his current position; the impending orgasm a combination of release, anticipation, reciprocation, and sheer utter joy.

He came with a quiet yell and time ran away for a while, taking the bedroom—the world—with it, leaving Aaron in a place where only pleasure remained. When he came back, Gray arched and shuddered beneath him, his cry of release deeper and throatier. A yell of wonder and satisfaction. A sound Aaron wanted to hear again.

Moments passed before a verbal objection to the inevitable separation issued from both their mouths. Afterward, Aaron flushed and laughed, and beneath him, Gray snorted. He was touching Aaron's cheek, the flat of his palm warm and slightly rough. Baker's hands.

Then they were lying side by side, panting, Gray half-heartedly mopping his midsection with a towel and Aaron hesitating to divest himself of the condom because it would hurt. He was always super sensitive after sex. Also, he kinda wanted to relax in the afterglow. But if he left it there, things would get less pleasant and not at all glowy.

Steeling himself for the interruption to his high, Aaron peeled and tossed the condom toward the wastepaper basket. He winced as it glanced off the side. Thankfully, he'd knotted it and it didn't seem to have popped. But now he had to remember to pick it up.

"How many points?" Gray murmured beside him.

"Total miss."

"Don't forget to pick it up."

Aaron flopped onto his side, facing Gray. If replete was an expression, Gray was wearing it. Aaron reached down to fondle Gray's spent dick. "What are we thinking about round two? Not that I'm unsatisfied with round one."

"We're thinking round two is going to be awesome." Gray bent close to brush their mouths together. Across Aaron's lips, he breathed, "Damn, I'd forgotten what it was like to feel this."

"Satisfied?"

"Well-fucked."

Aaron squeezed the cock in his hand. "Our chemistry is on point."

"It sure is. Keep stroking, I could be ready in a few."

A quick conversation about testing and status over the condoms and lube had revealed they were both versatile. With the right partner, Aaron didn't mind taking one role over the other, but the prospect of having Gray inside him had his ass clenching in anticipation. Topping him had been amazing. But giving himself over to the man he almost hadn't dared to fantasize about? Aaron upped his stroking game and reattached his lips to Gray's. Kissing, licking, tasting.

Familiar sounds poked at the periphery of Aaron's attention, but he didn't put them together until a "Yoo-hoo!" floated along the hallway.

He fell out of the kiss at the same time as Gray rocked backward. "Is that . . .?"

"My mother? Yes."

"Damn, one of us needs to move out," Gray said.

"I *have* moved out." Aaron pushed to a half-sitting position and raised his voice. "Kinda busy right now! Help yourself to pizza."

"You did not just give our pizza away."

"You weren't going to have any, remember? Too many vegetables." Personally, Aaron liked spinach and broccoli on a pizza. With a homemade crust and the sauce low in sodium, he hoped they'd turned a forbidden food into a treat Gray could enjoy.

They'd made the dough together after Gray expressed horror over the store-bought crust Aaron had pulled out of the freezer. As they mixed and kneaded, Gray had explained the difference between various types of flour. Apparently, the success of any bread came down to the flour. The flavor, especially.

While the dough was rising, they'd played a card game. Then it had been time to play with dough again. Aaron wouldn't like to say cooking with Gray was as much fun as sex with Gray, but it came a close second.

He still had a hand wrapped around Gray's dick, which had firmed from soft dough to . . . *Yeah, not going to finish that thought.* "I've got something better than pizza." Aaron bent to use his mouth.

He had just put his lips around the tip when his mom knocked on his bedroom door. "What did you say, hon?"

Beneath him, Gray groaned.

Aaron sighed. Lifted his head. "Give us a sec to get dressed. We'll be out in a bit."

"I'm not staying long. I want to grab something to eat before I meet a friend at the cinema," his mom said, her voice moving away from the door again.

"Quite the social life for a visitor." Gray arched a dubious eyebrow.

"Tell me about it."

"Is she expecting to see you before she heads back out?"

Flopping onto his back, Aaron let out another hearty sigh. "Maybe?"

Gray kissed his temple. "At least we got one round in. And this isn't forever."

Aaron's heart beat triple time for a few seconds until he worked out Gray's meaning. His mom staying wasn't forever. Right. Gray wasn't referring to what they were doing. Aaron shook all thought out of his head. Now was so not the time to get thinky. Or clingy. Or weird. He and Gray were having a good time. *Focus on that.* And how to make dinner end as soon as possible.

After pressing a quick kiss to the side of Gray's head, Aaron rolled off the bed and stepped on the condom. He felt it bulge and then pop before he gained the presence of mind to lift his foot away. Cooling semen oozed between his toes. "Damn it."

"Condom bomb?"

"Yep."

"Here." Gray tossed him the hand towel they'd used for cleanup. Aaron sat on the edge of the bed to wipe spunk from his toes. Now dressed in a pair of black jeans and a white V-neck undershirt, Gray crouched in front of him and inspected the darkening patch of carpet. "We should clean this up before it sets."

Aaron grinned. "I could set my mother on it tomorrow. Remind her of the good old days."

"Oh, man. Moms have fixes for everything, don't they?"

"Unsung heroes."

A flicker of sadness softened Gray's smile as he took the towel from Aaron and helped slide it between his toes. He finished by cupping Aaron's heel, lifting his foot slightly, and bending forward to kiss his toes. Glad he was already sitting, Aaron gripped the bunched-up bedsheets. The sweetness of that simple gesture unsteadied his world for a beat or two. Then Gray was rocking back and smiling up at him. "You should get dressed before I try to take advantage." He focused on Aaron's cock. "I think I see a freckle."

Aaron tugged Gray upward and they kissed again. As they moved back onto the bed, Gray's clothed body brushed Aaron's skin, the denim of his jeans rough and soft at the same time. His T-shirt, soft. The skin beneath, warm. The weight of Gray more pleasing than all the rest of it combined.

"I want you so bad," Aaron whispered.

Gray ground his hips down. Behind the fly of his jeans, he was hard. "I want you too. Will she knock again if we don't come out?"

"Probably not?"

Gray dipped down to kiss him, lips wondrously gentle but demanding. Aaron arched into the kiss, his body straining upward. Warm fingers wrapped around his dick and stroked. A groan moved through his body, riding the rising tide of his arousal, and then Gray was moving south, lips caressing a rib, a hip bone, and finally the tender skin high on Aaron's thigh.

"Definitely a freckle." Gray's tongue rasped over curls of hair, his warm breath washing across Aaron's erection.

Aaron crushed a balled-up fist to his lips in an effort to squash the shout ripped from his lungs as Gray's mouth closed over the head of his cock. Did his best to muffle another cry as Gray sucked downward. The weight of a firm hand pinned his hips to the bed as Gray worked his length. Aaron's toes curled. His balls gathered on a whimper. He came, far quicker than he would have liked, but the relentless pressure of Gray's lips and tongue gave him little choice.

A moment later, Gray was back on his heels, wiping his mouth with the back of a hand. "Mm, latex."

Aaron laughed and his limper-than-limp dick jerked almost painfully. He pushed off the bed, landing on his knees in front of Gray, and leaned in to kiss him. Gray tasted like semen and, yeah, a faint hint of condom and lube. Aaron grinned into the kiss. He loved the messiness of sex. He also liked that he and Gray were already in the thick of it, neither of them giving or receiving the sideways looks that sometimes cropped up during a casual hookup over an objection that might not get discussed. It meant that whatever they were doing wasn't casual. Well, it was, in a way. They weren't anywhere near talking about what they were doing. But outside of the sex there *was* talk.

"Where'd you go?"

Aaron stopped kissing Gray. He blinked at the face in front of him. Pressed a palm to Gray's cheek and dropped a gentle kiss to his lips. "Inside everything. Just for a sec. I'm back now."

For a moment, Gray seemed about to speak. Then, with a half smile, he leaned back and snagged Aaron's boxers from the floor. "Put your pandas on. I'm gonna go wash my hands." He reached for the hand towel. "Want me to rinse this out or put it in a basket or whatnot?"

"Laundry hamper is in my closet."

Gray dropped off the towel and then eased the bedroom door open. He looked both ways before disappearing into the hallway, pulling the door closed behind him.

Aaron finished getting dressed and collected Gray's dark blue denim shirt from the chair beside the closet, smiling at the color. It suited Gray's complexion. He met Gray in the hall, handed it over, and waited with him while Gray slipped his arms into the sleeves and did up the buttons. Helped out with the tucking and couldn't resist pressing another kiss to Gray's mouth before taking his hand to lead him into the living area.

The oven door squeaked open as they passed the kitchen. With a pot holder in each hand, his mom glanced up and smiled. "Just in time. I think this is hot enough!" She pulled the pizza out and set it on the counter.

"Mom, this is Grayson Clery. Gray, my mom, Hava Asher."

Gray extended a hand. "Nice to meet you, ma'am."

"And you, Grayson."

"Gray is fine."

"Call me Hava."

They smiled and Aaron smiled and everyone smiled until the moment got weird.

Aaron clapped his hands, winced at the sharp sound, and cleared his throat. "Should we eat?"

Putting aside the fact Aaron would rather lick sauce off of Gray's body than eat pizza with his mother, dinner passed pleasantly. Gray and his mom chatted about the café, and then Gray's health, in a lighthearted enough manner that it didn't feel as though Gray might have visited with death a few weeks ago. When Gray asked how she was enjoying Pennsylvania, Aaron's mom talked about the two book clubs she'd joined—*two?*—and the volunteer work she was doing at the library. *Wait, what?*

Gray raised an eyebrow and Aaron spread his hands. When his mom looked in his direction, Aaron tucked his hands back into his lap.

"What do you two have planned this evening? Aside from sex?"

Aaron choked on his water and spat the mouthful back into his glass, coughing. Gray patted his back. "I wanted to see some of these games Aaron's been designing."

Oh, no.

His mother's face lit up like the Vegas Strip. "He's so talented! Did you know he's made cards? The art and all the meticulous printing."

Heat stung Aaron's face as Gray slapped the table. "I knew it. He tries to hide his nerdy self, but the minute he starts talking about games, you just know he's got more than one cupboard of boxes he hasn't opened yet, and rules for everything he's ever wanted to play written down somewhere. I bet there's a shoebox of painted figurines too, isn't there?"

Aaron couldn't decide whether he wanted lightning to arc through the ceiling and end it all now, or to run downstairs and gather his collections into his arms so he could show them off. He managed to wait until after his mom left, before leading Gray to the basement.

As Aaron opened the series of closets he'd bought to line the basement walls, Gray went curiously quiet. Then intensely quiet as he stepped from shelf to shelf touching some boxes, turning others, pulling still others out altogether.

When they reached the end of the row, he quirked a brow in Aaron's direction. "Sporty."

"I know."

"I think you have more games than I do, and that should be statistically impossible."

How else to reply but blush?

"Where's the one your mom was talking about?" Gray asked.

Aaron led him back upstairs. He pulled out the box his mom had found and handed it over. The reverent way Gray took it sent another flush coursing over Aaron's skin. Gray levered off the top of the box and stared at the interior for a moment. He glanced up. "You made these?"

"Yeah."

Gray licked his lips. "All of these. You lettered them too."

"I wanted to maybe get them printed at some point. When I finished tweaking the game."

After putting the lid aside, Gray delved into the box. "Okay, tell me about this one." He held up an average deck-sized card featuring the portrait of a wood sprite.

Aaron read out the text he'd carefully printed beneath. "'Wood sprite, friend/foe. Nurture for plus three forest. Murder for plus two wood. Bribe for one of each.'" He reached for the card. "The game basically starts with your character washing up on an island." He plucked the rest of the deck from the box and shuffled through the cards until he found some terrain. "Every round, you draw a card and if you get terrain, you can place it on the map, building your island. Coast, meadow, forest, ravine, etc. A wood sprite is an action card. You place her on the map to either grow your forest, gaining another terrain card, so to speak, or to cut down one you already have, giving you the wood to build tools or a structure. I haven't decided whether the building card or the extra forest card have to come from your hand or if there'll be a separate deck of generic world tiles."

When Aaron looked up, Gray was staring at him.

"What?"

"Aaron, man. This is . . ." Gray shook his head. "This is *something.*"

Aaron shrugged. "It's just—"

"Don't do that. Don't act like it's nothing. I've been playing games all my life. I go to cons and I spend more on new crowdfunding projects than I've probably made over the past two years. I know games. I collect games. This is something."

"You go to cons? Which ones?"

"All of them, when I can. Though not recently. Is this playable?"

"Kind of?"

"Let's play it. I want to see how it's structured so far."

"I don't have all the cards illustrated or figured out."

"It's okay. We can write on pieces of paper for the cards you don't have yet."

Excitement bloomed in Aaron's gut. "What, design a few on the fly?"

"Sure, why not. For what you don't have yet. Do you have a story for the world?"

"Sort of?"

Gray's dark eyes gleamed. "We need to write it down." His next smile wavered. "I mean, we could. If you were amenable to that."

"Are you kidding? I'd love that. I've got a couple of pages written, but more notes than anything else. I figured I could do that part last."

"No, no. I mean, I guess you could? But what if you had the story first? Then all of your cards, the pop-up events, the heroes, the enemies, will have to fall in with your theme. It'll help with the overall balance."

"Have you designed a game before?" Aaron asked.

"Nope. But I've always wanted to." Gray tapped the side of his head. "This is full of stories I always meant to write down. I thought it'd be cool if I could write one around a game. I never got around to it, though. Sometimes I'll see a project to back that's close enough to an idea I wanted to try and I'll buy that instead."

Chuckling, Aaron gestured toward the basement. "Ah, yeah."

They shared a grin.

Aaron studied Gray's face a moment, the lightness there. The quiet intelligence and eagerness sparking in his dark eyes, the smile hovering about his lips. "Maybe we could work on this together a while. See how it goes."

It was only after the words left his mouth that Aaron realized he could be talking about the game or what was happening between them. He was gaming *and* sleeping with Grayson Clery! Sometimes he felt like a teenager who'd been invited to live his dream.

Aaron dug his phone from a pocket. "You know, there's, um, a con this weekend. Down Philly way. We could get some ideas."

Gray dipped his head forward in a slow nod. Then he lifted his chin with a smile. "Let's do it."

Chapter Twenty-One

How was it that Gray always forgot what a gaming convention smelled like? The Deck Builder Expo was a smaller event—as in passes were available at the door. But there were enough sweaty bodies milling about Hall A of the Philly Expo Center to create a funk. As they'd predicted, however, the convention wasn't totally dedicated to deck-building games. There was a corner devoted to board games, a few indie video game publishers had booths in a cluster toward the center, and vendors hawking related paraphernalia such as dice sets, gaming furniture, and highly caffeinated beverages ringed the outside. There were T-shirts for any pursuit ever tagged as nerdy, along with plushies, art posters, sticker packs, and key rings.

More than once, Gray felt drawn to a jigsaw puzzle or another time-centric hobby he'd put aside when he'd moved back to Stroudsburg. He paused in front of a booth filled with thousand-piece magic puzzles, most of them featuring a maze that could be rearranged once the puzzle was complete.

"How cool is that?" Gray asked Aaron, who'd paused beside him.

"Not cool. Not at all. I mean, it'd take me a year to place a thousand pieces. Then I'm supposed to rearrange parts of the puzzle and put more pieces down? No. Nope. Not happening." Aaron's grin said he appreciated the idea, though.

"I used to do a puzzle a week. Always had one spread out on a card table in my dining room."

"Not the dining table?"

"That was for games."

Aaron gave a sage nod. "Of course." He tapped his phone, bringing up the expo map. "Okay, so the corner we want to visit is on the opposite side of the hall."

Gray surveyed the seething crowd between them and their goal. Ugh. His head didn't feel quite right today. No speckled vision, but every now and then, the world floated, as if an invisible wave were rolling toward an invisible shore, lifting him off his feet along the way.

"Everything okay?" Aaron asked.

"Just the crowd." Gray forced a grin. "You'd think I'd be used to it. I have, like, what, at least this many people in the café at lunch every day?"

Aaron laughed. "There about." He indicated a narrow passage between neighboring booths. "Let's squeeze through there and walk the perimeter."

"Good idea." They'd miss a lot of the wares on display, but Gray didn't need any new nerd shirts. Even one with—

Aaron beat him to it, tugging the bottom hem of the T-shirt down to reveal the design in full. A grumpy, cartoon-style kitten, arms folded, and the words, *I need coffee.*

"It's you!" Aaron exclaimed.

"It's me." Even the fur was the right color—a medium roast. And the expression on the kitten's face? Priceless.

Aaron flipped the T-shirt aside to reach the folded stack behind. "What size? L, XL?"

"Get me a 2X if they have it."

"Are you sure? You don't look like a 2X to me." Regardless, Aaron found the right size and handed the folded shirt over.

Gray shook it out and squinted at the seeming yards of material. "Maybe the XL?"

Had he lost weight or were these shirts absurdly large?

With a grin that was only slightly smug, Aaron handed him a smaller shirt. Gray nearly dropped it when he saw the shirt behind it. Aaron in kitten form. "I found *you!*"

He balled his shirt under his arm and reached for the ridiculously cute shirt. The kitten wore a headband and reclined on a workout bench with a slice of pizza in one hand.

"Oh my God, that's adorable." Aaron flipped through the stack to extract his size and thrust it at Gray. "We need to get both of these."

"Buy three, get one free!" said the teenager who popped out of nowhere.

Who needed four shirts? Gray frowned at the display as Aaron held up another shirt.

"Patty?" he said.

Gray had already spotted one for Wendell. And the cats counting in French? "If this isn't Nick, then Nick in T-shirt form doesn't exist."

Aaron held out a powder blue shirt featuring a happy kitty dusted with flour and daubed with frosting. The caption read: *Bake it til you make it.*

"You're killing me."

"The worst part," Aaron said with a grin, "is that we can buy all of these online, but here we are, sixty miles from home, at a convention full of gaming goodness, and what are we doing?"

Gray was too busy freeing another T-shirt from the stack behind the display. He unfurled it in front of Aaron and watched Aaron's eyes widen and then narrow with laughter.

"Yep. We're buying that one," Aaron said.

Cats playing D&D? They were buying two of that one.

Roughly ten minutes (or what felt like a mad half-century later), they fought their way free of the T-shirt booth, having hit the ultimate discount of buy ten tees, get five free. That fifteen shirts didn't feel like enough was clearly a Jedi mind trick. Gray could only hope that distance from the booth would weaken the effect.

They stopped to grab a snack, and the debate over whether a saltless pretzel was heart-healthy nudged Gray's happy meter toward north, despite the fact a pretzel without salt was all sorts of blasphemy. The hall was way too crowded and he'd already spent too much money, but he was having a good time. Best part? He and Aaron hadn't even checked out the games yet, and whatever they bought, they could take home and play together.

The board games on offer were fun. Gray had heard of most of them, owned more than a few. There were dozens of new games on display, but most of them were reimaginings of old ideas. Some very creative, though. One had artwork that drew Gray across the aisle. But nothing excited him the way Aaron's game had. There were no tile-placing, deck-building, role-play survival games on offer.

When Aaron finally found a game he wanted to try, Gray was entirely too grateful for the opportunity to sit, and he almost didn't care if the demo was interesting or not. Thankfully, after he'd been sitting for five minutes, the floor stopped rolling like it was balanced on water and his head cleared. And the game demo was fun. A simpler concept than Aaron's game, but as a deck-based city-builder, along similar lines.

Aaron thanked the pair who'd guided them through the scenario and took their card. Then he guided Gray off to the side. "Anything else you'd like to see, because I think I'm about done."

"Yeah, me too." The floor now felt steady, but Gray was beyond tired. He nodded toward the demo table. "That's about the best game here, in my opinion."

"Yep. I'm going to sign up for their newsletter." Aaron was frowning at the card in his hand. "The name of their publisher is familiar." He showed the card to Gray. "Ever heard of Jatek Games?"

Gray felt his head bob up and down. "I have. I have a stack of their games at home. Good company. They crowdfund first, and most of their projects go wide after that. Sold in stores and online."

Aaron's expression was thoughtful. Then his forehead unwrinkled. "Kevin."

"Huh?"

"At the gym. A long-time client. He has a friend in the industry. I think this is them."

Gray indicated the two women setting up their game for another demo round. "Want to ask them about the company?"

Aaron pocketed the card. "No. At least, not yet." He met Gray's eyes. "I mean . . . should I?"

Gray grabbed Aaron's arm, intending to give his biceps a reassuring squeeze. The firm musculature, warm beneath Aaron's long-sleeve T-shirt, distracted him for a microsecond. When they got all nerdy, he forgot Aaron was built. "Doesn't hurt to dream a little, Sporty. If you've got questions, now's a great time to ask. But you have their card. I'm sure you could email them at any time if you want to work on your list first."

"My list?"

"Of what you want and how to go about getting it."

Aaron's face blanked for a second, and oddly, his shoulders seemed to draw inward, as though he were preparing to fold into a shell. It was so not the Aaron that Gray was used to seeing at the gym—open, friendly, buff—that he almost wondered if the invisible waves had started lifting Aaron off the floor as well. Especially when a hint of panic and vulnerability flashed through Aaron's eyes.

"Hey." Gray squeezed his biceps again.

Aaron seemed to come back to himself. Mostly. His eyes retained a slightly faraway cast and his smile still seemed vulnerable. "Sorry. I . . ." He shook his head.

"What is it?"

Aaron jerked his head toward the narrow corridor circling the periphery of the exhibit hall. "Want to walk and talk? I wouldn't mind a breath of fresh air."

"Sure." Gray fell into step beside Aaron, their bags of T-shirts and handful of games they'd bought bumping together. "What's up?"

"My whole family is sporty."

"Scary sporty. Even your mom looks fit."

"She's climbed K2."

"No kidding!"

"I'd never kid about that. If you laid out every hike or climb or walking tour my parents have done, end to end, they'd be close to circling the planet three times. My sister is probably nearing her first circuit. Heck, I'd be close to one from childhood hikes with the family. Point is, we're fit. It's a family theme. We're movers and we love to show others how to move."

"Okay." Gray wasn't sure where this was going, but he wanted to listen. Aaron had been patient with him as a newbie exerciser and had listened to him talk about the café a number of times now.

Aaron turned to look at him. "Sometimes, though, I want to sit and play games. I mean, don't get me wrong. I love my job. I love what I do."

"It shows. You're amazing at what you do."

"Thanks." Aaron's smile was sweet and kinda shy. His blush not quite fierce enough to disappear his freckles. "That means a lot. But it's not all I want. My sisters, though? My sister and sister-in-law. They're looking at a site for a third gym, and they've offered it to me. To run."

"That's great!"

The pained clinch of Aaron's features suggested it wasn't great.

Gray tried again. "It's not what you want?"

"I don't know. I've been thinking it through some, and running a gym would supposedly give me more time to myself. I wouldn't have to teach as many classes, and I could oversee personal training instead of taking on so many clients myself. That's what happens when you move up the chain. Thing is, I like teaching classes and I love working with my clients, even if I haven't had as much time to devote to gaming as I usually do. Lately, with the current expansion, we've been busy."

Plus, Aaron was still helping to close the café most weekdays. Guilt clamped down on Gray's middle. He needed to sort his own shit out. Stat.

"It's not that I don't appreciate what they're offering me," Aaron continued. "It's that . . ."

"You don't want it."

Obvious relief pulled Aaron's shoulders down. "I don't. I really don't. Like, I just . . . don't. I like what I have now."

"Then tell them that. Your sisters."

"I don't know how." They'd reached the doors to the hall. Aaron pushed through and held the door for Gray. Outside, he breathed out a sigh. "I don't want to disappoint them."

"It'd be a worse crime to disappoint yourself."

Aaron wore a frown of pained consideration. Then he nodded. "You're right. Damn."

"If you want to talk it through before chatting with them, let me know. But my best advice is to listen to your heart. Life is short, and we're nearly at that age where if we don't figure out what we want, and soon, we're going to spend what's left in regret." Wow. If that wasn't depressing, Gray didn't know what was. "Sorry, I meant—"

"No, you're right." One corner of Aaron's mouth twitched upward, giving him a wry look. "I think that's advice we could both use, yeah?"

Oof. But, yeah. "Truth."

A wider smile washed Aaron's face clean. "Okay, let's go home and play games." His smile spread even wider. "And not only the ones we have here."

Wiped out as he was, Gray couldn't help returning his grin. "I like the way you think."

"Oh, you like a lot more than that." One ginger brow curved over a now decidedly wicked smile.

Gray kept on grinning.

Chapter Twenty-Two

L ate on Sunday morning, about an hour after Gray had left, Aaron stood in the center of his living room torn between couch and door. With his mom in the house, and as busy as he'd been lately, it'd been a while since he'd spent an afternoon doing close to nothing. He could put on a movie or a season of TV he'd already watched for background noise, and spread a game over the coffee table. One to play, with him essentially competing with himself, or one of his projects.

He found it harder to laze about with TV and games when it was sunny outside, though, and it wasn't simply that he'd been raised to enjoy the outdoors. Despite the fact he burned at the thought of sunshine, Aaron loved the sensation of warmth against his skin on a spring day. Before the sweltering heat of summer and the buzzing of humidity and insects that came later in the season. Today, the weather was perfect. The air cooled by a breeze, the sun still stretching sunny muscles.

He should go out, but . . .

Aaron gazed at the box on the coffee table. Last night, before retiring to his bedroom for other fun and games, he and Gray had outlined a story arc for his survival game. Gray had an amazing imagination. He'd taken the elements of Aaron's world and woven them into the beginnings of a mythos that could carry this one single game into many iterations or expansions. They'd sketched a vague plan for that, and an idea for limiting the first game to a handful of terrain-types and resources to make the whole project less daunting. Aaron now had a ton of new ideas for hints and Easter eggs, in the base game and the expanded world.

But it was so sunny outside. A beautiful day.

His phone chimed, breaking the moment of indecision. After looking around, Aaron found it in the kitchen and woke the screen. There was a text from his sister.

Devorah: *We're taking Mom to see the new site. Will swing by in a few to pick you up.*

"I guess I'm going out, then."

Aaron glanced toward the window and the beckoning sun. Excitement did not unfurl within his chest. Instead, dread added a weight that threatened to pull clouds out of the sky. Putting a hand to his sternum, Aaron exhaled a long, slow breath. He needed to talk to his sister.

Ten minutes later, a horn honked outside. Aaron closed and locked the front door and jogged down his front walk. Dev and his mom sat inside the car. Both up front, with Dev driving.

Aaron contemplated the back seat of the Mini Cooper with distaste. "Maybe we should take my car."

"Oh, get in, it's not far," Dev said.

Thankfully, the tiny car had four doors. Aaron crawled inside the back to find half the tiny space taken up with a car seat. When he sat, his knees almost touched his chin. "With another kid on the way, you're going to need a bigger car."

"Maybe when they're older, though they might not be as tall as you."

"I'm not that tall!"

"Children, please," his mom put in.

"Ugh." Aaron flopped his head backward. "Mom. Having you here is like being a teenager again. It's not right."

"I am the fountain of youth," she said.

Aaron closed his eyes. When the world swirled around him, he opened them. He hadn't forgotten how cramped the back seat of Devorah's car was, but he had failed to remember how car sick it made him. Directing his gaze front and center, he found the horizon line and focused on that until his stomach settled. Dev was taking 611 west through Stroudsburg.

"Not taking the highway?" Aaron asked.

"Mom hasn't seen all the development around Bartonsville. I figured we'd go the long way."

"Yay."

His mom scratched around in her purse and handed a roll of mints through the seats. "Here. You always did get sick on long car journeys."

"I'm not sick." Aaron took the mints. "Yet. But it's cramped back here."

"Uh-huh." Dev caught his gaze in the rearview mirror. "Mom tells me you've been having overnight guests."

"Guests? No. Guest, yes. One guest."

"Grayson from the café?"

"Right."

"He has the most gorgeous smile," Dev said almost dreamily.

"Doesn't he?" his mother agreed.

Aaron wanted to close his eyes again. Drift into the daydream world that had carried him through the many, many, many family outings of his youth. He changed the subject instead. "So, when was the last time you spoke to Dad?" he asked.

His mom raised her eyebrows. "Last night. He's planning to stay on for the tour of Sleepy Hollow."

"Didn't we go there when I was, like, thirteen?" Dev asked.

The rest of the drive flitted by in snatches of past and present as the three of them relived childhood vacations in between Devorah and Aaron pointing out the new hospital, the new supermarket, and the old tire shop that was somehow still in business.

"Wait!" his mom exclaimed. "Where's the barbecue place?"

"It's a car dealership now." Aaron tapped his window to indicate the former restaurant on the left side of the highway.

"No." His mom gasped. "That makes no sense."

"It was weird for a while."

When they passed the flea market, his mom wanted to stop, but Dev argued they could stop on the way back. "The empanada stand on the corner of the lot will be open then."

So much for his day. Aaron gazed out at the sunshine and wondered whether he could argue for a walk around the summit of Big Pocono. Seeing as they were out and apparently staying out.

Then they were pulling into an expansive empty lot. Crumbling pavement lined the road, but whatever had been there before had been torn down. Most of the site was cordoned off, but the chain-link fencing outlined where the new buildings might go. They also indicated the size of the new development. It was going to be massive—nearly the size of the neighboring outlet mall.

Aaron unfolded himself from the back seat and stretched his arms and legs.

Dev whacked him on the shoulder. "Oh, come off it. You've only been back there for ten minutes."

"More like twenty. I can't feel my toes."

Grinning, she hooked her arm through his and led him toward the southeast side of the lot. "Here it is. Your gym."

A feeling like dread dropped into his stomach. No, it *was* dread—a cold, heavy stone of it. A boulder pushing through his intestines and bearing him to the ground. Aaron firmed his legs. Tugged on his arm.

"What's up?" Devorah regarded him with concern.

"Nothing. Late night."

She grinned. "From what Mom says—"

"Don't." He held up a hand. "I don't want to hear thirdhand what I sound like when I'm . . ." He shook his head. "Wrong, so wrong."

Devorah leaned in close and whispered, "Dad's got one more tour. Then we can send her home."

Aaron watched his mom approach the fence and hook her fingers through the wire. Dev tugged on Aaron's arm and they went to join her. Together, they walked the perimeter of the fence, and despite the ball of lead rolling slowly around his gut, Aaron could see the potential. The space was larger than either of the current gyms, and the land behind would be perfect for another outdoor jogging path and maybe a fitness trail. They could also put a gazebo out there and a picnic area where clients could relax before or after using the gym. Settle in for a bite of lunch or simply enjoy a breath of fresh air between classes.

While he contemplated the wide expanse of tufted grass and distant line of trees, Devorah was pacing off what would be the rear of the building. "You know," she called over, "we could put a pool in. Imagine that. This area could use another pool. One that's not part of a waterpark."

Something inside Aaron quickened. A pool would be awesome. He turned to watch as Devorah continued to pace off the lot.

"It'd mean hiring a lot of extra staff," he mused.

She glanced up. "Instructors, lifeguards, hydro-therapists?"

"Add it to the research list," his mom said.

Aaron exhaled. Pressed his lips together and surveyed the fenced-off site. What could be his gym. The spark of excitement he'd felt at the thought of a pool and his envisaged outdoor space flared brightly for a moment and then guttered. The site was just so freaking huge. Too huge. He could barely picture himself in charge of one of the gyms they currently had, let alone one this size. When he started thinking about all of the amenities—space for additional aerobics studios, a larger cardio area, an extended café. Free weights and stretching over there?—it was overwhelming.

He took a backward step.

Devorah arrived at his side as though drawn by a magnet and took his arm again. "Are you sure you're okay? You don't look well, Aaron."

"I can't do this," he said, his voice quiet.

"What do you mean?"

His mom started wandering back toward them, and Aaron pulled free of Devorah's hold. "I don't think I can run a whole gym."

"You wouldn't have to do it all by yourself. I couldn't run Stroudsburg without you and Stacy. Leili has a team of three helping her oversee Marshall's Creek."

"It's not the size. It's . . . It's not what I want."

"Then we'll change the plan. Instead of a pool we could do larger studios. Your classes are so popular we could totally fill a larger space. Pull in new instructors for the extra sessions. And we could have private consulting rooms for training clients. Imagine that!"

"No." Aaron patted the air with his hands. "That's not what I mean." He glanced at his mom and stopped. She remembered. He could see it in her face. She knew he didn't want this, and not only because they'd brushed across the topic themselves.

Meeting her gaze, he pleaded, silently, for her to give him a signal. To let him know it was okay to wreck his sister's dream. But she gave him nothing. How could she? His mom had helped both of them fight their battles for most of their lives. She'd always be on their side—against the world. But not against each other.

Also, this had to be his choice.

Aaron turned back to Dev. "I don't think I want to run a gym."

"You don't or think you don't?"

"I don't." Surely the ground had shifted beneath his feet. Cracked a little? With two words, Aaron had split his life into two permanent halves, and the space between them seemed to be widening. He had a foot on either side and had to jump one way or the other. But why did he have to choose? He'd been doing fine playing jock by day and nerd by night. No one person had to be all one thing, right?

His sister's expression begged him to reconsider. She was shocked, hurt, confused. Angry.

"Dev—"

"Why did you even come out here today if you knew you didn't want to be a part of this? Or to the trade show? When were you going to tell me, tell us, that you didn't want a gym? Aaron, we've started the financing for this. We've hired an architect."

Oh, his poor gut. The ball of lead had dropped through, taking essential pieces of himself with it. But although panic and remorse threatened to overwhelm him, Aaron managed to push both aside in favor of anger. "You said I had time to decide."

"Yeah, like a month ago."

"I told you I was going to think about it."

"I assumed you had!"

Aaron looked again to his mom for help, but she'd retreated to the car and stood leaning against the door, arms folded, watching them. He was on his own—as he should be. *Damn it.* He turned back to Devorah, who had her hands on her hips.

He sighed. "I'm sorry."

Devorah's chin wobbled.

"Dev, don't."

"I don't understand what you're doing."

"I'm not doing anything. I love working with you and I love what I do. But the idea of running a gym of my own is too much. It's overwhelming."

"But it's the next step for you. I know you've never been that interested in the financial side of the business, but you're an equal partner. Having your own gym will reinforce that. Besides, you don't want to be a trainer forever, do you?"

"It's always been about the people for me. I couldn't care less about the money. Just keep paying me to connect with my clients and I'll be happy. For me, that's the joy of this career."

"You could still do that as an owner/operator. Personal training could be your outlet. What you do to—"

"When was the last time you taught a class?"

Devorah pressed her lips together and gazed across the empty lot toward the trees. Aaron surveyed the grassy field again, sadness welling inside him now. The image of the gym he'd conjured, however briefly, was fading. It wasn't hard to let it go, though. He'd love to work in the place he'd imagined. Would find delight in the larger rooms, added space, and outdoor areas. But he didn't want ownership of it.

"I don't have the same drive and ambition you do, Dev."

"Sure you do." Her tone was pleading.

"I don't. For good or bad, I don't."

Eyes dark and sad, chin dipped toward her chest, Dev turned back toward the car.

Feeling as though he'd fallen into the crack, was still falling, skin of his palms and the edges of his fingers burning as he missed handhold after handhold, Aaron followed.

Chapter Twenty-Three

When Gray's alarm chimed at 3 a.m. on Monday morning, he opened his eyes, blinked at the ceiling, and contemplated the kernel of unrest in the center of his chest. He'd followed this ritual for three weeks now, making it out of bed and down the stairs several times only to choke by the back door to the café. The last time he'd made it down the stairs, he'd been almost ready to work. But the squeak of the oven door opening and the familiar odor of baking bread, present even in the rear stairwell, had sent him scurrying up the stairs and back to bed.

If someone else was baking, he didn't need to be there, did he?

This morning, the kernel lay quiet. Gray left his bed and pulled on the chef's pants and café polo he'd laid out across the desk. He'd showered the night before to give himself one less distraction, one less obstacle between him and the stairs, the stairs and the door, the door and the café, the oven. Today, he would bake bread. He would work. He'd return to his role as a functional adult and business operator.

Before he could second-guess himself, Gray keyed in the code to the café's rear entrance and pushed the door open. The kitchen was warm—the oven set to a timer that would have it pre-heated and ready to bake. He flipped on the necessary lights and fell into routine so easily he might not have missed a day. Starter for daily breads came first. Then he visited the racks of shaped dough in the walk-in: bagels and rolls that could be prepared in advance. Bagels were plunged through the boiler, seeded, and put on trays. Once he had a batch in the oven, he set a timer and turned to check on the starter and begin making dough.

The back door swished open and Wendell stood there, blinking. Then he smiled. "Hey. How're you doing?"

Gray smiled back. "All right." He then realized he could have saved Wendell a few hours' sleep and a drive if he'd, what? Texted him at three in the morning to say, *Hey, I actually feel like working today.* "Sorry I didn't call."

An easy shrug rolled over Wendell's shoulders. "It's no big deal." He started washing his hands. "Seeing as I'm here, what can I do to help?"

"Check the first batch of bagels? Maybe plunge the next? You've . . ." Of course Wendell had made bagels. He'd been making them for weeks now. Mixing, rolling, shaping, and baking. Wendell probably made better bagels than he did.

Gray pressed his lips closed.

Wendell paused, seemed about to speak, then turned away. Gray had lifted another bag of flour when Wendell spun back around. "It's cool," he said.

"What?"

"This is your café, Gray. I'm not looking to take your job. I get that how I've been doing things might not be the way you were doing things, but I always remember this is your place. What you say goes, and if that's me packing up and heading home . . ." This shrug was less easy. "Then it's me packing up."

Guilt and shame skewered Gray in the middle, though he hadn't entertained any such thoughts. Yet. Mostly, he was still trying to figure out his own place in a business that was supposedly his.

"Honestly, I'm not sure what's going on yet. This is the first morning I've made it through the café door without Patty sounding the alarm about me being here. The first morning I feel like baking. Things have been weird."

"No doubt."

"But I appreciate all you've been doing and I'm glad you're here." As Gray said the words, they became true. Wendell's arrival had lightened the burden of the morning. Gray had started the day with the best of intentions but when he contemplated all there still was to do? Heck yeah, he was glad Wendell had shown up. "It's going to take me a while to get to speed."

Wendell's expression remained uncertain.

"Whatever we're paying you can stay the same while I get my groove back," Gray assured him.

Waving a hand, Wendell said, "Nah, that's not it, but I appreciate it." He clapped his hands in a gesture that reminded Gray of Aaron. "Okay, I'll get on bagels. You stay on breads?"

"Sounds like a plan."

By the time the café opened for business, Gray felt as though he'd been working with Wendell for years. He combined efficiency and competence with a chattiness Patty did not possess. Gray hadn't realized that he and Patty rarely spoke outside of barking orders at each other until he registered Wendell's constant stream of banter. Not once did he feel as though he should ask the man for quiet, though. Gray welcomed the light conversation, especially as his part was mostly to listen. Wendell had observations about the weather, the traffic along 209 at the ass crack of dawn, the weird TV shows they were making for kids these days, and the lack of mountains in the Pocono Mountains.

"I mean, these are hills," he said. "Not a one of them is much over a thousand feet."

"Kistler Ledge," Gray put in. "It's got to be two thousand feet, at least." Not that he'd hiked it. But he'd had a friend in high school who'd done all of the trails and climbs in the area. He did remember they'd had much the same lament, though. That the Pocono Mountains weren't much as far as mountains went.

Wendell made a *pshaw* sound before dusting his hands off on his apron to approach the counter. He took a couple of orders, and Gray cooked breakfast sandwiches. The morning rush ebbed toward a trickle. Patty showed up sometime after eight and started on the dishes. It was as though the three of them had worked together for years.

Before All the Fuss, Gray would have taken a break shortly after Patty arrived. The café always experienced a lull between breakfast and lunch—time enough to refresh the bread trays, assess what needed to be mixed and rolled for the morning, and figure out the weekly orders, in and out.

So, despite wanting to prove he was up to the challenge of a full day on his feet, Gray filled a takeout cup with French roast and carried it back to the office. Wendell jumped up out of the chair. "Oh, hey. So, here's where the ordering's at." He swiped the laptop off the desk and started poking at a chart on the screen. "ProFoods order is in. Did you know they carry the same deli items you were getting from Linz?"

"Yeah, but their pricing isn't as good."

"I called 'em, and because you already order a substantial amount of flour and whatnot, they're willing to do a discount based on how much meat and cheese you order. They have the frozen chicken and steaks too."

Gray blinked. "Really?"

"In fact, just about everything you've been ordering from five different suppliers."

Gray leaned toward the screen, hoping the spreadsheet or chart or whatever would resolve into something he understood. It didn't. "They do?"

Wendell broke into a grin. "It's a new thing. Or most of it is. They've been adding lines. Bought out some other supplier from New Jersey and expanded their catalog."

"Oh."

"They could've sent out a notice, right?"

"You'd think."

"Anyway, if you want, we could go through what they have online. The more we order, the bigger the discount."

Gray glanced from the laptop to Wendell and back again. "Why don't you take care of it? You seem to know what's up with the, ah, website, and you know what all we need."

"Mostly." Wendell cocked his head. "You doing okay over there?"

The floor had started to shift beneath Gray's feet. "Yeah, I think—"

Shift and bump. Gray stumbled.

Wendell grabbed his elbow and guided him toward the chair. "Take a load off. It was a busy morning."

"It was," Gray murmured as he sat. Closing his eyes made the rocking worse, so he opened them and hissed as coffee splashed across his hands. It wasn't hot enough to burn, just to surprise. While he sat and swayed, Wendell bustled out the door only to return a moment later with a cloth, which he handed over. Gray spent a few seconds trying to figure out how he'd grab the cloth while he held a coffee cup before remembering he had two hands. Also, that the cup wasn't fused to his fingers. He could, like, put it down.

He did that. Took the cloth. Wiped his hands. Wondered whether the floor was going to settle and if he'd ever be able to close his eyes again.

Sometime between all of his wondering and wiping, Patty replaced Wendell at the door. "Everything okay in here?"

Gray tried for a smile and had to swallow a lump in his throat before he managed to get a few words out. "Thank you."

"For..."

"For keeping everything going."

Patty hustled inside the office to lay a hand on his arm. "This isn't just a job, you know? We're family."

"Who barely knew each other a year ago."

"And now we do."

"Wendell's a good man."

Patty's face rounded. "Isn't he, though?"

"You two like working together?"

She leaned a shoulder against the shelving unit behind them and nodded. "We do. Took us a bit of organizing at first. We kept getting in each other's way. But then we sat down and said, 'Okay, when we're at the café, we need to just do the work. Tell it to each other straight. Then, at the end of the day, we can apologize or whatever and go back to being husband and wife.' Ever since then, it's been easier. Sometimes we don't even get to the apologies because we get it, you know? Like you and me. Often, we have to yell to get each other's attention and can't always remember to be polite when there's a rush."

Gray nodded his agreement.

The world had stopped bumping and shifting, but Gray didn't feel any steadier. He was glad for the chair beneath his ass and the flow of Patty's words over his head and around his shoulders. Warm words, they were. Comforting. The cadence of Patty's voice familiar. From the beginning, he'd liked working with his cousin. Though they'd only met a couple of times during childhood, there'd always been an ease that came with being among blood.

Gray let that drift over him with Patty's chatter until someone gripped his shoulder. Startled, Gray opened his eyes and blinked up at Wendell. Where was Patty?

"I'd have let you sleep longer, but the angle of your neck was all wrong, man. I kept wondering if you were getting enough oxygen to your brain."

Smacking his lips and wincing at the taste of stale coffee, Gray gazed around the office. At the tidy desk where his note-scrawled blotter had been replaced with a collage of business cards under glass and the closed laptop. The dry erase board on the wall, one side devoted to a weekly shift roster, the other a shopping list. It was like he'd been transported to a parallel universe. He glanced up at Wendell. "What time is it?"

"Just after eleven." Wendell cocked his head toward the front of the café. "Things are starting to pick up out there."

"Oh, right." Gray put his hands on the desk, preparing to stand.

"It's cool. We got this kid helping out for the lunch shift Mondays through Fridays."

"What happened to Jacob?"

"Bad breakup with his girlfriend. He moved out."

Jacob had been the most reliable employee (after Patty) they'd found in a while.

"Varya is where it's at," Wendell was saying. "She's only seventeen, still in high school, senior year, but doing it online or whatever. She does her classes in the morning, works here for lunch, and does some other classes at the community college a couple afternoons."

"That sounds exhausting."

Wendell laughed. "It's how they do it now. School's all flexible."

"Huh." Though he wasn't needed, Gray still wanted to stand and stretch his legs. Restart the blood flow Wendell had been so worried about.

"Hello!" Oliver poked his head into the gap between Wendell and the doorway. "Hey. You look like you've been sleeping."

"I was."

"Dropped off while Patty was talking." Wendell grinned. "I'd say more, but she'd probably hear it and I'd have to answer for it later."

Gray laughed.

Oliver grinned. "Everything seems under control here. I wanted to check in before I deliver an order to Mount Pocono. Did I tell you I picked up a contract for a nursing home up there? Twice-weekly deliveries."

"Nice!" Oliver deserved his success. His pastries might have seemed weird at the start—what with no eggs or cheese. But he'd spotted a niche and filled it. Gray hoped he'd continue to do well. Especially because Oliver seemed happier than he'd ever been. "One of these days you'll have to catch me up on all your clients and what you're doing for them."

Oliver beamed. "It's a date." He smacked the doorframe. "Okay, I'm off." He glanced at Wendell, back at Gray, then at Wendell again. "If you need anything, I'm a call away, and Aaron or Nick should be over to help with closing. Or Cam? I can't remember who does Mondays."

"Aaron," Wendell said.

Gray's heart lifted and spun.

As though Gray had a window in his chest, Oliver and Wendell looked at him, at each other, and smiled. Then Oliver left and Wendell answered a bellow from Patty, leaving Gray alone in the office once more.

Gray contemplated the laptop, the neat row of supplier catalogs on the shelf over the desk, the reorganized stock shelves behind him, the rows of sodas, juices, cans of tuna fish and chicken, the plates, cups, napkins, and takeout boxes.

The stuff of business that had begun and ended his days for coming on two years felt almost foreign, and not only because everything had been rearranged. Sucking on his lower lip, Gray surveyed the office again and listened to the bustle of industry from the front of the café. Patty calling out orders, Wendell confirming them, a younger, higher voice popping up in between. The new hire. The one that actually showed up and worked.

They didn't need him here. He'd seen that last week when he'd stopped by to help Patty find the number for the refrigeration repair. Patty and Wendell had the place humming. They were the perfect team, like Gray's parents had been.

Maybe that was what he'd been doing wrong all this time. He hadn't been running the business with a partner. A spouse.

Gray frowned. That notion made little sense, but obviously something had been awry, because Wendell didn't look as though he was about to keel over with heart trouble and Patty was as cool, calm, and collected as she was on their busiest days. So, it had to be *him*. Gray.

He sucked on his lower lip again. Then, he pushed to his feet. Paused a second, waiting to see whether the floor planned to shift and ripple. When it didn't, he crept from the office. Spied the rear door across the kitchen. Checked both ways before heading toward it. He expected to feel guilt as it clicked closed behind him. Instead, he felt relief. And kind of sad.

The door at the top of the stairs opened, and Gray watched as his dad plodded quietly down. They faced each other in the hallway.

"How'd it go?" his dad asked.

"Okay," Gray answered. Then, "We need to talk about the café. And some other stuff."

His dad gave a long, slow nod. "I suppose we should."

"When's a good time for you?"

"How about tomorrow?"

As he bobbed his head up and down, Gray wondered whether his dad was as relieved as he was that they weren't planning to do this today. Then he wondered if tomorrow would actually come. Then he decided he needed another nap.

He should spend some time thinking about what would come next. Who he'd sell his dream bread to. Could he try a market stall? Make some connections the way Ollie had and branch out from there?

When the stairs rippled a little under his feet, Gray added a call to his doctor to his to-do list. Then he fell face-first onto his futon, closed his eyes, and let the world slip away.

Chapter Twenty-Four

Aaron flipped the notebook page and continued to read out loud: "World history is divided into three periods—the age of magic, the age of technology, and the age of dirt. Dirt?"

Gray didn't respond.

Aaron glanced over. Gray was sitting next to him on the couch, his posture similar: bent forward, elbows on knees, chin cupped in his hands. But his eyes were closed. His breathing soft and regular.

They'd barely sat down. Then again, good sex and good food could knock anyone out for a while. Also, Gray had started back at the café this week and had still managed to show up for his training sessions. Apparently, the café often experienced a lull between breakfast and lunch, giving Gray time to take care of personal business—like take a nap. Workout days, he replaced naptime with gym-time. Aaron admired his continued commitment.

Should Gray be this tired, though?

With a start, Gray opened his eyes. He blinked a few times, smacked his lips, and then yawned. He focused on Aaron a second later and frowned, as though he couldn't place the face in front of him. Then he smiled—somewhat sheepishly. "Needed to check out what was happening on the inside of my eyelids for a few."

"Apparently."

Gray leaned in and Aaron bent to meet him, touching their lips together. The kiss was soft, but a thrill still shot through him at the contact. He was kissing Grayson Clery—the guy who'd seemed to delight in scowling at him only a month ago, was now sitting on his couch, his lips pressed to Aaron's.

Nearly forty wasn't too old to fall in love, was it?

Aaron drew back a fraction. "So, what's all this about dirt?"

Gray's forehead wrinkled. "What?"

Chuckling, Aaron reached for the notebook Gray had brought over. He held up the open page. "The Age of Dirt."

"Oh!" Gray's face lit up. "Okay, so here's what I was thinking: We want— I mean, you might want—"

Aaron touched Gray's knee. "We want. We're doing this together."

Head bobbing up and down, Gray continued. "We want the island or continent, the land, to have a prior history? You've got cards hinting at lore and a time before, so let's define that as a part of the story. I chose three ages because it's simple and not a lot to flesh out. Magic, then technology, which maybe destroyed the magic or caused it to atrophy? Then I was thinking maybe a tech disaster. I know that's been done before, but we can put our own spin on it. Also, how cool would it be for adventurers to find artifacts from one of these two ages? Like technological artifacts that can either be used as they are or combined into new objects? We could choose maybe four or five building block pieces. In fact, we could do the same for magic, but make those pieces much rarer because they're older. But they'd be more powerful because the magic is coming back."

Wow.

Gray had paused for breath. "What? Why are you staring at me like that? Is it too much?"

"No. It's amazing. All of it." Aaron hefted the notebook—the one Gray hadn't referred to as he retold the history he'd mapped out. "How did you come up with all of this?"

A shrug rolled over Gray's shoulders. "I always sort of wanted to write, you know? I read a lot of fantasy and science fiction. Or I used to, before I came back up here. What I love about speculative fiction is that while you can make stuff up, like, anything goes, it still needs to hang together realistically. And that's because spec fic is so often a reflection of our own world but with the rules changed so that we can create stories that might otherwise be difficult to tell."

"I can see that." Aaron considered the box of game cards on the coffee table. He'd figured it'd be cool to put a band of people on a remote coastline together, give them a few tools, and see what happened. But now that he thought about it, he could see how the act of picking up the first tool—heck, taking the first step—started a story.

"Even here, on this island"—Aaron jerked his chin toward the box—"we'll be telling a human story. Like, we'll do what humanity does. Set up a home base, exploit the local resources, explore boundaries, and develop the technology to make it all easier."

Gray was smiling and nodding. "Yep."

"That's sad, when you think about it. That we do what we do, no matter where we are."

"Heh. So, we give players a goal. Or a set of them. Optimal outcomes or ways to win the game, although it could be a totally sandbox experience. We could have one for balance or harmony." Gray picked up the wood sprite card. "You can pillage the forest, encourage the forest to grow, or bargain to use a part of the forest. Three paths, like the ages. Maybe the middle path is balance."

Now Aaron was smiling and nodding. "Yeah. And, as with life, the middle path is also compromise." He blew out a breath. "This is all way more complicated than I thought it could be."

"Is it too much?"

"No. It's amazing." He bumped his shoulder to Gray's. "I had no idea how in depth we could go. Here I was plotting moves across a board, a board we'd make along the way, and you've given it all meaning. This game is going to be awesome."

Gray's smile had a weary edge to it.

"Do you need to get home?" Aaron asked. "I know you have an early start." Bakers' hours were nuts.

Gray's gaze seemed slightly out of focus. He turned toward the box on the coffee table, then leaned back into the couch and folded his arms.

"What's up?" Aaron didn't want to ask, but he also had to ask.

A heavy sigh settled Gray deeper into the couch. He glanced at Aaron, then away. "Although the café was always busy and working there sometimes felt like trying to hold water in a sieve, I thought it made me happy. At first, I found running a business fulfilling. I've always been more focused on the breadmaking than the moneymaking, but it was cool to see how it all came together." He licked his lips.

Glanced over again. "It also gave me a new perspective on my folks. Their relationship. New respect, too."

With a short nod, Aaron prompted him to continue.

"But ever since All the Fuss—"

"Your heart attack?"

"I hate that term. It's like my heart attacked me."

"It did."

Gray winced. Unfolded an arm to press his palm to the center of his chest, the gesture either conscious or not.

Aaron touched his elbow. "It's okay to slow down or not enjoy the things you once did."

"I get that? Intellectually. But in here"—he flattened his palm over his heart—"it feels . . . everything feels wrong. Like I'm letting a whole lot of people down, but mostly myself. And yet, at the same time, it's like it would be easier if I gave up because everything's running fine without me. I could, quite literally, pack my shit and head back to Allentown."

A sharp pain touched Aaron's heart. He resisted the urge to press his palm there.

"Problem is," Gray continued, "I'm not sure if that's what I want anymore, either."

"What about the job you had down there?" Aaron asked.

"Gone. I could reapply. They'd probably take me back. But it wasn't the job I thought it was."

"Right."

"I just wanted to bake. For as long as I could remember, I've wanted to make bread. There's something so essential about it." Gray leaned forward to grab the notebook. "But this." He tapped the open page. "Writing this has been the most fun I've had in months. Years, even. And meeting you. Or getting to know you. Doing this with you. It's all . . ." He trailed off with a helpless gesture.

Aaron spread his hands over his knees and counted the wrinkles across his knuckles. A lot of what Gray was saying, he related to. Hadn't he come to a similar point with his own career? He loved it, but he also didn't love it. Not right now. The training, yes. The pressure to do more? Not at all.

"Is this a forty-year-old feeling, do you think?" he asked Gray.

With a snort, Gray relaxed. "If I were to ask my friend Ollie, he'd say yes. Did you know he lost his job last year? Fifteen years he was with that company, and they let him go just like that. Some other firm bought them and his position ceased to exist."

"That's . . . not right."

"But it happens."

"The catering he's doing, that's new?"

"Yep. He sold his house, bought a building on Main Street, and put everything he had into making cheese-less, eggless pastries."

Aaron felt his eyes go round. "Seriously?"

"Pretty much. It's the bravest damn move I've ever seen."

"Okay." Aaron pulled in a full breath. "If you could do anything from this point on. Say the café is closed. It's done. Finished. What would you do next? Let's not say money is no object, but we can assume resources. What do you want to do?"

Gray met his gaze, his eyes warm and brown, and they gazed at each other for a long, quiet moment. Then Gray smiled and leaned in for a kiss. "If I look at you while I'm thinking, all I want to do is sink to my knees and suck you off."

Aaron grinned. "I'm flattered, truly." Now he wanted to press his palm to Gray's crotch and start fondling. Should he redirect them back to the topic of Gray's future?

Was that what they were actually discussing?

Gray widened the space between them enough to give them a moment to catch their breath. "This is what I want," he said. "I mean, not just the sex, but this. What you and I are doing. Building." He got an abashed look. "I can't believe I'm saying that. We're talking about my career and I'm saying I want to go to bed with you. Stay over. Make something."

Aaron wrapped a hand around Gray's nape and pulled their foreheads close. "I don't mind. I'm the one who stalked you, remember. In a totally not creepy way."

"Because ordering the same sandwich at the same time every other day isn't at all creepy."

"It's not. It's really not."

Gray's lips touched his. Aaron melted into the kiss for a while, enjoying the soft contact between them, the lack of urgency.

"This isn't helping me decide what to do with the café," Gray eventually said.

"Do we have to decide tonight?"

"Probably not."

Aaron pulled away but kept his hand behind Gray's neck. "We can pick this back up. Anytime. I mean it. I . . ." Emotion hit him front and center. "It's been a while since I tried a relationship, but I'll tell you one thing. I can't remember the last time I was with a guy I could talk to like this. Real talk. About real life." He tried out a smile. "I like it."

Gray was nodding. "I feel you, even though I'm the one who seems to do most of the heavy talking. You know it goes both ways, right? I can listen. If you want to talk about what's going on with the gym, I'm here."

Aaron most definitely did not want to talk about what was going on with the gym. But he did want to acknowledge the offer. "Thanks."

"This could be the beginning of the most adult relationship I've ever had."

Whoa, heavy. But . . . Yeah. "Where do we go from here?" *Not back to Allentown, please.*

But even if Gray did decide to give up the café and move back into his house, he'd only be forty miles away. And they *were* adults. They had cars. Aaron had to wonder, though, what he would do with himself if his sister decided to replace him with someone who did want to manage their third gym. Would he stay in Stroudsburg or move away?

"Hey, where'd you go?" Gray asked, bumping their noses together.

Aaron forced a smile. "Thinking about bed." He reached down to nudge Gray's upper thigh. "We can set an alarm if you want, or we could see what happens between now and 3 a.m."

Gray grinned. "Now that's the kind of future I can subscribe to."

The front door creaked open. "Yoo-hoo!"

"Oh, dear God." Aaron groaned.

From the doorway, his mom said, "Don't mind me, just going to bed. Have a good night!"

She slipped down the hall toward the bedrooms. Aaron flopped back onto the couch. "Maybe we could both move to Allentown."

Flopping back next to him with a grin, Gray tangled their fingers together and squeezed.

Chapter Twenty-Five

Gray upended the cereal box and shook precisely one flake into his bowl. Rattling the bag inside released a dust of crumbs. After frowning at the Barbie-sized breakfast, Gray flipped open the breadbox—he hadn't had time to bake for himself this week, but there'd been a loaf of sandwich bread in there. The breadbox was empty, though. He checked the freezer and found a leftover sourdough he'd made . . . When? Before Christmas? So, five—no, six months ago. He shook it out of the plastic wrapping and winced as ice crystals flaked off onto the counter. He could scramble a couple of eggs while the bread thawed enough for him to slice.

The inside of the refrigerator glowed whitely—a phenomenon that only happened when it was near empty.

No problem. The café ordered eggs by the tens of dozens. He'd hop downstairs and grab a handful. And maybe some bacon. And a couple of yesterday's bagels. Heck, he could eat breakfast down there like he used to. Before all this heart-healthy nonsense.

His head spun and his heart squeezed oddly, as though caught between beats. Gray massaged his chest. If he rubbed the same spot hard enough, his heart would behave. It'd worked before.

That his heart knew what to do without assistance from above did occur. Also, Gray didn't like being this in touch with the processes of his internal organs. Listening to his stomach and feeling the ache across his shoulders and up the back of his neck. The squeeze and release in his chest. The dizziness that was now so familiar, he barely noticed it. Or, at the very least, had become accustomed to working through it. He needed to eat was all.

The pressure eased and Gray breathed out. He leaned a hip against the counter in the almost dark kitchen and did nothing for about a minute. Then his stomach turned over, and his thoughts turned toward the breakfast that wasn't happening. With a sigh, he cleared away the remnants of nothing, putting the loaf back into the freezer, and grabbed a notepad and a pen.

Cereal
Bread
Milk
Eggs

He opened the refrigerator again, scanned the bare shelves, and continued his list: *Lettuce, tomatoes, vegetables, chicken breasts, fish . . .*

He'd have to consult the sheaf of handouts the doctors had given him to remind himself of the foods he was allowed to eat. There weren't many.

Although he hadn't been up for long, fatigue pushed at his shoulders. Sometimes just being alive was exhausting. Not that he'd rather the alternative. There had to be more than this, though. More than empty refrigerators and the dread surrounding the simple act of going to work.

Gray closed the refrigerator and jumped nearly a mile into the air at the shadow outside the kitchen. "Jesus, Dad. You scared the crap out of me."

"Sorry. Heard you banging about and wanted to check you were okay."

"Didn't mean to wake you."

The spectral form of his father shrugged. "Don't sleep so much, anyway."

"We need to go shopping. There's nothing to eat."

"Yep."

"Want to go later this morning? Like, around nine? Café is always quiet then, and we never did get to talking about the business."

"We can talk now."

Somehow, three o'clock in the morning didn't feel like the right time to ask his dad whether or not he wanted to sell the café he and his wife had dedicated their lives to. "It'll keep. We'll get an early lunch. Sit and catch up. I feel like I hardly ever see you, and we sleep, what, ten feet apart?"

"Could be more when your boyfriend stays over."

Gray winced. "Sorry."

Another shrug. "You're young. Why shouldn't you have a good time?"

Gray didn't exactly feel young, but he mustered a smile. "Shopping and lunch?"

"All right."

The café was busier than usual with two orders coming in for last-minute lunch platters. Today not being a gym day, Gray spent the hour he might have napped slicing deli meats and cheeses and arranging them around large plastic trays. He stuffed pickles, peppers, and olives into small plastic cups, filled paper sacks with mustard and mayo packets, and rooted through the bread baskets for a variety of rolls to stack opposite the deli goods. He'd just finished pushing the plastic lids down when Wendell called for the order.

Gray handed over the trays and glanced about the bustling kitchen. It was ten, an hour after he'd arranged to meet his father. The front counter was quiet, but the sink was full of dishes and no one had started scraping congealed fat off the bacon trays yet.

An earnest young man materialized by Gray's elbow. "Patty says to tell you absolutely not to start on the dishes."

"Who are you?"

"Lucas. I started yesterday."

"Huh."

Patty poked her head around the dividing wall. "Why aren't you gone yet? Your pop was at the door a while ago, waiting for you."

"I had to finish the trays."

She made a shooing gesture. "Go on, get."

Gray raised his eyebrows at Lucas, who regarded him with a combination of confusion and amusement. Gray got going.

His dad said nothing on the drive to the store and nothing for the first five aisles. They were standing in front of the jam when he finally spoke. "Not that one, the seedless."

Gray put back the jar of strawberry preserves and reached for the one beside it.

"Not Smucker's. Your mother likes Polaner."

"But this one has seeds."

His dad reached past him for a jar of what looked like strawberry gelatin. While he placed it in the shopping cart, Gray thought about the fact they were buying jam for a dead woman and how he could use that to begin the conversation he both did and did not want to have.

In the next aisle—pasta, rice, beans—his dad continued choosing products his wife had shopped for. Gray hadn't noticed it at home. The cans of beans his mom had liked were always in the pantry, so it hadn't seemed odd that they were. Here, on the supermarket shelves, they stood out. And as his dad faithfully replicated her monthly list, Gray's heart squeezed tighter. No amount of massage would make that pain go away.

They were in the dish soap aisle when his dad turned to him and said, "Why are you rubbing your chest like that?"

"I don't know."

"When was the last time you saw your doctor?"

"Two weeks ago."

"You should go again."

Okay, sure. Great talk. "Dad."

His dad was comparing the price of two different dish soaps and Gray found himself wondering which one his mom used to buy. Nearly asked that instead of the question balancing on the tip of his tongue.

"Dad."

His dad looked over.

"How would you feel about selling the café?"

Turning away, his dad nodded toward the soap. "I can't remember which brand she used to buy. It was a blue bottle, but they're all blue now. Except this one. But I don't remember it being that green."

Gray sighed. "It's just soap."

His dad picked up one of the blue bottles and flipped open the cap. Sniffed. "Not this one."

Sighing again, Gray sniffed dish liquid with him until they found the correct brand. When they added his mom's brand of toilet paper to the cart, Gray had to blink tears away from his eyes. Why now? Why today? They'd been filling this same order together once a month for two years. Why was he only now noticing that they always bought the same things? That the list hadn't changed significantly in twenty years.

His dad was living in the past, and Gray had moved up here to join him.

At the checkout, Gray packed the cold stuff into insulated foil bags, separated everything else by package size, and then extracted a handful of twenties from his wallet to pay his share of the bill, like he'd been doing ever since he moved home. His dad took the cash and wrote a check for the whole amount. Like he'd been doing ever since Gray moved home.

They packed the car and his dad went to sit in the front passenger seat.

Gray leaned in the driver's side. "Lunch?"

"I don't know why you want to eat lunch out when we bought all this food."

"Because it's a nice day and they have a deck."

"We could get a sandwich downstairs if that's what you want."

"I don't want to eat at Clery's, I want to eat somewhere else. With you. We haven't spent much time together lately."

His dad glanced in his direction. "We've spent forty-five years together."

Gray's chest hurt, and the pavement was all wavy again. Climbing into the car to drive home suddenly seemed easier. But he stood his ground. "I want to talk to you. I want to eat out and have a conversation."

Gray straightened and waited on his side of the car.

After a full minute his dad got out and stood on his side. They eyed each other across the roof. Then his dad sighed and jerked his head back toward the shopping center. "I wonder if they have curly fries."

"I'm sure they do."

"I like curly fries."

"I know."

This side of noon, there were still a few tables outside. Gray nearly fell into his chair, and the relief of sitting had his eyes drifting to half-mast until their server appeared with menus. His dad ordered a BLT with curly fries. Gray stared at the picture of the Reuben sandwich, saliva pooling around his tongue, before ordering the turkey club on whole wheat with no bacon or cheese.

His heart hurt for an entirely different reason as the server disappeared.

"You know you're going to pay the same, whether you have bacon or not," his dad said.

Gray sighed. "Is it like a thing you do? You wake up every day with a list of ways to make life unpleasant? Or does it come naturally?"

Eyebrows lowering, his dad glanced across the shopping plaza parking lot toward the traffic on 611.

Gray restrained the urge to apologize. Then he decided to speak his mind instead. "Are you truly as miserable as you seem? Like, do you scowl and brood at bingo or when you're out walking, or hanging with your friends?" Gray got a sudden mental image of his dad and his friends all scowling together. Maybe that was what old age was. Except his dad was the only one whose wife had died. Two of the others were divorced and the other two, from memory, were still married. They probably complained about the fact they still had women in their lives.

His dad's jaw was set.

Gray could feel the clench of his. Then he let it all go with a sigh. Spread his hands across the table. "I don't know how to talk to you. I'm forty-five years old, and I don't know how to talk to my own father. It's like Mom was the glue between us and now that she's gone, we're becoming two separate pieces. I'm not sure how you feel about that, but I don't like it. You're my dad and believe it or not, I love you. I came home to be with you because I love you and I wanted to help.

"But what I've been doing for the past two years isn't helping. If you were down there with me, taking care of the books and ordering like you used to, I'd be helping. I'd be doing Mom's job, taking care of the bread and the baking, while you did your job. But I've been doing all of it and I can't anymore. It's too much. Christ on a cracker, Dad, it nearly killed me."

Gray had been studying the table between them as he talked. The blankness of his father's expression had been too much to bear. But when he heard the soft, wet breath, he looked up and his heart squeezed so hard he thought it might give out. His dad was crying.

Gray reached across the table. "I'm sorry. I didn't mean—"

"Sell it. Sell the café." His dad grabbed Gray's hand, his grip strong and tight. "Sell it, Grayson, because if that café kills you too . . ." His lips trembled.

Their server returned with two iced teas, and both Gray and his dad fumbled with their napkins, trying and failing to hide the fact they were blotting at their eyes. Thankfully, the server left without comment.

Gray peeked at his dad over a fold of bright green linen. Laugh lines Gray hadn't seen in far too long wrinkled around his dad's eyes. Gray responded with a tremulous smile. Then, after a long swallow of iced tea, he pulled out his phone. "I have a list of details here. Things I need to talk to you about."

His dad nodded with a new seriousness. "All right."

"How are you doing for money?"

Thankfully, though his dad seemed to have checked out of life over the past couple of years, he hadn't let everything go. He'd been good with money in the past and he had a nice-sized retirement fund, which led Gray to his next question:

"Can you afford to finance a loan for someone who might be interested in buying the business? I've got some put aside. I can go in with you on it."

"Someone wants to buy the place already?" his dad asked.

"I was thinking of offering it to Patty and Wendell. Not only have they got that place running like you and Mom used to, but I like the idea of passing the shop on to family and keeping it Black-owned."

"Agreed. It's ours," his dad said.

"You should see what they're up to. I hardly recognize the office. Six weeks and they've turned everything around." Gray shook his head. "A businessman I am not."

"I couldn't have done it myself. Neither could your mom. It's a two-person job."

"Then why didn't you help me?"

His dad's eyes lost their focus. Before Gray could prompt him again, their meals arrived. They ate for a while. About the time Gray was deciding his sandwich could have used some bacon, his dad said, "You ever had your heart broken?"

Gray thought back to his past relationships. There weren't a lot of them. He'd spent his twenties perfecting his trade, his early thirties searching for the right job, and his late thirties settling into a career. So far, it felt like he'd spent the bulk of his forties at Clery's, despite the fact it wasn't an even split, yet. In all that time, he'd had only two long-term partners and his relationships with both had fizzled out rather than exploded.

"I think you need to be in love for that to happen," he said softly. A cheerful face, dotted with freckles and crowned by alarmingly red hair, floated across his mental landscape. Gray lightly batted it away. Not yet. He wasn't ready for that yet.

His dad was frowning. "Gay couples are supposed to be better at the whole commitment deal than us straight folks. Or so I read."

Gray smiled. "Yeah, I've heard that one too."

"Your mom and I . . ." His dad's eyes acquired a new sheen. "She was my heart, son. That woman beat and I breathed."

"I'm sorry we haven't talked about her much. I feel like I've let you down."

"Lord, no. You came home and made sure I didn't fall apart. I'll always be grateful to you."

"Then why all the scowling and frowning? Sometimes I feel like you woke and found a stranger in your home."

"Heh." His father paused for a sip of tea. "Feels like that to me sometimes too." He put his glass down and appeared to think for a moment. "I think it's because you were doing what I couldn't. My heart isn't broken, it's gone."

The hurt was almost too much. The loss and despair. Gray missed his mom too. The past two years had dulled the pain, but it was still there—a blade waiting to be polished. The emptiness in his dad's eyes, though? Probably the saddest thing Gray had ever seen.

His dad reached across the table and gripped Gray's hand. "Let's sell the damn café because if I lose you too, I'm done."

Chapter Twenty-Six

Aaron knocked once and opened the door to his sister's office, wondering why it was closed. Oh, she had a guest. Aaron raised a hand in a quick wave and mouthed, *Sorry*, before backing up.

Devorah gave a reflexive smile, as though her face recognized her brother before her brain reminded her that they weren't talking. Not that they weren't talking. *Good mornings* and *what's the plan for the days* were exchanged. Little else, though.

Before Aaron could shut the door, Dev called him back into the office. "Aaron, come meet Hector."

Aaron regarded her guest, a fit young man in his early thirties. He had dark, wavy hair, lightly bronzed skin, and a killer smile. Hector met Aaron's gaze of inquiry head-on before sweeping his eyes up and down in a familiar manner. He was checking Aaron out.

Crossing into the office, Aaron extended a hand. "Hello."

Hector rose to greet him, his shake short but firm. "Hi."

"Hector is here for an interview."

And you want me to meet him why? Aaron frowned at his sister.

Devorah addressed her next comment to Hector. "As I said, we still have a couple of candidates to talk to, but you're one of the most qualified applicants so far." She rounded the desk and held out her own hand. "Thanks so much for coming in, and we'll be in touch by the end of the week, either way."

"It was a pleasure to meet you both." Hector had a slight accent, one Aaron couldn't place. He directed a last smile at Aaron, one eyebrow quirked lightly in invitation, before leaving the office.

Aaron didn't have to fight an urge to check out his ass. The only ass he was interested in was Gray's.

Beside him, Devorah snorted. "Not sure I'd be able to show the same restraint."

"What do you mean?"

"That is one fine bod."

"Did you just objectify a potential employee?"

"Tell me you disagree."

"What position was he interviewing for?" A curl of discomfort writhed though his middle.

"The new gym." Dev turned back to her desk. "I'd like whoever we hire to work here first. So far, it will either be Hector or Clarice." Dev pushed the laptop toward him, and Aaron peered at the picture of a woman about the same age as Hector. Ebony skin, short-cropped hair, amazing cheekbones. She made Aaron feel pasty and wholly inadequate to deal with life. Then he read her résumé and the feeling solidified. Clarice had as much personal training experience as he did, at a younger age. She also had a business degree. What the heck did Hector have if they were considering him over her?

Aaron didn't dare ask. He also didn't like to enquire how his sister had possibly thought to turn over the management of an entire business to him rather than one of these applicants.

Then Dev's words filtered through. *"I'd like whoever we hire to work here first."*

He glanced up sharply. "Here?"

"They'll need to learn our management style. How we treat our members, our ethos and codes of conduct. Scheduling, optimum class sizes and balance, instructor training. The unique energy of our gyms."

All stuff he knew. A compulsion nearly caught him—the urge to say, *I'll do it. I'll run the new gym.* Thankfully, the impulse passed with a surge of relief but also sadness.

Dev was watching him. "Do you hate it so much?"

"Hate what?"

"Working here?"

"When did I ever say that? I love working here. You know that. I put in more hours than anyone else. I have more personal clients. I teach classes because I like doing it, not to fill gaps in the schedule."

"That's the sort of person who would make a great manager. Why can't you see that?"

"Why can't you see I'm happy as I am?"

"Because I don't! Yes, you're happy as you are, but you could have more. Be more." Devorah spread her hands. "Remember when the three of us were working for Imperial Fitness?"

An hour and a half east, in New Jersey. Leilani had been working for the large chain of gyms for a couple of years before Devorah started there. Following his sister, Aaron had taken the next opening, and the three of them had quickly hit it off, Dev and Leili romantically, the three of them as a team. Soon, they'd hatched a plan to open their own gym back in Pennsylvania, where they would be closer to family, and where Dev and Leili could raise a family of their own. Resources had been pooled, partnership agreements drafted, property found.

Aaron had never felt as though he were simply along for the ride. Back then, he'd been a part of the planning but always with the understanding that he wanted to keep doing what he loved: working with people on their fitness goals. Helping folks succeed, even in little ways. He'd been happy to let Dev and Leili take care of the business side of things.

"I always said it was about the people for me," he reminded his sister now.

Devorah regarded him silently for a beat or two, then nodded. Her smile was weary.

Aaron's phone chimed. Without reaching for it, he said, "My next client is here."

"Okay. Did you need me or the office?"

"I was going to update my files on your laptop."

"You could have your own office if—"

"How about we get me a laptop?"

Obviously pained, Devorah sighed and returned to her desk.

Aaron went to meet Gray at the gym's entrance. Gray's face was round with happiness as he passed through the sliding glass doors, his color good, a lightness to his step. Thank goodness one of them was clearly having a great day. Just seeing him changed Aaron's for the better.

Despite wanting a hug, Aaron extended a hand as he would to any of his clients.

Gray's smile widened as they shook. "Do you meet all of your clients at the door?"

"I try to."

"Should I be jealous?"

"You're the only one I eat lunch with." Aaron leaned in closer. "And sleep with."

Gray grinned again and hefted the bag he had slung over his shoulder. "Let me get changed. I'll meet you in the warm-up area?"

"Sure."

Over the past few weeks, Gray's program had evolved from stretching, light cardio, and some work with dumbbells into a substantial workout. Now, after stretching, Gray put in thirty minutes on a treadmill with a ten percent grade and a pace that alternated between a fast jog and a fast walk.

"How's the at-home part of your program working for you?" Aaron asked as he jogged alongside.

"Good, when I remember to do it. I always feel more focused when I'm here, though." Gray cut him a sideways glance. "I've been thinking about doing three sessions a week with you instead of two." He paused to catch his breath. "Which is kind of amazing. I mean, I hate the gym."

Aaron laughed. "You do love the high you get after a workout, though. Am I right?"

"You're not wrong."

"Well, you don't necessarily need to book another session. You could come in and workout on your own. Follow your program or change it up, if you like. Experiment with different exercises and classes."

"Heh, if you're not watching, I'll slack off." Gray's breath had shortened into a quick pant.

Aaron frowned. "Why don't you slow the pace? Take your next interval."

Gray adjusted the pace and slowed to a walk. After sixty seconds, he started to jog again, and quickly began gasping. When he reached for the center of his chest, Aaron all but panicked. He smacked the stop button on Gray's treadmill. "Tell me how you feel. Are you short of breath? Dizzy?"

He extended a hand to help Gray off the track and onto the floor, but Gray batted him away. "I'm fine." Then he lurched to one side.

Aaron hauled Gray's arm over his shoulder and led him toward a quiet corner. "Talk to me."

"It's this damn dizziness. It's been happening on and off for a couple of weeks, but it's more on than off, now. The floor starts moving under me and then my head spins. Heartbeat gets all concerned for a while."

"Have you talked to your doctor?"

Gray shot him a pained look. "I had an appointment a couple of weeks ago."

"And . . ."

"I was too busy telling her about my bruises and how I nearly bled to death when I cut myself shaving. The way my bones ache for no reason, and the endless fatigue. So, no, I didn't get around to the dizzy spells. I figure it's me, I dunno, adjusting to the medication."

Gray's skin had acquired a familiar ashy cast. His lips were pinched, his forehead wrinkled.

Aaron reached for the phone in his pocket. "This has been going on for more than a couple of weeks, then?" Most times, heart attacks didn't just happen. They gave warnings, weeks or months in advance. Gray had probably been feeling off for quite a while leading up to All the Fuss, as he called it. How could he possibly think ignoring symptoms now would add up to anything good?

"It doesn't feel the same," Gray said, obviously reading Aaron's thoughts.

Aaron had his phone out. "How do you know?"

"It's not a heart attack."

Aaron lowered Gray to a workout bench. "How can you be sure?"

"Because when the dizziness passes, I'm still alive."

Fuck me. Aaron sat next to him. "Why haven't you called your doctor?"

Gray said nothing for a moment. Just kept massaging the center of his chest and breathing. Then he looked over, and Aaron saw it in his eyes. The reason.

Gray was truly scared.

Ignoring the need to be professional, Aaron took Gray's hand and tangled their fingers together. "C'mon, let's go."

Gray opened his mouth.

Aaron squeezed his hand. "You can come willingly, or I can call 911. Your choice."

"Color of your Jeep is likely to do me in in the parking lot."

Aaron laughed. Then gave Gray what he hoped was a serious glare. Gray squeezed his fingers in return. "All right. Let's do it."

The nice thing about living so far out of the City—whether you considered New York or Philly the "City"—was that there was always plenty of parking at the hospital. Lehigh Valley Hospital–Pocono had a lot close to the emergency department, which meant Aaron was able to drop Gray off and meet back up with him while he was still checking in.

As he walked up to the counter, Gray turned to heave an overly dramatic sigh. "You didn't have to come in."

"I wasn't going to wait in the car."

"You could have—"

"Mr. Clery?"

Gray turned back to the windowed reception desk.

"Dr. Kassel is here today," the attendant said. "We've put a call in, and she'll be down shortly."

In hospital speak, that could mean early next week. "Are you still dizzy?" Aaron asked.

Without turning around, Gray nudged him with an elbow. "I can wait out here," he told the attendant.

She answered with the smile of a woman who'd seen things that would make others cry before pressing the button that released the door beside the desk. "No need. We can take you back now."

Gray turned to Aaron.

Aaron opened his mouth to offer to go with him, though he wasn't sure whether that would suit Gray. He closed his mouth without saying anything.

"I won't be long," Gray said.

"Okay. I'll be here when you're ready to go home."

Gray stared at him for a long moment, and Aaron wondered if they were both thinking the same thing—despite his brain being in some sort of holding pattern. Then Gray pressed a fast kiss to the side of Aaron's mouth and pushed through the double-wide doors leading into the interior of the emergency department.

Aaron tried not to lean around the corner to watch after him. Tried not to mentally replay the most dramatic scene of every hospital drama he'd ever watched. Gray had been fine in the car. A little worked up and anxious, but the dizziness had passed. Always did, he'd said.

Still, Aaron couldn't switch his brain off.

He went to find a seat and chose a row of chairs at the back of the waiting area, under the TV. Sat there trying not to think for the longest minute of his life before he pulled out his phone and accessed his notes app and the file marked *Game Notes*.

Setting his thumbs to the keyboard, he tapped out: *Winning Conditions*.

Under that: *For Gray to be just fine.*

Chapter Twenty-Seven

Arm throbbing slightly from the blood pressure cuff, his opposite arm busy clotting from the blood draw, Gray gave into gravity and relaxed back onto the narrow ER bed. He'd been determined to sit on the edge, as though he were visiting rather than here for any particular reason. Such as, say, a suspected heart attack. Which it wasn't. Which he'd told every person in scrubs. Multiple times.

Each and every one of them had given him the same answer: *"We'll do a few tests."*

Now he had sticky pads all over his torso, a cotton ball taped inside one elbow, and a cuff wrapped around his other biceps.

Gray hadn't spent a lot of time reminiscing over his last stay in the hospital. Like, who would? He hadn't exactly been on vacation, despite similar rules regarding leaving his room alone. There'd certainly been no French toast. But after being encouraged to turn his legs around and lie back, he'd returned to the blur of time after his heart attack. Thankfully, this fuss was quieter than that fuss.

The ER staff quickly came to the same conclusion as him: his heart wasn't infarcing or whatever it liked to do when it got fed up with regular duty. But his blood pressure was elevated, and combined with the dizziness he'd been experiencing and the myriad other symptoms one of the staff had wheedled out of him—stomach pains, nausea, and shortness of breath—it had been suggested that he might be experiencing adverse side effects to the blood pressure medication.

He'd pulled his phone out to text Aaron, let him know he absolutely, positively wasn't having a heart attack, when the curtain twitched aside and Dr. Kassel poked her head in.

"Mr. Clery." She smiled and extended a hand.

While they shook, Gray did his level best not to scowl.

Keeping her smile, she consulted the tablet in her other hand. "How are you feeling now?"

"Like a crash test dummy."

"You'll feel better tomorrow."

"Isn't that what you said last time?"

Ignoring his joke, she asked the same questions he'd already been through with the ER staff. As he related the history of his symptoms, she nodded and took notes.

"You don't seem very worried over there," Gray said.

She glanced up again. "Were you experiencing any of these symptoms at our last visit?"

"Yeah, but I figured it was me generally feeling like crap. I was tired for weeks after All the Fuss."

"All the Fuss?"

"It's what I call my, ah, heart attack."

A slim eyebrow arched. "I'm concerned that you're not taking your health seriously. Given the circumstances."

If Gray had freckles, they'd probably have disappeared.

"But your color is good." A half smile edged across her lips. "You're conversing in full sentences, and haven't clutched your chest once."

Gray reflexively opened and closed his fingers. "My heart squeezes once in a while."

"Mm-hmm. How often is 'once in a while'?"

"I don't know. It depends what I'm doing."

"More so when you're under stress?"

"Yeah, but also sometimes when I'm exercising."

Concern pinched her brow. She examined her tablet again. "I'm going to schedule a stress test. And I'm going to prescribe a different medication."

"Okay." Did his voice sound as small to her as it did to him?

"I'm not worried. That means you shouldn't be either, okay?"

Gray exhaled heavily.

"You've lost some weight and, otherwise, your numbers are good. I'm confident further tests will show the same results." Her smile narrowed to a professional degree. "It's natural to worry about every squeeze and odd palpitation, but you're more in touch with what's happening in your chest than you've ever been, so you're mostly noticing what's always been there. That's good, Mr. Clery. Paying attention to how you feel is healthy. But don't let it overwhelm you."

Easy for her to say. She looked fit enough to run two marathons back-to-back.

Gray exhaled a little less heavily. Hearing a cardiac doctor tell him everything was going to be okay—even if not exactly in those words—went a long way toward reducing the ever-present pressure over his heart. He wasn't going to die today. Probably.

Out in the waiting area, Aaron seemed engaged by the wall-mounted TV, where a pair of handsome young men were conducting an animated conversation over an antique toaster oven. He stood up as soon as Gray approached and quivered in place for a second. "Is it okay to hug you?"

Previously unknown knots of tension along Gray's spine began to unravel. "Please." As Aaron's arms settled around his shoulders, Gray murmured against Aaron's ear, "If someone objects, I hear the emergency department here is pretty good."

Aaron patted his back. "Stop, you. We're fine. You're fine." He pulled back. "You are fine, right?"

"Side effects. We're going to try a new medication."

"Okay." Worry creased Aaron's brow. "How do you feel now?"

"Like if someone else asks how I feel, I might snap."

Aaron took a step back and held his hands up in mock surrender. Chuckling, Gray caught him around the shoulders and tugged him into a looser, sideways hug. "I'd really like to kiss you," he said quickly.

"I'd like you to kiss me."

They shared a smile.

"Let's go home."

Aaron dug out his car keys. "I'm in the first lot outside."

When they were seated inside the offensively yellow Jeep, Aaron asked, "Which home?"

Gray dropped his head back and closed his eyes. "Can we go to yours?" His dad didn't know he'd been to the hospital. Would he wonder where Gray had been all afternoon? Gray pulled out his phone and shot off a short text. *Staying with Aaron tonight.*

His dad didn't respond, but he'd likely see the message the next time he checked his phone.

"How is your dad?" Aaron asked.

Gray glanced up sharply. "How did you know who I was texting?"

"I figured it was your dad or Oliver."

"Did you tell anyone where we were?"

"Just Stacy so she could cover my classes."

"Sorry."

Aaron put a hand on Gray's knee and squeezed. "Don't be. Your dad?"

"Not a lot has changed since we had lunch and talked, but I didn't expect him to start smiling and joking at the breakfast table. The man is dealing with a terrible loss."

"You are too," Aaron said softly.

"We talked about Mom when I first got back up here, but then we didn't, you know? I'm not sure we need to do that now, talk about her. But I do think we need to stop trying *not* to talk about her, if that makes sense."

Aaron hummed in agreement.

Gray watched the familiar streets of East Stroudsburg and then Stroudsburg pass by as Aaron wove through the interconnected towns, making his way across McMichael Creek and along Main Street, turning several blocks after the café and gym to wind back across the creek and into his neighborhood.

As downtown Stroudsburg disappeared over the hill behind them, Gray mused over how he always felt at home in these streets. Another of his school friends had lived on this road, and he'd dated a guy who lived over the next hill. Were they still around? If he planned to stay here, he should start looking folks up.

He'd been to weddings at the reception center off 191 and had had his picture taken at the weird cutouts in front of the Thai place on 611 more times than he could remember. He'd watched fall overtake the valley and roll up the sides of the hills. Listened to ice crack under the Seventh Street bridge. Fallen asleep to the distant sound of rushing water after the spring thaw and when it had seemed to want to rain a year's worth of water in one day.

He'd never felt as at home in Allentown.

He checked out Aaron's profile. If he moved, he'd miss Aaron, except *miss* wasn't exactly the right word. Before he could find a better one, Aaron was turning into his driveway and switching off the car. He faced Gray and Gray leaned in. Their lips touched, and the kiss seemed to convey a charge between them, lighting up a place inside Gray that had remained dull until this moment.

Aaron pulled away. "Inside?" His voice was soft, hesitant.

"Yeah," Gray affirmed.

Once inside the house, their clothes marked a trail to Aaron's bedroom. They didn't stop to check whether his mother was there— Gray didn't care if she was. Once the bedroom door closed behind them, his only goal was to have Aaron laid out on the bed beneath him. It wasn't even about the freckles now, or the miles of sleek skin over fine musculature. It was the breathy moans following every stroke. The laughter and quick smiles as Gray found ticklish spots. The way Aaron touched him in return, as though Gray's body was something to revere. How their eyes always seemed to connect and lock as one of them found their way inside the other—this time Gray between Aaron's upraised knees, his cock buried so deep, he might have touched heaven.

The almost sleepy set of Aaron's eyes suggested he had.

"You feel so fucking good," Aaron panted.

"So do you."

Aaron grasped Gray's hip, digging in with his fingers. "Not so . . . Oh, God."

Whether he wanted Gray to thrust faster or slower seemed not to matter. Gray was clearly hitting the sweet spot, and Aaron looked as though he was about to transcend. For his part, Gray felt pretty great. He was all in with a guy who turned him on like no one else had. But more than that, he was with someone who *mattered* in a way no one else had. This was more than sex. More than making love.

But as his climax crept along the backs of his legs and squeezed his balls, Gray let those thoughts become untethered. Because, for whatever Aaron meant to him, this moment simply was. And if he'd learned anything over the past month and a half, it would be that. Life *was*. Moments, reflections, happy dances of light.

And the ultimate sigh of release as two climaxes met in the middle, each trying to climb over the other and serving only to push them higher. Heart pounding with exertion, delight, and wonder, Gray yelled with his release, held firm over his lover as Aaron followed, and then collapsed down into arms that seemed to have been waiting to hold him forever.

Chapter Twenty-Eight

I t had been a while since Aaron's house echoed with so many voices. He didn't mind living alone—he spent so many hours of the day either at the gym or with his sister and her wife that his house had become a refuge or sanctuary. His space to spread out and be at peace. But when his mom wasn't vacuuming at stupid o'clock and knocking on doors while he was trying to have sex, Aaron had enjoyed having her around. And when Gray stayed the night, the house felt content, as though it had long wanted to accommodate multiple people.

The crowd gathered around his dining table filled the space, but the open-plan design of his kitchen, dining, and living areas managed the noise well as his guests got ready to play.

For the past week, Aaron and Gray had been putting the final touches on a playable version of the game. They'd tied the story to the cards, redesigning only a few. They'd figured out the resource and crafting systems, going for a simple design that could be expanded upon later. Gray had produced a multipage printout of the rules of play—again, there were few, with goals and motivations decided mostly by the players. Aaron had provided illustrations.

Now they were sharing it all with their friends. Mostly Gray's friends, as Devorah and Leilani hadn't responded to Aaron's invitation. His mom had, but she'd yet to show. She'd been spending time at Dev's place helping to decorate the new family room and nursery.

Aaron's house missed her.

Aaron kind of did too.

Gray's friends comprised Oliver; Oliver's partner, Nick; and Nick's brother, Cam. Gray had also brought his dad.

Aaron drew Gray into the kitchen to help prep the snacks. "Your dad really wanted to come?"

"He's the most competitive strategy gamer I know. Doesn't play so much anymore, bingo being his current jam. But I figured I'd ask." Gray shrugged as he sorted bags of chips along the kitchen counter. "It is cool to see him out of the house. And maybe even happy."

Aaron smiled. Gray looked good. His new medication seemed to have fewer side effects, though he'd been warned they could still impinge. But the hypervigilance of a week ago had been replaced with an ease Gray likely hadn't experienced in a while. Reduced hours at the café probably helped.

"How's the sale coming along?" Aaron asked as he grabbed one of the chip bags.

"We've figured out what we think is a fair price. Next step is to convince Patty and Wendell to buy the place." Gray filled two large bowls with corn chips.

Nodding, Aaron spooned salsa into two smaller bowls.

Earlier in the afternoon, Gray had taught him to make the focaccia with all the seeds. They had that in the oven, along with a twisted cheese bread Aaron had already forgotten the name of. The kitchen smelled amazing. Oliver had brought a platter of vegan enchiladas that looked suspiciously good, and Nick had contributed cookies so uniformly round, he might have printed them. Cam had brought beer.

"Label the spicy salsa," Gray said. "We don't want any injuries before anyone gets to play."

Aaron located a pair of index cards in the junk drawer and scrawled *Hot* on one and *Mild* on the other. He then contemplated the bowls. "Which one was which?"

Gray scooped up a chip, dragged it through one of the bowls and crunched. "This one is hot." He started breathing through a mouthful of half-eaten chips. "So freaking hot. Dear lord, is this ghost-pepper salsa?"

"Water?"

Between waving a hand in front of his mouth and exaggerated chewing, Gray managed a nod. After swallowing, he fused his mouth to Aaron's in a surprise kiss. Aaron laughed, parting their lips, before putting a hand to the back of Gray's neck to pull him closer. Gray tasted of salt and hot peppers. And, holy heck, the hot was hot.

"Hot peppers!" Aaron ducked out of the kiss. "We should make that a harvestable item. They could be like a wild card. Nutrition, poison, maybe they could have a medical property too. Or a cool effect on the soil."

"So much for being swept away by my affection." Gray was grinning.

"Like you're not thinking about the game all the time."

"Only all day, before I fall asleep, in my dreams, and when I wake up in the morning."

Aaron curled his fingers around Gray's nape. "When we're having sex?"

"*May*be."

The doorbell chimed. With a frown and flutter in his chest, Aaron went to answer it. His mom and sister stood on the doorstep.

Dev came!

"Hey!" But why hadn't they let themselves in? "It wasn't locked," he said. Also, his mom had a key.

Devorah answered for them. "This many cars in the driveway, we weren't sure if we'd be interrupting an orgy."

"What?"

His mom waved a hand. "I don't know what Gray's friends are like."

"Uh-huh. Why don't you come see for yourself? We're about to play a game." At their amused smiles, he added, "A board game. Which you knew, because I invited you to play with us." He directed a mock-glare toward his mother.

"And we're here to play."

Aaron peeked over his mom's head to check Dev's expression. "You too?"

She shrugged. "I guess I want to see what's keeping you from realizing your full potential."

"Ouch?"

"Sorry, that came out wrong." Devorah's frown was contrite. "Mom said you guys have been working on this day and night, so I wanted to see what all the fuss was about."

Aaron's thoughts immediately rolled toward Gray's health. Maybe they should call their still nameless game All the Fuss.

"Come on in." He stood aside to let his mom and sister into the house. Greetings followed, everyone introducing themselves—shaking hands, touching shoulders, and smiling. Gray caught his eye and sent over a grin. Aaron returned it. Inside, he felt like screaming. This many people were about to play a game he'd made. Why on Earth had they decided to do this?

Gray edged around the table toward him. "Let's show off what we have first, then maybe split the group into two?"

"We don't have two games."

"Then we'll have to take turns." Gray gripped his arm. "Breathe. Do you need to head out back and do push-ups?"

"Why would you ask that?"

"You're an active guy. I figured exercise might calm you down."

"I'm calm." *Hah!* If his heart beat any faster, it'd push through the front of his chest and take off for the moon. Aaron pressed his palm there. "Does your medication do anything for a heart that's about to head into space?"

Gray laughed. "Nope. But this usually works." He pressed his lips to Aaron's in a quick kiss. Then he clapped his hands twice and said, "Let's do this," in a weird voice.

Aaron blinked at him. "I do not sound like that."

"You totally sound like that."

"C'mooon," Cam whined. "Let's play."

Mouth suddenly so dry his tongue seemed to catch everywhere but on the right words, Aaron started explaining the premise. Gray jumped in when he got to the background story, keeping it short and sweet, giving just enough information to make sense of the world.

Nick asked for the printout and started reading that. Cam asked questions about the few cards on display. Aaron's mom was sitting close to Gray's dad and the pair of them seemed preoccupied by their own conversation. But when Gray's dad asked whether they planned to limit the resources, Aaron realized they'd been talking about the game. His game. Well, his and Gray's, but . . .

People were paying attention. They all appeared interested.

It was decided to play with a partner for the first game, meaning everyone got to join in. Aaron's mom paired with Gray's dad, Oliver with Nick, Gray with Aaron, and Cam scooted his chair closer to Dev. Watching Nick's brother flirt with his sister was almost as much fun as watching them play the game. Cam wasn't sleazy about it, though. He simply seemed to enjoy Dev's company.

Gray's dad and Nick asked the most questions.

"But what's the *cost* of magic?" Gray's dad wanted to know.

"And is there a regeneration penalty?" Nick put in.

"Is there a formula relating it to similar items of tech?"

"How about if you tie it to the DPS ratio?"

Aaron had his phone out to take notes, and Gray was scribbling along the edges of his printout. After about an hour and a half or so, the conditions they'd set at the beginning—a specific area of territory explored and secured, and a certain number of resources gathered—declared Nick and Oliver the winners.

Aaron sank back into his chair, deflated in a way that often happened after he'd become intensely focused on a game. Though their play had been interrupted by rule clarification and further explanation of the cards and terrain tiles, for a while there, he had managed to become caught up in the world he and Gray had designed. The story. He'd almost believed he'd been washed up on a lonely shore. He'd discovered a coastline and figured out how to exploit it. He'd made friends with a tribe of kobolds who provided him with ore in exchange for old tech items he found. He'd rediscovered magic—thanks to those same allies. Now it was over and he was back in his living room with empty chip bowls a mess of game pieces.

"What did you guys think?" Gray asked.

No one said anything for nearly a minute, and it was the longest silence of Aaron's life.

"Well, I loved it, if my opinion counts," his mom said.

A wave of enthusiastic nods rounded the table, then Nick spoke up. "The balance is off. You need to reexamine the comparable items for magic and tech."

Aaron sank into his chair, a heavy weight pushing him down.

Nick wasn't finished, though. "A third category could help. Modern, or whatever's made from old objects during the game.

You could then rock, paper, scissors the whole combat system. DPS wouldn't count for as much, then."

"Right!" Oliver piped up. "But it might mean nerfing a few of your bigger weapons." He frowned. "What if you introduced one ultimate per track? The dream weapon?"

Gray's dad flapped a hand. "But what if you're not aiming for conquest? Best weapon in the game isn't going to help you, then."

"Unless it's multipurpose," Cam put in. "Like an engine of some sort. You get one and you can use it to power your most valuable asset."

Seated next to him, Dev leaned over. "Am I supposed to understand what these guys are saying?"

Aaron flashed her a smile. "Not necessarily." He chewed on his lower lip, wanting to ask her what she'd thought of the game, but not quite wanting to hear it. "Thanks for coming over tonight," he said instead.

She shrugged one shoulder. "I'm not going to say I get it. How this could be more important to you than what we've been building together over the past few years. But . . ." Her dark eyebrows pinched together. "I guess it was sorta cool. Like, I can see how creative it all is."

"It's not more important than the gym."

"Used to be *our* gym," she said quietly.

"It's always been yours and Leili's. I just work there."

"That's not . . ." She frowned harder. "Is that how you really feel?"

He sighed. "I guess not? But when it comes to the business side of everything, yeah? I mostly follow your lead." She was, after all, his older sister.

"Leili and I always figured that when we started having kids, we'd scale back. And that you'd be there to, I don't know, make everything work."

Huh. "I wasn't a part of that conversation, Dev."

She gestured toward the game. "Is this what you want to do instead?"

"No." Maybe? Aaron studied the game spread across the table. His cards, Gray's history book. Their work. What if they did manage to sell it? How much money could they make? And would it stop with one game? Gray had already outlined two expansion models, and Aaron had notes for cards to match. They also had notes for a second game idea. But could he make a career out of producing games? Or was it just a hobby gone wild?

He glanced over at Gray, who was still scribbling furiously. Gray's dad and Nick were still offering suggestions, and Oliver and Cam chimed in now and again with questions and comments of their own.

Gray met his gaze. They shared a smile. All things considered, their first public playtest had gone well. Nick did have a point about the balance, which meant they might need to rework the magic and tech systems. But it would be fun. Work, but fun, like his job at the gym. Would the results be as accessible, though? The game wouldn't change people's lives the way exercise could.

"What are you going to call it?" Cam asked, drawing Aaron's attention. "The game."

Everyone had a suggestion.

"Wonders of the Wilds."

"Man versus Wild."

"Man versus Nature."

"Women versus Men," Dev put in with a sharp glance toward Cam.

He held up his hands. "Us versus Them." They shared a cackle.

"A Lonely Shore," Nick put in quietly.

Recognition fluttered through Aaron's chest. The beginning of the game felt like that.

Gray spread his hands across the table. "Shelf Life."

Aaron straightened in his chair. While he sounded out the words to himself, Gray added an explanation. "It's a fantasy game, but a title that doesn't scream fantasy could work in its favor. And everything in the game has a life span. The ages, the artifacts, the resources, the journey of the player. The whole game is about expired objects. Reusing forgotten items, repurposing them."

"What about Expired Objects?" Oliver mused.

Aaron shook his head. "No. I mean, that's a cool name, but I like Shelf Life. It's weird and different."

"Like the game," his mom said.

Aaron laughed. "Like the game." He met Gray's gaze again, and Gray squeezed his knee beneath the table. He mouthed words Aaron didn't quite catch, but might have been, *Like life.*

Shouldn't have been comforting, but, yeah. Life was weird and different. But that was what made it so entertaining.

Chapter Twenty-Nine

I n the nearly a year they'd worked together, Gray had seen Patty's happy look; patient look; what he called the mom-look, which she wore when talking to her kids on the phone or to customers who seemed to need maternal guidance; and his personal favorite: the *this is ridiculous* look. He'd mistaken it for anger the first time her lips pushed upward and her eyes rolled. But good humor always followed. Patty never seemed to get angry.

Right now, her mouth formed a perfect O. It was an expression he hadn't seen before. Then her lips clamped shut, but not before the top pinched in the middle. Was this—

"But, Gray . . ."

Her eyes weren't rolling.

"We . . ." She glanced at her husband, who was still open-mouthed. "We don't have that kind of money."

"We can finance it."

Patty shook her head. "With what? We have a mortgage and two college funds to contribute to."

"No. I mean Dad and I'll finance it."

Wendell pushed his hands across the table, palms facing Gray. "Oh, no. You don't lend money to family. That's how everything gets messed up."

"We haven't even decided to buy the place yet." Patty shot Wendell a sharp frown.

Gray took that as his cue. He scooted his chair back from the table. "Why don't you two talk about it for a bit? Like, regardless of the financing, whether you'd be interested in owning and operating a bakery. Before I step out, though, can I say something?"

Patty and Wendell stared at him, expressions somewhere between shock and consternation.

"Over the past month, you two have saved this business. You've got it running like I never could. For weeks, I stood in that hallway out back, wondering if I had the wherewithal to come back in here and get to work, and the only reason I could stand around back there was because you didn't need me in here."

"All your friends were chipping in," Patty said. "Aaron and Nick still come by most every day to sweep and mop. Oliver, too, when he can."

Wendell grinned. "We conveniently forgot to tell them we don't need them mopping and sweeping."

Chuckling, Gray said, "If it's in Nick's schedule, you've got someone mopping and sweeping for life. But, listen, I mean what I say. You two work well together, and that's what this place has always needed. Two. One to bake and one to do everything else."

"That's what we had when you were baking," Patty reminded him.

"Except I was baking and trying to do everything else instead of letting you handle it."

Patty shrugged. "Without another person besides Wendell in the kitchen, I couldn't have handled it. Finally getting additional staff in here regularly has been amazing."

"Staff you hired. Not me," Gray pointed out. "What did you say to Varya and Lucas in the interviews that made sure they showed up to work?"

"I didn't loom like you do. I think you forget you're six and a half feet of big scary baker sometimes."

Gray glanced down at himself, at the body that didn't feel as familiar as it once had. If it ever had? The body he'd been taking for granted until recently. Surprisingly, his gut wasn't the first thing he noticed. He put a hand there, as if to feel for the weight he couldn't see.

"Looking good," Wendell said with a grin.

Patty winked. "Working it with Sporty McSporterson, you mean."

"Stop right there." Gray patted the air. Then he smiled. Touched his midsection again. "Been a while since I could see my toes without leaning forward, you know?"

"I hear you."

Gray shot Wendell a withering look. The guy was all legs and arms and knees and elbows. Like Aaron, but without the miles of freckles and well-placed musculature. Not that Gray had seen Wendell in anything other than jeans, T-shirts, and Clery's aprons.

"You can take your eyes off my husband and upstairs with you while we talk this through," Patty said.

Gray snapped back to attention. "Ah, so, yeah, remember what I was saying. You two have got this. If money is your only concern, we'll figure it out." He turned to Wendell again. "And if family doesn't help family, then this world is in a sorrier state than we thought it was."

With that, he left them at the table in the front of the café and sauntered through the back to the door that had proven his barrier for so many weeks. On the other side, his phone rang. Gray dug it out of a pocket and answered without focusing on the screen.

"Hello?"

"Gray." It was Ollie. "That bread you had at Aaron's the other night."

"Which one?"

"The one with all the nuts and seeds. You made it from some Zika flour?"

Gray laughed. "Pretty sure Zika is a virus."

"Sorry, you were nerding out about the flour and all I absorbed was that it was low in gluten. High in protein?"

"Yeah, the Enkir flour. Why?"

"Do you have any? And can you show me how to make bread with it?"

"It's pretty pricey stuff. You'd have to sell the loaves at twice the price of your regular focaccia." Which reminded him. He'd been meaning to chat with Oliver about the cost of setting up and running a stall.

"Nick and I ran the numbers a couple of months ago and we basically doubled what I was charging for everything. Except to catering customers. But at the markets? I'm selling what no one else has."

"You mean pastries and cookies that lie."

"Don't make me reach through this wall."

"You're next door?"

"Yeah."

"Perfect. There was something I wanted to talk to you about. Be there in a sec." Gray hit the End Call icon and pocketed his phone. A moment later, he knocked on the rear door of the premises next door, the building Oliver had bought and refurbished at the beginning of the year. Downstairs was still a work in progress. The kitchen was up and running, but Nick hadn't opened the shop portion yet. He wasn't sure he would. His current business model kept customers at a distance—with sales and requests for custom dollhouses and models coming through his website. Nick thought he wasn't great with people and was hesitant to display his work and invite people to stop by to see it.

Gray agreed with Oliver that while Nick could be awkward with strangers, once he started talking about his work, he tended to relax. Mostly. Could be engaging. Sort of. He could also hire someone to do the talking, like his brother. Cam could talk to literally anyone.

Oliver finally opened the door to let Gray inside. Like the café kitchen, Oliver's was quiet and cool. Afternoons were when bakers and their ovens rested. Oliver held up a carafe of coffee, and Gray shook his head. "Have you got any tea?"

Oliver blinked. "Did you just ask for tea?"

"Better call 911."

"Seriously."

Smiling, Gray tipped his head toward the front of the shop. "Where's Nick?"

"Consulting with the Chamber of Commerce about the Downtown Stroudsburg project." A coordinated effort between local artists to represent the city through various mediums.

"I hope they all decide to go ahead with that. I'd love to see it." Nick's contribution would be Main Street, front Fifth to Eighth, in miniature. Three blocks of buildings on both sides of the street. "Are they still talking about including Seventh and Courthouse Square?"

Oliver shrugged. "Maybe? I don't know—you'll have to ask Nick. So, this flour. What's it made from? Some grass grown only in the droppings of mountain goats on the western slopes of the Himalayas every seven years?"

Gray laughed. "Something like that. Why do you want to know?"

"My clients are always asking me about gluten-free options. Mostly, though, I like the idea of a loaf that can be sold as is or sliced up and sold by the slice, sort of like an on-the-go bread-protein bar."

Oliver's business at farmers' markets mostly centered around handheld snacks for different diets, hence his eggless, cheese-less, joy-less pastries.

Gray hummed and pulled his phone back out. "How many pastries are you selling at one stall on a Saturday?" Ollie recited numbers and Gray did some calculations. When he finished, he was impressed. "You're doing amazing business."

Oliver's smile was pleased. "Speaking of which, have you talked to Patty and Wendell?"

"I just did." Gray tipped his head toward the adjoining wall. "They're discussing it now."

"If they accept, and they'd be crazy to say no—"

"Or crazy to say yes. Working at a business and running it are two very different things." Which could be the most succinct thought Gray had had about the café in a long while.

Oliver nodded. "Have you given any thought to what you might do if they do accept?"

Gray drew in a breath. In his chest, his heart gave a single, hard, extra beat, then calmed. He licked his lips. "Maybe, which is why I wanted to talk to you."

"Because you're considering going into game design full-time and you want me to talk you out of it?"

"What? No. But there are folks making millions with crowd-funding projects, you know."

"Uh-huh."

Gray frowned. "You don't agree that what we're working on is good enough?"

"Your game is great. But I'm not sure you should pin all of your hopes on it."

"Who said anything about pinning all my hopes on it? Right now, we're having a lot of fun with it. To me, that feels like the important part."

Oliver was quiet for so long, Gray started thinking—if that was what mentally chasing himself could be called. Should he be throwing all in with the game? And who was Oliver to suggest he shouldn't? *Shelf Life* was awesome. Every time he and Aaron played it through, it was like living a different story.

Their next step was to invite other people to play. Not just family and friends. They needed real play-testers; people who played games for a living.

Wouldn't that be a dream job?

"Gray."

Gray blinked and he was back in Ollie's kitchen. The kettle had boiled and Ollie was holding up two different boxes of herbal tea. Gray picked one at random (they all tasted like dead flowers), and Oliver plucked out a bag. He poured the water and handed Gray the mug.

"Anyway," Oliver said, as if they'd been conversing while Gray had spiraled into and out of his dream state, "I'm sorry if I sounded unenthusiastic. If anyone should advocate for taking chances, it'd be me."

"You have a point, but that's not actually what I wanted to talk to you about."

"Oh?"

"Not to steal your idea," Gray started.

Oliver's eyebrows rose.

"But I could bake that bread for you. The focaccia. Maybe some other loaves? Sell them at your stall and give you a slice of the action? Just until I organize a stall for myself."

Oliver's eyebrows rose another degree. "Are you still baking next door or . . ."

"No. Wendell has it handled. The guy's a natural. He's already started tweaking recipes and such. He and Patty got a babysitter last Friday night so they could spend the evening in the kitchen trying a different flour blend."

"Wow. If they don't buy the café, they truly are crazy."

"Right?"

Gray got it, though. Their need to talk it through. To consider the financial aspect not only in relation to now but their future. And it was that consideration that would make the difference between their ownership and Gray's. He'd fallen into it. They would choose it.

Gray cast a speculative look in Ollie's direction. "So, making bread for the markets. See what sells and how much." A warm glow, something like an internal bread oven, spread through Gray's torso. "I could use the stall as a test market for new recipes. Eventually, I mean. To begin with, I'd want to stock bread people might like to order in bulk."

"You should also connect with the Chamber of Commerce. I've made so many business contacts going to their events."

"I always meant to, when I got back up here. I just never had enough time. How many Black business owners take part in these events?"

"A good number and they already know you, through your mom."

A great sigh gusted out of him, and Gray let his chin dip toward his chest in a nod. "Do you think I've wasted her legacy?"

"No."

Gray waited for Oliver to say more, to qualify his short answer. When he didn't, Gray realized that single word was all he needed. "Feels like it's about time I got back to work."

Oliver smiled and lifted his coffee cup. "Here's to the best damn baker in the Northeast."

"I wouldn't go that—"

"Best baker I *know*. And everyone likes bread. Even people who don't want to eat bread like bread. My clients want bread." Oliver's smile warmed. "And you could make the bread you wanted to. The breads you never had time to experiment with."

Gray pushed his palm into his chest.

Oliver's smile dimmed. "Are you okay?"

After rubbing a soft circle over the deep pulse behind his breastbone, Gray drew in a long slow breath. Then he swallowed. And blinked. Because what Oliver had described sounded like his dream job.

Sure, he loved playing games, and designing one called to his creative side. But baking—it was in his blood. In his bones. Rooted deep. And all because of one person, which was why he'd had such a hard time giving up on the café, even when it seemed the café was ready to give up on him.

His mother had helped him shape his very first loaf. Giving up baking would be like forgetting that. Forgetting who he was.

He smiled at his best friend, then grasped his arm. "Thank you."

Ollie's smile widened again. "Anytime."

Chapter Thirty

Once a month, Devorah and Leilani organized a team lunch for senior staff. Aaron usually handled the catering, giving him an excuse to visit Clery's Café for more than a single sandwich. Gray hadn't been the one to fill the order last month. He'd still been recuperating. He wasn't the one to fill the order for May, either.

Patty handed over the bulging paper sack with a smile. "It's all there. Extra pickles and hot peppers in little containers, just like you asked for."

Aaron bit his lower lip to hide a wince. He'd hadn't imagined he was a difficult customer and he'd never meant to complain, but he had always made a big deal about making sure everything he ordered was in the bag. Not because there'd ever been an issue—he was that kind of guy. Annoying. No wonder Gray hadn't seemed to like him much.

After thanking Patty and paying for the order, Aaron hugged the bag to his chest for the short walk back to the gym. The clouds that had threatened the horizon earlier in the morning had retreated for now. May in the Poconos could be winter, spring, or summer, though, and with the breeze still fresh, Aaron wouldn't discount a storm before the day quit.

Back at the gym, he hustled into the conference room where everyone had already gathered, including Devorah's new favorite employee: Hector. Objectively, Hector was a great fit for the gym. He was good-looking, which might seem a shallow observation—and Aaron knew for a fact Dev didn't discriminate when it came to appearance—but attractive instructors were good for business. Hector also had an outsized personality to match his high-wattage smile, and he seemed to have already made friends with all the staff at both locations.

He was also sitting in Aaron's chair.

Aaron shot him a few narrow-eyed looks as he laid out the sandwiches and condiments. Hector seemed too busy talking with Leilani to notice. When he'd finished, Aaron cleared his throat and most everyone turned toward him. He gestured toward the sandwiches. "Lunch." He pointed left. "Veggie options." Right. "Omnivore options." Center. "Condiments and chips."

Leilani rose from her seat and crossed to hug Aaron's side. "Thanks, brother dear. You're the best."

He'd only picked up sandwiches. Still, with the whirlwind of the past few weeks, Aaron hadn't seen Leili as often as he was used to. He curled an arm around her shoulders and pulled her close. "You're welcome."

Dev was still chatting with Hector.

Sigh.

While everyone lined up for a sandwich, Aaron eyed Hector's empty chair. *His* empty chair. He thought about sitting there. Claiming his spot at the head of the table with Dev and Leili. Then, with another sigh, he stalked out of the conference room to steal a chair from one of the offices. He returned to find one lonely sandwich, no pickles (not that he wanted them), and no chips. And no space at the table for his chair. He looked pointedly at Hector, who seemed to ignore him just as pointedly.

Stacy eventually noticed his plight and made space for him at the other end of the table.

Aaron sat with his sandwich—tuna salad, which he did not particularly enjoy—and sulked. Silently.

Devorah kicked off the meeting by introducing Hector, "Our fabulous new manager," and Aaron's mood spiraled from there.

Hector half stood and waved. "I'm thrilled to be joining you all, and I hope the experience I bring will add further success to the Focus Fitness story."

Corny. Ugh.

Devorah tapped the tablet in front of her. "Okay, scheduling. We're making a few changes over the coming weeks. For those of you who see you have fewer classes, don't panic. We want to bring Hector up to speed as quickly as possible, so he'll be leading a number of classes over the next month or so. If you still want that slot, let us know and we'll attach you to the roster. But if you did want to take some vacation days, now is a great time."

Aaron checked his schedule and noted the gaping holes. Like, a lot of holes. In fact, the only class that was still his was the Saturday morning freestyle. Aaron opened his mouth. After meeting his sister's warning expression, he closed it again. Before he turned away, though, he noted the sympathetic glint in Leili's eyes—and that only made him feel worse, because it meant Dev had discussed the changes with her before making them.

The meeting moved on to discussion of the summer programming and an outline for the progress of the new gym, which they hoped to open in the late fall. "Just in time for Thanksgiving." Leilani touched her midsection. "I'll have my hands full with this baby, so Devorah and Hector will be taking care of that one."

Stacy shot a look at Aaron, eyebrows raised.

Aaron met her gaze but didn't engage. What was the point? He'd chosen this. What he hadn't chosen, though, was feeling like a stranger in his own family—because that's what the gym and the business had always felt like to him. Family.

As soon as the meeting ended, he pushed back his chair and left the office. Normally, he'd have been the one to clean away the lunch. Let Hector do it. Aaron needed fresh air. He made for the doors and stepped out into the weakening sunshine. The clouds were back. Perfect. If he was lucky, by the time he made it to the bench facing the woods, it'd be raining. The confusion and defeat swirling around in his gut only needed a quick storm to blow up into a full movie montage of depressive self-pity.

"Aaron."

He glanced over his shoulder to find Leili jogging after him. Shortening his stride, he waited for her to catch up. When she did, she touched his arm. "I should have emailed you about the changes before the meeting. I'm sorry. I meant to. But please don't take any of it personally. Dev's focused on getting Hector up to speed before we transition him to a new property."

Aaron stopped to face his sister-in-law. "She's using him to punish me for not falling in with her plans."

Leili grimaced. "Maybe a little?"

"He was sitting in my seat!" *And he ate my sandwich.*

"To be fair, you pretty much gave up that seat when you said no to the third gym."

That hurt more than it should have. "I didn't know that saying no meant I'd be pushed out of the job I already have."

Leili studied him for a moment before she said, "Dev and your mom seem to think you want something different. With the game you're making?"

Aaron gazed up at the gathering clouds and then closed his eyes because it wasn't the sky he wanted to see, but his life restored to what it had been six weeks ago.

Except for his relationship with Gray.

He returned his attention to Leili. "Don't you have a hobby?"

She shrugged. "Sure. I quilt. I'm not planning on opening a quilting shop, though."

"But do you make quilts for other people? As gifts."

"Ye-es," she hedged.

"It's like that. Kind of. I was making the game for me. Gray saw potential in it and now we're working on it together, as a hobby we can share. I'm not planning to make a career out of it."

He loved his current job and found it fulfilling. But he also liked the idea of taking his gaming ideas seriously. And what, exactly, would be wrong with that? And so what if his family didn't get it?

Leili touched his arm. "Hey."

He looked down at her.

"I get it. Not everyone wants to run the show. You're happy as you are." Leili delivered a squeeze. "Dev will come around. I think she's just . . . We started this business together, we three. She likely assumed that meant all the way. That all three of us wanted a gym of our own. A three-person empire."

"I don't know that I ever thought about it that way," Aaron admitted. "I was just along for the ride. Dev says jump and I say how high."

Sadness pulled Leili's eyebrows down. "You shouldn't think like that."

"It's true, though. She's my older sister and has always sort of been my . . . if not hero, then my icon. Who I wanted to be. Except now that I'm nearly forty, I don't want to be her anymore. I want to be me. I like me."

"I like you too." Leili tugged him into a hug. "In fact, I love you."

Aaron hugged his sister-in-law as hard as she hugged him. "Back at you."

After a good long moment, Leili pulled away and looped her arm through his so they could walk together. That she didn't rush off felt good. She hadn't come out here just to check on him but to properly connect. "Did you know your dad is on his way here?"

Aaron stopped walking. "What?"

"We're going to pick him up at Newark tonight."

"Why is he coming here?"

"To get his wife back, I assume."

Aaron had been about to take a step but stopped. "But they were doing their own thing, weren't they? I thought he was cool with that."

"Apparently not."

"Huh." He looked down at Leili. "Are they okay? Is there anything else no one wants to tell me about?"

"I don't think so? But your mom and Dev have had a few heads-together convos over the past week. You might want to check in with them."

"I'll call Dad." They'd chatted a couple of times over the past month, mostly about where his dad planned to walk next.

Leili shot him a sharp glance. Then she softened. "You know what? That's probably a good idea. Your mom and Dev can get kind of steamrollerish when they believe what they're planning is for the betterment of mankind."

"You think?"

She laughed lightly and squeezed his arm to her side. "I did hear a rumor your mom wants to move back up here."

"Now that makes sense. I mean, they travel so much, it doesn't matter where they live, does it?"

"And I never really pictured them in a retirement community. Even in Arizona. Did you?"

"Nope."

Leili looked up at him. "How is everything with you, otherwise? Your new boyfriend is completely adorable, by the way. I watched you two work out together on Tuesday. The way he looks at you is, well, adorable."

"You need another word." And to stop talking.

She laughed again. "Adorable! Is it lurve?"

"Oh God, why do you have to do that?"

"What? You used to tease Dev and me all the time. Can't I have a turn?"

"How's pregnancy so far? Is that what this is? You're feeling all maternal and clucky?"

"Hm. Maybe! It's nice to see you with someone, though."

"Thanks. It's nice being with someone."

She stopped walking then, and turned to gaze back at the gym. Aaron turned with her and stood in silence with her for a minute. Then she said, "If this game business doesn't work out, we'll always be here." Leili glanced over at him. "I don't really understand what it is you're doing, and I'm not trying to talk you out of it or whatever. But don't think Dev's little love affair with Hector means you don't have a permanent place with us. This gym, our first, is as much yours as it is Dev's and mine. And if you ever change your mind and do want to try managing a property, that option will always be open too. Okay? I want you to know that."

She was trying to be nice. Aaron got that. But somehow, her words felt wrong. As though she expected his dream to fail.

Or maybe that was just him. His gaming obsession had been a sort-of-secret hobby. His and only his for so long, it almost didn't matter if the game failed. But would Gray see it that way? Gray's whole life had been turned around, and he was now spending more time working on the game than he was baking. Maybe they should slow their roll. Not reach out to Jatek Games. Keep it as a hobby and make a few copies for friends as gifts.

That would sure avoid the disappointment of failure. And maybe then Aaron could look into doing more for the gym.

If only that idea didn't feel like some sort of compromise.

And if only trying something new didn't feel so scary.

If only his heart wasn't mixed up somewhere between the two, pulling between his sister and a man he was falling in love with.

Aware Leili was waiting for him to acknowledge her gesture, Aaron squeezed her arm to his side and delivered a warm, heartfelt smile. It almost worked. She returned his smile, but her eyebrows were still pulled low.

And so was the weird feeling behind his breastbone.

Chapter Thirty-One

"If we combine too many elements of the magic and tech systems, they'll no longer feel unique." Gray strived for a patient tone, but the jut of Aaron's jaw indicated he hadn't quite succeeded. He backpedaled. "If you don't feel that's important, it's cool. The ages as we've described them don't have to be as distinct."

"No, I think we should keep them the way they are: magic, technology, and dirt. I wanted the crafting system to be simple. It's a board game, not a computer game. Whatever inventory we have has to sit on the table in front of us." Aaron tapped his forehead. "Or up here, mostly. Unless we want to design a player sheet."

"But that would make setup onerous. I kinda love how freeform that is at the moment. You decide who you are and make a go of it."

Aaron tendered a brief nod, and Gray sighed out his relief. Finally, a point of agreement. Gray leaned away from the coffee table and sank into the cushions of Aaron's couch. "Okay, so let's examine the crafting system, then. What components do we have now?"

Mirroring Gray's pose, Aaron released a deep breath, tipped his head back, and closed his eyes. "I don't know. Too many, probably."

"Want to take a break?"

Aaron cracked one eyelid. "Sure. Sorry, work has been kind of busy."

"Are you short-staffed?" Why else would Aaron be at the gym longer than usual? His schedule seemed pretty fixed.

Shaking his head, Aaron let his eyes fall closed again. "The opposite, actually. Too many staff."

"Huh?"

Aaron didn't answer. Nor did he open his eyes. A weird sensation crept across Gray's chest—one that didn't involve his heart. Or not exactly. No extra beats or squeezing. More a sense of emptiness at the edges, as though he were grasping at a ledge he couldn't quite hold on to.

Further thought revealed that edge to be Aaron. They weren't clicking tonight. Not snapping together in a pattern that had become familiar and welcome. And Gray couldn't help feeling like it was his fault, although he wasn't sure why.

"You know you can talk to me, right? I've shared a lot of my work woes with you, whether you were ready to listen or not. I wouldn't even consider it returning the favor." Gray touched Aaron's arm. "I'm here for you."

Aaron considered Gray for a long, long moment, his eyes barely open, before he nodded and let them fall closed again.

Pushing out yet another sigh, Gray bent over the coffee table and scooped up their list of bug fixes. Third item was crafting. He pointed a pen at the line, unsure whether he could cross it out. They'd discussed the crafting system, but they hadn't exactly fixed it. Or come up with anything approaching a fix.

He wrote *more discussion* and moved down the list. "Okay. Terrain cards." Gray squinted at the next line. "You want to restrict the ways in which players can build off of each other's tiles."

"That was your suggestion." Aaron hadn't opened his eyes.

"Pretty sure it was yours." Gray peered at the list again, willing extra notation to appear. Like, maybe a name next to each suggestion. He probed his memory, but failed to come up with the scene where he said, *"Let's restrict the ways in which players can build off each other's tiles."*

Unless he had said it but forgot? Could be a side effect of his new medication. After his last scare, Gray had started researching every brand of blood pressure medication online and had joined a couple of forums where people compared side effects. The Heart Disease subreddit was the worst bedtime reading ever. Doom-scrolling did not lead to restful sleep. And he should figure out how to stop the update emails coming to his inbox.

Aaron opened his eyes and leaned forward, resting his elbows on his knees. "I don't even remember the issue, but I say we keep it as it is. Anyone can build off anything. Otherwise, there will be too many rules to remember."

"That's why we need a booklet."

"No one ever reads the booklets."

"Sure they do. Nick read everything we have written about the game before he started playing."

"I get the impression Nick reads everything printed on a cereal box before deciding to buy it."

Gray snorted. "Probably."

A half smile tiptoed around Aaron's mouth. Gray smiled back, and for a moment, everything seemed fine. He was happy, Aaron was happy, and they'd agreed on something. When Gray moved to check the list, though, he remembered that they hadn't agreed. Not about the game, anyway. He pushed the notepad back across the table.

After folding his arms, he looked at Aaron, who was gazing at him. "Does it feel like we're taking one step back for every two steps forward?" Gray asked.

Aaron's brief smile died. "Two steps back for every one forward."

"I'm sorry. It's probably my fault. You had this whole game in your head and I feel like everything I've added complicates it."

"Not true. You're trying to make it clearer."

"Uh-huh. By introducing distinctions you didn't have before."

Aaron blinked. "I thought I was the one arguing for more distinction?"

"I don't even know anymore."

Rocking forward, Aaron got to his feet and edged out from behind the coffee table. They'd pulled it closer to the couch to lay out game pieces, notes, and lists. "Want another iced tea?"

"Sure." Gray watched Aaron's ass disappear around the corner. Heat licked through him, warming his skin.

"Later," Aaron called out.

"What?"

"I could feel you watching my ass." Aaron leaned back around the archway with a grin. "If we ever want to do anything other than talk about making a game, we need to finish at least one page of your notes."

How were they Gray's notes? They'd worked up the list together.

Before Gray could say so, Aaron disappeared again. Gray listened to the sound of him in the kitchen. The clink of fresh ice inside the glasses. The thump of the freezer door closing and the whisper of the refrigerator opening. The pouring of liquid—almost obscenely loud in the quiet house.

Gray picked up his phone and put on some music. Not the best sound system, but not the worst, either. He'd just put it down, when Aaron returned, carrying their refilled glasses.

Aaron handed one over and raised the other in a brief toast. "Cheers."

Gray murmured a mostly nonverbal response before draining half the glass. Why was he so thirsty? Could it be a side effect? He reached for his phone to check, then decided now wasn't the time to contemplate what was going on with his body. He then nearly picked up his phone anyway, struck by the sudden urge to check wholesaler prices on artisan flours and ancient grains—the thought no doubt spurred by his need to research *something*. He gripped his knee instead.

"Everything okay?" Aaron asked as he sat.

No. I want you to talk to me. Tell me what's wrong. "Yeah." Had his lips stuck together on the side of his mouth or had he imagined it? "Just managing my new medication."

"How's that going?"

"I think everything is a side effect, including why tonight is so weird."

Aaron's eyebrows pulled down and across. "Why is tonight so weird?"

"I don't know. You can't feel it?"

"Feel what?"

Gray gestured between them. "This. Us. Do we feel off to you?"

Rolling one shoulder through a vague shrug, Aaron said, "Not really. Except that I'm tired and don't feel like talking about the game."

Or anything else, apparently.

Pushing that thought aside, Gray studied the pieces they had laid out. The cards Aaron had painstakingly illustrated, and the piles of notes Gray had penned. For a project that had seemed so big to start with, there wasn't a lot to it. Then again, they had too much material for a simple box—as it stood. Maybe they did need to simplify.

He couldn't remember if he'd been the one to suggest that, or Aaron.

Couldn't recall why it mattered.

He glanced up. "Maybe we should take a break."

Horror competed with sadness for control of Aaron's freckles. Whatever he was feeling, a flush of color declared victory, briefly. Then Aaron was simply pale. He turned away with a jerk of his head and put down his iced tea. He was pushing at the couch cushions when Gray made the connection.

"I didn't mean us." Gray frowned. "Why did you think I meant us?"

"Honestly, I don't know. I guess my mood is strange, is all. I'm having an off night. An off week."

Gray thought back over his own week. The samples he'd baked for Ollie to try, and his plans for the following morning: He'd set his alarm for three and wanted to have two dozen loaves cooling and ready for transport by the time Ollie arrived to pack for the Saturday market downtown.

Weariness edged around him, but it was the good kind. Not the overworked, sick-to-his-stomach stressed kind of tiredness that never seemed to abate. He could admit to some anxiety regarding the failure potential of his market plan, but not overmuch. As Oliver had pointed out, people generally went to farmers' markets to buy food. Providing exactly that was a sound business model.

He tuned back in to Aaron's funk. "Are you sure everything is okay with you? I know I'm the one who said tonight was weird. But—"

"No, I think we're both feeling off."

Not really? But—

"Maybe a break is a good idea."

Urgent panic fluttered in Gray's chest. He squashed it by reaching for Aaron's hand and threading their warm fingers together. "But not for us."

The butterfly smile was back. "Not for us."

"Not every night is going to be sex and seduction." Though Gray could totally go for some seduction about now.

"No." Aaron offered a half grin. "I mean, it could be. But real life is a thing and sometimes we're going to be tired and out of sorts, and it'd be easy to look for fault or blame."

"Right. But we're good." Gray squeezed his fingers. "There's nothing we need to talk about." Right? "It's just tonight. We've hit a place where we need to take a breath."

"It's not the shine wearing off."

Gray shook his head. "Absolutely not. Or the fact I might have counted every freckle you possess."

"Summer is nearly here. I'll produce more."

The thought of Aaron's skin acquiring new freckles was tantalizing. Gray's mouth almost watered. His dick definitely perked up—not so far as to harden, though.

"Is it the game?" Gray asked.

"What do you mean?"

"Do you wish you'd kept it to yourself? You can say yes, I won't be offended." A total, utter lie. But Gray would rather deal with that truth than any of the others surrounding this odd interlude.

"No." Aaron shook his head for emphasis. "No. It's not the game. I really do have a lot going on at work." He shared a smallish smile. "Besides, you have an early start, don't you?"

"I do."

"Then maybe we should turn in." His brow pinched. "Unless you wanted to—"

Gray cut him off with a kiss before pulling back to speak across his lips. "I want to go to bed. With you. I want to make love and fall asleep next to you. And I want to watch you complain sleepily about my alarm at three in the morning. Maybe kiss a few freckles before I leave you to wake up later and alone."

"You're evil." One dimple flashed.

Gray would take it. He moved his lips there, to kiss the hint of a crease beside Aaron's mouth. "Mm-hmm." He dipped a hand toward Aaron's lap. "I could leave now."

Aaron rolled backward onto the couch, pulling Gray with him. "Don't you dare."

Chapter Thirty-Two

Aaron raised his hands for the double clap signaling the end of class, and the class clapped back. The energy on his part was lacking, though. Thankfully, the multitude of adults mopping faces and swigging energy drinks didn't seem to notice.

Except Kevin.

"Not feeling it today?" Kevin pointed an elbow in Aaron's direction, as though to nudge his side.

Aaron tried for a smile. "Schedule's been full lately. Too much work and not enough play."

"I guess that's why I didn't see you for our session this week, huh?"

"What?"

Kevin held up his phone.

Aaron blinked at it, not sure what the gesture meant.

"I got an email explaining that someone called Hector would be taking the session," Kevin explained.

"You *what*?" The heat washing across Aaron's face had little to do with the workout he'd just finished. *He'd* gotten a text listing the appointment as canceled. "Can I see that?" Kevin handed over the phone, and Aaron read the email. "What the ever loving . . ."

Kevin looked confused as Aaron handed the phone back.

Tamping down every emotion but calm rationality, Aaron tried for another smile. It felt about as successful as the last one. "We're expanding the business and want to make sure Hector meets all of our longtime clients."

"Oh."

"How was the workout?"

Kevin shifted uncomfortably.

Aaron dropped his polite pretense. "I'm sorry. I didn't know about this."

"The workout was fine, but a part of the reason I keep renewing my contract is that I enjoy working out with you. I'm not as driven on my own, and you always seem to know when I need to push harder. And I like that we can talk about whatever. Like we're friends."

A real smile tugged at Aaron's mouth. "Thanks, Kevin. I appreciate that. I enjoy working with you as well."

Kevin leaned in, and Aaron squashed the sense things were about to get uncomfortable.

"Hector kept pushing me to download some app he'd designed. Like, a workout tracker? Said I could use it at home to keep up with my progress. I downloaded it because I'm always interested in new tech but— Oh, by the way, my friend Matt? Jatek Games? Sorry, this is why I wanted to talk to you. Not to complain about Hector, not that I am?"

"If you're not happy about any aspect of your training, I always want to hear about it, okay?"

Kevin clapped him on the arm. "See, this is why you're the best trainer they have here. I hope you plan to stay."

Alarm bells began ringing again. "Stay?"

"Hector kind of suggested you might be moving on."

"When?"

"When I asked why I was working out with him and not you."

Instead of heat, Aaron now felt cold. He smoothed a hand over his forearm and touched goose bumps. Also, he was suddenly really, really sad. A little angry—maybe a lot. But whatever upset he felt was almost buried by a deep trough of depression.

So, this was it. Devorah was replacing him entirely. The move didn't make much sense. If they planned to give Hector the new gym, they'd still need someone in Aaron's role here, at the flagship property. Unless Devorah planned to return to training and instructing full-time. With a new baby on the way and a toddler.

He needed to talk to his sister.

"Anyway, like I was saying, my friend Matt is in town. Passing through as he heads west. There's a convention next week in Denver, and he's decided to drive rather than fly so he can transport the games himself. Some mix up with logistics last time. We're having lunch, and I told him about your game, and he'd love to meet you."

Aaron tuned back into the conversation Kevin was having without him. "Me?"

"Yeah, you and your partner. Grayson, right? I wasn't able to tell him much because you still haven't given me a playable version to try out. But from everything you've described, I felt like I had a pretty clear picture. Dude is really interested, man. What do you say? Do you have time to swing by? It's a great opportunity. He usually schedules appointments only at cons or reaches out through a crowdfunding platform, but I talked you guys up."

"That sounds awesome. Thanks. Ah, when?"

"Today! Like, in an hour? I was going to grab a shower and meet him at Marita's. They have that outdoor deck?"

"Right." Marita's was one block along Main Street from Clery's. "I'll text Gray and see if he can meet us there. He had a market this morning, but he should be done by now."

Kevin touched his forehead in salute. "See you in an hour, then."

"Thanks again. Oh, and Kevin? I'm going to talk to Devorah about scheduling. I'll have your training switched back to my roster because I'm not going anywhere and long-term clients are a priority for me. I'm sorry about the mix-up."

With a grin, Kevin left.

Aaron switched on his phone and texted Gray. *You about? Kevin's friend, Matt from Jatek Games, is in town today only and wants to meet us for lunch to talk about the game. Marita's, 2 p.m. If you can come, I'll meet you there? I need to shower and change and get the game from home.*

Aaron checked the time before navigating back to his contact list to call Devorah. The phone rang over to voice mail. "Dev, we need to talk about Hector. Actually, no, we need to talk about me. Are you trying to get me to leave? Because if you are, be up front about it. I know you're disappointed by my decision not to run the new gym, but I feel like you're going out of your way to make me feel bad and it's—" *working.*

Aaron exhaled heavily. His phone vibrated in his hand. Gray had responded to his text: *See you there.*

He returned his attention to the voice mail in time to hear the prompt to send or rerecord his message. He hit Send and pocketed his phone. Then had to resist the pull of gravity. The workout studio was empty and quiet, and the fatigue pressing down on his shoulders was suddenly a lot heavier than it had been five minutes ago.

What the ever-loving fuck?

Blowing out a final sigh, Aaron scooped up his towel and water bottle and made for the door. He'd just left the gym when Devorah pulled into the parking lot. He waited by the curb for her to park and get out of her car.

"I got your message," she said.

"Can we make a time to talk?"

"Are you free now?" She checked her phone. "Leili took Cosmo, Mom, and Dad down to Easton for some book festival, so I'm free for the next hour or so. Then I'll need to be home for the afternoon shift. A two-year-old and Mom and Dad in one afternoon?" She tried for a smile.

Aaron attempted to return it, then stopped trying.

Obviously sensing his mood, Dev gestured toward the front doors of the gym. "Want to talk inside, or . . .?"

"I have an appointment to get to, so can we do it here? Or sit in my car?" Some privacy would probably be best. This was going to be a difficult conversation.

Dev started for his Jeep and Aaron followed. Once they were seated inside, him in the driver's seat, her as a passenger to nowhere, he turned to her and said, "I don't appreciate you taking one of my oldest and best clients and transferring him to Hector's roster. Kevin signed with me to train, and I should be the one to honor that commitment. I interviewed him and set the schedule with him. Hector doesn't know Kevin's goals or how he feels about being here in the first place."

"Wait, what? Slow down. I suggested Hector study your client files. You keep the most up-to-date records of any trainer we have."

"Seriously? That's how you're going to play this?"

"We've always operated the gym as a team, Aaron."

"But those clients are . . ." He wanted to say *mine*, but even unsaid, the word had an ugly echo inside his brain.

"Ours."

"It feels like breaking a promise!"

"The files aren't private."

"Are you listening to me? Hector scheduled a session with Kevin. With *my* client."

Devorah's eyes widened. "He what?" She pulled out her phone. Aaron touched her wrist. "You can deal with that later. Talk to me. Do you want to edge me out? Is that what this Hector business is all about?"

Devorah shook her head. "I just don't get what's up with you. We started this business together. The three of us. Now you want out to go play games for a living?"

"That's not what I want." Aaron sucked at the weirdly thick air inside the car. "But, hey, let's go there for a second. What if I did want to play games for a living? What would be so wrong with that?"

"Are you kidding me right now?"

"The gym isn't my whole life, Dev."

"What's that supposed to mean?"

"I'm not like you or Mom or Dad. I don't live and breathe fitness and health and walking everywhere my legs can take me. I love my job. I do. I love working with clients on their fitness goals. I feel like what we're doing is important. But it's not all I am. I also like gaming and other nerdy stuff. Quiet things. Sedentary things. Worlds I can build inside my head."

Dev's expression suggested he'd slipped into another language.

"You like to watch TV," he tried. "What's your favorite show?"

"What?"

"What do you like to watch on TV?"

"I don't understand the question or what TV has to do with what we're talking about."

"Stories, Dev. There's more to life than what we can see. There's what we imagine too."

"Sometimes it's like I don't know who you are."

A car backed out of the space next to them, and sunlight glanced off the driver's-side window and into Aaron's car, splashing over his sister's face, highlighting the deeper hue of her skin, the healthy tan that Aaron's freckled canvas might never approach, even by the end of summer. Her dark brown hair and eyes a stark contrast with his flame of red and lighter brown. The intensity of her expression and how closely she resembled their mother and father.

How he didn't.

"Even when everyone is related by blood, people can like different things," he said, unsure whether the words were for him or her.

Devorah's forehead wrinkle softened. "I know."

"Then why is this such a big deal?"

She chewed on her lip a moment, gaze directed forward, through the windshield. "I don't know. I think it's . . ." A frown marred her forehead, and for the first time in a while, Aaron was reminded of the gap between them. Dev might only be eight months older, but they'd each had ten years on their own before becoming siblings. "It's all going so fast, you know? The expansion, Leili and I having another kid. And sometimes I feel so old."

"You're not old."

"I'm forty, kiddo. I'm O-L-D old."

"Mom and Dad are O-L-D old and they're still walking all over New England. Well, Dad is. Mom's determined to join every book club between here and Arizona."

"Dad's walking-tour thingy is a book club."

"Our parents are strange."

Dev smiled. "They are, which is probably why we are."

And just like that, the differences between them faded a little again, as though a cloud had passed across the sun to leave the world in a less contrasted state. But the clouds gathering on the horizon were darker and more ominous, and Aaron didn't have time for them right now.

He checked the dash clock. He had twenty minutes left to go home, shower, change, grab the game, and get back downtown. He was going to be late. "Listen, I need to go."

Hurt flashed across Devorah's face. She could probably see the dark clouds too. Their argument, or difference of opinion, was not yet resolved.

Aaron cut off a sigh before it happened. "I know you don't get what I'm trying to do, but . . . Okay, here's the deal. Owning three gyms is your dream. It's what you and Leili planned. And you're super close to achieving that dream. You're excited about it. That's how I feel about getting to meet a game developer today. I get to show him my dream and hopefully that will advance my timeline. I'll be a step closer to achieving it."

She nodded, but said, "I get that. I do. But, Aaron, I thought the gym was *our* dream. All three of us. That's a part of what I don't understand. I thought you'd be thrilled about the expansion plan. You never said you didn't want to run a gym of your own."

Okay, one last sigh, then he was done for the day. "I never said I did, either. When we started this venture, the three of us, what I wanted was to work with you, Dev. My sister and best friend. My *family*. That's one of the reasons I love my job so much. I get to hang out with you every day."

Tears glistened in Dev's eyes, though frustration creased her brow. "How am I supposed to respond to that?"

Aaron shrugged. "You don't."

Dev just wasn't getting it. Aaron *did* want ownership, but not of someone else's dream, and if Devorah didn't understand that, then he'd have to accept the break between them. This permanent gap. Because the opportunity to publish his game was too important.

The *game* was his dream. His and Gray's.

Chapter
Thirty-Three

G ray checked the time on his phone and texted Aaron again: *Are you close?*

While waiting for a reply that might not arrive, he peered through the glass door leading out to the restaurant deck. Kevin, he recognized from the gym. The guy with him was a stranger, but he had a familiar look. It wasn't the pinched brow or glasses, the game logo T-shirt and soft-washed jeans. Not even the slight roundness to the shoulders—although all of these things added up to hours bent over a tabletop or keyboard. He was definitely a gamer. More interesting was the intense way in which he seemed to be listening to Kevin, as though Kevin's words were the most important he'd heard all day.

Gray wasn't at all sure he'd like to be the focus of that attention. Not alone. Aaron needed to get his ass to the restaurant.

He checked his phone again. No messages. Should he call? Or should he lift his chin high and walk into the meeting his partner had arranged and try to sell a game his partner had created?

Christ on a cracker, where was Aaron?

Kevin must be wondering the same thing, because he picked his phone up, frowned at the screen, and put it back down.

Sucking in all the air remaining in the restaurant lobby, Gray squared his shoulders, tucked his notebook of world history under his arm, and approached the doors. He'd just pushed through when Kevin glanced up and smiled.

Kevin filled the same mold of athleticism as Aaron: so fit he radiated good health. He was also lightly tanned and flushed with vitality. Attractive, if you were into the preppy type. Came across as an all-round nice guy.

As Gray arrived at the table, Kevin extended a hand and they shook vigorously.

"Grayson! So glad you could make it." Kevin turned to his friend. "Matt, this is Aaron's partner, Gray."

Matt stood with a smile. He was taller than Gray had expected, and his smile added much needed animation to his face. His skin was a cooler shade of brown than Gray's. His limbs long and lean, his handshake firm.

"Great to meet you." He checked the space behind Gray. "Aaron isn't with you?"

"I think he got caught up at work, then he wanted to run home and grab the game." Gray held up his notebook. "I have a lot of information here, though. I can definitely get us started."

Matt nodded quietly. He didn't seem disappointed, exactly. But not impressed, either.

A server stopped by to clear away the remains of Matt and Kevin's lunch. Gray ordered an iced tea. After she left, he flipped open the notebook, past a few pages of notes and stopped when he got to the best draft of their world history. He put on his most confident smile. "What can I tell you about the game?"

Matt's expression remained neutral. "Kevin mentioned it's card-based? Like a deck-builder survival game?"

Damn, if only Aaron was here. The pieces he'd designed, the cards and terrain tiles, were so much more impressive than a ratty old spiral-bound notebook. "Aaron has the cards and tiles and they are gorgeous. He did the art himself and hand-lettered them all. I think he's been working on the set for three years. We've been looking into getting everything printed for a few prototype sets to give out to game testers. Anyway, it was the cards that drew me into the game at first. I wish you could see them."

"Me too," Matt said.

Gray gathered all the enthusiasm he'd felt the first time he'd seen Aaron's game and pushed that into his voice. "The first card I saw was a wood sprite and while the art grabbed me—Aaron's style is very simple and neatly illustrative—it was the description underneath that was so exciting. You could fight the sprite for control of the forest, netting your character a raw material. Wood. You could live side by side with the wood sprite, effectively leaving the forest intact and gaining an important ally. Or you could trade with them. A middle-of-the-road or compromise move that netted ally points and resource materials. Obviously, a reduced amount of each."

Finally, Matt appeared interested. Beside him, Kevin was nodding.

"That's the beauty of the game, in my opinion. In that there's not one way to play. You don't land on this island and immediately set out to conquer it. Though, if you want to, you can play that way. Nor do you necessarily need to make friends. But you can do that too." Was he being too vague? "You, um, do you. What I mean is, that you pretty much play however you want."

"What's the goal?" Matt asked.

Gray opened his mouth, but no words came calling. Instead, a horrible blankness seemed to roll up out of his midsection. What was the goal? Had he and Aaron ever discussed it? Frowning, he flipped through a few pages of his notebook, searching for inspiration. "Ah, the winning conditions are—"

"No, I mean, why should I play this game? What do I get out of it?"

Glancing at Kevin provided no help. His eyes were wide and panicked. While Aaron had obviously discussed the game with him, it couldn't have been in great detail. Gray resisted the urge to flip through his notebook again and steepled his fingers together. Hopefully, he gave the impression of thought.

Fuck, where was Aaron?

"For me, it's about exploration." What was it Aaron had said? Discovery? No. Free will? Survival? "It's a survival game, but one that breaks the mold."

Interest again glinted in Matt's dark eyes.

"It's not about who wins the game, it's about what you do on the island while you're there. How you, as a player shape it. It's, ah, a story, that you're building yourself, and the tools you . . ."

Was that shine interest or were Matt's eyes glazing over?

A muffled thump and crash sounded behind him. Gray turned and nearly fell out of his chair in relief. Aaron had finally arrived—only to apparently trip through the door and lose hold of the game box, which had, of course, fallen open to spill cards and tokens everywhere.

People were hopping out of their seats to help pick everything up. Cards fluttered in the light breeze, and one slipped between a crack in the deck. Gray sank to his knees after it, but his fingers grasped only air. He hoped it hadn't been the wood sprite.

"Sorry," Aaron said as he flapped his hands around. He was blushing, his face nearly as red as his hair. He looked freaked out and stressed. More so than he should be.

Gray touched his arm. "Is everything okay?"

Aaron shook his head. "No. Everything is not okay. How about here?"

"Sort of okay? Can you see the wood sprite card?"

"What?"

"I started with that, and I feel like he needs to see it."

Aaron sat back on his heels. "Did you tell him about your history?"

"Not yet."

"I thought you'd start with that."

Gray pushed up to sit on his knees. "I thought you'd be here with the cards."

"Fuck. I'm sorry."

At a slight gasp next to him, Aaron glanced over. Gray did too and winced as the mother of a younger child remonstrated them with a glare.

Sorry, Gray mouthed.

Aaron had finished gathering up the cards and tiles but the box was a mess. Everything inside jumbled together.

"Guys?"

Matt stood over them. Gray got to his feet and offered Aaron a hand up. Before Matt could speak again, Gray quickly performed introductions. "Aaron, this is Matt Jatek. Matt, Aaron Asher, the genius behind the game."

Aaron shouldn't have been able to blush any harder, but he somehow managed. At this rate, his hair was going to disappear or catch fire. Aaron mumbled and shoved the box at Matt.

Matt frowned at the mess of cards and tokens. Gray thought he might be about to shake his head and make excuses, but then he snagged a card. It wasn't the wood sprite. It was a terrain tile—mountain meets coast line. A jagged line of rock curving from one corner to the opposite corner with an impression of blue water on one side, and shadowed stone on the other.

He glanced up at Aaron. "You drew this?"

Aaron made a soft gasp.

"He did." Gray sifted through the box for a creature, any creature, and pulled out a rock troll. "And this. All of them. It's beautiful, isn't it?"

"Excuse me." A server with a tray as wide as the space they all stood in wanted to get through.

"Let's head into the lobby," Kevin said, leading the group off the deck and into the cool and relatively dim vestibule between the deck and the restaurant proper.

Matt dropped the card back into the box. "Listen, I need to hit the road. I want to make it to Pittsburgh tonight. But it was great to meet you guys." He slipped two fingers into his back pocket and pulled out a wrinkled card. He held it out between Gray and Aaron.

Gray took it. Aaron seemed unable to move. Or speak.

"When you've got a game to show me, give me a call." Matt's smile was friendly. Not sympathetic or empathetic or slanted in any way that might convey how he felt—whether he imagined Aaron or Gray would ever have a game to show him or if he even cared. He was just a nice guy. A really nice guy.

And somehow, Gray and Aaron had absolutely failed to impress him.

Kevin's face told the truer story. Mild disappointment mixed with embarrassment. He spoke softly to Aaron as he passed and shot a quick, sympathetic look in Gray's direction. Gray glanced behind him to confirm the wooden bench lining the wall was still there, and sat.

Aaron continued to stand in front of him, hands clutched around the box, which was missing a lid.

The doors to the deck flipped open again. The server. She had Gray's notebook. She brightened when she saw him. "There you are." In her other hand, she held his glass of iced tea. "Did you still want this?"

Twenty minutes later, Aaron still hadn't said a word. Gray had started to speak several times, managing only "What...?" "Where...?" and "Fuck." Which, really, was the word of the day. Now they were sitting across from each other in the nook off Gray's kitchen, two glasses of water on the table and an open canister of peanuts in front of Gray because he was hungry, damn it, and peanuts (in moderation) were on the heart-healthy list.

He'd rather a burger and about half a bottle of bourbon, but dying right now would only make things more awkward.

"I'm sorry." Aaron finally looked up from his box. He hadn't stopped clutching it or staring into it since they'd left the restaurant. "I'm sorry I was so late. I got caught up at the gym, and then I couldn't find anything to wear." He was dressed in jeans and a long-sleeved T-shirt. How hard had those been to find? "Like, I didn't know if I should dress up or down or in gamer-type stuff or workout gear or a suit. I just, kind of, like— Have you ever had a panic attack?"

Whatever Aaron had experienced while choosing his outfit was clearly still happening. His eyes were wide, face still flushed an unhealthy shade of red, lips somehow pale and cracked.

Gray reached across the table to grip his hand. "No. Unless a heart attack counts."

Aaron's eyebrows twitched together.

"Sorry. Bad joke." But was it? "What happened? What got you so rattled?"

"I don't know if this is what I should be doing."

Gray strove for calm before answering. "What do you mean?"

"The game. I was making it for me, before. No one was ever supposed to see it. Then my mom found it and you saw it, and everyone made such a big deal out of it, and I don't feel like it's ... It's not what it was."

A ball of lead took up residence in Gray's gut. "Shit." He was going to exhaust his modest collection of curse words in one day. "I'm sorry."

"Don't be." Aaron sounded so dejected, though. "I mean, did we really think we could make something out of this? It was a hobby. Not my job. And now I might have to rethink my job and for what? A box of badly-drawn cards."

Oh, boy. "First of all . . . No, fuck it. Seriously?" Gray let the anger fizzing through him take hold for a second or two. "I get that today sucked. Bad timing and maybe we weren't ready. Doesn't mean we can't try again. But if you're so down on the game, if you didn't want to do this project, why didn't you say anything?" He beat the anger back again and felt frustration slip into the space left behind. "I've been writing and revising history stuff for weeks now. How long have you felt this way?"

Aaron looked pained. "I don't know. Awhile?"

"Awhile? How long?"

"Today? Yesterday? Last week? I don't know!"

Rationally, Gray knew Aaron was upset about . . . Actually, he didn't know what Aaron was so distressed about, only that he was. Well, Gray was upset too. And he also didn't exactly know why. Lunch had not gone well, but Jatek Games wasn't the only publisher and a publisher wasn't the only path to launching a game. If they wanted to do this, they had a dozen ways of getting it done.

The question, it seemed, was whether they wanted to keep trying. There might also be a *what*, as in what should they be trying. Because Aaron was upset about more than the game.

Aaron's chair squawked as he pushed it back. "I think I'm going to go." He glanced up from the table. "I'm going to . . . go."

Gray got up too. "You don't want to talk about it?"

"About what, Gray?"

"The game, or what happened today." *Us.* "Are you—"

"No, I'm not okay. I need to go home and get changed and go for a run. I feel like my life is spinning out of control, and I need to get back to what works for me."

"Can I help?"

Aaron shook his head. "No. I'll call you."

Uh-huh.

Before Aaron could disappear through the front door, Gray grabbed his wrist, circling the knobby joint gently but firmly. Aaron's sleeve pulled up just enough to reveal the trailing end of one of his elaborate tattoos.

"Aaron."

Aaron looked at him.

"I know today didn't go how we wanted it to, and I understand needing time to think. But if you don't call me later, or at least text, I'll text you. Or call. Because I care. A couple weeks ago, we talked about what we were doing, outside the game, and I thought we were on the same page with that. About friendship and more. I'm telling you now—" he pointed between them "—it's more. Don't go bailing on that without talking to me first, okay?"

He half expected Aaron to shake him off. The guy was obviously in distress. Instead, Aaron gave a slow nod. He leaned in, touched his lips to the corner of Gray's mouth, and then he was gone.

As Gray shut the door, he worked to put aside a feeling of finality. A familiar band of tension squeezed his chest. Had Aaron's kiss meant anything, besides being a way to end the conversation? Would he answer Gray's texts? Should Gray text at all?

Keys scraped against the lock, and the door pushed into his hands. Gray stepped out of the way to let his dad in.

He took one look at Gray's face, glanced toward the stairs—he'd have passed Aaron on his way up—and turned back to Gray. "How did the market go?"

Gray's mind blanked for the second time that day. Then he remembered how his morning had started. With a three-o'clock wakeup call. The quiet solitude of Oliver's kitchen, breakfast with Ollie while they packed for the market, and the fat wad of cash still stuffed into an envelope on the desk in his bedroom. He hadn't baked a lot for his first time out, but he'd sold everything and had taken a couple of orders for the week ahead.

His day had started well. The market had gone *well*.

Then Aaron had texted.

Gray couldn't describe the tightness in his chest except to say it wasn't a heart attack. Must be close, though. He turned away from the door and saw the game box still sat on the kitchen table.

Not a heart attack, no. The soreness that came after, as though his chest was bruised. He glanced back at his dad.

"So, this is what love feels like," he mused.

"What did you think it was going to feel like? Falling off a log?"

Well, no. But . . . "We were just getting to the good stuff." Planning for the future was supposed to be the good stuff, right?

His dad squeezed his arm. "Wish I could tell you it gets easier."

Thanks? But what did he expect, really? Life wasn't easy. He and his dad both knew that.

Chapter Thirty-Four

When Gray didn't show up for his Tuesday workout, Aaron was more relieved than disappointed. As promised, Gray had texted over the weekend. Aaron hadn't answered. Twice, he'd begun to, and then he'd started thinking about the lunch, what a jerk he'd been afterward, the situation with his sister and the gym, and had ended up lost for words.

Until he finished sorting out how to manage the difference between his and his sister's ambitions, the rest of his life was in a holding pattern. And sorting the situation with Dev was going to take more than a text. More than the stiff, not-really-there smiles they forced upon each other around the gym. It also couldn't happen at the gym. Too many glass walls and none of them thick enough to muffle the sound of argument.

As Tuesday wound toward a close, Aaron tugged his phone from his pocket. Gray hadn't sent his evening check in, yet. Aaron read over the morning one.

Making walnut bread this morning. Thinking about you.

Aaron's smile hurt. He returned to his contact list and poked his sister's name. Sent her a quick text. *Can you stop by my house tonight?*

A shadow moved in the periphery of his vision. Aaron glanced toward the glass wall of Dev's office and watched as she picked up her phone. After reading his text, she gave him a nod through the window.

When he pulled into his driveway that evening, light shone from the living room window of his house. Devorah knew where he hid his spare key, but it was doubtful she'd have let herself in. Not while they were whatever they were. That meant his mom and possibly his dad were there.

He'd spoken to his dad on the phone yesterday, but the conversation had been strained. Mostly on Aaron's end. And when his dad had asked him what was wrong, the familiar need to say nothing had closed Aaron's throat. Why was it so hard to share what he was feeling? Thinking, even?

And now, when all he wanted to do was fall facedown onto his bed, his parents were camped out at his house.

With a sigh, Aaron heaved himself out of the Jeep and gazed up the driveway toward the front door. Maybe he could sneak into the basement and hide out in the laundry until everyone left.

The front door opened, and his mom poked her head out. She waved. "I thought I saw your lights. C'mon. We saved some dinner for you."

Aaron lifted one hand in a wave. "Be right there."

Once inside, Aaron caught the aroma of meatballs and his mom's signature red sauce. His stomach rumbled. Pasta wasn't generally on his menu—not that he didn't love his carbs. Everything in moderation and all. But he did try to pack his meals with as much nutritional bang for his calorie buck as possible, so pasta rarely made the list. But after the day he'd had, he could go for a big bowl of comfort food.

He glanced around for his sister and noted the newspapers, real estate flyers, and architectural drawings spread across the dining room table. The rumor his parents were thinking of returning to Pennsylvania appeared to be true. His dad cleared a space by one of the chairs, and his mom set down a bowl of reheated spaghetti for him.

"What can I get you to drink?" she asked.

"A glass of milk." Aaron nodded toward the paperwork. "So, what's all this?"

His mother and father shared a smile before his father answered the question. "Your mom wants to move back to Pennsylvania."

Aaron immediately imagined a future where his parents never found a house and lived with him forever.

His mom sat next to him and squeezed his shoulder. "Don't worry, we're not going to stay with you while we look for a house. We're thinking of building, and that could take months. Maybe a year."

Aaron swallowed a half-chewed meatball and winced as it threatened to lodge in his throat. "You're always welcome here. You know that. It's been great having you here for the past six months." She laughed and patted his shoulder. "You. It's been six weeks."

More like eight. He aimed a tired grin in her direction before resuming his meal.

His dad sorted through the paperwork until he found a plan and slid that across the table. "Check out this one. There's a community out near Hazleton we like. They have two lakes, a ski slope, mountain bike trails, hiking paths, three pools, and an eighteen-hole championship golf course."

Aaron blinked. "That's . . . a lot of amenities."

"They also have a huge social calendar. Clubs galore." His mom beamed.

"Book clubs and walking clubs?"

His parents exchanged another look, and the smile they shared pulled at his heart. That they'd evidently resolved the issue that had led to separate spring vacations didn't surprise him. His parents had been married for fifty-five years, after all. They were one of those couples who communicated in paragraphs without saying a single word. Another chunk of meatball caught somewhere between his tonsils and esophagus, and Aaron forced it down with a painful swallow. The hurt moved from his throat to his chest, where it lay heavily over his heart.

He wanted that, the deep connection his parents shared. He always had. He'd thought he had something like it with his sister, but the events of the past couple of weeks had left him drained and unsure, while his dream of establishing a similar connection with Gray had been reduced to a series of texts Aaron was too self-absorbed to answer.

Undigested spaghetti stirred in his gut. Aaron burped and winced.

"Everything okay?" His father wore his concerned-dad expression: eyebrows bunched and pinched together. Chin tilted to the left. His dark brown eyes held myriad emotions, and Aaron could absolutely see why his parents were such a good match. His mom was the talker, his dad the listener.

Aaron put down his fork. "I asked Devorah to come over tonight. To talk about the gym. I thought she'd . . ." A sigh gusted out as he pushed back from the table and got to his feet. "I think I'm going to get a shower."

His mom touched his arm. "You can talk to us."

"About what?"

"About whatever is going on with you. You've been quiet all week."

"It's only Tuesday."

"Since Saturday, then." Her brow pinched. "You had something on Saturday, didn't you? I'm sorry—to do with your game?"

"What game?" his dad asked.

"Oh, Aaron's been developing a board game with his boyfriend."

Aaron squeezed his eyes shut. He had no idea what his face looked like, but when he opened his eyes, both of his parents were staring at him.

"I'd ask about trouble in paradise, but I don't want to sound flippant." His dad patted the table. "Sit back down, son. Let's talk."

Aaron shook his head. "I'm fine. I just need some sleep."

"I'd really like to hear about your game."

His dad's tone didn't render the words *your game* into anything diminutive or unimportant. Aaron's imagination did that. Still, he couldn't help replying, "It's not important."

Except it was—and not only because he'd messed up a golden opportunity. He'd failed before. Maybe not quite so spectacularly. No one got through life without a few missteps. But right now he needed to sit with himself for a while and figure out what he wanted.

"Aaron." His mother's tone wasn't exactly sharp, but it did catch his attention.

The doorbell rang. They all turned to the door, before his mom went to answer it.

Even from the dining table, Aaron could see Devorah's eyebrows fly upward. "Mom." She peered over their mom's shoulder and saw Aaron and their dad at the table. Her gaze landed on him, and the years crumbled away as Aaron clearly read her thoughts.

Devorah assumed he'd called in reinforcements.

"I didn't know they were going to be here," Aaron said.

His mom and dad exchanged a glance. Devorah seemed to hover over the doorstep, indecision buzzing around her like a cloud of mosquitos. Then her forehead creased. "You made Aaron spaghetti and meatballs?"

His parents laughed, and his mom pulled Devorah inside. "We had a favor to ask him, so I thought I'd cook his favorite dinner first."

So they *were* planning to stay with him for a while. Somehow, the thought wasn't as awful as it should have been.

The inertia holding Aaron by the table dissipated. "Can we talk?"

He beckoned Devorah toward the other end of the house, the short hall leading to the bedrooms. She followed him into his room, and he shut the door after her.

"Sorry, I didn't know they'd be here."

She waved him off. "They'll do what they do, no help from us."

"Well, it's official. They're planning to move back to Pennsylvania."

"I figured they would."

"Oh?"

Devorah took a deep breath and held it. Then she nodded toward his bed. Aaron sat and she sat beside him. Exhaled slowly. Then she took his hand, and the gesture was so unexpected, Aaron nearly snatched his fingers back.

"I'm sorry, baby bro."

He gaped.

"I hate that we're still not okay. You're my best friend too and not being able to talk to you about *you* has been driving me nuts."

"You have Leili."

"Believe me, she's tired of hearing it. And of saying I told you so."

"What did she tell you?"

"That you didn't want to run a gym of your own."

Aaron let his head flop backward on his neck so he was gazing at the ceiling.

Devorah cupped the back of his skull. "God, I hate it when you do that. Your neck looks broken."

He straightened and shot her a weak smile. Then he issued an apology of his own. "I'm sorry too."

"For what?"

The shrug was reflexive, and Aaron thought about his answer a moment longer before giving it. "Not talking to you, I guess. I mean, we've talked, but we've mostly been yelling about what we want and it's clear, or should be by now, that we want different things."

"What do we do about it?"

Aaron turned slightly so he could face his sister. "If I refuse to head the new gym, are you going to continue forcing me out?"

Devorah's mouth opened, her chin dropping almost to the point of dislocation. Then she smacked his shoulder. "Aaron Anton Asher. How could you ask that?"

"Hector."

"Hector is history with a capital *H*. We've already contacted our other top candidate to make an offer."

"And me?"

"I couldn't run Stroudsburg without you. You are the life and soul of that gym." A light frown wrinkled her forehead. "That's why I thought you would be so good at running a gym of your own. Your energy and enthusiasm. But I do see why it's what makes you perfect where you are. I do. And I'm sorry I pushed you so hard."

"Why did you? Push me so hard?"

"I . . . don't know. I think a part of it was wanting something to go forward."

Aaron took a turn at frowning. "Is everything all right with you and Leili?"

She gripped his hand. "Yes. I just . . . House renovations, a new baby, and a new gym? It's a lot and I feel like I'm running in place. Doing a lot and getting nothing done."

He could see that. Devorah and Leilani had put enormous pressure on themselves to do everything at the same time. But they often worked that way. They were the sort of people who thrived under pressure and withered when life was too dull.

"It is a lot," he said. Her lips pulled into a wry smile, and she leaned her head against his shoulder. Aaron curled an arm around her back. "You know I'll help out all I can. But."

"But."

For one shining moment, his immediate future felt clear. Purpose had found him, and his next words came easily. "For the foreseeable future, my after hours focus is going to be the game I'm developing with Gray."

"It's that important to you."

"It's a dream, Dev. One I've harbored for a long time."

"One you never shared with me."

"No."

"I'm sorry you didn't feel you could." She studied him for a long, quiet moment. "Want to tell me what happened on Saturday? I gather it wasn't good."

Aaron told her about the disastrous non-lunch. After the conversation they'd just had, he expected she'd show some sympathy regarding his big break into board-game publishing having gone sideways but the tight curl of her arm around his shoulders surprised him.

"I'm so sorry, Aaron. That must have sucked."

Tears stung his eyes. "The worst of it is that I feel like I let Gray down. He's all in on this game, and I messed up the meeting so badly." He aimed a quick glare in her direction. "And dealing with you and Hector on Saturday morning didn't help."

"No. I guess not." She rubbed his shoulder. "Again, I'm sorry I've been so inflexible." She jerked her chin toward the bedroom door. "I was worried about them, too."

"Yeah."

Devorah drew in another deep breath. Let it out. "Let's not do this again. We're going to fight. Family does that. But let's not . . . If I start to get unreasonable, if I'm not listening to you, tell me to take a step back. Those exact words. I'll try to remember anyway, but if you remind me, I'll think of this conversation and how awful the past few weeks have been, and I'll remember to step back, take a breath, and examine why I'm so upset." She caught his gaze. "Because it wasn't you. I mean, it was totally you. I wanted so badly for you to run the new gym. But it also wasn't you."

Aaron grinned. "That's clear."

With a suspiciously choked-up chuckle, Devorah withdrew her arm and nudged him in the side with her elbow.

"Take a step back, big sister."

"You first, baby bro."

She fell on him, and they mock wrestled for a few seconds before a knock rapped at the door. His dad called through. "Are those sounds of murder or laughter?"

Aaron sat up and pulled his sister up with him. "Both?"

Devorah stood and tugged him off the bed. "C'mon. I want some spaghetti."

"Mom didn't make it for you."

"Says you."

Outside the open door, their dad looked from one to the other and smiled. "That's better."

Aaron shoved Dev gently forward. "Go on, I need to make a call."

"Gray?" she asked.

"Gray?" his dad echoed.

"Boyfriend," his mom supplied. She'd arrived to join the party in the narrow hall. "Lovely man. Bakes the most amazing bread." She faced Aaron again. "Everything's okay between you two, isn't it?"

"No, it's not. I was an ass on Saturday. Completely wrapped up in this B.S. with Dev, and I messed up this lunch deal where we were supposed to show the game to a developer. Then, afterward, I kind of blew him off, and Gray so does not deserve that. Especially from a guy he took a chance on." Aaron smacked the wall lightly. "He has a ton of his own stuff going on and . . . God, I am not the person I thought I was."

His dad was now wearing a full grin.

"What?" Aaron snapped.

"Welcome to forty, son."

"I am not having a midlife crisis."

"Of course not. You're just questioning everything you ever thought and believed and finally figuring out what you want. Happens to the best of us." His dad's grin managed to spread further. "Good news? Once you sort everything out, you'll get to do it again. It's called life."

"Gee, thanks." But though Aaron didn't have time for a *this is life* speech from his father, the words were already burrowing into his consciousness. He'd been coasting for a while now, living in a bubble of his own making. Now it seemed as though everyone had a pin: his sister, parents . . . Gray.

Aaron could go in search of a patch kit, but there was another path open to him. The braver course, and it definitely wasn't the road less traveled. Or maybe it was? He needed to learn to live outside the lines. He wanted to. And the first step along that road was getting in touch with Gray.

"I'm going to grab that shower," he said.

"Can I see the game afterward?" his dad asked.

"Ah, it's at Gray's place. But I've plenty of others."

"I want to see yours."

"Tomorrow, then."

His family retreated toward the living area, and Aaron locked himself in the bathroom, head throbbing a little, but his heart light. While he waited for the shower to warm up, he sent off a text: *I'm sorry about how I've behaved. I'd like to explain why I've been such a mess. If you're interested in listening? And to talk.*

Then he sent another one. *I miss you.*

Gray's evening check-in still hadn't arrived. Good. He'd see Aaron's text first. Before Aaron could obsess over how and when Gray might reply, he switched off his phone and gave himself over to the steam rolling out of the shower.

Chapter Thirty-Five

"**I**f you could sign here, Mr. Clery? And then turn the page and sign at the bottom. There. Thank you. I need two more signatures."

The lawyer overseeing the sale of the café turned to the next page marked by a perky yellow tab, and Gray's father touched his pen to the indicated spot. With each signature, Gray's stomach collapsed further. By the end of the document, he had a black hole in his midsection and his heart was beating an irregular tattoo.

"You doing okay?" Patty touched his arm.

Gray swallowed against the bitter fluid in his throat and nodded.

"Wendell, will you get him a bottle of water?"

The lawyer's assistant jumped up from the table. "I'll get it. Sorry, I should have offered you all something when you sat down. We have bottled water, sodas—"

"Water is fine." Gray didn't think he could listen to the other suggestions, let alone make a choice. Had his breath felt this weird when he'd been having an actual heart attack?

As opposed to whatever is happening in your chest right now?

He massaged the tender spot over his sternum. Was it sore because he kept subconsciously pressing his fist there and then rubbing the same place afterward? Or was it sore because his heart sometimes beat hard enough to leave a mark? Or was it not sore? Maybe he only imagined it was sore. Or the pain over his heart could be muscle tension referred either from his shoulder or neck.

How many times had Aaron shown him exercises designed specifically to relieve that?

You're so tense.

Yeah, well, he was watching his father sign away a lifelong dream. Gray's legacy. And, no, he was not okay.

The assistant returned with several bottles of water, which he handed around the table. After he retook his seat, the signing continued. Now it was Patty and Wendell's turn, and with every turn of the page, Gray felt as though he were disappearing.

He glanced over at his father. Did his dad feel the same? Could he feel part of his life draining away every time Wendell and Patty touched their pens to the page?

A sudden urge to jump up and cry *stop* warred with the need to start laughing.

He really did not feel well.

Gray uncapped his water and chugged half the bottle. A bubble of fluid caught in his throat, and he coughed trying to swallow. His father thumped him on the back.

"Never could drink water properly," he said, voice quiet. "Tried to drown all the time when you were a kid."

"On water? Like, as a drink?"

His dad smiled. "You don't remember?"

Vaguely. It was hard to turn his thoughts to the long ago with everything that was happening in front of him now. How did one compare with the inexorable death of a dream?

"You okay?" Gray asked his dad.

His father blinked a couple of times before answering with a slow nod. Beneath the table, he sought Gray's hand. They caught fingers and squeezed briefly before letting go.

Patty and Wendell both signed the last page. Now it was time for money to change hands.

The lawyer hefted another thick stack of paper from the pile to her left. "This is the loan agreement."

"That wasn't a part of the sale contract?"

"It was, but the actual terms of the loan are a separate contract."

More signatures. More little deaths. And Gray was a part of this one. He was helping his father finance the loan Patty and Wendell needed to buy the café. Felt like he was giving money to Patty so she could give it back to him—and then pay him a monthly sum for the privilege.

Patty caught his eye as the lawyer moved the contracts over to her side of the table. Silently, she asked him the question of the day. *You okay?*

Gray nodded. He'd like to excuse himself from the table. For all intents and purposes, the deed was done. He didn't need to sign anything else and wanted to go. But he stayed until the last signature was applied and the bank draft for the deposit was passed across. Pleasantries followed, with everyone shaking hands and being polite.

Gray felt as though he was floating. Or some sort of ghost—one able to interact with the real world, but not really a part of it. Then they were outside in the oddly cool afternoon, and everyone was talking about plans for Memorial Day weekend, which was only a week away.

Patty appeared beside him. "Thank you."

"I should be the one thanking you." He put on a brave smile. "You're taking the damn café off our hands."

"Only because you're helping us do so."

Tears misted his vision for a second. Gray blinked them away. "Take care of it, Patty." He hadn't meant to say that. "Don't . . ." He couldn't continue.

She squeezed his arm again. "I won't."

"You don't even know what I was going to say."

"Don't run it into the ground? Don't ever forget your mother started this business, and that her stamp is all over the shop, from the menu to the fixtures to the bell hanging over the front door."

"I remember the day she hung that bell." Gray winced into a smile. "It's one of the few things that hasn't changed over the past twenty-five years." He touched Patty's hand, the one she had wrapped around his biceps. "Change whatever you want. The café is yours now."

"Just you remember it's still in the family and that whatever changes we might eventually make, we'll continue to honor her memory. We'll never change the name."

Gray nodded, although he didn't really care about the name, did he? Heck, he didn't know what he felt about anything, except for the fact his heart hurt and his head hurt too.

And underneath all of it, he missed Aaron.

He'd answered the texts from last night with a simple: *Missing you too. Can we get together to talk?*

Aaron hadn't replied, resuming the pattern of the past few days. But despite the hurt, Gray was determined to wait at least another hour before checking back. He'd never been the needy type. What he didn't get, though, was why the mess of lunch had impinged so heavily on their relationship. And why Aaron had been the one to make that decision for them. After all, Aaron had been the one to pursue him, not the other way around. Didn't make sense that Aaron would be the one to call for a break. Unless it did?

No clear answers today, my friend.

Gray touched the bruise in the center of his chest. When he looked up, his dad was waiting by the corner for the four-block journey back to the café. Gray fell into step beside him, and they ambled toward Main Street in silence, crossed at the light, walked another two blocks, and turned into a street with access to the alley behind their building.

The sun wouldn't set for another two hours, but it hung low enough in the sky for the air behind the café to grow cool, despite the warmth of the day leaking from the brickwork to either side. The shadows were long and deep, Main Street relatively quiet in that odd lull between late afternoon and the dinner hour.

Gray's thoughts skittered over the wide avenue of possibility that had opened up before him with regards to his career and his personal life. He'd told Patty and Wendell he'd hang about (unpaid) until they were up to speed. He also had plans to start tinkering with the top-floor apartment. And he had new bread recipes to try. Markets to bake for and a couple of personal orders.

Things weren't *all* bad.

His dad cleared his throat and Gray glanced up.

Aaron was waiting by the rear door of the café.

After muttering to himself, his dad turned back to him and said, "I'm going to walk back across the street to Freeman's. I feel like a burger. You're both welcome to join me when you're finished here." In other words, *Clean up the freckled mess by the door.* "I'll be at the bar."

His dad disappeared around the corner of the lane, leaving Gray alone with Aaron and again contemplating a canvas he found intimidating. This one wasn't blank, though. Delicate images scrolled out from the edges to leave the middle empty. Aaron was a project half done.

Before Gray could say that, or figure out how he felt about anything at all, Aaron stepped forward and held up his hands. "I'm not only here to talk at you. I'm going to listen to what you have to say. Every word. I know some of it I'm not going to like, but I'll listen, because I deserve whatever you have to throw at me. But if it's okay with you, I'd like to say something first. A few somethings, actually. Then you can do or say, um, whatever."

Gray breathed out quietly. Relief that he didn't have to go first warred with a niggle of anger he couldn't quite place.

Aaron lowered his hands. "To begin with—"

"Can we do this upstairs?"

"Oh." Aaron looked at the building behind him as though he hadn't noticed it before. "Yeah, sure. I mean, if you want me to come in."

"It's not like you killed my dog or anything. Of course you can come in."

A brief smile visited Aaron's mouth, tight and uncomfortable. He followed Gray upstairs, through the door, and into the dining nook, where they sat across from each other at the small table.

Folding his hands in front of him, Gray waited.

Aaron said nothing.

"To begin with," Gray prompted.

"Right . . ." Aaron swallowed, his Adam's apple bobbing sharply against his throat. "I'm sorry. About lunch, the mess I made of it, my attitude afterward, not answering your texts, and generally being absent and assholish over the past few days. I have no excuse. I'm not going to try to offer an excuse. But I would like to explain where I was at, if I could."

Was Gray supposed to respond or—

"I told you a bit about what's happening at the gym," Aaron continued. "With the new expansion and how my sister and her wife wanted me to head it up, and that I didn't want to do that. I told them I didn't want to manage the new gym, and Dev didn't take it well. Even though we're months away from opening the new property, she hired someone for the job and he pretty much took over the gym where I work now. I have . . . I'm not taking *that* well."

A grimace pushed dimples into both cheeks before his expression faded to worry once more.

"See, through everything I've tried and tried to be, being a personal trainer and gym instructor is what fits best. That and playing games—which is probably because when I play, I get to be someone else, and when I started making my game, it was to serve that need, I guess. I could be anyone. I could do anything. The island was a fresh start, each and every time."

"That could have been our pitch." Gray flexed his fingers. Was his notebook close by? He should be writing this down.

"Huh?"

"Sorry, didn't mean to interrupt."

"Oh, okay." Aaron seemed off-kilter. Eyebrows lowering, he peered across the table at Gray. "You . . . don't seem all that upset. Or angry." Complicated emotions ran across his face. He started pushing his chair back. "Should I—"

"Sit down, Aaron."

Aaron sat.

Gray let the sigh building inside his lungs gust out. "My dad and I sold the café today. Signed, sealed, and delivered." He pulled the folded cashier's check out of his pocket. "This is all that remains of my mom and dad's dream. My legacy." He smoothed the crease in the middle. "What I can't decide is whether this simple piece of paper represents success or failure."

A groan exited Aaron's lips. "Damn. I'm sorry." He touched Gray's knuckles. "I should have been there. How are you doing? Do you want to talk about it?"

"There you go again." Gray shot Aaron a sideways smile.

Aaron looked confused. "What?"

"I appreciate the offer, but right now, I'd rather you talk. Or keep talking. Let me in, Aaron. You're always there for me. Always. I want you to let me be here for you."

Panic flittered across Aaron's face. He shook it away. "I . . . How did everything get so messy? I mean, last week, everything was fine, and now everything is so not fine. Like, I don't even know what 'fine' means anymore. What happened?"

Gray snorted. "Life™. By the same people who bring you All the Fuss and Love Makes No Sense."

"What did you say?" A flush crept across Aaron's cheeks.

"You heard me, Sporty."

"Should I, um . . . Do you want me to acknowledge that?"

"What?"

Aaron rolled a hand through the air. "The last thing you said. The, um— About love."

And there it was. The spark. The glint of humor that had been missing from Aaron's eyes and the corresponding shine from Gray's soul. The connection—the one he'd been so sure had been lost.

Gray leaned back in his chair and smiled. "Oh, I think you should talk awhile first."

Chapter Thirty-Six

R ight, so, where was he? Apologizing. How creative could he get? And when could he stop using words and start using his body to show Gray how sorry he was?

As though sensing the direction of Aaron's thoughts, Gray let his smile tilt up on one side. "After. We should finish talking first."

Aaron reached across the table to brush Gray's hand. "I have spent a good part of my life wondering who I am and what I want. Know what I figured out last night? I already know who I am. I'm me. I know—huge stuff, but sometimes it's hard to grasp the disparate parts of yourself and imagine them as a whole. As for what I want?" He tapped the back of Gray's fingers. "You. Ever since I first saw you, I've wanted you. Not just physically, though I'm willing to spend the next however many years scratching that itch."

The corresponding heat in Gray's dark gaze suggested that had been, if not the right thing, then a good thing to say. Aaron allowed a sliver of a smile and extended one finger to stroke the back of Gray's hand. Just once, though. He still had some explaining to do, and then he had to work out whether Gray's calm and reasonable demeanor was good or bad.

"Working on the game with you has been— I want to say an honor and a privilege, but that makes it all sound way grander than it is, and as though we're planning a funeral. What I mean is that I had no idea we'd click so neatly."

Gray caught his hand, and slid their fingers together. "Am I allowed to talk, or do you want me to wait until you're done."

"Go ahead."

"That bit about the itch?"

Aaron winced.

"Nah, don't do that. It's . . . Yeah. I get what you mean because, if I'm honest, I thought that's all you were at first. An itch I needed to scratch. Me being into you made no sense whatsoever. You're so damn fit, sitting near you feels like a competition."

Before Aaron could articulate his thoughts on that, Gray moved on. "Listen, I get it, okay? I know how much you've put into the game and Saturday was bad. I was pretty crushed and it's not even my project."

"But it is."

At Gray's gentle glare, Aaron snapped his mouth closed.

"Let me finish. Yeah, I'm involved now, and Saturday sucked. But I've been thinking about why I was so down about it, and I think it's because I literally have no idea what to do next."

"Now that the café is sold?"

"Yep." Sad was not a good look on Gray.

"Want to talk about the itch instead?"

Gray laughed and squeezed Aaron's fingers. Sobering, he said, "I didn't want to want you. I'm not sure why. Probably because I was so caught up in the day to day of the café and the feeling of it bouncing out of my hands like a collection of marbles. I couldn't keep them together. Every aspect of running the business made me feel like a failure. Then, in one horrible moment, I nearly lost it all."

"And you realized how much you cared?"

Gray was shaking his head. "No, that was just it. I didn't. Care, that is, about the café. Once I had an excuse not to go in every day, I found it ridiculously easy not to go. The most torturous part of my recovery, apart from your workouts, was trying to make myself go back to work."

"You're glad you sold the business, then?"

Gray gazed at the check he'd left on the table and shrugged. "I . . . don't know. Right now, it's a yes and a no. I'm relieved, but I don't know what's next."

"Let's talk about what you don't want, then. Narrow it down?"

"I thought we were talking about the itch."

Laughter bubbled up inside Aaron's chest and it felt good. Being with Gray felt good. "Damn, I should have stayed on Saturday. I'm sorry, Gray. And I'm sorry I didn't answer your texts."

"Ain't no big thing."

"How can you say that? I love being with you. I have no idea why I didn't want to be with you this week. I think . . ." Aaron sucked in a sharp, self-revelatory breath. "I was embarrassed. I didn't want you to see me so wrecked."

"Man, you saw me nearly die and helped me recover afterwards. Want to take that back?"

Gray's eyes were kind, but the set of his shoulders, the tension in his neck, urged Aaron to be vulnerable.

Aaron found himself nodding in agreement. "You're right."

"Mm-hmm."

"Where do we go from here?"

"We decide whether this is us getting at what itches, or more."

"I want more." Wow, that was fast. *Could we think about it a little first, please?* But when Aaron consulted his self, his core of deep-down wants, the answer was as immediate. And the same. "With you. That's why I'm here, now, asking you to forgive me for being an ass."

Gray smiled. "Good. Because for all we shouldn't fit, we somehow do. But if we're going to do this, we need to do it right. I want to see you vulnerable too." He moved his thumb over the inside of Aaron's hand, teasing his palm. "You know all about my health, my career, my dad, my mom. Let me in, Aaron. Share it all with me. Not just the sexy parts, but the messy parts."

The thought of opening himself up to Gray—to anyone—had tension creeping up the back of Aaron's shoulders. But the warmth of Gray's hand around his served as a perfect metaphor for how Gray made him feel. Exposed, yes. But not necessarily in a bad way.

Gray saw him. Gray knew who he was. Aaron could be utterly himself—had been. And Gray would not turn away.

Aaron exhaled. His shoulders sank from a height he'd been unaware they'd attained. He nodded slowly and repeated his earlier words, as though in affirmation. "I want more." Then. "I want this. I want you."

"I want you too." Gray frowned, his eyebrows pinching up and together.

"Should you look like you're in pain when you say that?"

With his free hand, Gray massaged the center of his chest. "That expression, you know the one. Love hurts? I can confirm that it does."

Warmth flowed between them, sparking from the connection between their hands, flickering over Aaron's wrist, and zipping up his arm. Piercing the center of his chest. "It's a good hurt, though." Aaron touched the spot over his heart. "It's not a pain. It's more a feeling of a breath being held and the strain inside your lungs."

"And not knowing whether to breathe out or keep holding it in."

Aaron grinned. Gray *did* feel the same way he did. "I never expected you to like me back. To maybe love me. You were a dream, Gray. Someone I thought I'd always have to admire from afar."

"If there's one thing All the Fuss has taught me, it's that sometimes you need to consider life from a different angle."

Aaron decided to test the words out loud. "I love you." That feeling of holding his breath? Oh, yeah. And he might not ever exhale again.

"I love you too."

Okay, phew, air was rushing back out. Aaron laughed over his relieved sigh.

Gray grinned back at him. "Now we've got that part sorted, let's figure out what we're going to do about everything else."

Aaron groaned. "Ugh, can't that be enough for one day? We should be pulling off our clothes. Figuring out a way to have sex on that thing you call a bed."

"Or we could wait until we get back to your place. Your bed is much more accommodating."

"I now have my mother *and* my father staying with me."

"Dude."

"I know. I know."

Laughter rolled across the table. Gray's eyes squeezed nearly shut, his lips spread wide, and his gorgeous skin glowed with health and amusement. He looked about as good as Aaron had ever seen him.

When he finally sobered, Aaron tapped the table. "I think the first order of business is what to do with our parents."

"Speaking of which, my dad is waiting at the bar for us."

"Is he, though?" Aaron wasn't even sure whether Gray's father liked him. But the simple nod of acknowledgment as Robert Clery had approached the building and seen Aaron waiting there—the way he'd immediately made room for them to talk—had alleviated a little of his worry. That, and the quick smile as Robert had turned away.

"Maybe not, but, if it's okay with you, I think I'd like to join him. We sold his dream today, and as much as I want to get you naked and update the freckle count, I also want to be with my dad for a bit."

"Okay." As much as Aaron wanted Gray to count his freckles, he got it. He slapped his palm lightly against the table. "Okay. Well, I'll be home if you want to call later or come over."

Gray caught his hand. "Come with me."

Hearts did actually leap. *How about that.* "Are you sure?"

"This thing we've got." Gray pointed between them. "No shelf life. We had a misunderstanding and we fixed it. As long as we keep talking, we'll always be able to fix it."

Speaking of shelf lives . . . "What about the game?"

"Let's ask my dad for advice. He's been around. He's started and sold a business. He knows stuff." Gray looked him square in the eye. "What I do know? I'm not ready to give up on the game after one bad outing. What we have is good, and we can make it better."

Aaron's heart twirled again. "Are you sure?" He'd supposed Gray might be done with that part of their relationship.

"I have a unique opportunity right now. My renter is paying my mortgage and I'm living rent-free. My plan is to refurbish the upper-floor apartment and eventually move up there. I can work on the game some and make bread for markets and whoever else when I'm not stripping and sanding and thinking. Good bread. Bread that makes me feel alive."

"Walnut bread!"

Gray laughed. "I saved you some. Don't let me forget it later."

"Are you sure you want to keep working on the game?"

"Do you want me to? Like, are you still interested in— Mff."

Aaron had leaned across the table and kissed him. He pulled back far enough to say, "Our game, okay?" before kissing him again.

The familiarity of Gray's kisses, his lips, the poke of his tongue, went a long way toward healing the rift inside Aaron, and he mentally kicked himself for not staying on Saturday. But he had needed time to think, and to settle everything with his sister before being able to approach Gray with such an open heart.

Or had he?

Gray eased back. "Where'd you go?"

"You're right. You've never been shy about sharing your ups and downs with me. I'm sorry I didn't share mine with you."

Gray's smile was instant and wide and beautiful. "There's the apology I was waiting for."

Relief flooded Aaron. He touched his forehead to Gray's. "Want to head across the street?"

"Yeah."

There would be other issues. That was life. Aaron could almost hear his dad in the back of his mind listing what he'd have to deal with next: Another new manager at the gym and continuing to develop the game. How to go about acquiring a publisher. Helping out Gray with the upstairs apartment, and then convincing him that Aaron's house was big enough for two—after his parents moved out, of course. Learning to love, fully. Embracing his actual self and delighting in who he was.

Being with Gray.

Facing him, his expression an eerie echo of Aaron's pensiveness, Gray seemed to be coming to a similar conclusion. "It's about the bread," he said.

A different conclusion, then. Aaron tilted his head in question.

"I just want to bake."

"Then bake. Everyone likes bread. We'll have no trouble finding someone to buy your bread."

"'We'?" Gray asked.

"We." Aaron pressed a fast kiss to Gray's full lips. "Because this is definitely a 'we.' And an 'us.' That's what this itch was always about."

"Yep." Gray nodded. Smiled. Kissed Aaron again. "Let's go discuss the future, then."

Heart and mind almost breathlessly light, Aaron tipped his head back and smiled. "Let's do that."

Epilogue

"**D**o you have any sourdough left?" The customer, an elderly man, wistfully surveyed the three loaves in the last upturned basket.

Though he was unsure whether his customer could see him, Gray held up a finger and hustled toward the back of his stall to the box where he kept a few loaves aside for his regulars. There, he retrieved a small sourdough loaf and carried it back toward the low table, where his customer was still making sad faces at the detritus of another successful Saturday market.

"Here you go. I saved one for you."

The old guy looked up and sunshine broke across his face. "For me?"

"You're here every week. Small sourdough. Thought you might not make it today."

"Thank you. I . . . Thank you." He pulled out his wallet with a shaking hand and sorted through the money inside the billfold. "It lasts all week, you know. I eat it fresh on Sunday night with my supper and Monday morning for breakfast. Then I toast it on Tuesdays and Wednesdays." He hesitated. "I put the rest of the loaf in the freezer, then, and have one slice a day until Saturday. That's when I eat the crusts." He glanced up as he held over his money, his expression somewhere between embarrassment and dignity.

Gray had seen the same expression on his father's face. He leaned in. "You slice it before you freeze it?"

"Oh, yes. Otherwise, I'd have to microwave it and microwaved bread is the worst."

"Ruins the crust and makes the crumb tough," Gray agreed. He made a vague gesture that encompassed the remaining three loaves. "I'll slice these and freeze them. They'll last about three days."

The old guy's eyes widened. He'd lost his embarrassment and was now simply engaged.

"My partner"—the word *boyfriend* might shock the old gent—"is a fitness instructor. He says he shouldn't eat carbs, but he can inhale half a loaf without blinking. Then there's his family, of which there are a lot. They all love bread. And who doesn't? My dad? If I don't save a loaf of rye for him, he threatens to leave me out of his will. Then there's my cousins who run the family café. As if they don't have enough bread of their own, they're always after mine. So, yeah, I freeze it, for all the good that does."

"So freezing bread is okay, then."

"It's okay."

His customer nodded, his head wobbling around on his neck. Then he smiled. "It was nice talking to you. And thank you for saving me a loaf."

Gray extended a hand. "Grayson. And you're welcome."

"Arthur." Arthur's shake was light but firm. "See you next Saturday."

Gray watched Arthur make his slow way past the next stall only to stop in front of Bee's Hive. Honey for his toast, no doubt.

At a gentle poke in his side, Gray turned to find Oliver standing beside him.

"What's up?" Gray asked.

"Did your sourdough guy come?"

"Yeah, that was him. Arthur."

Oliver nodded in the direction of the honey stall. "I've seen him. He's asked about my pastries but doesn't seem to understand the no-cheese, no-egg thing."

"You don't say." Gray offered his best friend an arched eyebrow.

Oliver picked through the three loaves left in the last of the wire baskets Gray used to display his bread. "Can I take the rye?"

"I wanted to save that one for my dad. Take the whole wheat? Hey, have you seen Aaron?"

After his Saturday freestyle class, Aaron usually stopped by to help Gray pack up the stall. They then spent the afternoon together working either on the game or the upstairs apartment, the choice entirely dependent on how much energy they had. Given Gray was usually up at three to bake on Saturday mornings, the game often won out.

"He's at my stall chatting with Cam. Want me to send him over?"

Gray waved dismissively. "When he's ready. I can start."

"You might need to bake more bread for these markets," Oliver said.

"I know. Though, realistically, I can only make about a dozen more loaves before I run out of oven space and have to think about making dough on Thursdays too." He already worked most of Friday mixing up the dough that could "wait" overnight, the rise halted by the refrigerator. Gray didn't want to go back to baking all week.

Oliver was nodding. He got it. Gray smiled.

"What?" Oliver asked.

"This time last year, you were baking failures in my café. Now you've got your own pastry business. And I can talk bread dough with you and you get it."

Oliver grinned. "It's kinda cool that our friendship still has places to go."

"It is."

Oliver tucked the whole wheat loaf under his arm. "I better get back. Nick likes to start breaking down the stall at exactly 11:52."

"Because it takes eight minutes."

"It takes exactly eight minutes."

Laughing, Gray waved him off. Oliver disappeared behind a knot of people hoping for last-minute bargains. Another man stepped around their other side, his hair catching the sunlight between market umbrellas and bursting into flame. Metaphorically. Gray's entire chest lifted. Unmetaphorically.

Aaron caught his gaze and smiled, lifting a hand. Gray waved back and then stood there, smiling, feeling slightly silly (embarrassed but dignified?) until Aaron arrived at his side. They hugged, cheeks brushing—the Stroudsburg version of PDA—and then stood and continued to smile.

"We're ridiculous," Gray said.

"Eh, whatever." Aaron turned his smile toward the upside-down baskets lined up along the table. "Wow. You're going to have to start making more bread."

Gray snorted. "Or I could be satisfied with what I have, remembering I still have an apartment renovation to complete and a game to refine."

"There is that. Speaking of the game, I was chatting with Cam. He showed *Shelf Life* to a few people last night."

"What version does he have?"

They were up to version sixteen triple-a or something, with the true number being somewhere like thirty. But they'd stopped assigning new numbers with minor tweaks and number sixteen felt pretty good. It should. Sixteen included most of the changes implemented upon the suggestion of real, live beta-testers.

Matt from Jatek Games had reached out over the summer with the names of some testers who had time for a new project, and had been keeping tabs on the results. If everything went to plan, they'd send him the next version to see what he thought.

"Sixteen double-a, I think. He didn't mention the points change."

"I thought triple-a was the points change."

"That's what I said."

Gray stared blankly at Aaron, who kissed him quickly. "Awake now?"

"Sorry. Early start."

"I know, I was there."

If not for the public venue, Gray would frame Aaron's lovely face with his hands and kiss him much more thoroughly than appropriate. Not that he was afraid of displaying the gay. But what he wanted to do with Aaron should be kept behind a closed door. And while equipped with little things like lube.

"I love it when you think dirty at me," Aaron murmured.

Gray laughed and sobered. "I want to kiss you so bad."

"And I want you to kiss me. Later, okay? Let's get this stall broken down while I pass on Cam's notes."

They did that, Aaron sharing the few comments Cam and his friends had put together the night before. Once they were done, Gray gestured across the Courthouse Square. "If we're going to yours, I need to stop home and get a change of clothes."

Aaron shot him a look Gray interpreted as the opening salvo of a conversation they'd been having on and off over the past few weeks. Gray offered a sheepish smile in return. Aaron lifted his chin. Gray sighed.

Aaron let out a chuckle. "We can have this whole conversation without words now."

"I'm still thinking."

"It's not like I've asked you to move to Siberia."

"But it's *your* house."

Aaron stepped in so close their clothes almost brushed together. "It could be *ours*. But if it's important to you that where we live is somewhere we both chose, I'm open to moving. I've told you that."

Several times, and Gray appreciated the offer. It wasn't that, though. He wasn't entirely sure what it was—the reason he was reluctant to let go of the shitty office/bedroom and futon that barely accommodated them. Maybe it was the idea of the upper apartment, of finishing a place and then being able to live in it.

Or maybe it was simply leaving his father alone.

"Hey, are we interrupting?" It was Cam, accompanied by Nick and Oliver.

"Want to get together for a game tomorrow?" Oliver asked.

"I've got some friends coming up from Allentown to play *Shelf Life*," Gray said.

Oliver brightened. "Fresh blood." He clapped his hands together. "Can I join?"

"Hah. Maybe next time. I want to reconnect with my old crew for a bit, introduce them to Aaron."

"Sure."

"Besides, you're going to get sick of playing our game sooner or later," Gray said.

"But it's different every time we play," Nick pointed out.

Aaron grinned like a proud papa. Gray nudged his shoulder into Aaron's and let the rosy glow of happiness and contentedness filter in and around him. This was how his life was supposed to be. Exactly this. Friends and games and bread.

"Yoohoo!"

The shudder was reflexive. Aaron nudged his shoulder back, and they shared another look, this one less about whether they should live together, and where, and more about being thankful that Aaron's mom and dad had moved to Hazelton.

Hava and Tamir Asher were walking arm in arm, plastic bags swinging from both their wrists. Behind them, Gray could see Devorah and Leilani, a toddler and baby carriage between them. New nephew proximity alert obviously pinging, Aaron darted around his mom and dad, totally missing the fact that Hava had reached for him. Gray followed, catching up in time to hear Aaron cooing.

Little Caio was cute. Cosmo and Caio. Boy were these kids going to have a fun time in school. Rather than fuss over the baby, Gray turned to Hava and Tamir. "How's Hazleton?"

"Fine, just fine," Hava answered. "The house won't be finished until spring, but the condo we're renting is in the same development, so we're already getting to know the neighbors."

"Joined a few book clubs?"

"Only one so far!"

"We're scheduled for a hike through Rickett's Glen tomorrow," Tamir put in. "Hiking club."

"Sounds perfect." Behind the knot of Ashers, Gray spotted yet another familiar face, and for a moment, his heart didn't do what it was supposed to. That regular, average, normal beating gig. Then the squeeze in his chest eased and he was able to take a breath. "Excuse me, I think I see my dad."

Hava touched his arm. "We picked Robert up an hour ago. We're all heading out to lunch after this. We stopped by to see if you boys wanted to join us." She lifted her chin to include Oliver, Nick, and Cam, who were still standing by Gray's packed stall, chatting. "Your friends are welcome too. The more the merrier."

All he needed was for Patty and Wendell to show up with their kids, and everyone he cared about in the world would be in one place—and apparently planning to have lunch together.

Gray offered a quick nod and smile before excusing himself to catch up with his dad, who'd stopped to chat with a guy Gray vaguely recognized from around town. As he drew closer, it became apparent it was one of his father's bingo buddies. He waited for their conversation to end.

His father said goodbye to his friend without introducing Gray, then turned in his direction. "Missed your stall. Sorry. Did you save me the rye?"

"Yeah, I did."

"Huh. Did you sell enough?"

"All but your rye, just about."

Robert Clery took a moment to process that before offering a nod. "Good. I knew you'd do good." He indicated the Ashers. "They all think we're having lunch together. You coming?"

"Sure."

"Good. I've got some notes for your game."

His dad had only made it to the market once before. About four weeks after Gray first set up. And he didn't show up to every game night, though Gray made a point of inviting him. Most nights, anyway. But now Gray understood something fundamental.

His dad was always around. Not here, but there. Thinking about his son's ventures and being involved in his own way.

And he wasn't as alone as Gray had always assumed. His life now consisted of more than walking by the creek to check on the beavers. More than bingo and bowling. He'd started reaching out to his friends again. And this wasn't the first time the Ashers had picked him up and taken him out.

His dad pulled out a small notepad and pencil and started flipping through pages. While he waited, Gray glanced over at Aaron. Arms full of baby, Aaron caught his eye. They shared yet another look, one that didn't have a meaning. But Gray knew this one as well—as intimately—as the others. Sometimes it was as though an invisible string connected him to Aaron, and that it had, perhaps, always been there. Shortening when they came into closer proximity; stretching when they moved apart. Strengthening over time, with new strands overlapping.

No one could predict the future, and Gray rarely wanted to. That was why he liked gaming. Sitting down with a set of conditions and seeing what happened. But him and Aaron? Gray liked to think their future was this. That they were already there. Because regardless of where their lives took them, they were connected. Through their love of games, through the complications of their families. Through the love they had for each other. Because of the constant buzz of attraction and the simple joy Gray found in Aaron's company.

But mostly because they fit. They'd been two pieces of a larger puzzle and only together did the picture make any sense.

Aaron brought the baby over. Caio was only six weeks old and apparently delicate. Gray had heard him howl and would beg to differ. Still, he was careful as he lifted a finger to caress the baby's cheek. "Hey there, little fella."

Being asleep (and therefore an utter delight), Caio didn't respond.

But Gray's dad did. "You two look good with a kid. You should think about one." And he flipped a page in his notebook as though preparing to add that to his list of game tweaks.

Gray glanced at Aaron, who shrugged gently.

"Okay," Gray said.

Aaron's eyes went weirdly round. "Okay what?"

"I'll move in with you."

The relief on Aaron's face was comical. "Right, great . . ." He breathed out. Smiled. "Awesome."

"You thought I was saying we should get a kid, didn't you?"

"I nearly had a freaking heart attack."

Gray winced.

"Too soon?" Aaron handed the baby back to Leilani.

Gray circled an arm around Aaron's shoulders and pulled him close. "Nope. I was grimacing in sympathy."

"Yeah?"

"Yeah."

Aaron leaned in. "You want to skip lunch and go back to my place to celebrate?"

Man, he was cute. Too cute. Perfectly cute.

"Nah. We'll pack the rest of my clothes tonight and then celebrate until dawn. Right now? This is where it's at. You, me, everyone. And they've all got notes."

Aaron cackled. "We've turned them all into game freaks."

"We just might have."

After sharing another grin, they joined hands and stepped after Aaron's mom.

"Ah, guys?"

Gray looked over his shoulder to where Cam was gesturing to their packed-up market stall. "Whoops."

Aaron laughed, and Gray fell a little harder. Could almost feel the pavement coming up to meet him. But he didn't panic. Not this time. His heart was doing fine. Doing what it was supposed to do. Beating. Squeezing and contracting. Laughing and loving. Getting on with it.

Gray put a hand to the center of his chest, breathed deeply, and joined his heart in life.

Explore more of the Hearts & Crafts series:
riptidepublishing.com/collections/series-hearts-crafts

Dear Reader,

Thank you for reading Kelly Jensen's *Shelf Life*!

We know your time is precious and you have many, many entertainment options, so it means a lot that you've chosen to spend your time reading. We really hope you enjoyed it.

We'd be honored if you'd consider posting a review—good or bad—on sites like **Amazon, Barnes & Noble, Kobo, Goodreads, Twitter, Facebook, Tumblr,** and your blog or website. We'd also be honored if you told your friends and family about this book. Word of mouth is a book's lifeblood!

For more information on upcoming releases, author interviews, blog tours, contests, giveaways, and more, please sign up for our weekly, spam-free newsletter and visit us around the web:

Newsletter: riptidepublishing.com/newsletter
Twitter: twitter.com/RiptideBooks
Facebook: facebook.com/RiptidePublishing
Goodreads: tinyurl.com/RiptideOnGoodreads
Tumblr: riptidepublishing.tumblr.com

Thank you so much for Reading the Rainbow!

RiptidePublishing.com

ACKNOWLEDGMENTS

In 2018, thinking we had too much time on our hands, my husband and I bought a small business—a bagel shop and café—and learned very quickly that any spare time is a blessing and one we would never again take for granted. When we shared the horror stories of almost daily trials with friends and family, they inevitably had one response, "You should write a book about it!"

At first, I thought that book might be a memoir called *Remember the Time We Bought a Bagel Shop?* with the subtitle: How our marriage not only survived but actually seemed to grow stronger, despite everything that damn shop threw at us.

Honestly? Sometimes I'm surprised we lived through the experience, and all I wanted to do after we finally sold the place was a whole lot of nothing. Then Gray, best friend to Oliver from *Sundays with Oliver*, needed a book, and seeing as I'd already started taking out my bagel shop frustration with his character, I figured he could continue the story. So, my first slice of gratitude goes to Gray for letting me ruin his life. I think you'll agree he's all the better for it.

A second hefty slice of gratitude goes to Kris T. Bethke for being so generous with her time and expertise regarding Gray's health. We brought him down, and built him back up again.

To my beta readers, Sahar Abdulaziz, Liv Rancourt, and E.J. Russell: Thank you for your unflagging interest in reading my early drafts. My books always benefit greatly from your notes.

To my editors, Veronica Vega and Caz Galloway: Thank you for your patience as I wrestled with these characters' voices. I know, I said the same thing last book, but I really mean it. Veronica's insight into Gray, as a Black man, was invaluable. And Caz always pushes me hard enough to want to quit. My books are always better for it.

To L.C. Chase: Thank you for helping me show Gray the way Aaron sees him. It's all about that smile.

To the rest of the team at Riptide: thank you for your brilliant work and support.

To the friends and family who said I needed to write about the bagel shop: Here it is, the book you asked for. I hope you like it!

To my husband and daughter: We *are* the dream team. Together, we can accomplish anything.

To my dad: Thank you for being you. You've inspired more than one parent in my books and are the reason I enjoy writing families so much.

To my gaming buddies, the Shaolin Pirates: Win or lose, it's all about the journey. Right? Right!

To my readers: As always, thank you for reading. I hope you love this book as much as I do.

ALSO BY
KELLY JENSEN

Hearts & Crafts Series
Sundays with Oliver

Out in the Blue
Wrong Direction
When Was the Last Time
Best in Show
Block and Strike
To See the Sun

Let's Connect series
Let's Connect
Let's Go Out

This Time Forever series
Building Forever
Renewing Forever
Chasing Forever

Aliens in New York series
Uncommon Ground
Purple Haze

Counting series
Counting Fence Posts
Counting Down
Counting on You

Chaos Station series (with Jenn Burke)
Chaos Station
Lonely Shore
Skip Trace
Inversion Point
Phase Shift

ABOUT the AUTHOR

If aliens ever do land on Earth, Kelly will not be prepared, despite having read over a hundred stories of the apocalypse. Still, she will pack her precious books into a box and carry them with her as she strives to survive. It's what bibliophiles do.

Kelly is the author of fifteen novels—including the Chaos Station series, co-written with Jenn Burke—and several novellas and short stories. Some of what she writes is speculative in nature, but mostly it's just about a guy losing his socks and/or burning dinner. Because life isn't all conquering aliens and mountain peaks. Sometimes finding a happy ever after is all the adventure we need.

Connect with Kelly online:

Website: kellyjensenwrites.com

Facebook: www.facebook.com/kellyjensenwrites

Twitter: twitter.com/kmkjensen

Instagram: www.instagram.com/kellyjensenwrites

Enjoy more stories like *Shelf Life* at RiptidePublishing.com!

LOGAN MEREDITH

Alex Danvers

The Weight We Carry	*A Teaspoon of Desire*
The journey from friends to lovers is hard enough without baggage.	As the competition heats up, these men need a recipe for romance.
ISBN: 978-1-62649-943-0	ISBN: 978-1-62649-927-0